SHADOW
OF THE MOON

SHADOW

OF THE

MOON

Douglas C. Jones

Henry Holt and Company | New York

Henry Holt and Company, Inc.
Publishers since 1866
115 West 18th Street
New York, New York 10011

Henry Holt® is a registered
trademark of Henry Holt and Company, Inc.

Published in Canada by Fitzhenry & Whiteside Ltd.,
195 Allstate Parkway, Markham, Ontario L3R 4T8.

Library of Congress Catalog-in-Publication Data

Jones, Douglas C. (Douglas Clyde), 1924–
Shadow of the moon / Douglas C. Jones. — 1st ed.
p.   cm.
I. Title.
PS3560.0478S47   1995   95-21735
813´.54—dc20   CIP

ISBN 0-8050-3654-7

Henry Holt books are available for special promotions
and premiums. For details contact: Director, Special Markets.

First Edition—1995

Designed by Betty Lew

Printed in the United States of America
All first editions are printed on acid-free paper. ∞

1   3   5   7   9   10   8   6   4   2

*You shall not see water or wheat or axe mark
on the tree without remembering them, for
they won every shadow of the moon.*

—Stephen Vincent Benét

Foreword

Most of the people already knew or soon found out after Roman Hasford died that he left an illegitimate daughter sired out of a girl named Diana Chesney.

They generally called this daughter the Bastard, but certainly not to her face, especially after her inheritance which made her one of the most powerful people in the whole state. In the newspapers, she was called Queen Burdeen of Catrina Hills Farm.

Not many of her neighbors every gave much thought to Burdeen's genealogy beyond what they knew of her grandfather, who had brought the Chesney name into the county during Civil War times. But once she became the Queen of Catrina Hills Farm, and hence having the money and the influence to hire expensive detective work, *she* gave it a lot of thought. And as a result collected much material on her mother's family as far back as anybody could trace it.

This material has been made available. And is the basis for what follows.

Douglas C. Jones
Fayetteville, Arkansas
1994

This story is fiction, and the characters are from imagination. Except for those events and those people you recognize from your close attention to history lessons in high school.

Part I

THE BALLYMENAS

Chapter 1

Afterward, they called him Old Sergeant Bobby. Because they didn't know much about him or where he came from or why. Maybe they didn't really care. And it was a lot of trouble trying to blow away all that mist of time, clear back to Ulster. So they just called him Old Sergeant Bobby and let it go at that, as though he was like some Greek god who had risen right out of the sea, not only full-grown but old as well. Some called him Old Robert.

Of course, Old Robert wasn't always old. And he hadn't risen out of the sea, either. For the time in question here, he was just coming into his manhood. It was a short while after the Seven Years War, when Britain defeated France in the contest for control of North America.

Robert Chesney was not unbecoming. Rather tall and with a typical Scots face that had more planes and sharp edges than curves. Hair of a color difficult to describe. He was distinctive in one way. Whereas most Scots were taciturn, Robert Chesney was as garrulous as an Italian, so some people said.

Like most lowland Scots, he was threadbare poor. On most days he had no idea where his next bowl of oatmeal was coming from. Everybody blamed the bloody English, who were trying to pay for their last war, and maybe the one before that, too, which meant higher taxes and a deep cutback on government purchases of everything from potatoes to wagon tongues to carded wool. Plus, the British army was no longer recruiting and in fact was releasing veterans of the French war faster than the civil population could absorb them. A man couldn't even join the army anymore to avoid starvation.

So Robert Chesney did what a lot of his compatriots had been doing since before the time of King James I. He crossed the channel to Northern Ireland and became a man of Ulster.

Nothing is known of any family he left behind in Gretna Green or Dumfries or wherever, but in Ulster he apparently had an uncle or cousin or some such relative near Ballymena, to the north and west of Belfast.

There was a public house in Ballymena called the Kitty Whiskers where Robert Chesney began to appear from time to time. Everyone assumed he was a Presbyterian, like most of those who came across from lowland Scotland, but nobody ever recorded having seen him in church.

At the Kitty Whiskers, he met a young man his own age named Miles Urie, who was married to a girl called Maudie, and she tagged around after him like a whipped dog. She was a tiny thing, eyes big as saucers in a narrow face. Later, Robert Chesney could not recall a single instance in Ulster when she uttered a sound. At least not in his hearing.

Maudie wore on her head what most women of the time did, whether they be still in the cradle or laid out for the grave. A cotton or linen cap pulled down tight over the hair and with a pucker string to hold it firm in place, at the edge a ruffle of lace. For the rest of her, she wore exactly what Miles and Robert Chesney did. Rough linen shirt and home-sewn woolen long jacket that looked like a smock except it was open down the front, trousers of sheepskin coming only halfway down her calves, and low, blunt-toe shoes with a buckle at the front. In winter, heavy woolen stockings.

She was thirteen.

All Miles wanted to talk about was America and how to get there. It had to be better than Ulster, he said. But you couldn't just walk down to Belfast and get on a ship and be taken to Charleston or Philadelphia or Boston. It took money to buy passage. Which meant that most people never got the opportunity to go to the land of opportunity.

Such a small detail didn't bother Miles Urie. He would find a way to immigrate, he said, and everybody who knew him figured he would, too, because Miles Urie was the kind of young man who generally found a way, fair or foul, to reach his ends. Everybody who knew him figured he had a touch of Welsh blood in his veins because he would burst into song after only a half dozen drinks. Besides, you could always see that crazy glass glint in his eyes when he started reciting poetry in unrecognizable Welsh, which he always did after he'd had a full dozen drinks.

So it didn't surprise anybody when Miles Urie took his wife and Robert Chesney down to Belfast to talk with a man named Axel Muir, and with his wife Cordelia as well, who did a lot of the talking in all matters pertaining to her big, burly husband. He'd been bos'n mate on HMS *Vanguard,* a seventy-five-gun ship of the line during the campaigns against the French in Canada back in 1757 to 1760. You could tell just from looking at him that he likely had a few *Vanguard* splinters still in him from the times French cannons had taken aim with solid shot.

With the single exception of Cordelia, when Axel Muir talked, everybody else listened until he was finished. Maybe because he always wore silk stockings below his knee-length breeches and hence appeared to be a gentleman. Or maybe because he always had a belaying pin shoved into his thick leather belt.

Axel and Cordelia were set up in one dingy corner of a waterfront warehouse, using a large wooden crate as a desk. Lettered across the front of the box-desk were five words: "Recruiting—Ballymena and Virginia Cooperative."

Axel and his wife were identically clothed, most noticeably with pea jackets and turtleneck sweaters. The only difference was head-gear. His a hard little narrow-brim first mate's hat, hers a blue silk scarf tied tight down over red hair, a few ringlets of which usually escaped to frame her ears.

"So it's America for you, is it?" shouted Axel Muir.

"That's what it is," Miles Urie said, shouting just as loud as Axel Muir had. "The three of us, off to the New World."

"There's the money, you know," said Cordelia. "You don't get off these docks without the money."

"I'll speak to the money, my dear," Axel Muir said. He cleared his throat and slapped a stack of papers on the packing case before him. "We are a part of a company formed by certain gentlemen in the city of Philadelphia. Members of this company forming here will sail on a British merchantman to the city of Baltimore, where a gentleman of the company will meet us and provide funds for provisioning us."

"We go through the wilderness to the place Mr. Muir knows of," said Cordelia.

"Yes, my dear, on the river Monongahela. I know it not now but can find it. By God, if I can make a compass course over ocean waters, I can do it over timbered mountains.

"If you ship with us, you will be at my direction, like that to captain of a vessel. We find our spot in America and make a town and share in the land with our gentlemen from Philadelphia. We clear the forest, we till the soil, we breed the livestock. Hogs and chickens and cattle and sheep. Once in with us, you don't get out. We all depend upon one another."

"Like a family," Cordelia said. "And it costs ten pounds. I don't suppose you've got anything like ten pounds among you, and it costs ten pounds each."

"For all that money, what will you give us to eat on this long voyage?" asked Miles Urie. "Roast beef and hasty pudding?"

"Don't be a smart mouth pippinsqueak, young man," Axel Muir roared. "Navy hard crackers and salt pork."

"You want to be uppity," snapped Cordelia Muir, "you can bring rye bread and oatmeal, but you buy that yourself!"

After the French were effectively run out of America, a few people in the British colonies saw that it was a good time to make a lot of money. Expansion into the frontier would be easier now, what with no Frenchmen and their pesky Indians causing trouble on all sides, from Canada and from the Louisiana Territory, which France had ceded to Spain at the end of the Seven Years War to keep the British from getting it.

There had to be ways of making a profit out of expansion. Well, there were a lot of ways, and one of the best was land speculation.

Many solid, enterprising businessmen formed stock companies to take advantage of this opportunity. One such man was Vanderbilt Tigert, of Dover, Delaware, who, with a number of associates from Philadelphia, founded Ballymena and Virginia Cooperative.

It worked as all other such companies did. The investors provided the lion's share of initial capital in return for claim to a certain percentage of the land developed. Then they found people who were willing to do the lion's share of work for a smaller percentage of the real estate. It was easy when there were so many people in Europe anxious to immigrate but too poor to do it on their own.

Vanderbilt Tigert knew a great deal about the Ulster Scots because he'd made a point of doing so. He knew these were a people who made excellent frontiersmen because a great many of them had already done so. Hence, he formed the European side of the company out of Belfast, with Axel Muir as his agent and the man who would lead the company to its destination in America and through the founding of a settlement.

Across the mountains west of the Piedmont plateau where Philadelphia was the principal city there were vast, wild, and unclaimed lands. Unclaimed by any white men anyway. Nobody was sure yet who owned this land. Virginia claimed it but so did Pennsylvania, both by original colonial charter, they said. But thus far there had not been enough settlement throughout most of that country for any of the colonies along the East Coast to bother with setting up a government and administering it.

So Mr. Tigert and his friends figured this was a good place to stake out a settlement, and then eventually whoever ended up with that area would simply incorporate the settlement into their government, whether Virginia or Pennsylvania or New York.

The people who actually colonized the place would get everything started and running well, to include some basic form of township. When later arrivals flooded the area with kids and goats, Mr. Tigert hoped, the original settlers would have their lands and the new people would buy theirs from Mr. Tigert, who of course would hold title to all real estate in the area not owned by the Ballymenas.

Everybody was happy. Except maybe new arrivals who might think they had to pay too much for their acres. But the businessmen were certainly happy. Profit without being shot at by a single wild Indian. The original settlers were overjoyed because the scheme got them to America in the first place and then provided property for them to cultivate or mine or trade or sell.

Certainly the men in the first organized government who got there were delighted that there was a town and farms and whatever, with people settled and running their affairs just like it was back in real civilization and all needed was to absorb the whole bunch and call it Ballymena County or Muir Court House or Tigertville.

Axel Muir said you'd have to look real hard to find a slicker system for building a whole country out of a savage wilderness. And he was pretty near absolutely right.

But Robert Chesney didn't have the ten pounds it took to buy into Virginia and Ballymena. Nor did Miles and Maudine Urie.

Axel Muir wouldn't get the company onto shipboard for a fortnight, which gave Miles Urie time to work a plan, so he said. His father owned a black bull calf that he kept on the Urie hay patch near Carrickfergus. Not a long walk from Belfast itself.

8

"Your daddy ain't going to never part with such a calf," said Robert Chesney, for although he'd never seen the animal, he knew that in hard times such a thing could be the complete measure of a man's worth.

"We'll see," said Miles Urie.

And so they did! In two days, Miles Urie had the calf, bawling, on a rope, leading him about the county and telling everybody that he was going to raffle it. After they figured most of the people around the Belfast countryside had seen what a fine prize was being offered, Miles Urie took slips of scrap paper collected from alongside roads and in alleyways and whatnot, and wrote numbers on them. Watching Miles Urie write on the lottery tickets fascinated Robert Chesney because writing was a thing Robert Chesney had not yet learned to do.

For a week, they went their separate ways, selling chances. And each day Robert Chesney wondered how in hell Miles Urie expected that little girl wife of his to sell anything without talking. But it was Miles Urie's calf, so Robert Chesney didn't say anything. Still he wondered some more how in hell Miles Urie had talked his daddy into letting go of that calf.

From Ballyday to Glenarm to Moneymore they sold, and a lot in Belfast. It was hard times, but as is always the case, in such straits there were plenty of men willing to spend their last three pence on the chance to win something more than they had to start with, so before Axel Muir collected his immigrants at shipside, there were thirty pounds and some left over in Miles Urie's pocketbook.

Miles Urie's father won the calf, the slip of paper lifted out of a burlap potato bag by Maudine as they stood on one of Belfast's docks, Axel Muir and Cordelia themselves acting as witnesses, and a great many men who had bought into the lottery.

As Farmer Urie led his prize away, a good many of the men standing about grumbled and a couple picked up paving bricks, and Axel Muir glared and fingered his belaying pin, but there was no need for Royal Navy bluster and oath making because Maudine Urie came close to the men and Robert Chesney figured that when you looked at that sweet yet listless little face with the big, sometimes sad eyes,

9

you had to figure such an innocent, poverty-buffeted child could never be a part of something fraudulent.

Well, Robert Chesney wasn't so sure about all that innocence. He had noted as they came in from various places each night with the money from lottery ticket sales, Maudine always had the most. Finally, he asked Miles Urie. When Miles Urie's wife was out of earshot, of course.

"Oh my," Miles Urie said and laughed. "That girl! When she looks up into a man's face and a tear runs down her bonny cheek and she tells him of her poor mother just in her grave and her poor sister having to sell herself on the waterfront to keep food in her stomach and her poor, dear little brother coughing away his life with consumption and nay hot soup to soothe him, why these stout, brave men canna do much else but dig into their duffel for a penny or two, can they?"

So Robert Chesney looked at the girl where she sat across the empty hog's shed they'd been sheltering in while they conducted the raffle and waited for sailing date, and he knew from past conversation with Miles Urie that this child was an orphan and had no known sister or brother, nor dear dead mother just in the grave, either.

It was something else that astonished him most. Hearing of this girl pouring out a story wet with tears enough to make hard men dig for pennies.

"Hell," he said. "I thought her dumb. I didn't know she could talk."

The *Swallow* was the size of a small frigate, displacing about one hundred fifty tons according to Axel Muir, who was supposed to be an expert in such matters. She had two masts and a shallow draft, and when the sea began to run a little rough, she responded to the helm like a blind mule, as everyone would soon see, whether they were experts or not.

Swallow was licensed out of Philadelphia, engaged in the commerce between Britain and the American colonies. Outbound from

English ports she carried metal fittings for shipbuilding, sail canvas, navigational instruments, nails, and a lot of woolen cloth. In the ports of the colonies she took on lumber, cotton, cheeses, potatoes, and sometimes items of already famous Baltimore furniture like highboy chests of drawers.

What all this meant to the Ballymenas who boarded her on a rainy morning in April 1772 was that even though they would be confined to crowded quarters in the forecastle when they needed cover from weather, it wouldn't smell bad. As it most surely would had *Swallow* been carrying such things as turnips or livestock or slaves.

Because they were moving at last, the Ballymenas were happy, and they stood along the railings, even in the cold rain, laughing and pointing out landmarks on the shore as they moved toward White-head. The land was gray in the failing rain, as though they were see-ing it through cheesecloth.

As they rounded into North Channel and moved toward the open sea, the laughing and pointing stopped. Waves were running strong in the narrows between Ulster and Scotland. *Swallow* began to yaw and pitch and groan and dip low enough in the water to send sheets of salt spray across the deck to accompany the rain.

Well before they were into the North Atlantic, Robert Chesney said to Miles Urie, "If the good Lord sees fit to get me off this thing alive, I swear I will never get onto another one!"

Axel Muir was astonished. In all his experience in the Royal Navy, he had never seen so many people so dreadfully seasick at one time.

In that company were forty-six Scots-Irish people: twelve married men, their wives, and fifteen children, one maiden lady of nineteen years, and six bachelors, three of whom were of an age with Robert Chesney, which is to say nineteen. Well, one of the single men was Welsh.

For six weeks they subsisted on hard crackers and salt pork, when they were able to get anything down at all. For six weeks they huddled in the forecastle to avoid what was a stormy season in the

North Atlantic. For six weeks they were soaking wet most of the time, as was all their duffel, and no sooner spread their belongings on deck to dry in sunny weather than to have them soaked again. For six weeks most of them wondered why they had ever been crazy enough to board this bucking, heaving, sodden ship.

And for the last three of those six weeks, the drinking water, stored in oak casks, became so foul they had to add ginger to it before they could gag it down.

There were Sunday services, on the open deck, usually in the rain. Axel Muir would read a few lines from the writing of John Knox, and they would sing a hymn. Usually, these holy proceedings were punctuated by the loud and profane oaths of the sailors, as in the manner of all seamen while working their ship in bad weather.

Miles Urie said these religious rites were a wonderful interlude in the monotony of gray sea, not only because of the sinful interruptions of the ship's crew but also because Axel Muir always wore his knee britches and silk stockings instead of the usual navy duck trousers.

"It is a beautiful sight, our leader's legs in those puke-splattered stockings," he said.

"He could preach with no trousers at all for all the good it does me," said Robert Chesney. And he thought he heard Maudine giggle.

It was June 6 when *Swallow* rounded Cape Charles and headed into Chesapeake Bay with a following wind that blew gently toward the land from the sea. It was nightfall, but clear, and they could see the rise of the American continent as they made across the bay and dropped anchor off Point Comfort, with the wide, dark mouth of the Rappahannock off the port bow.

Axel Muir held a service of thanksgiving on the open deck. After prayer and a hymn, he spoke to them in the gentlest tones they had thus far heard from him.

"Friends, let me tell you. The Spaniards came with their Franciscans to enslave the Indians and mine gold for their king. The French came with their Jesuits to manipulate the savages and harvest furs for their monarch. With our women who hold the Bible of good King James in their hands, we come praying to stay clear of the red heathen and them to stay clear of us. But whether they do or not, we come to build homes for our children!"

There were many "A-Mens" and a shiver of warm feeling, and Robert Chesney figured it was the best speech he'd ever heard and thought how wonderful it was that a man could join the Royal Navy as Axel Muir had done and there learn all those things about the Spaniards and the French.

Two of the crew rowed ashore for casks of fresh water. Axel Muir went with them and returned with almost a bushel of golden yellow apples, crisp and firm from storage in some Virginia cellar all the past winter.

Each of the Ballymenas had two apples, and Robert Chesney ate his, core, seeds, and all.

They slept on deck that night and for the first time in many days had no seasickness. The black vault of sky was sparkling with stars, and they wondered before they closed their eyes if those they had left behind in Ulster might be looking at the same stars. For without the constant struggle to keep from rolling about as the ship pitched and yawed, they had this moment to realize the first pang of homesickness. Then out of the dark came the voice of Axel Muir.

"Safe in our new homeland, you pioneers. The worst is over."

It would be a long time before he ventured such a prediction again!

With morning, some of them rose to discover welts on cheeks and necks. A few spring mosquitoes had come out during the early morning hours to greet them. But it was a glorious day so nobody cared. The lower Chesapeake was a dazzling panorama of dark green timberland coming down to shining water, cobalt and turquoise and azure and every other species of blue imaginable, and there were long ripples of transparent flow that looked like greensward at the mouth of the many freshwater streams that emptied into the bay.

But as *Swallow* sailed, holding her course near the western shore that was Virginia at first but would soon be Maryland, it was the forest that held them at the rail, mouths agape. For none of them except Axel Muir had ever seen such trees. Not only were they large, the canopy rising more than one hundred fifty feet, they were everywhere. They covered the earth like a blanket of green.

There were a few settled sections, a few individual farms, where land had been cleared and was cultivated right to the water's edge, and there were small bay-side villages with fishing boats in clusters around the quays. But it was the timber that fascinated, clearings serving only to emphasize how vast this woodland was. And wherever they could detect dry land, they could see trees.

"Sweet Savior," whispered Maudine Urie, "look at it. So big and so clean!"

Startled to hear the girl speak, Robert Chesney looked and saw a small smile on her lips and a shining in her eyes that had never been there before.

They sailed past the mouth of the Potomac, then the peninsula of St. Mary's, where old Leonard Calvert had built the first capital of Maryland back in 1634. And the mouth of the Patuxent River where the bay narrowed enough for them to see the eastern shore, but then on into broader waters.

There was a rain squall as they passed Henry Bay, but it cleared by the time they reached the narrows at Annapolis and they could see clearly the far-shore trees, oaks and hickory and elm with their high canopy and beneath those and growing down to bay beaches the black willow and hawthorn and chokecherry. There were clusters of bloodred nandina berries shining in the sun, and they would stay red all summer then turn brown and drop off to be replaced in the fall by the brilliant crimson clusters once again.

It took three leisurely days, but finally they headed into the mouth of the Patapsco River and there was Baltimore spread like a piece-quilt counterpane in many shapes and colors. They had seen cities. They had seen Belfast from these same decks, in the rain looking cramped and soot covered, the streets crooked and narrow, the people hurrying with shoulders drooping.

But Baltimore! It seemed to pulsate in the bright sunlight, the wide streets leading off past high houses, some three stories, painted, with window shutters, and the people everywhere, and church steeples, all kinds of churches, for although this was predominantly a Catholic place, there had been religious toleration written into law for more than a century.

The waterfront was like a leafless forest, the masts of many ships rising about the docks where there were piles of lumber waiting to be loaded onto vessels for shipment to tree-starved Europe. Maybe for most of the Ballymenas, that lumber helped them form a first impression. Belfast was like an old, battered, varnished oaken desk, misused and long ago past its good day. Baltimore was fresh-cut pine, waiting to be built into something for the first time.

Even the odors that came to them on the soft land breeze were different. It was the smell of the New World.

The Ballymenas spent their first night in America in a mule pen. Just off the waterfront. It was a confusing maze of stock pens and corrals, some empty. In one of these, they would bed down, happy to have a chance to sleep anywhere other than on the decks of that damned ship, which they had been cursing every moment since the first wet morning in Belfast.

They gawked at the mules, just as they had the tall trees along the shores of the bay. Like the trees, these mules were gigantic. Well, they seemed so. There were not many mules in Ulster and hardly a one anywhere in Ireland, maybe, that stood as much as seventeen hands high at the withers, as these mules did.

"What are those?" Maudine whispered.

"Mules," said her husband. "All with jackass for Da."

The Ballymenas would lie down that night separated from half a dozen of the big brutes by nothing more than a rather flimsy looking pole fence. If the Ballymenas had never seen such beasts, maybe the beasts had never seen such people, for they stood with their heads over the top corral pole and with yellow eyes glared menacingly at the intruders.

"They don't look too friendly," Robert Chesney said.

"They'll stand back," Miles Urie said, and whipping off his broad-brim hat, waved it in the mules' faces. The mules stood motionless, unblinking. Miles pulled the hat back on his head. "To hell with em."

"You gonna be a lot of help in this here New World, you know that, Miles?"

"Bite my foot," Miles Urie snorted, and Maudine was giggling and maybe that broke the tension for the mules, too. They casually turned and ambled away from the corral fence, once passing a great explosion of wind, as only a well-fed mule can do.

Axel Muir and Cordelia had gone off in search of the Philadelphia representative of the cooperative who was to meet them, referring to a fistful of notes and papers Cordelia had produced from her duffel.

They'd finished their supper, the last ration of hard navy crackers and raw salt pork from *Swallow*'s larder, and were unrolling blankets on the ground when the black man came. It was almost total night by now, but they could see it was a black man. He was carrying a lantern in one hand and a long walking stick in the other. The lantern was the kind you'd expect to see on the quarterdeck of a sailing ship. Indeed, the man was dressed like a sailor, complete with a little flat, narrow-brim hat with a black ribbon that fell down the back. He wore a striped shirt and a jacket without sleeves and duck trousers cut just below the knees. He was barefoot.

The walking stick had a large brass knob at one end in the fashion of something a British infantry regimental drum major might carry on parade. Nobody suspected this man had ever been a drum major in a British regiment. They may not have seen many men such as this, but they'd seen British regiments enough.

He went to the center of the mule pen and squatted, placing the lantern on the ground, and looked at the dark circle of Ballymenas who were all watching, the eyes glinting in the shine of whale oil light.

"You all is gone to Kaintuck, is you? It's what the sailors say who brang you on that ship today." He did not shout, but his words had a growling resonance that demanded attention. After a moment, the Ballymenas silent as gray tombstones, he took a small tin from some inner pocket and fingered a pinch of snuff from it. With the snuff pocketed firmly in his lower lip, he laughed. "I done been to Kaintuck, I is, so now you need me, Young Bone Trudeau, to show you the way up the ole Susquehanna."

It was deathly quiet. Today a few of these people had seen a mule for the first time. Now most of them were seeing an African for the first time, for although there were sailors of color on the docks at Belfast, few of the Ballymenas had spent much time away from their potato patches in the surrounding hills and the things in Belfast, to most of them, were as foreign as Persian princes.

"Whatsa matter, white folks? Cat got your tongue?" Young Bone Trudeau laughed again.

Finally, a dark figure rose and moved out to stand in the light of Young Bone's lantern, but he moved tentatively, cautiously, as though he had little appetite for it. This was Silas Fulton, whom everybody considered to be second in command of the group because he was the oldest man among them and had more children than anybody else. Besides that, he and Axel Muir were cousins, both having a maternal grandmother whose name, as you would expect, had been Reed. All Scots-Irish, it seemed, had a grandmother named Reed.

Anyway, Silas Fulton stood a long time shuffling his feet. He cleared his throat twice before finding any words.

"What was it you wanted? We have na food to give you."

"No food, no, no! Bone Trudeau gone lead you to Kaintuck. Young Bone Trudeau. Me!" And he touched his chest with fingers that looked like long, brown sausages in the lampshine.

"I am a free nigger. My daddy, Ole Bone Trudeau, he bought his freedman paper a long time before the last French war. After one of those other French wars, when we captured Louisberg, and Ole Bone Trudeau was there and fought, and Constable Mathews sold him his freedom, and me, too, Ole Bone Trudeau's little chile, and then the English give Louisburg back to the French and Constable Mathews saz he so mad bout that he gone take that freedom paper back again, but he was joshin my daddy. So we all went to Kaintuck with Constable Mathews and come back. So now Ole Bone Trudeau dead. Me, I'm here so I gone help you with them troubles you gone have in Kaintuck!"

A few more of the older men detached themselves from the dark circle of Ballymenas and moved to stand beside Silas Fulton before Bone Trudeau. As he talked, the African smiled constantly, a great, broad smile that revealed an astonishing number of white teeth.

"Trouble? What trouble?"

"Some folks tell you trouble with The Line," Young Bone said, and he said it in capital letters. He was speaking of the Proclamation Line of 1763, and maybe he knew the name for it, maybe not. It didn't matter. He knew what it meant.

"Constable Mathews, he saz after the last French war the bloody Englishmen who get license to trade with red savages want to keep all that Kaintuck land like it is, all woods and trees, so red savages there will hunt and trap and bring pelts in to trade for guns and whiskey and hatchets and wool coats. Because it makes them bloody Englishmen traders lots of money, like it did the French up north there, in that Canada, and where it makes lots of money now for all those bloody Englishmen traders, Constable Mathews saz, since the French was run off from there. And so all these bloody Englishmen traders want the same thing in Kaintuck so they get Old King George's people across the water to make a line along the top of the mountains, and a law says you and me and other colony gentlemens can't go across that line so we can cut trees and make farms in Kaintuck."

Now more of the Ballymena men had moved closer to Young Bone's lantern and were listening intently, frowning, licking their lips with quick little flicks of their tongues.

"You mean," asked Silas Fulton, "that somebody will arrest us if we go across the mountains?"

Young Bone Trudeau threw back his head and laughed.

"They supposed to, but they won't. Gentlemens like Constable Mathews, he the one aroun here supposed to arrest anybody go off west of the mountain ridge. But he won't. Constable Mathews, he saz let the bloody Englishmen traders get their furs up north and leave these Kaintuck woods for us colony gentlemens who wants to cut trees and make farms."

The Ballymena men standing around the African glanced at one another in confusion, and finally Silas Fulton voiced their question.

"Then what kind of trouble be it?"

"Why, my gracious, the trouble is some of them red savages in Kaintuck, mostly who fought for the French in all them wars we've had and who know about King George's line on the mountain, and sometimes when they see any of us colony gentlemens, they take in to causin trouble. They a contrary bunch, them red savages, and they just simply don't like us colony gentlemens much!"

"Exactly what manner of trouble?" somebody asked.

"Oh maybe not much. But maybe if they drunk, they steal a cow or a hog. Or maybe shoot somebody in the dark. Or sometimes drag a woman off into them big woods and make her scream. Or maybe catch up a little child so they can take it off and grow it up in their tribe."

There was a lot of gasping and swearing and stomping around after that. Young Bone was given to understand that he'd have to wait until Axel Muir returned before he could have an answer on accompanying the Ballymenas. The men who had come out to the center of the pen to listen fused back into the dark circle, where the more imaginative ones began developing stories of red atrocities until some of the children were sniffling and crying, and through all that

Young Bone Trudeau squatted in the center of the pen, grinning and dipping snuff into his lower lip.

Most of the furor finally died down, and many of them were asleep when Robert Chesney heard his name whispered.

"What's the matter?" he said, a little sharply because his nerves were somewhat frayed from thinking of screaming women and Indians with hatchets in their hands.

"Don't make so much racket," hissed Miles Urie. "Listen, I was looking at all the windows in this Baltimore town. You ever see so many windows? And glass in them, too."

"Hell's fire! Glass windows? I want to get some sleep."

"Listen, I've got a few silver pieces left from that black calf. What say we slip out of here and go see what's behind all them bright windows. It may be our last chance before them red devils catch us and eat us up!" Miles Urie was snickering.

"Yeah, you may laugh out the other side of your head when we meet some of them red savages you seem to take as a big joke."

"Are you coming, or not?"

"Help me find my shoes."

And thus did Robert Chesney and Miles Urie go off on their first great American adventure together, in the city of Baltimore, and having two companions of a like age unto themselves, Calvin Reed and Luke Baird.

Chapter 2

According to Baltimore's constabulary records for June 6, 1772, there occurred in the Anchor and Chain tavern on Dundalk Road a serious difference of opinion between sailors from His Majesty's Ship *Trident* and four rather uncouth young men just arrived in America. The reporting official could be no more precise because he didn't know from whence the young men came but remarked that one of them did a considerable amount of what had to be cursing in a language unknown.

The sailors were taking recreational shore leave from the *Trident*, at the time tied up at the Baltimore docks. They were enjoying the famous Maryland soft-shell crabs and washing them down with vast quantities of equally famous local stout and whiskey.

Cause of the conflict had been the sailors' talk of all the waterfront mischief in Baltimore and other places by ruffian American mobs who seemed to make it their business to taunt and discomfort members of the Royal Navy, troops of His Majesty's regiments, and customs officials sent to America from the court of St. James to collect money the colonists certainly owed to pay for the recently ended French war.

And further, that despite all their glorious little slogans, these American mobs were nothing more than a drunken rabble recruited from among dockside bums, most of whom were recently arrived scum from Europe who had been too lazy to earn a living in Great Britain and would be as indolent on this side of the ocean once shantytown Whigs stopped paying them in whiskey to go out and make trouble for honest, honorable Englishmen!

It was at this point, the constabulary report indicated, that the four young men entered the conversation.

The same records also reveal that later a certain Mr. Muir came to the Baltimore jail a little after dawn and paid not only the bail required for the release of the four young men but an additional sum for the restoration of broken property like chairs and beer kegs and windowpanes in the Anchor and Chain tavern. It was noted that Mr. Muir was in a towering rage.

Only one casualty was noted. A young man named Chesney, who had both of his upper middle front teeth knocked out. Hostilities at one point had apparently erupted into an alley and adjoining cowshed, where this Chesney was struck in the mouth with a milking stool.

One of the arresting officers said Mr. Chesney presented a rather distinct picture as they escorted him off to jail, shouting colorful curses and spraying blood on everybody nearby, his wide, crimson smile marked in the center with the gaping void where the two teeth had been.

Some of the Ballymenas said the events of that night were sufficient to turn Axel Muir's disposition raw and leave it that way for the next two years. It wasn't just the affair at the Anchor and Chain. It was that pipsqueak representative of Mr. Vanderbilt Tigert of Dover, Delaware, with whom the Muirs had been in conference for most of the night in his room at the Gaston Inn on Front Street, during which time he gave Axel Muir enough instruction to fill a book the length of *Pilgrim's Progress*. And worse, provided a bag of gold which he said must not be spent until the party reached their next rendezvous upstream on the Susquehanna. Except for a few rations.

Mr. Vanderbilt Tigert had suggested the party continue to subsist on navy biscuits and salt pork as they had been doing, and soon they would be able to supplement this rather dismal diet with game they would be taking from the forest with the fine muskets to be furnished at that earlier mentioned rendezvous. And they could fish along the way.

All of this was supposed to be taken happily, in view of the fact that Mr. Pipsqueak had brought a half gallon of fresh honey to soothe the prospect of more keg pig and hard dough crackers. But it didn't do much for Axel Muir's peace of mind, even with Cordelia doing what she could to placate him.

So finally, Cordelia stowed all the notes and the bag of gold in her huge duffel purse, and they returned to the mule pen. In time to be informed about the happenings at the Anchor and Chain. And after that was taken care of, the sun already blazing down on them, Cordelia Muir said to hell with Mr. Vanderbilt Tigert's suggestion and sent two of the party's young women to a bakeshop in sight along one of the waterfront streets to buy hot buns, enough for all to have a nice breakfast of bread and honey. Even though it was actually going onto dinnertime by then.

The African freedman, Young Bone Trudeau, was still hanging about during all of this, giving advice and showing his acres of teeth. At some point, apparently Axel Muir agreed that Young Bone could accompany the Ballymenas, although later, Axel Muir could never recall doing so. Anyway, Young Bone got his bakery bun and honey along with everybody else, and his wish. To go along to Kaintuck.

Young Bone took a great interest in Robert Chesney's smashed mouth. From time to time as he moved about the group, talking incessantly, he would stop before Robert Chesney and bend close and peer intently at the swollen lips and make clucking sounds and blink his eyes rapidly.

"Me oh my," Young Bone said. "You done gone an made a mess of that mouf, ain't you?"

Finally, still red-faced and smarting with fury, Axel Muir lined up his charges, each carrying their own personal belongings, yelling at them much as he had likely bellowed at His Majesty's sailors on board that frigate during the last French war, and lined them out and began to march them across town, in fact, through the very middle of town.

Soon, people along the sidewalks stopped to stare at them as they passed. Soon, a mob of urchins began to follow them, shouting, "Rag Tail, Rag Tail." Soon, dogs began to run out and bark at them.

You might wonder why the Ballymenas would attract such attention. They really looked no different from the people who stood aside and watched them pass. The women wore their hair up and covered in caps or scarfs. The older ones held dark knit shawls across their shoulders; the younger ones wore bodices. Their dresses were ankle length and of rough linen or wool. There were many half aprons.

Among the men, triangular hats or low-crowned ones with floppy brims were the style. They had on collarless shirts, long jackets, wool once again, and knee britches or sailor-style trousers that came to shoe tops. And the shoes were untanned slip-ons or buckle pumps or calf-length boots. Footwear for the women was the same.

Maybe the onlookers sensed something illusive, as the odor of wood smoke caught only briefly by a sharp breeze, something strange that told them these passersby were foreign. Or maybe something that told them these newcomers and their like soon would be the Americans and they the foreigners. So maybe their laughter and scorn was part fear, too, or at least apprehension because they might just be looking at their own replacements.

After about six miles, they arrived at Back Bay and found there at a dilapidated wharf three large bateaux and a dozen men on the bank, grouped around himself, Mr. Pipsqueak. As Axel and Cordelia

Muir went into counsel with Pipsqueak, everybody else stood along the muddy bank and stared at the fat, blunt-edged boats. There were two men in each boat. They wore heavy stocking caps more suitable for salty gales off some winter coast than for spring in Baltimore.

"Them sure is ugly boats," Robert Chesney said through his swollen lips.

"I don't like the looks of all those oars," said Miles Urie. "Who you allow may be usin those?"

"You can wager it won't be Muir or Cordelia."

There lived in the city of Philadelphia a doctor named Benjamin Rush. This was perhaps the best-known physician in all the colonies, and he was active in the movement for separation from the mother country, too. He would one day sign the Declaration of Independence. Nobody in the colony of Pennsylvania was better known or enjoyed higher reputation than he excepting only Benjamin Franklin.

Dr. Rush was not adverse to earning money from time to time. To that end, he invested modestly in the land speculation scheme of Mr. Vanderbilt Tigert, and suggested to Mr. Tigert that before sending a party into the wilderness, they should all be vaccinated against smallpox.

This mission was passed to the Ballymena and Virginia Cooperative in Baltimore. Thus Pipsqueak, who on that afternoon in his last meeting with Axel Muir indicated the recommendation of Dr. Rush and the instruction of Mr. Tigert and therefore appeared before Axel Muir with a rather fat, wheezing man who wore a powdered wig and carried a small, black valise, a certain Dr. Vincent.

Actually, the procedure did not require a medical man. Anybody could do it. Dried pustules or scabs from a smallpox victim were kept in petit cans, such as those used for snuff and candied fruit, and all doctors carried such a can in their valise and all apothecaries displayed them on their shelves. You simply scratched the skin to bleeding, placed some of the scab residue in the wound, wrapped the wound to keep the smallpox debris from falling away, and waited.

Sometimes the patient died, probably most generally from infection because nobody had the vaguest notion that such a procedure needed doing with clean fingers and instruments. But usually there was a minor manifestation of the disease, and once the fever from that subsided, the patient had developed immunity to fight it off when the real thing came along. Smallpox inoculations had begun in the British Isles in the first quarter of the eighteenth century. So it was nothing very revolutionary, although there were few Ulster Scots who had been vaccinated.

But Axel Muir had been while serving in the Royal Navy and knew the benefits, so quickly he had his charges passing before the good Dr. Vincent who sat on an up-ended water cask performing his magic. There were many scowls and sour faces, and all the children were crying and let loose horrible shrieks when the tip of the scalpel touched their arms.

When Robert Chesney came before him, the doctor looked at the swollen lips and made a clucking sound.

"Well, well, well, young man," he puffed. "Have a look at that battle wound in a moment."

And so it came about that Robert Chesney had nine stitches taken in his gums, although after almost twelve hours from the Anchor and Chain combat they were tightly swollen and of course it didn't help any that the effects of the grog and rum had worn off.

When it was over, Calvin Reed, who had two stitches taken in his left ear, said to Robert Chesney, "By Old Holy Hoxie, Robert, it were a lot more fun gettin my ear pert near torn off than it were getting it put back on again!"

"When that needle did its work, you two bellowed like stuck hogs," said Miles Urie.

Dr. Vincent instructed Maudie Urie on how to remove the sutures after about two weeks and left her a nice pair of tweezers to do the job. Then he gave the two wounded veterans a sip of brandy from a fat bottle he produced from the valise.

"Doctor, I was in that same affair," Miles Urie said, licking his lips.

"Sorry, son," said the doctor. "Only for those with marks of battle on them."

His eyes watering from the sting of the brandy, Calvin Reed gasped, "Doctor, that bein the case, I be willing to let you sew some more on me."

Maudine Urie was smiling, holding a hand over her mouth as though ashamed to let anyone see.

"By God, I don't think it's very funny," Miles Urie said and stomped away in a huff, his boots making indignant squishes in the muck along the riverbank.

Dr. Vincent chuckled and slipped the fat bottle from the valise again and handed it to Maudie.

"Can't let a man get into a pout, can we little lass," he said. "You hide that until after dark, and then you'll know what to do."

"Oh, oh, oh," Maudie gasped and quickly covered the bottle with her waist-length apron and hurried after her husband, looking like a pregnant child with the bottle under her apron.

It hurt like hell when he laughed, but Robert Chesney laughed anyway and from that day always had a fond regard for doctors, even in those times ahead when he'd see them hacking off the arms and legs of friends.

The six men the Ballymenas found waiting at the boats were Portuguese. They were a disgruntled and sour lot because they were open-sea fishermen who harvested the cod and the halibut off the coasts of their New England homes and now, owing to economic chaos in the colonies, had been forced to take this inland water job. They made no effort to hide their irritation.

Only one of the Portuguese spoke anything remotely resembling English, but he spoke plenty of it and constantly bombarded those in earshot with his personal analysis of what was wrong with everything and how to fix it.

Revealing another reason for his recently upset stomach, Axel

Muir confirmed everything the sailor said, and added a few things himself, all of which he'd heard in that first-night session with the Ballymena and Virginia Cooperative's Baltimore representative.

"We've come to these shores in the worst possible time," he said gloomily. "The devil himself is loose on this land!"

"Now, now, Mr. Muir," said Cordelia. "You make it out more terrible than it be."

But maybe not, Robert Chesney figured. Maybe there was even more that Axel Muir didn't know about. It sounded like that kind of a situation. And the more he heard and the more he thought about it, the more he could understand the bitter words of Englishmen in the Anchor and Chain when they spoke of Americans.

Little time to think of such things now. With first light on their third day in the Western continent, the Ballymenas pushed away from the dead fish smell of Back Bay's muddy shore and into the Chesapeake Bay. That's when they discovered how clumsy and obstinate bateaux could be and how short a time it took pulling on oaken oars in rusty oarlocks to raise blisters the size of gooseberries on their hands.

The two Portuguese sailors in each boat hardly touched an oar. They were at the tiller or fiddling around with the short mast and canvas lateen sail. This was the ancient triangular sail of the Egyptians, with a spar on the top edge of the sail, the spar attached to the mast at a forty-five-degree angle.

It was a tribute, the sail, to the Portuguese genius for moving vessels across the surface of water. From as far back as the twelfth century, any maritime technique useful to them they either invented or copied from somebody else.

All of which was completely lost on the Ballymenas, who neither knew nor cared about Portuguese marine initiative.

They had a following wind and with full sails moved quickly over the smooth surface of the bay. They reached Spesutie Island by nightfall and pulled the boats up on the sandy shore and turned them bottom-side-up for shelter during the night.

They needed the shelter. Clouds had begun to obscure the sun at midafternoon, and by nightfall the rain was coming in a steady downpour. It was cold, without blankets, and they huddled together under the boats like packs of sleeping dogs.

It rained on them through most of the next day, and the wind died, and they were left with only the oars. They had taken to wrapping their hands in whatever strips of cloth they could find, and the wrappings were soon soaked red with the rain and the blood from burst blisters. They passed Aberdeen and turned into the mouth of the Susquehanna, beaching the boats at the western end of the settlement of Havre de Grace.

"To hell with Mr. Tigert's suggestion," said Axel Muir and went into the town and bought blankets and woolen coats for everyone in his party. And two cured hams and a bushel of potatoes. And the rain stopped.

They built fires and were drying out around them when they got a taste of the troubles brewing in the English colonies. A group of seven redcoat British soldiers and an officer in a plumed hat arrived and demanded to look through all their duffel. It caused a lot of hair to stiffen on the backs of necks, especially with the younger men, but there wasn't much they could do. The soldiers were armed with muskets, and ominously, their bayonets were fixed.

The British officer wanted to know where they were going and what they intended doing there, and Axel Muir, red-faced but controlling his temper, answered as he had been coached to do. Just to Lancaster to settle and find employment in the tanning trade or perhaps take up farming if there was any land available.

"You know you are prohibited by Royal proclamation from going west of the mountains," the officer said.

The soldiers spent an inordinate amount of time poking the tips of their bayonets into duffel and bundles, their eyes hooded but bright as they looked at the women in the party, and the Ballymenas knew enough about soldiers to understand what the redcoats were thinking.

Finally, the detail departed, looking over their shoulders, some of the soldiers grinning and winking at the women now.

"Bold as brass, ain't they," muttered Calvin Reed.

"Looking for smugglers," said the Portuguese. "Plenty much damn smugglers now."

It was true. Axel Muir had heard in Baltimore about the British customs cutter *Gasspee* pursuing a suspect ship just a week before, running aground, and patriots going into boats and rowing out to burn her before she could work her way off the rocks.

"That Parliament put a tax on about ever'thing us colony gentlemens use," Young Bone Trudeau said. He was sucking the marrow from a ham bone. "Lead and glass and tea and paper. Us colony gentlemens saz no siree, we ain't gone pay all that tax you put on us."

"Around here, they say these are Crown Colonies," said Cordelia Muir. "They say all these colonial charters are from the king, so Parliament isn't supposed to tax them. And they have no representatives in Parliament."

It was more than that, too. James Otis in Boston making a loud seditious speech, saying not even a king could infringe the natural rights of man. Nobody was sure what the natural rights of man were, but it made a good rallying call.

And this Sam Adams organizing little groups in all the towns, groups of very literate men, who would write very treasonous things and circulate them and nail them to barn doors and publish them in newspapers. He called these groups Committee of Correspondence.

And even before they'd left Ulster, some of them had heard a rumor of British troops guarding a customhouse in Boston. A mob of citizens began throwing cobblestones and chunks of firewood at these soldiers and the soldiers fired into the crowd and killed half a dozen of them.

"An so them Parliaments send more lobsterback soldiers an they put them soldiers right inside the houses of us colony gentlemens to sleep and eat," said Young Bone.

"God, anybody hates it when the army quarters troops on you," Silas Fulton said.

"Them British tole they send more troops to protect us," the Portuguese said. "Protect from what? We tell them, French is gone now. From Indians protect, they tell us. Goddamn red heathen, we can protect our own self from him!"

"Oh," growled Axel Muir. "From all I hear, those red hellions you speak of has been raising the smoke of a lot of settlers' farmsteads on the other side of those mountains. And taking as much hair as ever, only difference now being they don't come with Frenchmen leading them."

The Portuguese sailor sputtered and blinked and swore in his native tongue.

"And we supposed to go right into the middle of all this, and those red hellions and the very devil himself loose on this land," Axel Muir said, and his face was getting redder and his voice was raising to a shout. "And by God, we will, too!"

"Now, now, Mr. Muir," said Cordelia. "You'll upset our ladies."

"Well, I don't want anybody to get taken unawares about what the hell we're gettin into," Axel Muir roared and turned and walked off into the dark.

In the shadows well back from the fires, Robert Chesney and Calvin Reed were smoking. For in addition to the other things, Axel Muir had bought a number of clay pipes and twist tobacco.

"I can see one thing now," Robert Chesney said. "A thing that caused us to carp somewhat earlier."

"Yes," said Calvin Reed. "Waiting so long to buy our plunder, all the plunder we'll need going to this Promise Land. Monongahela, or whatever it is."

They both knew, coming to terms with all this New World quicker than they would have thought possible, that had they already bought their full load of wilderness supplies, the British soldiers would have confiscated some of the more important items. Like weapons and ammunition.

And whiskey, if there had been any. And Robert Chesney and Calvin Reed hoped that when the time came, Axel Muir would remember to buy some whiskey.

Maybe they had been reminded of the whiskey because from under one of the boats, even as all the serious discussion was going forward, they could hear Miles Urie singing one of his sad Welsh songs and they knew Maudine had given him Doc Vincent's medicinal brandy.

"Holy Hoxie," Calvin Reed whispered. "I surely hope they ain't enough of that doctor's medicine left to get Miles into the poetry recitin mood!"

The Ballymenas soon found that the Susquehanna was not the best of rivers for quick and painless passage. There were riffles, whirlpools, rapids, hidden rocks, falls, and sometimes current so swift that oars could make no progress against it.

The lateen sails were useless now so they were rolled and stowed, but the six Portuguese still managed to find a way to stay on board, one at the tiller, the other in the bow poling. For most of the way, long lines were attached to the bateaux, and the Ballymenas walked along the bank pulling, like oxen along a canal. The Portuguese called this process cordelling.

The worst was portage. When no other way would work or the falls were too steep for even cordelles, they carried the boats around the bad water, women working with the men to manually heave the heavy burden through underbrush and briars and mud and jumbles of rock to some point upstream where they could get back into the water.

It was during a short rest after one of these gut-wrenching portages that Robert Chesney found Axel Muir to one side, away from the others, and voiced a concern that had grown in his mind since Baltimore.

"Captain," Robert Chesney asked, that being what all the Ballymenas now called the former Royal Navy man, "all this uproar over taxes. We get to the back country, that won't be unsettling for us, will it?"

Axel Muir stared at Robert Chesney for a long moment, blinking rapidly, as though it was a crazy question never before considered.

"Taxes? Hell, boy, it's not taxes will be unsettling." Axel Muir snorted. "Taxes, those are just the current excuse. If not taxes, it'll be something else to shout against. These people want independence, don't you understand that, boy? Independence, that's what it is. Independence!"

Independence! It hadn't entered Robert Chesney's mind. Independence from what? Everything he'd seen so far looked pretty good. Compared to Ulster anyway. And what troubled him most was how the hell do you go about getting independence? Was Axel Muir talking about war? The very idea of war made his mind reel. A few friends drunk and enjoying fisticuffs was one thing. But war?

He figured he'd best discuss it with Miles Urie and Calvin Reed and Luke Baird. But hell, what did they know? And how could he start such a damn-fool conversation? So he put it out of his mind. Well, he tried to put it out of his mind.

It was about seventy miles from the mouth of the river to Harris' Ferry, and it took them eight days to make it. The last seven of those days they were on nothing but salt pork. The navy biscuits had been drenched in the rain on Chesapeake Bay and had to be thrown away. The Havre de Grace hams and potatoes had lasted twenty-four hours.

Well before they reached Harris' Ferry, they could see mountains rising to the west, deep green in their late spring foliage. Increasingly, as they struggled upstream, the land around them on both sides of the river showed steeper and steeper slopes and higher and higher ridges. Now, coming into the foothills of the Appalachian range, the heavy timber closing in around them, they were for the first time feeling held fast by the wilderness. Not trapped by it exactly, but enclosed as you are when a thick muffler is wrapped around the neck. In the bay, they had seen the great trees from afar. As the river narrowed, the trees marched in closer to them on all sides.

Now they were close enough to see the texture of bark and the shape of leaves and the markings on birds' wings. They could see the undergrowth and its berries and tangles of briar and the deep shadows far back from the sunlight, the tree trunks like dark pillars and the blue and purple unknown between, capable of hiding any mystery, any terror.

Yet no matter how foreign the deep timber was to anything else they had ever experienced, many of them felt drawn to it, many of them saw its beauty, many of them tried to imagine what it hid, many of them could smell it, an odor unique in all their lives and with a pleasant freshness.

And all of them, maybe because of some long-forgotten or never-known Scots-Irish instinct, became at once on entering that great forest, a part of it. Maybe that great forest with all the wilderness that lay beyond was something they had been waiting for down all the generations and now at last had found it.

Robert Chesney thought so. Not in those words exactly and not at that moment, but years later.

"We hadn't come to a strange land," he would say. "We'd come home!"

The colony of Pennsylvania had awarded a license for trade with the Indians to Englishman John Harris back in 1718 on the Susquehanna in the vicinity of the mouth of the Juniata, which flowed into the big river from the west. He built his trading post on the east bank of the Susquehanna and twenty miles south of the Juniata. In the same year he began operation of a ferry, hence the name by which this place was to be known until years later when it would be incorporated as the city of Harrisburg.

When the Ballymenas arrived, the elder Harris had been long dead, and all he had begun was operated by his son. It had been some time since Indian trade had amounted to much here, but a sizable community had grown around the old trading post and young Harris was now a typical merchant among the white settlers coming to claim land in the rich valleys of the Appalachian's eastern foothills.

For every disadvantage he had suffered in the declining Indian trade, Harris the Younger had earned double in providing for land speculators.

Harris the Younger had been alerted by yet another of Mr. Vanderbilt Tigert's ubiquitous agents and so was waiting. No sooner had Axel Muir turned his little flotilla toward the west bank to beach on a gravel bar beside the ferry slip than Harris had his indentured servants loading the ferry on the far bank with those things he knew the Ballymenas would need for a trek into the wilderness and would buy with the gold he knew Mr. Tigert had given them.

It was just past midday so Axel Muir's people figured they would stay here through the night, and already many of them were finding places to sleep. Not under the boats now because the bateaux never left the water. With small fanfare, the Portuguese turned the big clumsy vessels back in the direction they had come and were away, very busy now what with only two of them to man each empty boat.

"Goddamn, people," shouted the Portuguese talker as he stood in his boat. "You don let them devil red heathens scalp your hair off, you kill em good you kill em fast."

It wasn't very reassuring, but they soon forgot that and their exhaustion and the disappointment that they hadn't gone ashore on the town side of the river, because the ferry was coming to the slip. They could see what they had longed to see. Food. At the very front of the ferry were bushel baskets filled with potatoes and apples and onions and a box of loaves of rye bread and a whole quarter of beef, recently slaughtered, they knew, because there was still free-running blood at all the exposed joints.

So while Axel Muir and Cordelia sat on the ferry and talked with Harris the Younger, the rest of the party began fires, and the talk and laughter was infectious and it was a special time for celebration. They didn't know celebration for what, but it felt like such a time.

And Axel Muir had bought whiskey. And beer. Not enough for a long trek, but enough for that night. They brought out mandolin and the French harp, and Luke Baird played spoons, tapping them together in time to Cordelia Muir's and Old Ma Fulton's singing, and they danced on the ferry, Harris the Younger leaving it on the south bank for that purpose. By midnight the whiskey was gone, the beer was gone, two strings on the mandolin were broken, one of Silas Fulton's children fell in the river but didn't drown, Young Bone Trudeau's trousers caught fire when he did a jig too close to the flames, Cranston Shook threw up on himself, Calvin Reed and Miles Urie got into a minor fistfight, and Robert Chesney danced with Ma Fulton and Maudine Urie, and Cordelia Muir kissed him square on the sore mouth while they were doing a reel. He forgot all about independence and what it might mean.

When the euphoria passed as the sun came and they began to prepare for the next leg of it, they realized for the first time, maybe, just how much Americans were willing to invest in land speculation. In the hope, naturally, of making a lot of money. As they sorted and packed the various items Harris the Younger had brought on his ferry the evening before, it was impossible to ignore how serious Mr. Vanderbilt Tigert and his associates were about acquiring interest in real estate beyond the Appalachians.

"How much gold are we dealin with here?" asked Miles Urie. "To buy all this truck?"

"We ain't dealin in no gold atall," Calvin Reed said. "Cause it's all in that Harris man's pocket now."

"Well, it was in Axel Muir's pocket til yesterday," said Robert Chesney.

"It was in Cordelia's pocket," Miles snickered, and he cut a quick glance and a wink at Maudine. "And we all seen how you was kissin her last night."

"I was not," Robert Chesney said, and he knew his face was going brighter than the new sun. "She just did it once when we was . . . well, dancin, that's all."

"Don't you try to josh us, you ole speckle rooster you," Miles said, and they were all giggling, including Maudine. "We know what you want, struttin around Axel Muir's chicken coop even with that mouth still all puffed up like a big rose flower."

"You wanta hush now, you son of a bitch," Robert Chesney said, and his voice was quivering and the veins on his neck standing out, and he raised up from his work holding one of the new hatchets from the supply of tools Harris had brought.

That was the end of any teasing about Cordelia Muir. Later, Calvin told Luke Baird he figured Robert Chesney would have used the hatchet if Miles had said another word.

"It scared the pee-waddin outta Maudine," Calvin said. "In fact, it unsettled me a mite, too."

It was obvious that their mode of transport was about to change. Harris the Younger had brought over four small dugout canoes that Young Bones Trudeau said were the kind once made and used by the Powhatans along all of Virginia's major rivers. There was a rope for cordelling, too.

But mostly they would carry their truck in three carts, the kind with two large wheels and a single tongue. There were six oxen, one of which looked sick already.

There were breeding stock. A dozen shoats, two boars, and ten sows, and they'd be ready to breed in the spring. And a willow twig cage with chickens, and a milk cow and a bull.

Hard soap, needles, cast-iron cookery, tin plates, salt, coffee beans, dried chickpeas, dried beef, cured bacon. Fishhooks and line. Three bolts of rough-weave wool, buckskin jacket-smocks for the men, with long fringes across the shoulders at the back.

"Not for decoration, those fringes," said Cordelia Muir. "For string. You need string for anything, you cut off a fringe."

Moccasins, winter style with uppers that reached halfway up the calf. Two bolts of flannel. A box of threads. Shears. Woolen blankets. Seeds for planting. A medicine chest with a small booklet from Dr.

Rush in Philadelphia detailing care of the sick. There were salts and paregoric and laudanum, these last two based on tinture of opium. For diarrhea, give paregoric, Dr. Rush had written. For all else, give salts, laudanum, and bleed the patient. The good doctor had included an anatomical chart to show where to make the incisions and a German silver scalpel for the cutting. Dr. Rush believed, it seemed, that anything could be cured by opium, bowel movement, and bleeding. Especially bleeding.

Then the tools. A crosscut saw, hammers, wedges, axes, hatchets, augers. A twenty-pound bag of mixed nails. Empty oaken barrels. Two lanterns.

Then the weapons. Two kegs of powder, bars of lead, a sack of flints, a can of whale oil. A dozen large knives. And twelve Brown Bess muskets. The standard weapon for the British army at that time. It was almost five feet long, weighed twelve pounds, had a bore of .75 inch, shot a lead ball that weighed almost one-sixteenth of a pound or half a dozen buckshot or both. When fired, there was a flash of flame three feet long from the muzzle and a great cloud of smoke and a smell of sulphur.

When Axel Muir set the men to practicing with the muskets, which he knew they needed because only a couple of them had ever used a firearm and he wanted them ready when the hostile Indians came, and he was convinced they would come, the younger men thought it was a hell of a lot of fun shooting these things even though most of them, at one time or another, got too much powder in the pan and singed off their eyebrows.

Silas Fulton had served with the British army during one of the French campaigns, so could advise them.

"At fifty paces, you can hit a target big as a French sergeant major. Sometimes. Beyond fifty paces, just point it in the general direction of the target and hope. Beyond one hundred paces, wait til the target comes closer.

"If he's close enough to hit and you miss anyway, and he's chargin at you, you won't have time to reload before he gets close enough to jump on you. So then the old Bess makes a good club. They didn't give us no bayonets."

And that was all. Everything they needed, or at least everything they were going to get, to make a new life in the wilderness. If something else was required, they'd have to make it themselves, or grow it, or shoot it, or steal it.

And they knew that, Axel Muir told Cordelia. That second day at Harris' Ferry as he watched the women and the children packing everything in cart and canoe, and watched, too, the men learning how to use the Brown Bess, Axel Muir had been as proud of them as he had ever been of a well-drilled gun crew on one of His Majesty's frigates.

"Just before goin into the unknown where hostile peoples lurk," he whispered to her as they lay in their blankets beneath one of the packed and ready carts. "And now they come together and work together and laugh together, against all things, together. They are a bloody good bunch, like ducks to the water in this wild, new country."

"Is it true, really," Cordelia whispered, "that hostile people wait in the forests?"

"Yes! You've heard the talk. Yes! They wait!"

And whether or not it was a fact, the Ballymenas thought it was, so hence, to them it was true.

In the dark before dawn the next day, before the Ballymenas started upriver to the mouth of the Juniata, Harris the Younger brought across two horses, one with a saddle the other with a canvas pack.

In the growing light, which illuminated Axel Muir's mounting irritation, Harris the Younger explained that their guide for crossing the mountains, a certain Mr. Popjoy, was indisposed, having gotten unreasonably drunk the night before, but these were his horses and they should be taken along and cared for and Mr. Popjoy would join the expedition as soon as he felt up to it.

What's more, Harris the Younger said, it was best that the Muir party lose no time getting into the mountains because a British army detachment, out looking for deserters and tax evaders and who knew what all, was only a day's march away from Harris' Ferry, and if they caught the Ballymenas there would be hell to pay because it was obvious they were going to violate the Line of Settlement Proclamation of 1763, in addition to which they were in possession of firearms which in these troubled times the British would take to mean somebody was planning serious mischief. And would not only confiscate weapons and other supplies they viewed as contraband, but also arrest everybody in sight and take them all off to some prison hulk floating at the mouth of the Schuylkill River in Philadelphia.

"You needn't paint such a black bloody picture, Mr. Harris," Axel Muir growled. "We aim to get off here with sun up."

And they did, after Axel Muir said a long, John Knox–style prayer, in which he called on the Lord to help any way He could as these, His Ballymena children, set off to establish a good Presbyterian church among the fierce red savages, and if any of the aforementioned red savages tried to interfere, He might please give the young men the fortitude to stand firm against aggression as well as the sharp eye and steady hands to hit what they aimed at!

One of the elder children of Silas and Ma Fulton was assigned responsibility for the two horses. It was an easy job. The child, twelve-year-old Enoc, tied the lead ropes to the rear of a cart, mounted the horse with the saddle, and sat having to do nothing except view the lovely Susquehanna as they moved along leisurely at the pace of the oxen.

It was that first day out from Harris' Ferry when Robert Chesney saw that Maudine Urie's little-girl body had begun to change. Unnoticed until now, her belly under the white linen half apron had taken on a decided bulge. And this time, Robert Chesney knew there was no bottle of medicinal brandy hidden there.

Later, when Maudine had Robert Chesney sit on a stump while she stood between his legs to remove the stitches from his lip, he was terrified that she might touch him with her stomach.

Chapter 3

They were three days up the Juniata before Noble Popjoy caught up to them. He looked like a wilderness guide all right. He wore a wide-brim felt hat with two long turkey feathers stuck in the band and trailing out behind, and they bobbed up and down when he walked. He had on a very long hide smock with fringes at shoulders and sleeves, woolen trousers, and deer-hide moccasins. Young Bone Trudeau said they were likely Narragansett.

The first thing you'd notice was the face. It was high boned and very dark, and the hair, long and braided alongside the ears, was black but with a few streaks of gray. It was exactly the right face for the body, which in that skin clothing had the look of a forest animal that might move fast or slow but always carefully.

Then you'd notice the weapons. He carried a rifle. Not a musket but a rifle, about a .50 caliber. Across his back was a sawed-off musket, and at his sides were hatchet and knife. The hatchet was actually a pipe tomahawk, English made. The knife was very long and probably French.

At the neck were bandanna, glass beads, and a string of wildcat claws. At various places, front, back, and sides, pouches hung. It was anybody's guess what was in the pouches.

As he came up to the Ballymena party from the rear, on foot, he was among them before they realized he was near, and even then, what with their savage red Indian spookiness, they almost opened fire on him. Which would have meant mostly shooting each other. But he held up his free hand, the other occupied with carrying the rifle, held it palm out, and said, "Whoa! Whoa!"

It wasn't exactly a loud voice, but it had an edge on it. They all paused, wide-eyed, muskets half raised.

"I be Noble Popjoy," he said, hand still held palm out in the peace sign and his eyes darting from one to the other of the Ballymenas without his head moving very much. "Which of you be Axel Muir?"

And already Axel Muir was running to the wagon trace from his party of cordellers at the river.

Later, Calvin Reed would say, "Did you notice how everything just stopped when he come in here, sudden, unexpected, even like the birds stopped singin just that instant."

"Like everything froze solid in a twinkling," Luke Baird said.

"Hell, boys," Miles Urie laughed. "That was your heart stopped. Pure dee ole fright. And I expect you best get accustomed to that feeling."

Noble Popjoy was their first direct contact with the wilderness where they intended to establish a community. So he got an intense inspection from all sides, but at a distance because at first everybody was suspicious of him and maybe a little afraid of him besides, and it would stay that way for a while, as Calvin Reed said, until the paint had time to dry.

Popjoy sensed that and told Axel Muir it might be best if he, Popjoy, stayed a little apart initially, maybe camp each night where he'd be each day, a little ahead of the column.

"There ain't much for me to do for you right now, so long as this little trace alongside the river lasts. But it won't last long. Day or two, and with them carts, we'll have to cut all the road we get. You'll still follow the river pretty much, but as the country gets rougher, more hills and valleys, that's where I can help with some cutoffs."

Most visibly upset with the arrival of the wilderness man was the African freedman Young Bone Trudeau. Not because he was afraid of Popjoy or held him in any awe but because he had supposed all along that he was himself this outfit's guide. Although Axel Muir had never said so. Young Bone was on this trek because nobody had the heart to run him off, and besides that, with all the red savage Indian scare talk, they figured the African was another adult male who would pitch in if there was ever a fight. Although Axel Muir hadn't issued Bone one of the Brown Bess muskets.

Well, Miles Urie, who quickly became the most ardent Popjoy watcher in the group, noted that the frontiersman sensed Young Bone's dissatisfaction and made the most of it for everybody's benefit.

"Now lookee here, Ole Dog, I figured to have a number-two man for scoutin and such, and you appear to be him."

And Popjoy took one of the turkey feathers from his hat and gave it to Young Bone. Which immediately brought the broad smile back to the African's face.

"Stick that in your hat, and take them pins out of it so the brim flops down all around, that's the way us scouts wear a hat, Ole Dog. Now we'll take all my plunder off that yonder nag and throw it up on one of Boss Muir's carts, and you can ride him, and we'll scout and guide and camp and cook together. You know how to cook on open coals?"

"Mr. Noble, I can cook on nothin but a hot breath!"

"I knew it as soon as I laid eyes on you," said Noble Popjoy. And he slipped the sawed-off musket from his back and handed it to Young Bone. "This is my buckshot musket. We'll get into my duffel directly and find you some pellets and flints and a powder horn."

Something happened with that transaction. Afterward, Young Bone Trudeau didn't jabber so much, as though he needed to entertain. He still smiled, but quietly, as he moved among the Ballymenas with a stately step, turkey feather bobbing above the floppy brim of his hat, the sawed-off musket slung from his shoulder. He seemed to say, without saying it, that now he was not only a freedman but a freedman with a weapon and a feather!

Cordelia Muir watched all this with a curiosity so hot she thought it must surely singe her eyelashes. The first night after Popjoy joined, she started on her husband at once.

"He looks like a savage Indian himself," she whispered.

"He is. Halfway. His daddy was a soldier, Harris told me. He was here in this part of the country with the French army during Queen Anne's War. That's what the colonists call it. We called it the War of the Austrian Succession. And he lived with this tribe of savages, and his squaw had a baby boy, who was Noble Popjoy."

"A French da, then. A papist?"

"I doubt it. He learned French speech from Jesuits who came among his Indian people. But Harris didn't say anything about him being a papist."

"Where'd he learn to talk English, then?"

"Harris didn't know. I asked him. He didn't know. Quakers, he thought."

"Quakers? How'd they get into this?"

"Popjoy ran off when he was still a boy. Somehow, he ended with some Quakers, and they schooled him for a while. Harris wasn't sure about any of it. But Popjoy's been guiding people into this Kentucky country or Pennsylvania country or Virginia country, whatever it is beyond the mountains, for a long time. A lot of people on the coast want to invest in this land out here."

"Like our own Mr. Vanderbilt Tigert."

"That's it. Now go to sleep."

"Popjoy. That's no French name. Is it?"

"I asked Harris about that, too. He said he thought Popjoy just made up his own name after he came out of the wilderness and got with the Quakers. Now go to sleep."

But it took Cordelia a long time. There were still so many questions.

The Juniata River line wasn't a very good route over the mountains, but Noble Popjoy said it was as good as any other. As the river trace petered out, they started taking the line of least resistance for the carts, hacking out a primitive road for oxen as they went. Sometimes the carts traveled some distance from the river and at other times so close the wheels cut ruts in the steep banks and sent rocks and dirt cascading down into the water.

Silas Fulton was in charge of the cart train, and Hobe Spencer, a married youth who was likely the strongest man in the group, was with the boats. The young men and most of the women alternated between hauling on dugout ropes and going ahead of the carts with axes to clear a way.

Axel Muir went back and forth between the two. Popjoy and Young Bone had begun to range out a quarter mile ahead, looking for any Indian sign now. They rode horseback when the undergrowth allowed, but much of the time they were on foot.

They had no choice but to continue cordelling, but the dugouts were more and more unstable as the land lifted toward high ridges and the river grew increasingly turbulent. They lost one load with an overturned boat before they got into the real Appalachians. There were tools in that boat, and Young Bone and Calvin Reed spent the better part of a full day diving in the cold water to recover them. Tools were as important as the seed they carried. After that, Axel Muir consigned the tools to a cart.

Nobody expected much work from Maudine Urie. She was such a tiny thing and now it was common knowledge that she was pregnant, and she started each day back in the woods, looking mortified when she returned to the main party, sure everyone had heard her throwing up. But frail or not she seemed determined to do her part, pulling on a cordelle or helping shove a cart over rough and rising ground.

"That little lassie, got iron in her back," Luke Baird said. "Ain't nobody gonna tell her what she can or can't do."

Well, Robert Chesney thought, if she belonged to me, I'd tie her in one of those carts if I had to. She got no business thrashin around here like she was as strong as Hobe Spencer's mama.

"It ain't my business," he said aloud, and Luke looked at him in surprise at the tone of his voice. Robert Chesney had his mouth set in a hard line, and Luke said no more. Maybe remembering when Robert Chesney grabbed a hatchet because Miles Urie had said something that upset him. And at the moment, these two were in front of the carts clearing trees, and Robert Chesney already had a hatchet in his hand.

From what he could remember of the affair with the British sailors in that Baltimore saloon, it had been Robert Chesney who struck the first blow. So Luke Baird just figured discretion might be a good policy with any friend who was that quick to tie in.

They were near the Appalachian Mountains divide when it started to rain. The Juniata had become less than a river, less than anything except a rushing, narrow, foaming ribbon of water boiling down steep-slope ravines. Their dugouts had become useless.

Many of them would remember that time, having to give up the boats and at the same moment, it seemed, the rain making them all miserable and cold, even though it was supposed to be summertime.

"I thought they wasn't no wet season this time of year in this place," Silas Fulton said, the water dripping off his shaggy beard.

Losing the dugouts meant having to decide what to throw away. Everything was unpacked, reloaded. Popjoy and Young Bone would operate on foot from here on so their horses could be used as pack animals. All the men fashioned shoulder packs, each of them carrying what they deemed most essential. They did such a good job of it they didn't have to leave as much behind as they'd feared.

Most of the foodstuff left them was for seeding in their new home. So they started hunting seriously, Noble Popjoy teaching them as they went. But in the rain, game was staying put, as Popjoy said, and on the eastern slopes of the mountains they killed only one white-tailed deer.

So they were glad then that Axel Muir had had the foresight back at Harris' Ferry to buy a couple of kegs of salt pork. It was Young Bone Trudeau who showed them how to collect and roast white oak acorns. It was a lot like eating hard candy because the white oak acorns had a sharp little sweet taste. Not so the black oak acorns. They were bitter as mortal sin. But the pigs thought they were fine.

The livestock wasn't faring well. The ox that had at first shown little enthusiasm for pulling got worse as the altitude increased. So they killed it and had a stomach-bulging feast and roasted the ribs and carried them for the next day. And the pigs had a cow-gut banquet.

Then, in one of those vicious little ravines choked with underbrush, the milk cow fell and broke at least one leg. There was no need to check for further damage. The one leg was enough. So they slaughtered the cow, too, and had another brief period of gluttony.

Maybe there was something about beef innards that didn't agree with pigs. Two days after the milk cow was consumed, the pigs doing their share again as they had with the ox, one of the pigs died. The next day another died.

They were afraid to eat the pigs. It was not unknown for somebody to die who'd eaten a pig taken off by some kind of disease. Dr. Rush's little booklet had nothing to say on pigs that ate acorns and cow innards and then perished.

The chickens hadn't lasted long. Twice, hens found a way out of the twig coop, wandered off into the woods, and according to Young Bone Trudeau were likely eaten by red wolves. Weasels broke into the coop three times during the night, and that was the end of any chance for a brood flock or of eggs.

Before long, a few of them were looking at the two horses. But Axel Muir explained that these animals did not belong to the Ballymenas. They belonged to Noble Popjoy personally. Which put an end to any ideas they may have had about a big feed of horse steak.

Axel Muir absolutely refused to consider slaughtering the little bull, telling them this was the necessity for a herd of beef cattle.

"Where in Holy Hoxie's name does he think he'll find a cow out here in all this wilderness?" Calvin Reed asked.

And Hobe Spencer, whose faith was as strong as his biceps, overheard the remark and said, "The Lord will provide."

"Hobe," Calvin Reed said, "I sure hope you're right. I get the impression that this place is been plumb forgot by the Lord."

"No," said Hobe, a serious frown on his face as he looked up into the overhang of hardwood branches. "This here is the Lord's own chapel. I had a dream about it."

Later, and out of Hobe Spencer's hearing, Calvin said, "Well, boys, there is a man who'll make us a fine pastor one of these days. He's already got all his prayers made up."

They'd learned to make wickiups, bending saplings to form an arched framework on which branches and bark and blankets were laid. It could be done quickly and offered a little protection from rain, but not much. The youngest Fulton child, five-year-old Lucretia, developed a cough that wouldn't go away, even after the rain had.

Their appearance was changing, most noticeably in the faces of the men. They'd stopped shaving because at night they were exhausted and during the day it was hard to find time. They began to look pretty barbaric, but it gave them something to laugh about. Most of them swore that as soon as it was convenient again, they'd remove all facial hair. Except for Miles Urie, who said he'd likely save his mustache because it made him look like a Barbary pirate.

"More like an Egyptian camel merchant," said Calvin Reed.

Noble Popjoy, maybe due to Indian blood, had almost no facial hair to begin with, and any he found he plucked out with mussel shell tweezers.

Popjoy was slowly teaching them woodcraft, whether they realized it or not. The young men in particular took to it quickly, learning to read more into the forest around them than the eye alone recorded. The result was more game brought in so that usually at night there were venison haunches over the fire. Well, once the rain stopped, which it did about the end of July.

The frontiersman Popjoy continued to fascinate even though now he was no longer considered to be a cutthroat foreigner. They heard a lot about him from the man who was in his company more than any other, Young Bone Trudeau.

"Oh yesiree," Bone said to some of the young men gathered around a fire one night, smoking clay pipes stoked with shaved tobacco. "That Noble been here before. He come out with Colonel Washington when Colonel Washington here in Kaintuck surveying the land for Virginia."

"And just who might Colonel Washington be?" Robert Chesney asked.

Young Bone's eyes widened, and he stared at Robert as though the question caused a pain in his belly.

"Why, good Lord, Mr. Robert, Colonel Washington a fine colony gentleman. Why, good Lord, Mr. Robert, us colony gentlemens in Virginia sent him out here with soldiers to tell the French to get on back north where they belonged. That was before the last French war. The French built Fort Duquesne on Virginia land, and when Colonel Washington come with his soldiers, the French and their soldiers and their Indians captured Colonel Washington. And Noble Popjoy, too, cause Noble Popjoy was scouting for Colonel Washington.

"But they turned Colonel Washington and Noble Popjoy loose, and after that us colony gentlemens and the English army had the French war and run the French plumb out of all this land. And the French burned their Fort Duquesne and run off, and us colony gentlemens and the English built it up again only called it Fort Pitt now.

"*Thas* who Colonel Washington is!"

"How do you know about all this?" asked Luke Baird.

"Why, good Lord, Mr. Luke, everybody know about Colonel Washington. And your man Tigert, he knows Colonel Washington cause they both tooken a great liking to this Kaintuck, and for all we knows, Colonel Washington is one of the colony gentlemens put some money with Mr. Tigert on this whole shebang that gets us out here in Kaintuck."

"Are we there now?" Robert Chesney asked. "Are we in this Kaintuck now, Bone?"

"By God, Mr. Robert." And Young Bone laughed. "As soon as we gets on the west slopes of the mountains, we is. You betcha sweet life.

"Now time to get on over yonder to scout's wickiup where us scouts sleeps, Young Bone Trudeau and Mr. Noble Popjoy. Yesiree!"

They were past the headwater springs of the Juniata and moving down the western slopes of the mountains when summer weather finally arrived, and with the heat and sweat came gnats and wood ticks and brush flies of all kinds. Cranston Shook's wife Caroline was sensitive to insect bites, and on most days her eyes were swollen almost shut.

"Maybe we ought to bleed her," said Axel Muir.

"No, we won't," Cordelia said in a way that left no room for argument. "I'll make a salts solution and bathe those eyes each morning."

The salts solution didn't help, but Noble Popjoy came up with a remedy. In a lightning scar where persimmon trees were growing he found a black bear feeding on last fall's fruit overlooked by birds. He killed the bear and skinned him out, and there was a lot of fat that the women rendered into grease over that evening's fires. The odor almost ran everybody out of camp.

They roasted the bear meat, and it was tough and gamy and nobody much cared for it, except for Popjoy and Young Bone. But they ate it anyway.

When the grease had cooled, it congealed into a grainy lard, and Noble Popjoy showed them how to rub it on exposed skin to discourage insects. The smell of it was so violently foul that everybody said they'd take the bugs.

Well, Cranston Shook applied some of it to his wife's face, and she didn't complain much, and he did it again the next day and the next, and Caroline had no more trouble with swollen eyelids because the insects avoided Caroline Shook. So did everybody else.

They could tell now that they were going down into a major valley system. Sometimes, when the timber thinned or in lightning scars where trees had not yet had time for full growth, they could look toward the west and see mile after mile of mountains, ridgelines blurring and turning deep blue then smoky gray with distance.

Streams grew less turbulent as the degree of slope lessened, and the water was clear and cold even now, in early August. The mountain creeks were becoming rivers. They all flowed directly across their line of march, which here had turned almost due west. They took a lot of fish from these streams, and there was now plenty of game in the deep woods. No night passed without the smell of meat cooking over their open fires.

They were near the headwaters of a river called the Canemough the day Noble Popjoy and Young Bone Trudeau found the moccasin tracks. They were walking along a narrow sandbar at the water's edge, scouting ahead of the main party for a night campsite when they saw the imprints in the damp sand. As Popjoy stood looking at them, two of the prints closest to the river slowly filled with water so Popjoy knew whoever made those prints had done it only a few minutes before.

"Let's get back out of here real easy," Noble Popjoy whispered, and they did, their weapons up and their eyes casting like snake tongues through all the shoreline trees.

On the far side of the river and in the shadows of heavy timber, they squatted and watched. There was still nothing. But there had been something just a few heartbeats ago. Finally, they moved back toward the main party, and then Popjoy told Young Bone what they had seen and what it might mean.

He figured there were about ten in this party, all men probably. There was no way to tell if they were part of a larger group or out on their own looking for mischief.

There had been only those few seconds to read the prints, but he knew the moccasins were Iroquois. He didn't know which tribe. He hoped they weren't dealing with one of the Five Nation Iroquois. That could mean Seneca or Mohawk.

Most recently, in the last French war, Senecas and Mohawks had been allies of the English, and one might expect they would still honor that friendship with people from the British colonies. But the French were out of it now, which threw the whole equation into confusion. Besides, you never could tell what a small war party might do, even if the head men back in the longhouses professed peace. Especially if whiskey was involved.

"All right, Ole Dog," Popjoy said. "Let's keep this to ourselves for a spell yet, except for the three unmarried young men."

"Mr. Robert an Mr. Calvin an Mr. Luke."

"That's right. And we'll keep them mum, too. No need to fret the whole party. This bunch we almost surprised on the river washin their asses, they may be scared of us as we are them. Maybe it's just a hunting scout."

"What if it's not a scout? What if these red heathen mad at somebody?"

Noble Popjoy looked into Young Bone's eyes for a long time before he spoke.

"We'll just have to wait and see, won't we? In the meantime, we'll have our young men be sure the women and children don't get too far away from the cart."

They lost another pig almost within sight of their destination. It was something they'd always remember, not because of the pig but because of the circumstances of its departure.

It was mountain country still, but the ravines and gulleys were not so deep and the ridges not so sharp and high. The Ballymenas thought of it as foothills to the rough terrain they'd spent a month passing through.

The land had become a washboard topography, with valleys and hills parallel for miles, running east-northeast to west-southwest.

Which meant, now that Popjoy had turned their line of march due west, they had to traverse each corridor. Up and down, up and down, up and down. Like rowing crosswind to lines of breakers running toward a rocky shore.

That's how Axel Muir put it, using another one of his open-sea salt-spray metaphors.

Trees were not so close packed on these gentler slopes, and there were great swaths of scrub and second growth. Noble Popjoy said it was an old burn scar from what had been one hell of a forest fire back about ten or fifteen years ago, he figured.

There were some young pignut hickory and a few red mulberry, nothing over about thirty feet high. Mostly it was the kind of low, bushy tree that sprang up quick in a lightning scar. Their roots would hold soil in place for about a decade, giving the big hardwoods time to mature. Black locust and witch hazel. Sassafras and other mountain laurels.

Cordelia Muir kept pestering Young Bone to name these trees and bushes. Like the other Ulster Scots, the only thing in all the hundreds she could identify was a black oak here and there.

There were plenty of birds for him to identify as well. Dozens of warblers and almost as many woodpeckers and finches. They were everywhere, most of them finished nesting and now in flocks feeding on maturing forest berries and fruits. Wild cherry and crabapple. Huckleberries and gooseberries.

Not only the birds, either. Each day, the children, even though kept close to the carts by Popjoy's young men, had a sweet, juicy-mouthed feed of wild blackberries, going after the seedy ground fruit headlong, without regard for sharp thorns.

The day came when they arrived on the first knoll above the creek that they would later call Hog Gone Branch in their oral histories of the time. The rise of ground had few trees, but they grew dense along the stream and everything there was in deep shadows.

It all started after they camped there and the next morning just before dawn the little Fulton girl Lucretia died.

From his almanac, Axel Muir reckoned it was Sunday, August 22. So because they'd have to bury the child anyway, he called for a full day of rest and religious worship before pushing the last few days toward the Monongahela.

They made a crude wooden box from slats taken out of the cart sideboards. The hole they dug at the crest of the little hill under a young red gum tree, and Axel Muir spoke over the grave. It sounded suspiciously like a burial at sea. With a heavy dose of Calvinism thrown in for good measure.

"We commit this earthly remain of Lucretia Louise Fulton with conviction of resurrection when the earth gives up its dead. And remembering her glad smile and gentle demeanor our faith that she was chosen by the Lord God Almighty on that day before the earth and heaven were created to come and sit by His side in Paradise."

Some of the women cried. Calvin Reed said Nadine Spencer carried on better than anybody. But Silas and Ma Fulton remained stony faced and tearless, as you might expect from good Scots, but anybody who looked closely could see a terrible agony in Silas Fulton's eyes.

They rested then and were glad for it. The women washed clothes and laid them out on blackberry bushes to dry in the sun. Some of them baked bread, using ground white oak acorn flour. Axel Muir called them together for another service, and they sang a hymn and he read scripture from Cordelia's King James version. Then Hobe Spencer preached a sermon that would have made old John Knox proud. And they sang. As far as anybody has been able to determine, it was the first time the melodies of Presbyterian hymns were heard in those mountains.

Some of the young men moved off a short way into the shade of the woods to smoke clay pipes. Nobody noticed that about midafternoon, the woodpeckers in the timber along the little creek stopped pounding the trees in their search for grubs. And jays had gone strangely silent. Even the buzz of summer insects seemed suddenly suspended.

Robert Chesney, Miles Urie, Calvin Reed, and Luke Baird moved leisurely down the slope toward the stream, where the trees and underbrush were thick, the shadows dark. They were speaking of things young men often speak of, remembrance of good times past. They were almost to the edge of the timber at the creek bank when Robert Chesney was aware of voices ahead. He paid it no mind.

Then they stepped out of the brush and trees, and Robert Chesney's thinking suddenly stopped, like a clock's pendulum suspended in midstroke. He saw them, about half a dozen of them, who seemed to have popped up out of nowhere, like naked dolls from a child's jack-in-the-box; they were armed with muskets, and their faces were painted, and their eyes were black and shining beneath heads sheared bald except for long roaches.

One of the Indians held a pig in both arms, and standing close beside him was Young Bone Trudeau, his hands on the pig, too, and the African was trying to speak in some language the Indian could comprehend. In all that flash of light and shadow and confusion, one of them, likely Miles Urie, shouted, "Alarm, alarm!"

Everyone froze in place, like figures on a vague tapestry, weapons up. Young Bone Trudeau's eyes shone white as he looked across the creek and saw the Ballymenas. Young Bone may have tried to shout something, Robert Chesney wasn't sure, but he heard someone running down the slope from the main party.

It was Darrel Stark, the party's blacksmith, and just as he broke out of the trees, his foot hooked a tangle of briar and he pitched forward, and as his musket hit the ground, it fired, sending a flash of flame toward the sky and shattering the silence.

Robert Chesney was never able to remember thinking anything. But his musket was coming up and he saw the line of men across the creek leveling their weapons, and it seemed that everyone fired at once, a great exploding smash of sound and fire and smoke. Never could Robert Chesney recall even the kick of the Brown Bess against his shoulder or the quick, jerky movements of reloading, yanking out the ramrod, pouring powder down the bore.

Before the swirl of smoke obscured his vision of the far bank, he saw the African down and beside him the Indian who had held the pig, and the Indian's face was mostly shot away, and there were the shadows of the woods and nothing more, the line of Indians gone like a windblown scarf, flowing, gone like smoke. And the piercing scream of the pig, and Robert Chesney saw the pig then, thrashing on the ground beside Young Bone Trudeau and the Indian without any face. And as the smoke drifted off through the trees, he saw another half-naked form a short way back in the trees, lying deathly still with one arm up, caught in a blackberry bush, the hand still clutching a musket.

His thinking only started then, with someone sitting beside him saying, "They've shot me, Bobby, they've shot me." It was Calvin Reed, and his woolen shirt had a red patch of blood along the left side under the arm.

His next conscious thought had Noble Popjoy running back through the woods in the direction the Indians had gone, and Axel Muir and the other men of the Ballymenas all around, ready with their muskets. And Young Bone Trudeau shouting. "You Scot gentlemens best come help Young Bone now, yesiree, cause Young Bone got a sore wound and he got half this savage heathen's head splattered all over his shirt!"

Well, Axel Muir figured, it wasn't such a bad score. Two dead Indians, two wounded Ballymenas, and a dead pig. Young Bone Trudeau had a pellet that had barely punctured the skin below the left nipple, there striking a rib and skittering around toward the breastbone. The pellet made a lump under the skin large as a robin's egg.

Calvin Reed had taken a ball glancing across the ribs under the arm, maybe cracking one rib, but only laying open his hide like the skin of a tomato left in boiling water. Painful, but not serious. Cordelia had it stitched shut with some of Dr. Rush's sutures in no time and then turned to the African, who sat against a cart, his shirt off, laughing and telling the circle of children who stood around what a wonderful Indian fighter he was.

"Young Bone try to talk that red savage heathen into lettin that pig go. Then all Young Bone's friends come runnin, and Young Bone see Mr. Darrel comin down through them woods and fall down, and Young Bone say Lord Gawd that musket gone shoot all by its ownself."

Hearing that, Axel Muir's wrath fired up again almost to explosion, but not quite. He kept muttering about damn-fool accidents and this one could have caused two of his own people to be killed, maybe more. And God only knew what reaction they might expect from the tribe those pig thieves came from.

Cordelia made a small incision over the lump on Young Bone Trudeau's chest. There was a small spurt of blood, and she had the pellet, with a spoonful of blood, in the palm of her hand. Only it wasn't a pellet. Nadine Spencer, who had been helping, drew back and gasped, "Dear God!"

"What's the matter?" Axel Muir asked. His wife rose and held out her hand, and Axel Muir saw what she was holding. A tooth. A large human jaw tooth. He took it gingerly between thumb and forefinger.

"By heaven, I never thought I'd see such a thing again in this life," he said.

"What does it mean?" Cordelia asked, and she was visibly shaken.

"That musket ball," said Muir. "It shattered the red infidel's face, and this tooth flew out just like another bullet. I saw it once on the old HMS *Vanguard*. Off Antigua back in '46. We surprised a French sloop, and she got off a few shots before we sank her. Solid shot."

He wiped the blood off the tooth, and now the African was watching him, listening, wide-eyed.

"Well?" Cordelia asked impatiently.

"Two men in our gun crews, standing close, when a ball struck one in the head. The man standing next to him was killed, too. With a flying tooth. Just like a bullet."

"Are you spinning tall sea tales, Axel Muir?"

He had a hard little grin on his face, the only grin Axel Muir had displayed since Belfast. He held the tooth, shining clean in the sunlight, before her face.

"Do you see it, my pet?" he asked. "Do you think our young men are loading their muskets with teeth now? No, this is truly, before God, the tooth of a red savage heathen. And our good scout the freedman Young Bone Trudeau is lucky he's alive!"

Axel Muir offered the tooth to Young Bone, but the African would have nothing to do with it. He wouldn't touch it. He wouldn't look at it. He finally walked off into the woods, holding the place on his chest where the tooth had wounded him, stabbing the ground at each step with his long walking stick. The walking stick the Ballymenas had first seen in the Baltimore mule pen when the African had come to them. It seemed a long time ago. The stick then had had a brass ball at one end, long since lost somewhere in the Appalachian Mountains where one day somebody would find it and wonder how it came to be there.

So Axel Muir kept the tooth as a token of one less red savage inhabiting the land obviously meant by God to be taken and nurtured by good Calvinists. It was said a certain tribe in the Ohio Valley offered to pay many good furs for the head of the man who wore on a chain around his neck a tooth that belonged to them!

There was the question of two dead bodies to dispose of and the pig. The pig was no problem. They ate it. And that's when they named the place Hog Gone Creek. Perhaps with a rare touch of Scots humor. Well, the pig was gone all right, even though they did get the benefit of it.

The two dead men presented a different kind of concern. Savage infidels though they were, Axel Muir believed that some biblical ethic required that they be buried and read over. Noble Popjoy disabused him of that notion. Not with arguments that there was no such biblical ethic but rather that good common sense dictated otherwise.

Popjoy had returned after following the fleeing Indians for a short distance, saying they looked to be scooting out of the area at high speed. By then, the Ballymenas had the two dead men laid out in a grove of locusts nearby where the confrontation had occurred. Everybody, including the children, had come to make their inspection, standing well back to avoid the swarm of blackflies.

Once Axel Muir had his wounded tended to, he appeared on the scene and scolded everyone back to the campsite, leaving only himself, Popjoy, and two of Popjoy's young men. They stood around the bodies and discussed what needed doing.

And Robert Chesney had the strange feeling that he could see the dead men actually beginning to rot before his eyes as their killers stood over them and watched.

Well, he figured maybe one has to expect such outlandish things in peculiar times. After all, these were the only dead men he'd ever seen except for a few laid out in a coffin dressed in their best clothes.

"We can't just leave em out here in the woods for the varmints to eat," said Axel Muir.

"Best we do," Popjoy said. "That bunch *could* come back for these two. They don't like leaving their dead on somebody else's ground. And if they do come back, they need to see how serious it is to cross our track."

"You think they'll be back, then?"

"Only to pick up their dead," said Popjoy. "And another thing, if that happens, I want em to see that we play this game just like they do. We take trophies, just like they do. Now, if you take offense at lifting hair, you best look off yonder somewheres."

"You mean you're going to . . ." Axel Muir didn't need to finish his question. Popjoy was already giving him an answer, pulling out his long French butcher knife and bending to the bodies.

He did it quickly, as though he'd done it many times before. He peeled back a patch of scalp the size of a buckwheat cake from the top of each head, about the middle of the roach of long hair. Rising, he stuffed the trailing ends of the hair into one of his waistband pouches, allowing the flesh portion to hang free where wind and sun would strike it. There was almost no blood on it.

Later, at the shank end of this day, Robert Chesney would watch Popjoy flesh the scalps with a mussel shell, just like preparing a hide for making hair-on buckskin, then stretch each of them on a small willow hoop. They would hang like that at Popjoy's side until the skin had cured to the consistency and texture and color of old parchment.

But first, after Axel Muir reluctantly agreed, Robert Chesney and Luke Baird each took a dead Indian by the heels and dragged the bodies farther into the woods away from the camp, Noble Popjoy leading them. It was not a pleasant task, and going back across the creek toward the carts, Chesney and Baird took a long time at the stream washing their hands.

Axel Muir was still uneasy, and after dark he and Robert Chesney went to the campsite of Popjoy and Young Bone Trudeau. They had no fire this night. Which didn't do a lot to reassure Axel Muir, which is why he'd come. For reassurance.

"Indians always measure their chances before they fight," Popjoy said. "If they figure to get hurt, they wait til another day. That's why they use ambush and surprise attack and hittin home where the women and kids are, the things you whites think is bad. Of course, you do it now, too.

"But you people come from a land where they fight a war by both sides standing up and whaling away at each other until one is so bloody he's gotta back off. Indian thinks that's stupid. So he'll only fight that way if he's forced to."

"It sounds pretty sensible to me," said Robert Chesney.

"Why hell yes, it's sensible. And that little jamboree this afternoon was what he hates like smallpox. Him lined up, you lined up. He knows you like that, all of it strung out in full view like washin on a line. He knows you don't need to get ready, like consultin with your medicine, like singin to work up your power, like dancin a few nights to get your friends to follow you. All them things he thinks he needs before he fights. Hell no, you white people just wade right in, drop of the hat, dog eat dog, devil take the hindmost.

"Well, *that's* what he thinks is barbaric. You don't ask your gods for help or at least let your gods know what it is you aim to do. Like you ain't even *got* any gods."

Popjoy had worked himself into a white rage suddenly, talking about this, and nothing like it had happened before, and it frightened Robert Chesney a little. After all, here was this man telling them about how Indians thought white men were godless, and he's half Indian himself.

Noble Popjoy rose abruptly, and Young Bone with him. Popjoy took up his rifle and glanced at the pan.

"I'll take a walk around," he said and was immediately gone into the night.

Axel Muir wheezed a sigh of exasperation.

"By damn, I didn't intend to give him the colic about this, but I gotta think about all these people depending on me."

From the darkness, Young Bone Trudeau laughed.

"Don't you fret none, Cap'n," he said. "Mr. Noble saz them red savages ain't gone come back. An if Mr. Noble saz it, you can believe it be true."

Robert Chesney slept with his musket primed and under his hand that night. What little sleeping he did. There were more strange and dangerous-sounding noises from the dark woods that night than Robert Chesney could recall in all their past experience across the Appalachians.

He tried bravely to identify each sound from what Young Bone Trudeau and Noble Popjoy had told him on other nights along the trek. That's a horned owl. That's a red wolf, far off. That's a vixen and her pups, must be close to a den hole. That's a fish jumping. But what the hell was that? And that? And that?

Axel Muir, anxious to be rid of this place, had them up and moving just at dawn. There were a lot of men with red eyes, so Robert Chesney knew there had been others who had found sleep difficult.

As the carts lumbered off into the gray woods where mist was lying like a thin gauze, Robert Chesney, his heart up in his throat all the way, ran back through the woods to the place where they'd left the two dead men.

The bodies were gone.

Chapter 4

Two days after they left Hog Gone Creek, Robert Chesney found the courage to tell Noble Popjoy that the Indian party had come back. Noble Popjoy actually smiled, and Robert Chesney saw it even though the wilderness man tried to hide it behind his hand.

"Maybe it was a bear," Popjoy said. "Or a couple of red wolves. Come and drag em off."

"No, it wasn't either," Robert Chesney said, and his temper flared a little. "The ground wasn't tore up or anything. Neat and clean as a needle."

"Well, no use gettin puffed up over it," Popjoy said.

Then he reached out and touched Robert Chesney on the shoulder, and that made it all right again and Robert Chesney felt the heat going out of his face.

So they sat down on an old fallen log and had a pipe of tobacco and looked out into the valley opening below them. They were on high ground now, in scattered hardwoods, but the slope pitched away sharply toward the west and they could see a long way. There was a heavy, dark green timbered area about three miles off, meandering through second growth timber, and Popjoy said that was it. That was the Monongahela.

Then Noble Popjoy told the young Ulsterman about the Indian wars in this Ohio River country, this country that Young Bone Trudeau called Kaintuck, this country that nobody was sure who owned. On the basis of an old Iroquois treaty ceding much of this ground to the British, many land companies had been licensed to sell or settle certain sections of it. They were land companies with boards of directors favored by the Crown or powerful members of Parliament. But the Ballymenas were not the effort of a company favored by Crown or Parliament. They were sponsored by a wildcat outfit, unlicensed by anyone. Hence their movement into the area west of the mountains was illegal under the provisions of the Proclamation Line.

And Robert Chesney felt it an honor being told such things by this wilderness man. Because this wilderness man didn't talk freely to many people about anything beyond what he considered his job as guide and scout.

"This valley is pretty quiet now," Popjoy said. "South of the Ohio anyway. With the French gone. Just a few hunting parties now and then, like that one we saw. There was a time when there was war here. Not because the French and the English were gouging one another, either. An Indian war. Before there were any white men in this valley."

As he smoked and talked, Popjoy was cutting his fingernails with the same big French knife he'd used to scalp those two Indians at Hog Gone Creek.

"What was the war about?" Chesney asked.

"Trade," Popjoy said. "The fur trade. White man wasn't here yet, not many, but he was over to the east of here. And he was trading metal pots and knives and hatchets and guns for furs, mostly beaver. So the tribesmen brought in the furs, and for it they got all those things. And once a tribe started getting white man's goods, they had to keep doing it, because if they didn't, their enemies would, and that'd be the end of them."

"You mean their Indian enemies?"

"Onlyest enemies they had was other tribes. I just said, white man wasn't here yet."

"All right. So the tribes were fighting each other so they could trade with the English."

"Or the French or the Dutch," said Popjoy. "But it wasn't just a fight so they could trade. It was a fight to *control* the trade."

"Wanting to be the middleman. The jobber?"

"I don't know what you call it," said Popjoy. "But it's like this Mr. Tigert in Dover who hired me and who put this whole Ballymena thing together. He sits at the center and deals with both ends and makes a big profit. You got to understand, Bobby, Indians may be savages in your view, but in no view at all be they stupid. They can see how to profit from trading. Hell! They been tradin with each other back beyond the grandfathers. Before whites was anywhere on this side of the water."

"I guess wherever you got business, you gonna have them that tries to control it."

"The people as was fiercest on trying to control it was the Iroquois. And not just any Iroquois but the Five Nations. And not just any of them, either, but the Mohawks. Before white man in any number got here, the Mohawks would make sweeps through this country wipin out the competition. They was almost as bad as your smallpox when it come to wipin out Indians."

Popjoy was finished with his manicure, and he sheathed his knife and knocked the dead tobacco ash from his pipe and spat. Robert Chesney had the feeling that the scout was so wound up that if he had walked away Popjoy would have kept right on talking.

"Those two men you people killed back there, they were Eries. I didn't know there was any Eries left. Not around here. All poxed out or killed by the Mohawks or scattered and gone west. I grew up in an Erie tribe."

Robert Chesney felt a little shudder go up his back. He would have asked a question or two as Popjoy paused, but when the wilderness man said "you people," Robert Chesney knew there was a separation between them, that even though he might be employed by white men, Popjoy did not consider himself one. So Robert Chesney suddenly felt himself outside, looking in on the world being created for him by Popjoy's words. So he didn't ask anything. He kept quiet, and although he knew it was silly, he tried to make himself as inconspicuous as possible.

"My mother was a Delaware," said Noble Popjoy. "My pap was a Frenchman. A deserter from their army in Canada. They moved around somewhat because I guess he was afraid if he stayed in one spot too long, the French would find him and hang him.

"So for a long time we were with a band of Eries. They had a town just off the south shore of the lake. Lake Erie. When I was half grown, but still a boy, I left there and I left the Erie or anybody else I figured might get caught in what the Erie got caught in. I moved on east, and after a long time, some Quakers had me in one of their schools and they taught me everything the Jesuit priests had left out when I was with the Eries. Then, from there, I started scouting trails for the white man."

Popjoy stopped suddenly and looked at Robert Chesney and grinned, and it was so startling, Chesney almost fell off his log seat.

"I met Mr. Ben Franklin. Now there's a man wants to know what's west of the mountains. I reckon Mr. Ben Franklin is interested in just about everything."

Now Noble Popjoy filled his clay pipe again and lit it with a flint fire starter. He puffed a few clouds of blue smoke before he took up his story, watching each puff whipped away by the gentle breeze blowing from the west out of the Monongahela Valley.

"Yes sir, Bobby, I left. It was spring, and we'd heard rumors that Mohawk war parties were out. But hell, you always heard those stories. We were about ready to leave, move down into the main Ohio Valley and grow some corn. No hurry about it. And this one morning

66

about dawn, I was out in the woods close to the town looking into some rabbit traps I'd set."

Popjoy puffed a half dozen clouds of smoke out for the wind, as though he were feeding it.

"I heard this yell. Just one yell, all by itself. Then a musket shot. That's when the wailing started. It was a high whining wail, and with it were shouts and more musket shots. But the wailing was what made me know. I'd never heard it before, but I knew. That village was being slaughtered.

"It didn't take long. There must have been a couple hundred warriors attacked the village because they did it all so fast. I lay in the bushes listening to it and cold water fear along my back, and before the wailing stopped, I could smell the smoke from burning wickiups and longhouses. I didn't think about much. I just lay there chewing the dirt under my face and hoping they didn't find me and wishing the damned wailing and squealing and squawking would stop. It finally did."

Popjoy puffed on his pipe again and stood up, but he wasn't finished. As he looked out on the large valley, Robert Chesney could sense that Popjoy wasn't seeing this country but that Erie village on the lake after the Mohawks came.

"Everything that could burn was burning. I peeped around good before I went in there. The war party had moved right on. I knew there was a Miami village a few miles down the lake. I don't know what Miamis were doing that far east, but I expect they were sorry they ever left their home country before it was over. I figured that's where the war party went. They went in such a hurry they didn't take any of the food left in winter baskets. Just the weapons. They took all the weapons. They didn't even take all the hair. There were a lot of dead, most of them hatcheted, who hadn't been scalped. So I knew the Mohawks were in a hurry!

"I'll never forget it. The first time I'd ever seen what war could be like, up close. There were bodies all around, some still wiggling. Young and old. Man and woman. Babes. Bodies without heads, an arm here, leg there, heads scattered around. Pieces of my friends. Some roasting in the fires like bear meat. Even the village dogs had been killed."

He turned and stepped across the log, back in the direction where Robert Chesney knew the Ballymena column was coming on. Then paused again.

"I've heard that some white men who have come onto a village like that, a village just struck by an enemy war party, have wrote about it and what they saw. I'd like to read one of them someday. I wonder if they got the smell of it in there. You never forget the smell."

Well, it gave Robert Chesney plenty to think about. It might have been incongruous, but the whole thing reminded him of his own fascination with memory. For example, he had never been able to bring the image of his mother's face to mind, her having died when he was still a babe. Yet sometimes, when he dreamed of Scotland, he could hear a soft voice and he knew it was the voice of his mother.

And then the journey ended.

There was a small stream coming down to the main river channel, cutting a soft little valley, heavy timber on both slopes and along one ridge. They planned their community on the high ground with fewer trees overlooking the Monongahela and started laying out foundations for houses, a blacksmith shop, a large barn, and a meeting hall which would also serve as a barracks for the unwed men.

Along the main riverbank, Silas Fulton and his entire family did a slash-and-burn planting of winter wheat while the others cut and planned and drilled and notched. There were plenty of trees for all purposes.

Red cedar for shingles and a stand of white pine less than a quarter mile away for logs. Shagbark hickory and slippery elm. Beech along the creek in the moist soil there, along with the sandbar willow.

And across the river, a number of paper birch. Noble Popjoy and Young Bone Trudeau made a raft to cross and brought back sheaths of bark. They began to make birch bark canoes, and Popjoy asked Robert Chesney to help them. Axel Muir said canoe making might be handy once Popjoy left the party, so Chesney found himself with the wilderness man and the African while his young friends blistered hands with saw and hammer and adze.

And hunting. Those three, Popjoy, Young Bone, and Chesney, became the regular hunters for the settlement. Game was plentiful. Deer and black bear and turkey. Fish, too, and small game and upland birds.

Popjoy said he would stay with them well into winter or until he was sure the freedman and Chesney had learned all the things they needed to know.

The other young men looked at Robert Chesney with a little chagrin and a lot of envy in their faces. He was aware of it. He was aware of the special thing Popjoy was doing for him. It was more than just keeping a saw and hammer out of his hands. It was making him a woodsman instead of a farmer. Of course, there was nothing wrong with being a farmer, but Robert Chesney liked the thought of working with musket and skinning knife rather than plow and hoe.

By the first frost, there was a roof over everyone's head. On that day they woke to find Noble Popjoy gone. He'd left a special decoration nailed above the main door of the meeting hall where the young bachelors and the African lived. The two Erie scalps, the hair long and shining and beautifully oiled.

"Just as a warning, I'd expect, to any others who might pass by," said Robert Chesney, and Axel Muir, knowing Chesney understood Popjoy's forest wisdom better than any of the others, including himself, let the scalps stay, although he worried a little that the place where they held religious services each Sunday was now festooned with human hair.

In less than a week, they woke to find a powdering of white on the ground. It was their first snow in the new land, just a few days before

Christmas. The hills around them stood cold and gray, the leafless hardwoods stark against the colorless ground. Even the cedars were a dull blue-green on this sunless day.

The sky was as inhospitable as the ridges, and a rook of crows flapping above the barren birch trees across the river added little warmth of life with their harsh cawing.

Axel Muir decided it was time to hold a town meeting and get things organized. So everybody, including the children, filed beneath the two Erie scalps and into the barnlike meeting hall. A cold west wind moved the long hair like black silk pennants on the jack staff of a ship's stern castle. At least, that's how Axel Muir saw it.

The meeting opened with a prayer. A council was chosen. This was accomplished by Axel Muir naming himself, Silas Fulton, and Loy Ennis as councilmen and asking if anyone objected. Nobody did. Axel Muir said he'd act as chairman for the time being and that Cordelia would be secretary and take down minutes, and in about a year they'd have an election and vote another group in if they wanted to, because, he said, from now on everything would be done the way things are supposed to be done in a democracy!

Chairman Muir said that they had to be concerned with the peace and dignity of their town, and there followed an argument and near fistfight over what law they were supposed to respect, who were the policemen, where was the jail, and who were the judges to put people there if they acted up.

Using his belaying pin to bang on the railing they'd built around a pulpit at one end of the barn, the chairman regained order after a few moments and said the council would look into the problem and report everything to the community at large.

Next, the common defense against Indians. Somebody said they could organize a militia, but somebody else said there wasn't any sense in that, all the men now would fight if the settlement was threatened, so the first man said all right but they needed a bell or something to give a warning to people working out in the fields or in the homes some of them would eventually build at a distance from the town.

The chairman said the council would look into it.

Now the big one. Land ownership. Axel Muir had a map, or rather a chart, from Vanderbilt Tigert, and it showed what was Tigert's investors' land and what was theirs. So they had the broad area in mind, but how to distribute the slices, that was the rub, Cordelia said.

How much could a man and his family have? Could he have land in both town and country? Would tenure and improvement on the land be required before title would be recognized? Would he have to pay for his part of the public domain? How much? Could he be taxed on it? Could it be taken from him? What happened to it when he died? Who set the value on it? Who kept all these records, and who established legal title?

Thus the Ballymenas, whose only contact with real estate until then had been the hated pennies rent they'd had to pay some absentee English landlord, butted headfirst against Property! Property! Father to much of the law in civilized countries, be it constitutional, statute, or common.

"And what I want to know," said Cranston Shook, "this talk about pay for property, and then taxes. Who do we pay this to? The squirrels?"

The look on the chairman's face made Cranston Shook realize he'd made a mistake. The chairman explained that in the course of time the community would need a little money to operate and that the Ballymenas would be growing crops for sale, and surely Fort Pitt couldn't be too far down this river, so they could find a market for their stuff and have cash money, and he said all of that staring at Cranston Shook as though Cranston Shook was an idiot.

For now, the chairman said, the council would look into all these things.

Finally, they gave themselves a name. Hobe Spencer stood up and prayed and testified a little about his coming to grace, and Calvin Reed whispered that it sounded like one of those new Methodist exhorters, and Hobe said it had come to him that the name of their town would be New Jerusalem.

This created a storm of protest, and some of the more powerfully individualistic among them shouted that nobody had told *them* it was supposed to be called New Jerusalem. When the chairman finally regained some form of order, Hobe was very meek in suggesting Beulah Land. They all agreed it sounded all right, even though some still said no voices in the night had told them it ought to be called that, either, and the first law the council needed to enact was one that made it a whipping offense for anybody to try and influence public decisions by claiming to hear voices of the Holy Ghost or an angel or anybody else along those lines.

So they accepted Beulah Land because it was late and getting cold in that barn and coming on close to soup time. Thus learning another operating principle of democracy, to wit, that nothing moves a debate along faster than the approach of dinnertime!

Maybe Cordelia Muir was the only one there who had a chuckle over the Beulah business, being as she was somewhat of an expert on the written word in James I's Bible, even the Old Testament. So now she figured that Hobe Spencer might be a fine preacher but maybe a sneaky one. Because the prophet Isaiah, who was a very large prophet indeed, had suggested once that when the captive Jews came out of Babylon and returned to the city of their fathers, they would name it Beulah. And the city of their fathers was Jerusalem!

As the others filed out, Axel Muir took Robert Chesney aside and introduced him to responsibility for the first time in the young man's life. Robert Chesney would go downriver until he found Fort Pitt and there tell all that there was a settlement at this certain bend of the Monongahela. He gave Chesney almost all of the last of the Tigert money and instructed him on items he and Cordelia thought should be obtained, if possible. Get all the news, don't get too drunk, stay out of jails, and get back within a week. Provided Fort Pitt wasn't two hundred miles away. In which case, get back when you can.

It was a stunning thing! Robert Chesney lay awake most of that night, thinking about having become a grown man, trusted with the business of the community. Such things were supposed to place a leaden weight on a man's shoulders. Robert Chesney kept trying to feel a leaden weight. But no matter how hard he tried, he couldn't do it.

They built three canoes before Noble Popjoy departed. Paper birch bark on ash-and-cedar frames. These were the durable little vessels no heavier than a sparkle of sunlight that were amazingly easy to handle even while carrying very heavy loads.

One was about twenty-five feet long, a three-foot beam at midship, a true cargo canoe. It could carry eight paddlemen, but two were sufficient to control it in the stream. Each of the other two canoes was about fifteen feet long, a three-man, high-speed canoe, but one man could easily manage such a boat.

On that cold, black February predawn, the big canoe and one of the small ones moved away from the riverbank at Beulah Land. There was a sharp cracking noise as they pushed off because now a thin ice sheet formed along the riverbanks each night. But soon they were in clear water and turning downstream, their wakes etching two black lines in the pale quicksilver surface of the river.

In the small canoe, and leading, was Robert Chesney. In the large boat was Young Bone Trudeau at the stern, Miles Urie in the bow, and Hobe Spencer sitting amidship. All moved rhythmically with their paddles except for Hobe, who sat hunched like a sleeping bear, his musket muzzle above his head like a short mast.

Chesney figured Axel Muir had insisted that Hobe Spencer go on this trip because he was a Bible thumper and would keep everybody else out of any whiskey or woman trouble. Or whatever trouble there might be in this Fort Pitt. Providing they ever found Fort Pitt.

It wasn't only Hobe who looked bearish. They all did, dressed in the winter fur hats and jackets and leggings the women at Beulah Land had made from the various hides they'd brought in during the fall and early winter. Wherever daylight found them, a close inspection would reveal that their clothes made no pretense of matching.

Each wore a patchwork of skins. Bear, beaver, squirrel, rabbit, deer, cougar, and a few other things that nobody could likely identify.

They had no idea how far they were from Fort Pitt. They had been told it was on this river, and if it was, they'd find it. But they didn't know how long it would take.

All day, under gray clouds, they paddled. They didn't see another human being. They suspected that maybe a few other human beings saw them. The solitude and stillness of the vast country inching by as they paddled didn't do much for their piece of mind. Each of them had their muskets primed and lying at hand.

During the entire day, they saw three crows. And once, in an eddy of the main stream, a coot or cormorant or some kind of bird that ran along the surface of the water for twenty feet before lifting on flapping wings. That was all. No other sign of life. They felt completely alone in this frigid, endless wilderness.

From time to time, Robert Chesney halted for rest, but they floated in the stream, away from the shore. They ate fish caught and dried the past fall. It tasted like hell. Once, on one of these rest pauses, they held their canoes together, side by side.

"How far you figure we've come, Boss Bobby?" Miles Urie asked.

"I don't know. This river bends and twists back and forth," Chesney said. "For all I know, we might be just over the hill from where we started."

"Plague take this cold," said Hobe Spencer. "I hope we don't still be looking come night. I'd hate havin to go on the bank to make a camp."

"Bone, you said you been out in this country," said Robert Chesney. "How far you figure this Fort Pitt is?"

"Mr. Bobby, I ain't ever been down this river," said the African. "But I bet you a fresh honeycomb we is closer to Fort Pitt than we be to Beulah Land."

"Praise the Lord," said Hobe Spencer.

"Yeah, well, let's dig into it," said Robert Chesney. "Forget them sore shoulders there, Miles, just dig into it a little longer."

"Yesiree," the African laughed.

So they attacked the river once more. But not for long. There, around one of the huge, sweeping bends of the Monongahela, was Fort Pitt.

You could see immediately why the French had built a fort here. Not only to control traffic on three rivers but because the fort itself was open to attack from land on only one side. Otherwise, it was surrounded by water.

The Monongahela and the Allegheny came together to form the Ohio flowing off to the west. So the projection of land between them was actually a peninsula, a finger of solid ground pointing down the Ohio. It was low ground, rising only far enough above the water to be safe from flooding. Here, the French had built Fort Duquesne but burned it in 1759 during the French and Indian War. At that time, the lower extension of the peninsula had been cleared of all timber. It was still treeless when the Ballymenas came.

This bare plain rose to much higher ground within a half mile of the point, and here it was thickly wooded. Beyond that the terrain rose higher still, forming the ridges and valleys endemic to the area. Across the Allegheny, the land was well above any flood stage and the crest was covered with timber, to include cedar. On the opposite bank of the Monongahela there was high ground, much of it faced by a sharp cliff that began at the water's edge.

Drawn up on the bank of the point were many small boats, mostly canoes, arranged in long rows with keels up. There was a scatter of Indian shelters along the narrow beach, conical lodges covered with woven reed mats or bark, and between these the usual litter of campsite debris as well as dogs, children, cooking pots suspended on pole tripods over fires, women with blankets over their heads going about their chores, men in various costumes designed either to keep them warm or to show off battle trophies or beads or pendant metals or especially cherished designs of yellow-and-red-and-blue paint on chests and shoulders and arms. Some wore roached hair; others covered their heads with hide and fur caps. Almost all of them carried weapons of one kind or another.

These were not large tribal units but family bands come in to trade. They represented many dispossessed peoples who had been ravaged and separated and scattered by decades of fur trade war with the Five Nation Iroquois. There were fragments here from many tribes. Delaware, Mosapelea, Honniasont, Susquehanna, Erie.

The Ballymenas drew their canoes up on the bank some distance from the nearest Indian camp and moved onto the point where Fort Pitt sat like a square matchbox, poles upright for a stockade with two blockhouses at opposing corners. A gate faced the point where the rivers came together. The gate stood open, and sitting just inside they could see a small brass cannon. A church steeple rose above the palisades. It was the only structure in sight made of rough-cut lumber. Everything else was mud-chinked log or stone and mortar.

Lounging about the gate were a number of Indian men and women, a few frontier-clad white men, and two red-coated British soldiers. The soldiers were leaning on their muskets and seemed involved in animated conversation with all the others.

Robert Chesney led them well clear of the fort, maybe to avoid the soldiers, and into the town that squatted near the rear gate in the palisades. The buildings were laid out along two streets that had been churned and rutted while the ground was still soft and muddy, and now they were hard as iron and made for difficult footing.

There were many signs hanging from the fronts of the low log buildings, some rather elaborate and looking out of place in such a primitive setting. There was a tannery, a shoe shop, a jail and two stocks set in the ground but they held no criminal now, a hut labeled "Royal Charter Land Claims," a fur and hide warehouse, a blacksmith shop and stable, and a number of taverns. Everything a new town needed.

"A man pinned in them stocks right now wouldn't take long to freeze solid," said Miles Urie.

"Remember that if you take a notion to get into trouble in this place," Robert Chesney said.

The largest building, made of logs and with only two tiny windows at the front, was the trading post of one Abner Maddox, who, they found, had a license from the Crown for trading with the Indians, but who was also an agent for the Virginia House of Burgesses, which was supposed to be secret, and who did more trading with immigrants than he did with the Indians, all of which was highly illegal, including the fact that the immigrants were there in the first place.

The British army commandant was representative of the Crown and of Sir William Johnson, who was Britain's best Indian relations man in America and married to a Mohawk, and who therefore spent most of his time in New York among his wife's people. In fact, Sir William had built a rather grand manor house and fortress in the country of his wife's kinfolk with money some people claimed came from strange sources.

Anyway, with Abner Maddox telling it all as a wonderful joke, this British army captain who was supposed to be overseeing the Crown's interests at Fort Pitt had discovered that in an American frontier station, a civilized gentleman could retain his sanity only with liberal doses of whiskey and loose living. To such an extent that a captain of the line did not make adequate wages to cover it.

With the initiative of many British officers on frontier duty in America, perhaps even Sir William Johnson, the Fort Pitt commandant found additional ways and means. For example, he was willing to suffer temporary blindness any time there was occasion to observe even the least malfeasance of office where it concerned King George III's official Indian trader if a little money or whiskey or both were left in places where he might find it, places such as just inside the back door of his headquarters hut at the fort. This was a spot well known to Abner Maddox, his two indentured servants, and his three African slaves, all of whom, at one time or another, had left little gifts there for His Majesty's Fort Pitt representative.

So Abner Maddox was never arrested, either for his illicit dealing with illegal immigrants or later for his increasingly strident vocal outbursts against the mother country.

His most recent tirade had to do with the damned East India Company, and he was glad to air it out at full force for the Ballymenas when they arrived with their lists of requirements. Woolen coats and leather boots and salt and sugar and bacon and corn and rye seed and lead and powder could wait, bellowed Abner Maddox, until he'd enlightened these new arrivals to his mercantile territory with a few horror stories about the glorious jackasses in London who were trying to enslave America.

So standing at a rude plank counter in Fort Pitt's largest and only trading post, drinking apple cider out of tall pewter mugs, smelling the bacon rind and old leather and sawdust odor of the place, feeling the welcome heat from the huge fireplace across the room, Robert Chesney and his party got the full serving of Abner Maddox's fury.

Of course, there is no record of how much the four Ballymenas understood of such a biased personal summary of current events, but it didn't matter. What mattered at the moment was the warmth of the large cluttered room and the tingle on the palate of what Abner Maddox called cider but was in fact a rather potent applejack that would test out at about eighty-proof alcohol by volume.

"It's tuning up, boys, it's tuning up," Abner Maddox began. "The English got a stout whack in Boston just before Christmas. That damned East India Company, you know about them!"

None of the Ballymenas knew anything at all about the East India Company.

"A damned stock company where friends and relations of the Crown and Parliament invest with the thought of becoming rich, and now it's bankrupt. So the government makes one of their damnable policies, and this one gives the East India Company a monopoly on all tea shipped into the colonies.

"By God, the colonies get humpbacked and say they won't *take* any of that tea," Abner Maddox shouted, waving a fist in the air and getting warmed to his subject. Two old Indian men, wrapped in ragged and filthy blankets came to stand at one end of the counter and listen, black eyes shining in faces the color and texture of oak bark.

"Well, three ships loaded with East India Company tea come to Boston and nobody will take the tea, and the king's customs man says the ships can't leave until the tax is paid on the tea and I suspect said the Boston merchants would pay that tax whether they took the tea or not. Anyway, you can bet that's what the Boston merchants thought!

"So one night a group of fine Bostonians dressed like heathen savages row out and board those ships and throw the tea into the harbor! By God!"

"Us colony gentlemens," Young Bone Trudeau laughed. "We gonna do like we wants, not how English wants."

"The Lord only knows how those aristocratic butt boils in Whitehall will react to *that*!" Maddox said. "Why, remember how they said their Admiralty Courts would prosecute anybody in the colonies who violated the tax laws? Remember that? Americans tried by Crown-appointed judges, not American juries?"

"Ho!" shouted one of the old Indians, and the Ballymenas gave a start and gripped their muskets.

"Pay no attention to them," Maddox said. "They don't understand a damned word being said."

He poured a clear liquid from a crock jug into two tin cups and carried them to the Indians and set the cups before them, and two brown, long-fingered hands appeared from the blankets and grasped the cups.

"Ho!" one of them shouted again.

"Well," said Robert Chesney, "I'm glad we're out here in the woods away from all the ruckus back there in the big towns and all."

Abner Maddox looked offended. "Hell, Son, you ain't away from it. You're right in the middle of it."

"How do you figure such a thing?" asked Miles Urie.

"It's already started," Maddox said. "Just last week, news from downriver, a war party of Shawnees burned out a couple of farms. It's happened more and more the last year. This summer, just you wait. They'll be out and burning up and down these rivers. From Fort Niagara to the Illinois country. And the British army ain't going to help."

"Why not?" asked Hobe Spencer.

"Because," Abner Maddox said, becoming exasperated with such ignorance, "the English want the red savages to be let alone so they can hunt furs. Hell, since the last French war, the English have been licking their lips over having the kind of fur trade the French had. That's why they tried to keep folks like you from coming over the mountains and into this country. So nothing would bother the game and the tribes who trapped and hunted them. Furs is money, boys, furs is money!

"But my God, the English don't know how to handle Indians. Now the French, they'd send one or two men, these men would go right in amongst the tribes, learn the lingo, marry the women. The red savages would bring in furs, these Frenchmen would have the goods to trade, guns and knives and wool blankets and whiskey. Then the Frenchmen would go away. All they wanted was to trade. And mostly, the French *liked* Indians.

"But the English, *they* don't like Indians. They want Indians to stay far away. Just bring in the furs to a trading post like this one and swap their goods for hides. Then the Indians go back into the woods and leave everybody alone!"

"Well, what's wrong with that?" Robert Chesney asked.

"Not a thing, if it worked. But it don't. Remember how the French came with a few traders, single men? But with the English owning the country, now Americans come, only they ain't interested too much in furs. They want land. And they like Indians even less than the English do. Because at least the English figure the Indians can make a little profit for them. But the Americans don't really give a damn about trading with Indians at all."

"Yesiree," shouted Young Bone, and now it was the two old Indians who jumped.

"And when the people from the English colonies come, the Americans, they ain't single men only. They's got their women with em, and the Indians know this bunch has come to stay. And it's more complicated than that, too.

"With the French gone, some tribes are confused. They traded with the French for years. They fought for the French. The French told them the Great Father, the French king, would love his children forever and bring trade goods, but the French lost, finally, after more than a hundred years of fighting about it, and now the red devil got a new Great Father across the big waters.

"They don't know what to do. And old Sir William Johnson ain't much interested in anybody but Mohawks. So all these Ohio River and Great Lakes tribes watch, and pretty soon they see all these Americans coming with their women and kids and cutting down timber and putting in crops and building towns, and finally it sinks in. They're about to be pushed right out of their homeland.

"Boys, maybe for the first time these red savages around here are ready to burn us out for something besides the trade. Oh, they understand conquest. They been taking territory away from one another for as long as memory serves. Only now, instead of somebody like the Mohawks inchin in on em, it's you boys!"

"Us boys?" Robert Chesney asked. "What the hell about you?"

"Me?" Abner Maddox asked, and he lifted his arms and shrugged and his eyes were wide and innocent. "I'm just a simple storekeeper. I trade with one and all."

"Yeah," Robert Chesney said, and his face was getting red and the veins had begun to stand out on his neck. "Well you sure'n hell are hoopin and hollerin like you want somebody to start shootin the British. And now it turns out you don't want any part of that; you just want to sit here on your fat arse and trade with whoever wins."

"Now, now, Boss Bobby," said Miles Urie, and he had a hand on Robert Chesney's arm. "Remember those empty stocks out there in the cold."

Robert Chesney almost choked, and his face got redder and he shook his head and then ducked it. Suddenly, surprisingly, Abner Maddox laughed.

"Why hell, young man, don't you worry about sayin what you

PORTVILLE FREE LIBRARY
Portville, New York 14770

think around here. My land! Have some more cider and let me tell you about this damned Sir William Johnson."

"Well, Mr. Maddox, we best start going down my lists," Robert Chesney managed to mumble.

"Very well, boys," said Abner Maddox, obviously disappointed that they didn't seem more interested in his observations. "Too late in the day now to start back. Unless you want to have a go at that river in the dark. No? Well, by God, I'll have my three nigger boys load out your canoes in the morning."

They were offered pallet space for the night in the loft over the trading room. After leaving their blanket rolls and weapons there, they went out to see if there might be a friendly tavern at Fort Pitt. They found one, of course, a low-ceilinged room, smoky and cold and primitive. The tables were old barrels, and they made a supper of hard-boiled eggs.

"Say, Boss Bobby, what was all that whooping and hollering about back there?" Miles Urie asked.

"Independence," said Robert Chesney, his mouth full of egg. "And stop calling me Boss Bobby."

"Independence? What the hell do that mean?"

"I don't know. Ask Axel Muir when we get home. I guess he knows all about it."

What happened in that crude Fort Pitt tavern was ever after bewildering to Robert Chesney. He recalled vividly that on entering they had seen a large, burly man sitting in one corner, a barrel table before him, bellowing about his prowess at arm wrestling. Beside this man, who was an Indian fur trader left over from the French period, there was a new rifle, much like the one Noble Popjoy had carried only newer. Probably manufactured by one of the already famous Philadelphia gunsmiths.

Robert Chesney remarked to his companions that someday he hoped to own such a weapon so that he might become a true wilderness man. Then he forgot it and sat down to whatever drinks they might enjoy with the few pence he had left from what Axel Muir had given him.

Some months later, he learned of the proceedings from Miles Urie himself, who had orchestrated the scheme. And who claimed it as even better than the one he had done in Ulster when he raffled his father's black calf.

The gentleman of the rifle and arm wrestling was the object of attack. With Miles Urie doing all the talking, after conspiring with Young Bone Trudeau and Hobe Spencer, there was discussion of a wager.

Perhaps the question immediately arises of how even a smooth talker like Miles Urie could persuade a man of Hobe Spencer's Christian leanings to participate in betting. But apparently Hobe had consumed a considerable quantity of applejack which left him in a weakened condition. At least insofar as standing firm to his moral convictions.

Anyway, Miles Urie explained to the arm-wrestling gentleman that Mr. Hobe Spencer, there present, owned a wonderful African slave, also there present.

At this point Young Bone Trudeau grinned and nodded and said "Yesiree" a number of times.

That indeed, this slave had originally been brought into bondage in one of the French sugar islands and was strong as a swamp alligator. And that Mr. Spencer was desirous of testing his own arm-wrestling ability and would entertain doing so with this champion if they could make it worthwhile with a small wager. Say the African slave against the fine Pennsylvania rifle.

Throughout all of this, Hobe Spencer stood with his eyes unblinking and his face like a pale, innocent moon in the fur nest of his jacket collar. In the great bundle of his clothing, any hint of his bulging biceps was concealed. So the man of the rifle agreed, two pins out of three.

It didn't take three. The first pin happened so fast that Hobe

Spencer's opponent leaped up afterward and threw aside his coat, surprised but determined not to be surprised again.

"I think ole Hobe broke the bastard's collarbone on the second pin," Miles Urie would say later.

So Robert Chesney, in a cider haze by then, was suddenly and unceremoniously ushered out of the place and back to Abner Maddox's loft, where the other three presented him with the rifle, all grinning widely, even Hobe Spencer now that the time for acting innocent was past.

Robert Chesney had no idea what had happened, but having the rifle made him so excited, he didn't care. And rolled in some of Abner Maddox's blankets was soon asleep and perhaps dreaming of becoming a real wilderness man.

Or maybe not. Anyway, before this night was finished, he would be wakened by Miles Urie and taken to his first close experience with the degradation that sometimes came to those unfortunate enough to be on the losing side.

When Robert Chesney stumbled out of the murky darkness of Abner Maddox's trading store, the cold struck him in the face like a hammer, shocking him fully awake. The clouds had broken enough for the moon to shine through in spots, making a silver dapple pattern across the point of land where Fort Pitt stood.

"Where we goin?" he asked, his voice thick with sleep and with the dregs of his drinking.

"Just you wait," Miles Urie, hurrying along beside him, said.

They followed two bulky figures, and Robert Chesney assumed they were Young Bone Trudeau and Hobe Spencer. He could see the turkey feather bobbing behind Young Bone's fur cap. But as they hurried past the fort palisades, he could tell that the other man was not large enough to be Hobe Spencer.

"Who the hell is that?" he asked. "Where we goin?"

"Hush, just hush and come long." They were moving quickly in the arctic night, and they trailed huge clouds of white vapor with their breathing. "This night air will give us all the vapors if you don't come on quick."

They moved across the open plain between the fort and the line of Indian shelters along the river's edge, then the strange figure leading them went directly to one of the larger cone lodges and pulled aside the hide door flap.

As soon as he stepped into the warmth of the wickiup, something stirred Robert Chesney's senses, and it took a few heartbeats for him to realize it was the smell. Like wood smoke and charred logs and cooking meat and something else foreign. It was an odor completely new to him yet not unpleasant.

There was a woman at the central fire, but she quickly moved behind a blanket that hung across the back of the lodge, like a partition. There were bedding rolls along one quadrant and at one of these an Indian child's face, bright black eyes looking at them, and when Robert Chesney's gaze touched it, the face disappeared, like a turtle's head suddenly withdrawing into the shell.

The man who had led them there dropped his robe and coat and squatted at the fire. He was naked above the waist, and there were triangular designs of blue tattoos across his chest. His hair was not roached and hung loose to the shoulders.

From his belt, he took two hatchets, and Robert Chesney recognized them as Ballymena hatchets that had been purchased at Harris' Ferry. The Indian man did not speak or look up but sat stoic as a tombstone staring at the hatchet blades as he turned them in his hands.

Miles Urie had gone behind the hanging blanket where the woman had disappeared, and as Young Bone Trudeau and Chesney squatted, they could hear a laugh or a cough or some kind of sound, and now Robert Chesney knew why they were there. And knew why Urie had waited until Hobe Spencer slept to come out on this mission because even though Hobe might have been persuaded to wager, he would never agree to what was happening here.

Very soon, Miles Urie reappeared, straightening his clothes and grinning, and there was a glistening sweat across his forehead.

"Yesiree," Young Bone said and was up and going behind the blanket himself. Miles Urie squatted beside Robert Chesney, still grinning. He reached out and squeezed Chesney's knee and winked.

Young Bone took more time than Urie had, but still, it was over quickly, and when he pushed out from behind the blanket he was grinning, too, and sweating.

"Now you, Boss Bobby," said Miles Urie, and he squeezed Robert Chesney's knee again.

Robert Chesney hesitated for only a moment and then rose, shaking his head.

"I'm back to bed!"

His last impression of the place before hitting the icy outside night was the child's face, black eyes watching from the bedroll again.

He was far up the point toward the fort before the other two caught him. Young Bone trailed behind whispering "Yesiree, yesiree," but Miles Urie grasped Robert Chesney's sleeve.

"What's the matter?" he said loudly, indignant. "We traded the two hatchets for all three of us. What's the matter with you? You making us to be wicked?"

"I don't care what you do," Robert Chesney said. "I just don't feel like it, that's all."

"Don't feel like it?" Miles Urie's voice was high-pitched now, half between anger and laughter. "You want to belittle us here?"

"Leave it lie, Miles!"

They were past the fort and into the town now, and a dog braving the wintery weather was out and barked at them as they passed. Then at the door to the trading post, Miles Urie managed to turn Robert Chesney toward him.

"By God!" Miles Urie said. "You ain't ever done it, have you? You ain't ever *done* it!"

"Now, now young gentlemens, time for sleep, it's all right," said Young Bone.

"I'm damned! You ain't ever *done* it, have you, Boss Bobby?"

That's when Robert Chesney surprised Young Bone Trudeau and Miles Urie and even himself. He hit Miles Urie in the face with his fist, straining to put all his strength into it, his lips peeled back to reveal the gap between his front teeth. Miles Urie hit the frozen ground on his rump and sat there a moment and then felt his nose.

"My God, it's so cold my nose won't even bleed!"

Robert Chesney reached down and Miles Urie lifted both arms to protect his face from further blows, but Robert Chesney grasped both Urie's shoulders and lifted him to his feet.

"I said don't ever call me Boss Bobby no more," he said.

"Yesiree, it's all right, young gentlemens, it's all right." Young Bone laughed.

Robert Chesney slept no more that night. He tried to prevent it, but no matter how hard he tried to think of other things, the image was still there, of that cone of orange, smoky light, the sounds from behind the blanket, the Indian man squatted beside the fire, and the child's eyes on him, burning like pinpoints of black flame.

It troubled him deeply. It troubled him more than having helped kill two men at Hog Gone Creek. Seeing Indians, hearing them, touching them as he had at Hog Gone when he'd helped drag the dead away from the Ballymena camp, all had made ripples of goose-flesh up his spine.

But the smell of them in the place where they lived, that was the strongest sense of all. Their smell. He thought it might haunt him down the fullness of all his days.

By the time they had their canoes loaded and pushed away from the point of land at Fort Pitt, it had clouded over again and was a gray, cold day. But there was almost no wind.

Young Bone Trudeau was the only one of them in any sort of decent disposition, and he entertained them for a while with song, in a language none of them could understand. It did little to cheer them so he finally stopped.

About halfway to Beulah Land, as they came round a long bend in the Monongahela, they saw a whitetail buck drinking at the river's edge. Still leading in the small canoe, Robert Chesney waved them onto the bank, and although the canoes were full of Maddox trading plunder, they still handled well at the touch and both boats came to the bank quietly.

The buck was about two hundred fifty paces from them, and he seemed unperturbed. He lifted his head once to look toward them, then drank again.

Robert Chesney had wormed the rifle that morning and now reloaded. Two thimbles of powder and a conical bullet. He had a pouch of greased linen patches and used one of these to wrap the bullet. Unlike a musket, it was hard to drive the bullet home. He struck the base of the ramrod with the palm of his hand. Then primed the pan, and still in the canoe, lay forward on some of the duffel.

The buck had stopped drinking and now was turned and slowly walking back up the sloping gravel bar toward the wooded shoreline. Robert Chesney wanted a neck shot. A heart shot always left the body cavity full of blood and made for a mess when dressing out the carcass.

He whistled once, a low whistle, and curiosity made the buck pause and look downstream and Robert Chesney shot, and the buck, hit at the spine just behind the jawbone, dropped without a quiver.

They paddled to a gravel bar, erected a conical frame from poles cut at the woodline, chopped off the head, and hung up the carcass to bleed it out as they skinned it.

They were getting good at this kind of thing, and it didn't take long. They saved everything, even the hooves for glue making, lay the hide flesh-side-up in the cargo canoe, and put the meat and innards on top of that.

It made Robert Chesney feel better. It made him forget that orange light and the smell. When he looked at Miles Urie's swollen nose, he laughed aloud, and then Young Bone started singing again.

The rifle had felt good against his shoulder, natural, as though it belonged there. A wilderness man, he kept thinking, a wilderness man!

They were treated like warriors back from serious battles when they got to Beulah Land, and Robert Chesney felt as though they were. Before they had the canoes unloaded, it had begun to snow.

They had never seen this much snow. It was a long, white winter, and they learned how to ration their meager food supplies. The men learned how to wear their hair long, in a queue down the back. The women learned how to make buckskin smocks and thick-soled moccasins.

They formed a militia company. Twice more they sent canoes to Fort Pitt and once returned to Beulah Land with a gaggle of breeding geese. In the spring, they planned a trail overland to the fort so they could bring back a milk cow and perhaps some horses.

During the second week of snow, Maudine Urie went into labor. Cordelia Muir and Ma Fulton did what they could. But the baby boy was stillborn.

They chopped a grave out of the frozen ground and held the first funeral at Beulah Land. They had located it on a high knoll behind the settlement, where one could stand and look down across the river and see the white trunks of the paper birch across the Monongahela.

There were soft, blue-green cedars close to the grave, and on the day they prayed and sang their hymns and Axel Muir said the burial-at-sea service, the sun broke through the overcast for a moment. There were brilliant flashes of scarlet around them as cardinals played in the cedars.

Part II

REVOLUTION

Chapter 5

After General Thomas Gage, the British commander at Boston, sent that flying column to Lexington and Concord looking for Rebel cannon and shots were fired and blood spilled, there was a war whether anybody wanted one or not.

As always has been, once there are shots and blood, it is near impossible to turn back and things are only going to get worse. Even when a lot of good people with honorable intentions try to reverse time so unpleasant events can be forgotten. Shots and blood are not easy to forget.

There were many among Young Bone Trudeau's colony gentlemens who didn't want a war. Although he never would have believed such a thing, it seems that generally one could say there was a three-way split in opinions on the issue.

About a third of the people were what John Adams of Massachusetts called fence sitters. Those who either were waiting to see which opinion had enough advantage for them to choose the winning side, or else were sincerely unsure of their convictions.

Another third were hot for revolution. Not the kind of revolution that destroys everything in order to build it back, but one in which everything remained about the same except for any and all ties to Great Britain. An end to royal appointments, an end to Whitehall interference with American trade, an end to taxes imposed by Parliament.

As Axel Muir said, it was independence.

Then there were those who believed nothing was so bad that with time and patience all problems with Crown and Parliament could be worked out with diplomacy rather than with violence. And they were right, except there was no time or patience left after the shooting and the blood.

These last called themselves Loyalists. They called the folks screaming for independence Whigs, a slightly pejorative term.

The independence crowd called themselves Patriots. They called the Loyalists Tories, a completely pejorative term.

The British called the Loyalists good subjects. They called the Patriots Rebels. Or Vermin.

The fence sitters hadn't decided what was safe to call anybody.

Patriots had the upper hand. They had Committees of Correspondence so they could distribute information throughout the colonies about British wickedness. They had a lot of money, what with rich merchants disenchanted with Whitehall tax policies. They controlled the Sons of Liberty.

Many times, newspapers sympathetic to the Loyalists were wrecked, publishers sent fleeing for their lives. Crown-appointed officials like customs collectors had the windows in their homes smashed, their privy burned, their cat skinned and hung on the front gate.

Nothing like this happened to Rebel newspapers or to Rebels elected to some office by the colonists, and no Rebel cows were mutilated and left bawling pitifully in the night, and no Rebel lady was obscenely taunted as she passed in her carriage, and no Rebel brewery was sacked and the barrels rolled in the streets, open bungholes spewing foam into the cups and mugs of liberty pole dancers.

Mr. Vanderbilt Tigert, whose enterprise supported the Ballymena trek to Fort Pitt, was a man for independence. And his enterprise helped support things other than land speculation. His enterprise helped support the Mob.

Every large city on the coast had a Mob. Except for a few street leaders, membership might change from day to day. When powerful men behind the scenes, men who never, never appeared with the Mob on the streets, decided there was a job to be done, the word and the bribe money and rum were sent to the street leaders, who recruited as many men as they needed from among those along the waterfront, in taverns, and in jails. These stalwarts were not at all interested in the issues, only the rum, and they, along with a few youngsters looking for thrills, made up the Mob.

If that wasn't enough, the Patriots had enthusiasm. They were wild-eyed and frothing at the mouth for a break from England.

Maybe some of the Loyalists were just as enthusiastic about staying in the Crown's fold. But they seldom showed it, and they never organized. Sometimes in protest over a particularly brutish Mob action, a Loyalist would write a pamphlet. Maybe to the effect that everybody hadn't had it so bad for the past three centuries, so why break it all up? They wrote these using Greek pen names and then undoubtedly hoped the Mob wouldn't come looking for *them*.

Of course, using Greek pen names was fashionable at the time, and the Patriots did it, too. But they didn't have to worry about the Mob.

With the increased attention of Whitehall on the colonies and the increase in troop concentrations in America, you'd think the British were at least as well organized as the Patriots. But they weren't. They were no match for the Rebels when it came to taking advantage of the opposition's blunders. In fact, they made most of the blunders themselves and were somehow incapable of realizing they were blunders.

At the very lowest level, the British could never avoid irritating the colonists, even the ones who were Loyalists. As with all those troops. No measures were taken to make their presence unobtrusive. Just the reverse. British regulars and Hessian grenadiers wore highly distinctive uniforms, gaudy and bright, and could be spotted a long way off. They drank in all the taverns, insulted people, figuring that by God, *they* would not yield the sidewalk to some yokel just because he wore silk stockings below his knee britches and a tricorn hat.

The Rebels called the king's soldiers Squareheads or Lobsterbacks. Terms both intentionally and extremely pejorative!

When the violent ripples of conflict crossed the mountains and came to Fort Pitt and Beulah Land, there was no three-way split among the opinions of Ballymenas. The Ulster Scots had good reason to become Patriots or Rebels or Vermin, and they really didn't care what the label might be.

As yet, there had not been time for them to think themselves "free," as colonists who had been in America for two or three generations did. They were not yet upset about taxes or quartering of troops in their homes or Crown-appointed men judging them instead of juries in both criminal and civil cases. They'd never yet elected any colonial legislatures or town councilmen.

So all in all they didn't have much reason, it would seem, to start shooting at British soldiers.

But they had memories. Like most Celtic people from the British Isles, they remembered that even though they could worship otherwise, if they were not members of the English church they could not hold office or vote, and any prospect of ever owning land was small if they were not Anglicans. And no matter their faith, they had tithed annually to the king's church.

Some could remember when catching a rabbit on an English lord's estate was a hanging offense.

"Englishman" left a bad taste in their mouths, and it was hard to pass an opportunity to shoot one or two of them without the certainty of hanging.

Besides, among the young men there was the mistaken idea common among young men that war was fun.

Therefore the young men would march off to the east, looking for the town of Lancaster, where they had heard anybody of sound mind, healthy body, experience with a Pennsylvania rifle, and with a solid dislike of the English, could join a military unit being formed for action in the developing war.

If there hadn't been the threat of Shawnee war parties against white settlements in the area of Fort Pitt and the greater Ohio Valley, all the Ballymena men would have answered the call to arms in the east. But as Axel Muir said, you've got to protect the home port!

During the past winter, the troops at Fort Pitt had been withdrawn to Oswego or Fort Niagara or Detroit, where there were substantial British garrisons. All of these places were dangerously close if the time ever came for Englishmen to lead Indian war parties into the Ohio Valley.

So before the young men departed, they helped start construction of an upright pole palisade enclosure with the large council house inside, a kind of last redoubt in case hostiles appeared at Beulah Land.

Actually, the smoke of burning settlements and farms had already risen from Fort Pitt and Oswego, and more still downstream along the Ohio. These were largely Shawnees, but there were other tribes, too, some of which had once been traders and allies with the French. But also some who had been friends of the English during the fur trade wars.

"By God," said Silas Fulton, "these red devils don't have no loyalty. Whether they fit for the French or agin em, now they pitch in with the redcoats!"

"It don't matter," said Hobe Spencer, remembering what Abner Maddox had said at Fort Pitt. "Them heathens gonna pitch in with anybody agin Americans. They just simply gotta be agin Americans."

"Why?" asked Silas Fulton.

Hobe Spencer looked blank for a moment. He blinked a few times, trying to remember the rest of what Abner Maddox had said.

"Cause we brang our women, I expect," he said.

So they formed up to go, the young men. Only Robert Chesney had a rifle. But other than that, they were pretty much the same.

Cordelia Muir had seen to it that everybody was properly equipped, and Miles Urie said she paid more attention to Boss Bobby Chesney then anybody else.

In addition to a firearm, each had powder horn, bullet-and-flint pouch, and oiled patches. Hatchet and long knife. A tin cup and a water bottle, which they'd soon be calling a canteen. A blanket roll. Extra moccasins. Tricorn or slouch or fur hat. Buckskin smock with long fringes. Rough broadcloth trousers, leather leggings, also with fringes. Soap, razor, fishhooks.

In addition to Chesney, who Axel Muir said should act as their sergeant until they got to Lancaster because he was the best woodsman and had the only rifle, there was Young Bone Trudeau, who had taken to going anywhere Bobby Chesney went and was a good shot with Chesney's rifle. Then Luke Baird and Calvin Reed.

Darrel Stark wanted to go, but Axel Muir said the community blacksmith would leave only over his dead body. Loy Ennis, too, but Axel Muir said a town councilman should stay at home and help organize defenses.

Little thirteen-year-old-Enoc Fulton would go. They said they'd get him a drum to play while the older men shot Englishmen. Hobe Spencer had to decide which needed his spiritual guidance most, the settlement or the young men, and it didn't take long to figure it was the young men. Including Cranston Shook, the oldest at twenty-eight.

And finally, Miles Urie. And Maudine, to take care of all the men, she said, and was pretty stubborn about it, and everybody knew armies went around the countryside with a long string of women following close behind or even right in the ranks, so Cordelia gave Maudine some motherly advice, which forevermore remained a dark secret.

Six Ballymena men, one African, one boy, and one woman.

There was considerable hugging and kissing, and they set off.

This time they didn't fight timber and terrain as they had coming west. There was a fair road that went from near Fort Pitt all the way east to York County, Pennsylvania.

"Holy Hoxie," Calvin Reed shouted as they marched along. "Where was this here road when we come out to this country?"

"It was right where it's at now," said Robert Chesney. "Only I expect we never taken it because if we had, they'd been plenty of British troops along it to arrest us."

"I heared Axel Muir say it," said Luke Baird. "This here road was built by the British army during the old French and Indian War."

So they marched in the hazy July sunlight, pausing at night to sleep under the trees after eating their frugal ration of ground corn and dried venison. At first, their weapons and equipment jabbed and poked and rattled and jingled, but soon they fell into a steady rhythm, a natural kind of drumbeat marching that a group of men will almost always come into, without the drum, like a heartbeat.

Which is when the singing starts. And they'd heard a few songs on their frequent visits to Fort Pitt, mostly songs sung by militia veterans of the French wars.

A few of them not at all obscene.

> Come on with your rifle, let gray wolf and fox
> Howl on in the shadow of primitive rocks.
> Let bear feed securely from pigpen and stall,
> Here's two-legged game for your powder and ball!

At Lancaster, they weren't sure they liked being in an army. There was a lot of confusion. More of that than anything else. There were a few recruiting officers from the Continental army, and there were a lot of militiamen, and there were politicians making speeches and pickpockets and whores and dogs barking and horses and cannons and local German farmers with barrels of kraut and bushels of potatoes arguing about whether or not the money issued by the Continental Congress in Philadelphia was worth a damn.

There were a lot of colorful flags of one kind or another and young ladies wearing large bonnets and the low-cut gowns fashionable at the time in evening drawing rooms but not often seen on the street in broad daylight, all of which perhaps had something to do with patriotism and which caused Hobe Spencer to blush and prompted Calvin Reed to exclaim that he had never in his life seen so much naked tittie.

On the sidewalk before one tavern, people were dancing in the street as a fiddler sawed away on his instrument. There was a vendor selling pies out of a dog-drawn cart, and a horde of children ran about in the streets among the legs of many horses carrying well-clad gentlemen in the saddle or else hitched to various types of wheeled vehicles, of which there was every kind imaginable.

Hanging from a limb of the large oak tree that stood near the public well in the center of the town square was an effigy of King George III, splattered with mud and horse shit. Sitting on the ground, leaning against the tree trunk, were a number of militiamen, napping from the effects of too much drilling or too much rum, their tricorn hats tilted over their eyes, muskets lying across legs clad in blue knee britches and dirty white gaiters with large buttons up the side.

"I ain't ever seen so many different kinds of soldiers," said Maudine Urie.

They found their own kind on the porch of the Presbyterian parsonage, a log building like the church beside it, where riflemen were being recruited. There were two men in elaborately fringed buckskin smocks who were taking down the names. There was a doctor who apparently was to see that each man had the required number of body parts in the right places. There were a number of men standing around who looked as though they might have come from Ballymena themselves, Scots-Irish or Welsh.

It was here that they received their issue of rifles, turning in their muskets for distribution to the Continentals, the troops organized by Congress and the only "regular" army the Rebels had.

And it was here they found Sergeant Arvil Philips.

This rifle battalion, Sergeant Philips explained, was being recruited by Captain Daniel Morgan, a New Jersey–born man but from the name obviously Welsh, and Ulster Scots were pretty near kinfolk to any Welshman.

"An oak tree of a man," Sergeant Philips shouted. "Face as square as his honor, boys, and a rounder, too. Why he was in the British army during the late French war, and they had him be a teamster, he was, and when an English snoot of an officer did him an unfair turn, Danny simply beat him good with his rocky fists.

"The bloody English give him lashes, they did, about a hundred they tell, and lucky Danny was the bastards didn't hang him!"

Now, the Ballymenas learned, Captain Morgan was with General Washington his own self, just appointed commander in chief of Continental forces by the Congress. And Calvin Reed allowed it was a small world because it had been that same George Washington who fought the French on ground pretty near the sight of where their own Beulah Land now stood.

"Yesiree, yesiree," said Young Bone Trudeau. "Colonel Washington and my pappy, fit them French right there where three rivers meet. Now he gone be *General* Washington!"

"Well, where the hell is this Washington at?" asked Luke Baird.

"Don't worry," said Robert Chesney. "I expect you'll find out soon enough where he's at, and this Captain Morgan, too."

And they did, about two hundred of them, each looking pretty much like the other, with buckskin jackets and woolen trousers and leather gaiters with fringes and moccasins. Only their headgear varied. Fur caps or tricorn or slouch hats and a few with only a tied scarf with a bow in back like a sugar island pirate. The Ballymenas felt at home because all these other riflemen, no matter where their homes, were mountain people, mostly Celts, and with that distaste for the English brought over from the British Isles.

They found Washington, and Danny Morgan, too, in Massachusetts, where the army was laying siege to Boston.

There were half a dozen women with the riflemen. They soon learned that this was a very small number compared to the militia units and the Continental army, and the British army, too. In some of those other outfits, the baggage trains moved with crowds of women, wives of soldiers or hangers-on, and some with their children. When the troops stopped for night bivouac, the women moved into the camps and there cooked or washed clothes or offered companionship of one kind or another.

The Ballymenas had no notion how it worked in other encampments, but for themselves, they had recent memory of their trek over the mountains when the women were part of the column and nothing much thought of it. Women moved to one side of the line of march, usually after dark, and did their necessaries in the woods.

So having Maudine Urie with them posed no particular problem and in fact seemed natural enough. Except for Robert Chesney. Who often late at night thought he heard giggles and frantic whisperings from Miles Urie's bedroll.

When they were on the move, she trooped right along, carrying a load of duffel as heavy as that of the men, and when they crossed streams, she took all the canteens and filled them as the men marched on, then caught up, running with all the water bottles bouncing against her hips. Often, she carried her husband's rifle. At night, she made a fire quicker than any of the men could and always seemed to have a pot of hot root tea.

She carried a lot of buckskin and thongs, and she mended moccasins each evening. Calvin Reed taught her how to load a rifle, and before long Robert Chesney noted that she was carrying a couple of powder horns he'd never seen before and suspected she'd borrowed them from one of the other outfits in their army.

Robert Chesney wondered if she ever thought of that little baby boy she'd had, born dead. If she did, she showed no signs of it. She was as cheerful as any of the men.

So they moved with their long strides, Wilkes-Barre to Scranton and into New York. They ferried the Hudson at Kingston, on into Connecticut, and crossed the Connecticut River at Hartford. Now Massachusetts. Milford, Waltham, and Suffolk County where now and then they had a view of the sea and Boston Bay.

Feeling every inch an army by now, designated a part of Morgan's Rifle Regiment, they could call themselves the Riflemen with a capital *R*. They were placed in the line of revetments and entrenchments and began to pick off British officers at long range with their Pennsylvania rifles.

You would suspect that in an army made up of soldiers armed almost exclusively with smoothbore muskets, such marksmanship would attract attention. After all, it was nearly impossible to hit a target the size of a man's head with a musket unless he was standing close enough to spit on him, so Calvin Reed said.

And attract attention they did. They had been attracting attention all the way from Lancaster.

General George Washington would become known for many things. But one talent that was usually ignored had to do with his colorful and forceful language when he lost his temper. Young Bone Trudeau said that back when Washington had only been a Virginia colonel, he could blister the paint off a Masonic lodge hall with his cussing.

"If that fine gentleman do so good when he only colony colonel," Young Bone laughed, "jus you think how fine he gone do cussin now he's a Continental general!"

Dealing with Congress, on the one hand, and the various local colonial governments on whom he depended for troops and supplies, on the other, was enough to keep the general in a constant state of ill disposition, but he was diplomatic in these matters and handled them with admirable restraint.

But when troops under his command were vexatious, the restraint often disappeared in a purple haze of furious temper, and by the time the Riflemen had arrived at Boston, the very mention of them was enough to stiffen what was already a famously stiff lip!

The fame that preceded them into the works at Boston had nothing to do with marksmanship. It seemed that even before they had completed their passage across Pennsylvania, a shock wave of apprehension ran through the civil population along their line of march, much as you might suppose happened during the Middle Ages as the horsemen of Genghis Khan approached.

The record shows that twice during their march to war, the Riflemen paused in a community they were passing through to tar and feather a Tory. Well, the victims were pointed out as Tories by local Patriots, who provided the tar and feathers. That was good enough for the Riflemen, who had no notion yet that their commanding general might take the view that organized troops in a civilized army do not go around applying tar and feathers to civilians.

"I tell you," said Cranston Shook, "that first one sure put up a fight when we taken off his clothes."

"Better watch your politics," said Miles Urie, laughing. "Else you might get your gonads a bath in coal tar!"

"I don't know much about all this politics business," said Hobe Spencer, "but I sure don't like what we done to them two men."

That was only part of it. Somehow, the Riflemen had come to believe that they were entitled to those things they needed, like food, so wherever they found any that was convenient, they took it. Pigs, lambs, chickens, ripening corn in the field, apples on the trees. Generally, they did not take these things by force but rather by stealth. At night.

By the time they reached Connecticut, the Ballymenas had become boastfully proud of Maudine Urie, who had a kind of instinctive talent for stealing geese without the birds setting up an ungodly squawking and honking. Miles Urie, most boastful of all, said proudly that his wife had developed her technique as a child back in Ulster.

Also, most observers watching them pass said the Riflemen were always at least moderately drunk.

To cap General Washington's wrath, as soon as the Riflemen got into the line of siege, they began killing British officers at outlandish ranges, a practice the general had specifically forbidden. At any range.

The first hint they had of wrongdoing was the occasion of their initial meeting with Morgan, now their regimental commander. As Sergeant Philips had said, Morgan was a big and forbidding-looking man, especially when angry, and he gave the Riflemen a little speech on how to conduct themselves in future to avoid being treated like hostile Mohawks by the civil population. Not to mention the commanding general.

"If we aren't here to shoot bloody Englishmen," asked Luke Baird, "why the hell did we walk all the way from Fort Pitt?"

"Now lad, back away from that," said Sergeant Philips. "Didn't you see Danny Morgan wink?"

Then they met Captain Edmund Barclay, who would be their company commander. Captain Barclay issued blankets and little hats. Thinking the hat a joke, they laughed, which brought a roar from the captain who said they would by God wear this hat or face him and Danny Morgan and the lash.

Having already seen Morgan when he was only about half angry, and certainly having no stomach for the lash, they put on the hats.

It was a round sort of skullcap made of leather with a raccoon tail and feather attached to the top so they trailed down the back. There was no brim except at the front where a triangular piece of heavy leather stood straight up, making their faces look like extensions of a cone. The initials *RR* were burned into the snap-brim leather, which Captain Barclay said stood for "Rifle Regiment." There was a wide chin strap to hold the thing in place.

"We get to wear these silly damn hats," complained Luke Baird, "and he won't even let us have a little fun with the English?"

"Oh you people are famous on both sides of the line now," said Captain Barclay. "General Washington has in hand a note from Sir Henry Clinton, one of the British generals in Boston, and Clinton said you are all savages and shirttail bandits, sneaks and the most infamous widow makers in North America, ambushers and poltroons."

"What the hell's a poltroon?" asked Robert Chesney.

"Bobby, I don't know what a poltroon is," said Calvin Reed, "but I take all them other things they call us as a great honor, by Hoxie!"

"Lads, lads," said Sergeant Philips, "remember, Danny Morgan winked! He's one of us."

Whether Danny Morgan winked or not, they kept shooting at British officers. But not for long enough for General Washington to completely lose his temper and have some of them hanged.

As a lot of people were saying all the nasty differences between colonies and Crown could be ironed out with compromise, compassion, and copious correspondence, the Continental Congress authorized an invasion of Canada.

Invasions of their colonies not in revolt weren't viewed by the British as sincere expressions of peaceful intent.

It would be a complex plan, with two American armies converging on Quebec City. The Ballymenas knew and cared nothing of plans at the time. The first indication that something was afoot came with the order to form up and move out. They would march to Newburyport, about fifty miles up the coast, not much more than a one-day walk for the long-striding Riflemen.

They had been assigned to one prong of the invasion, the army that would be led to Canada by Colonel Benedict Arnold. Benedict Arnold, from Connecticut or Rhode Island, depending on who was telling the story.

Arnold, they had heard, came from a hard-nosed Yankee family of John Calvin Puritanism, and it was said that his mother had assured him as a child that he'd been picked by the Almighty as one of those predestined for paradise. So long as he didn't mess up too seriously. They were happy to discover that he was not a religious zealot. Hobe Spencer was delighted that his leader had been assured a seat in heaven and sent up a little prayer of thanksgiving to a gracious God.

Arnold had an excellent reputation as a great tactician and leader of men, having been at Ticonderoga with Ethan Allen, whom it turned out he disliked intensely, maybe for good cause.

They'd seen Arnold in the works around Boston. He cut a fine figure in always expensive uniforms. He wore his tricorn hat well down on his forehead over a rather impressively large hook nose, which gave him the appearance of constantly being about to crash his way through a Tory's yard fence with such force as to send shattered pickets flying all over Suffolk County.

The army would be composed of four divisions, which were really small regiments, the rosters filled with men of every colony from Maine to Virginia. There would be about fifteen hundred of them, not counting women camp followers. Morgan's Riflemen were the first division.

One of Arnold's aides was a smallish man, dark and handsome, named Aaron Burr. The Ballymenas had seen him, too, and his lovely, nineteen-year-old Abenaki Indian woman named Jacatacqua. Her buckskin smocks were elaborately decorated with beads and dyed porcupine quills which, even though fine, were as revealing as any Indian woman's attire, giving the troops an excellent view of her legs when she assumed certain positions in following her man about the town of Cambridge. They called her Golden Thighs.

Arnold chose a Presbyterian minister as army chaplain, educated at Princeton, of course, where many supposed all good Presbyterians were educated, and Hobe Spencer sent up a long prayer of thanksgiving.

Before departing the Boston area, Arnold paraded his army in review for the commander in chief. The Riflemen missed it. They had already been ordered forward because General Washington was constantly furious with them for raising hell, carousing in the streets and stealing everything they could lay hands on and singing drunken songs that were lewd even for a lewd army. And all that sniping at British officers. Hardly the conduct expected of gentlemen, in the opinion of the Great Virginian. So at the first opportunity, he sent them as far away from Boston as possible.

So they missed the parade.

They discovered that the appearance Colonel Arnold gave of rapid movement was not only apparent but real. An advanced party had alerted the citizens of Newburyport that troops would be arriving, and when the Riflemen marched in they were so fussed over and feasted that Hobe Spencer said now he knew how the Prodigal Son must have felt.

They were lodged in the Presbyterian church, Hobe Spencer by now almost in tears. When the rest of Arnold's little army arrived, they would be billeted in the town's two ropewalks, the council house, and a number of private homes.

The locals came forth with their best viands, the likes of which the Ulster Scots had never seen on either side of the Atlantic. Saltwater perch chowder, smoked eel, roast teal, broiled woodcock, all washed down with gallons of cider and no small dose of hot buttered rum. The Riflemen had to steal hardly a thing to satisfy their hunger.

The waterfront, which was the mouth of the Merrimack River, was crowded with small sailing craft. It was there that Luke Baird found the dark side of this wonderful September picnic.

"Look at them damned boats," he said. "I expect they will have us in them soon now, and all sick as bloody pups!"

The destination of Arnold's army was secret, of course. Which meant that within two days rumors were flying about Quebec. Arnold's local agents tried with some success to convince tavern keepers and barbers and young women who brought food to the troops that the real target was Nova Scotia.

The Riflemen didn't give a hoot where they were going, according to Calvin Reed, so long as the grub went along with them. But Luke Baird had a sour taste in his mouth about that, too, and wanted to know how far Quebec was and if the roads to it were worth a damn.

"Roads?" a Newburyport shipwright said and blinked and laughed. "You lads, this soldier fella wants to know what roads they be to Quebec."

A number of local men paused in their work there on the dock and looked at Luke Baird much as they might have looked at a bearded lady in the circus.

"Mister, there be nary a road twix here and there."

"Well, how far is it?"

"As the crow flies, maybe two hundred miles by way of the Kennebec."

"We ain't birds, though, so don't you know any closer than a maybe?"

"No. Can't say any white man does. Ain't nobody I know ever went up the Kennebec all the way to Canada. Abenakis has, but Indians don't know miles from pea pods."

After the rest of the army closed on Newburyport, Arnold arrived with a whole string of his aides, including Burr and Burr's Abenaki princess Golden Thighs. It gave Robert Chesney a thought, seeing that Indian woman.

"Sergeant Philips," he asked. "I saw some Indians when we were in Cambridge. Did their hair a little strange to what we've seen out along the Ohio."

"Sure, Penobscot Abenaki. I guess they hate the English. Fought with the French all along, now wanted to be a part of our army. But General Washington sent em home. Said he didn't want no Indians."

"Why not, for God's sake? The damned English use em sure enough."

"I don't know, lad," said Sergeant Philips. "I get the sense that General Washington don't much like Indians. Or maybe he just wants to whup the English all by his own self."

They didn't leave Newburyport for a number of days, which suited all the well-fed soldiers. Arnold had his boats out looking for Royal Navy patrols that came along these shores every day. Trying to figure a good time to slip past them.

"See?" said Luke Baird. "They're gonna get us in them little boats and we'll be sick as hell, and all the while the bloody English looking for us so they can blow us to pieces with cannons."

Finally, Arnold had a parade, his entire army tramping right-about along the banks of the Merrimack and all the young ladies of the town waving handkerchiefs and weeping, and one observer reported that the men of the Rifle Regiment were almost completely sober.

The troops were loaded in the boats, and they shoved off in darkness, a single small lantern at the fantail of each ship. And of course it rained and there were gale winds and lightning, and some of the ships got lost and the Riflemen were sicker than bloody pups. But the British didn't find them, and a few days later when they discovered that Arnold had eluded their patrols, they shelled a Maine town until it was in flames. All in a fit of English pique, one must suppose.

Fog covered them as they approached their destination and the wandering ships came in, and when the fog lifted, the troops on board saw Maine. Here there were many rocky islands covered with hemlock, and the water dashing against the rocks was gray and cold, and seaward were herring gulls and coots, the little sea ducks, flying wavering line formations just above the foaming crests of waves.

As the tiny flotilla moved cautiously between the rocky islands, bows pointed inland, they came to a settlement called Parker's Flat and there saw a company of Maine militia formed up along the shore and cheering.

There were maples here, and they were beginning to show orange and flame-red color in the crowns of the foliage. The expedition was in the mouth of the Kennebec, and Quebec was almost due north, more than two hundred miles away. As a crow flies. And it was past mid-September, and there was already a hard bite in the wind.

Gardiner was a settlement just inland from the coast, and there they saw again how Arnold had planned well. There were bateaux waiting for them, boats constructed by locals under a contract made with them less than a month before.

They took to the river and for a while some of the smaller sailing boats moved with them, but then the Kennebec became mostly white water, with many rocks, so moving by sail was impossible. The entire army began rowing and cordelling and polling. Here they had the luxury of what, with a little imagination, might have been called a road—a crude trace through the heavy growth of red pine and tamarack and beech alongside the river.

Colonel Arnold with his aides, including Burr and the Indian wife, were in two large cargo birch bark canoes with Abenakis paddling, four to each canoe.

"I thought General Washington said we wasn't to have Indians," said Robert Chesney.

"We're a long way now from where General Washington's at," Captain Edmund Barclay said. "Besides, these be from a different clan. Arnold trusts Jacatacqua's people. And he's paying these out of his own pocket so it won't show up in the army's accounts where Washington and the Continental Congress would see it. What they don't see won't give em the colic, will it?"

"We have to pay these Indians?"

"Hell, you get paid, don't you?"

"Not much."

"Well," said Barclay, "that fistfull of money I paid you at Newburyport came right out of Arnold's pocket, too. Someday, the Congress will reimburse. Arnold hopes."

In those first few days, before the army strung out like a worm stretching to full length, there was a lot of mingling with other units. Usually they camped at night around settlements, where they were made welcome. Here, there were opportunities to get acquainted, a chance to take a look at one another.

And the last chance they would have in a long time to sit dry and warm around a fire and exchange rumors and cuss unpopular officers and gripe and bitch, the second thing all soldiers learned. The first being the source of food.

The rumor of the moment was that a huge war party of Abenaki warriors was waiting in ambush somewhere up the Kennebec, having thrown in their lot with the English in this war even though they'd fought against the English in all previous ones. It was a fine rumor, one that could be enlarged in every direction and one that made ripples of gooseflesh creep up the back.

When the talk turned to such things, Maudine made her frail body into a ball, gripping her knees with both arms and leaning tight

111

against Miles Urie's back, her eyes large and luminous as she stared at the dark wall of trees surrounding them.

Robert Chesney was always aware of this, and he found himself wishing that Maudine would go off to the side, away from the firelight, and wrap herself in her blanket and sleep and stay away from where the men were talking.

Maybe even more fun than the scary rumors were the fault-finding sessions they had. Because as with all soldiers, when they didn't have an enemy immediately at hand to fight with, they fought with each other.

"These Connecticut men sure act like they might hate a Pennsylvania man or a Virginia man as bad as they hate the English," said Cranston Shook. The Ballymenas were grouped around a large fire, drying out from a day that had seen them fighting the unwieldy bateaux through rapids.

"Snooty, that's what they are," said Maudine Urie. "Almost as bad as them Princetons."

"New Jersey, that's where them men are from," said Sergeant Philips. "Only a few of the officers is from Princeton."

"Where the hell is Princeton?" asked Robert Chesney.

"Close to Philadelphia. In New Jersey."

"Well, the Massachusetts men, they're the ones I can't stand," said Luke Baird. "They act like they're sittin right beside of God Almighty all the time. And they ain't no closer to God than me and my hound dog Thomas!"

They laughed. It felt warm to laugh in this night that was turning bitter cold.

"The thing that takes the cake is these Maine people," said Calvin Reed. "When they talk, I can't understand hardly a word of it."

"Talk?" Miles Urie asked. "When did you hear one of em do anything but quack like a duck?"

Another laugh.

"Sergeant Philips," said Robert Chesney, "maybe you can tell me. Why is it I hear so many of these New England boys saying nasty little things about Colonel Arnold?"

"Lad, you've bought yourself a real bedtime story," said Sergeant Philips. "It's mostly to do with Ethan Allen."

"The one captured Ticonderoga?" asked Cranston Shook.

"The same," said Philips. "He be scattering bad stories about our Colonel Arnold everywhere, and he's good at it. Colonel Arnold was at Ticonderoga, too, and they had no sweet harmony sung between them. So these New Englanders are kind of divided in their loyalties.

"Some of Allen's boys think their own should have got the commission Arnold did. And every New England legislature's got a different idea of how to run things and issue orders accordingly. Which usually conflict with Arnold's orders from General Washington.

"So, Allen plays this little game. And Arnold knows all about it."

"What little game is that?"

"The game of beating his own drum and the drum of the Green Mountain Boys, to make them look damned good, so the Continental Congress will do a big favor," said Philips. "Oh, they have done a good job now and again, but they are not the saviors of the Revolution, as Allen'd have every colonial legislature and the Congress think.

"Some time ago, old Benning Wentworth was Crown-appointed governor of New Hampshire. While he's in office, Ethan Allen comes into possession of a lot of real estate. Most of those Green Mountain Boys, too. Governors sell titles to land, you see; that's where Wentworth comes in.

"Well, I don't know the wheres and whys. But I do know this land Allen laid claim to was west of the Connecticut River, which is in the colony of New York, lads. You can just imagine what the New York legislature thought about some Yankee yahoo claiming he owns a great hunk of their land because the governor of New Hampshire says so.

"It's almost a shooting war between New York and New Hampshire over these land claims, and finally the king's council, these being Crown Colonies both of them, gets their two cents in and says Ethan Allen's claims are void, and Benning Wentworth gets a nasty note about him being naughty but he don't care. He retires with all the money he's made as governor, and it leaves Ethan Allen in a real funk. Which you can understand, his having been hornswoggled!

"He's been trying ever since to get his land titles. So now, with the war, Ethan Allen sees a chance to make a big name for himself so that the Continental Congress will be beholden to him and, once the war is over, will give him and the boys title to that land.

"And somebody like Colonel Arnold, who makes Ethan Allen's star a little less shiny bright, because his toenail parings got more good soldier in em than all of Ethan Allen put together, and both of them operating side by side, it's natural that the worse Arnold comes out in all the stories, the better Allen will look.

"Also, Arnold's got a lot of friends in New York, and right now anybody from New York is a worse enemy to Allen than three barrels of rattlesnakes.

"Plus, Arnold's got a lot of men in Congress and the rest of the army who envy him because General Washington thinks Arnold hung the moon, so anything nasty can be said about Arnold by anybody, especially the hero of Ticonderoga, is going to get plenty of listeners.

"Now, there's a lot more to it than that, I expect. But you've got the nut of it."

"My God," said Robert Chesney. "I never thought they could be men who would use a war to get something for their ownselfs."

"Look around in any direction," said Sergeant Philips. "Look at yourself!"

"Me? I ain't got no argument with anybody about land titles!"

"You're fightin for liberty, ain't you? Well, that's something for yourself. You're fightin to get the Crown tax collector off your back, ain't you? That's something for yourself. Look at these men. Everyone figures he'll be better off, fightin this war. Or he wouldn't be here."

"That's not the same. Fightin for liberty, not land."

"Well, maybe liberty to Ethan Allen is a plot of land west of the Connecticut River!"

They struggled against the Kennebec's wild current, and every day they were soaked through and shoulders ached and hands were blistered from the poles because rowing was almost impossible. The boats Arnold had contracted for had been badly built and were made mostly of uncured lumber besides, and they warped and shrunk and popped seams.

Much time was wasted hauling the boats onto dry ground and repairing them. Supplies were soaked.

There were fewer and fewer white settlements and farms as they went up the Kennebec. All this area had been thickly settled until the last French war, and then the whites moved back toward the coast or were scalded out by Indians, usually Abenakis, usually led by white-coated French army officers. The two major war trails from Canada into the New England colonies had been the Kennebec and the Connecticut Rivers.

It began to rain almost every day. The rain came in slow, dismal sheets. It was cold rain from low cloud cover, and it turned everything to gray, the western mountain crests seen as through a thick veil, the woods around them dripping and dark even at noon.

"Sweet Jesus," Miles Urie said, "we pay our good money from my da's black calf to come here for something better, and as soon as we get here they run us out in this muck of a forest to fight a war we don't understand against somebody we don't know."

"Think of the sunshine," said Robert Chesney, grinning so the gap in his front teeth showed like an open gate.

"Now listen to the big sergeant," snarled Miles Urie. "A real Boss Bobby now, huh?"

Robert Chesney only grinned, which surprised some of them, but it was true. Only the night before, Captain Barclay had come to their pitiful attempt at a fire in the rain and told Robert Chesney that from now on he would be Sergeant Chesney, with an increase in pay that amounted to about two dollars a month. A fortune.

"My God, Captain, I don't know nothin about being a sergeant," Chesney said.

"You yell at your people so they do right."

"I already do that!"

"So now you get paid for it," said Barclay, smiling a little as the rain dripped off the snap-brim of his hat and into his face. "And now, if they don't do what you say, we can tie em to a tree and flog em!"

As Barclay walked away into the darkness, Robert Chesney looking after him, all the Ballymenas around the fire were watching their new sergeant. He became aware of that, and his face flushed.

"We ain't gonna flog nobody," he mumbled.

"Yesiree, yesiree," Young Bone Trudeau said, laughing. "No floggin round here all these fine colony gentlemens such good soldiers in Sergeant Bobby's army."

They all laughed with the African. Even Sergeant Bobby.

And at last they came to the old abandoned fort at the mouth of the Sebasticook. This was the western edge of any white settlement. From here, there was only the primeval country blanketed in hemlock and black spruce, never mapped and most of it never trod by white men, where no one except the Abenakis knew what ground lay dry under pine needles and what was covered with three feet of standing water, where footing was solid and where spruce and hemlock bogs sucked moccasins off feet at every step.

They were organized for the march now. Morgan's regiment would go ahead as advance guard to sweep any Indian ambushes aside and hack trails around portage sites. Even so, some of the Ballymenas would still find themselves thrashing along with the main column because Arnold would use them as couriers between the divisions of his army.

Morgan was supposed to get rid of his bateaux, which would have delighted his men, but he disobeyed orders and kept a few of them. As the Rifle Regiment hurried away from the head of the main body, trying to put distance between themselves and the others, the men

spent hideous hours carrying the big, awkward boats along the riverbank, even past water where they might have poled successfully.

"Dammit, Hobe," Miles Urie said. "How could a merciful God allow such things as these bateaux to be put on a man's shoulders?"

"They ain't God's vessels," said Hobe Spencer, who was almost
strong enough to carry one of the boats by himself. "These surely be
the boats of Satan."

They'd had one day of dazzling autumn sunlight, and then the gray
clouds came again. They were bedding down on a sandy point of high
ground above the river when it began to rain. They were too tired to
struggle with a wet wood fire and ate a mouthful of raw salt pork as
they rolled into blankets under whatever shelter they could find under bending hemlock boughs.

It was then that Morgan sent a courier to Robert Chesney instructing him to come forward. Chesney found the hulking, two-
hundred-pound Rifleman commander trying with small success to
stay dry under an upturned bateau propped against a tree trunk. As
usual, Morgan didn't mince any words as Robert Chesney stood beside the bateau in the rain.

"We've added a few Indians of our own," Morgan said. "They've
been waiting here, on my instructions, for us to come up. You'll find
them just upstream, about a hundred paces, in a little wigwag they've
built of willows, which I wish they'd built enough of while they were
waiting for the whole outfit. They want to talk to you."

Robert Chesney stood there with his mouth open, the rain dripping off his chin.

"To me? Colonel, I don't speak any of this Indian lingo." He called
Morgan Colonel no matter what his rank because that's what they all
called him.

"They speak some of yours," Morgan said. "Get on over there.
This courier will guide you. They're back in the timber a ways off the
river."

As they moved through the dripping woods, Robert Chesney was aware that another man had fallen in behind them. He thought he caught an unfamiliar odor, yet hauntingly familiar, too.

It was a bark-covered wigwam with a deer skin for a flap door, and Robert Chesney pushed it aside and stepped into the small dome of the room. The smell struck him hard now, and the bristles along the back of his neck rose. The same sensation and the same odor he'd experienced along the riverside at Fort Pitt over a year ago.

There were three people sitting around the small fire that was more smoke than flame. One hunched figure wearing a tricorn hat with feathers trailing behind had his back to the door. The others faced Chesney, and now the man who had been following was inside and took his place on the far side of the fire.

This one dropped a rain-soaked blanket from his head, revealing the strangest roach Robert Chesney had ever seen. On one side of the head, from crown to ear, the head was shaved. On the other side, the hair was long and hung down in black cascade to the shoulder. The exposed right ear was pierced from lobe to crown, and dangling from it were polished bits of freshwater mussel shell. He wore no paint, but his chest was tattooed with blue and green circles.

Next to him was an older Indian, hair roached in a stiff line along the crown with rattles from rattlesnakes and short feathers of blue jays worked into the hair. He wore yellow and ocher paint across high cheekbones which emphasized Oriental eyes. He had many brass and glass beads hanging from his neck and copper wire wrapped as bracelets on both wrists.

Each gazed unblinkingly into Robert Chesney's face, with no hint of friendliness.

The third person was much younger, with long hair, center parted and braided along each smooth cheek. This one held a blanket around the shoulders, and the eyes were cast down.

It was a quick appraisal, and all the while Robert Chesney's skin was crawling under the exotic, somehow guileless effluvium.

"Well, Bobby!" Without rising, the man turned, and there was the small, crooked smile that Robert Chesney remembered. It was Noble Popjoy. "Come sit."

"Good Lord! Good Lord!"

Robert Chesney sat, and they shook hands and clapped hands to shoulder and made all the senseless yet meaningful short comments that old friends always make after being apart for a long time. Noble Popjoy looked just as Robert Chesney remembered him.

In these first moments, the older Indian across the fire passed a long calumet with dangling feathers attached to the stem, and Robert Chesney took it. From the bowl there was a tendril of blue-gray smoke, and as he puffed on the pipe, Popjoy introduced the others in the wigwam.

"This here is Cohegog," said Popjoy, indicating the man with the strange hairstyle. "Don't matter what it means. Whites call him Ear Shells. You can see why."

The man who had passed the pipe was Memphreme, and because of the slant to his eyes, Popjoy said, whites called him the Chinaman.

"These men be St. Francis Abenaki," the wilderness man said. "Not Penobscot, like Arnold's Indians, but St. Francis. They ain't many of them left. They are my friends, and they wanted to help as they could against the English. Their people fought the English through all the French wars, so they want to keep at it. Especially now that the Mohawks are going to fight for the English, my friends here want to fight against them. They don't take much liking to Mohawks."

Noble Popjoy laughed shortly, and so did the two Abenakis. Robert Chesney didn't know what the joke was, but the little exchange of laughter let him know these men could speak at least some English.

"Morgan says you may be working with us some. We'll be mostly looking out for any hostiles on the route. Just like we did, you and me, going to the Monongahela."

"What kind of hostiles?"

"Any kind. Maybe Abenaki. Some of the old confederation may have decided this time to fight with the English. Maybe Iroquois, if the English have brought some over here from the Mohawk Valley. And by the time we get close to Canada, Huron and Ottawa, who once fought against the English but are now going to fight for them. Are you keeping up with all this, Bobby?"

"Maybe better than I did when we were on that last trek together."

"Good," said Popjoy. Now he waved one hand toward the line of Indians across the fire. "This here little one is Narragansett and Erie and French. Name of Nalambigi, which means 'quiet water' in Abenaki. In remembrance of a mother who was treated well by the St. Francis Abenaki after they captured her in a raid down the Connecticut River and found her, just a girl, working for a white man farmer who had bought her from somebody along the coast. We don't know who. A good mother that one was, to this chile."

For the first time, the young Indian's face lifted, and Robert Chesney could see now in the firelight features finely sculpted with delicate lips and high cheeks and skin the color of maple syrup. The eyes were black and shining as obsidian glass.

"Good tracker. Good shot with a rifle," Popjoy said. "Good for drying fish and cooking venison, too. Nalambigi! She's my daughter, Bobby!"

The warmth and fellowship of that wigwam would be in Robert Chesney's memory for a long time. Forever, maybe, as the Abenakis might say. He woke there the next morning, warm and dry and feeling that he was beginning to understand Indians and that now he had three of them he could actually call friend.

With Noble Popjoy encouraging it, the two men and the girl were soon uninhibited with this new white man and spoke and laughed with him enough so that he began to see that Indians were not necessarily the hard-visaged, stoic, taciturn beings most whites thought they were, but garrulous, laughing, emotional people like anybody else.

Under this stimulation, Popjoy talked and laughed more than he ever had in Chesney's presence before.

They ate chestnuts and dried moose meat and the men smoked, and although the tobacco was the rough Indian-cured kind that usually seemed harsh to a white man's throat, on this night it was good.

When Robert Chesney stepped out of the wigwam after a short sleep, the gray predawn was bitter and his breath was like a solid before his lips. He hurried to where his Ballymena companions were rolled in blankets like huge larvae in their cocoons. He began to call them awake, shouting their names, and at once there were the groans and grunts and moans of people waking to pain.

During the night, their wet clothing and blankets had frozen. As they sat up and rose to their feet, the sheet of ice enclosing their blankets popped and cracked and fell to the frozen ground like glass crystal being shattered.

"Hobe," said Robert Chesney as soon as he recognized Spencer shaking himself out of his ice sheath. "What's the date?"

Hobe Spencer shook himself like a great, burly dog, and particles of ice from his clothes clattered on the ground. He frowned and shook his head.

"October. About twelve October. I think. Why?"

"Just the middle of October. And look, Hobe."

Robert Chesney had his head tilted back, and seeing that, Hobe Spencer looked up through the spread of ghostly hemlock limbs toward a sky still mostly dark.

"God help us," he whispered.

They both knew it was more than a hundred fifty miles to Quebec City.

And it had started to snow.

Chapter 6

While the Ballymena boys were on their great adventure with Arnold, many things happened at Beulah Land. Twice, the home folks repelled Shawnee attacks. They didn't amount to much and were not led by British officers. But another scalp was added to the two already hanging on the wall above the door to the meeting house.

There was an election, the first of many that would follow. All the officers who had been named by Axel Muir at the start were reelected without opposition. Cordelia Muir continued as town recorder. She was the most conscientious of all the selectmen, being careful to keep a ledger of events in a large accounting book somebody had brought her from Fort Pitt.

Cordelia wrote with a goose quill pen, the settlement already renowned for its great flock of white barnyard geese. She made her own ink of lampblack and whale oil. Once she tried oil rendered from bear fat. It had a fine texture and was very bold, but she only brewed one batch of the stuff. When she opened that first, and only, bottle of bear fat ink, she had to place it so far away from her nose she couldn't reach it with the quill. She had to do this because it smelled so bad.

Having been so meticulous with local affairs, she felt compelled, when the heroes of Canada returned, to have their story recorded, too. She began a long series of talks with each of the boys who came home, plus Maudine Urie, in the kitchen of her new log house where sassafras tea and oatmeal cookies prepared on her new cast-iron stove hauled from Fort Pitt by ox sled and served on new shiny tin plates from the same place seemed to encourage recall of memories both fair and foul.

And so the Ballymena part in the attack on Quebec was chronicled in the great, sweeping penmanship of Cordelia Muir.

Maybe the others didn't notice. Not even Axel. But Cordelia had a kind of urgency about that journal of hers, as though there was some passionate requirement to get all memories recorded. Just recently, they'd heard of the document a man named Thomas Jefferson had written, called the Declaration of Independence. And maybe she figured the trials and triumphs of her tribe had to be written down in order for them to become a legitimate part of Mr. Jefferson's expectations for their new country.

A new country! It scared Cordelia a bit. When was the last time anybody had started out with a new country that had to be built without the help of all those smart men in London with all their tradition and history and legend from the dark mists of an ancient past?

Well, maybe that was it. Maybe she was building a tradition and maybe even some history and legend with her journal. Whatever she was doing, she figured it best not to say anything to Axel about her thoughts. He might not understand urgency and passion for words written on a sheet of paper.

For whatever reason, it was done.

Enoc Fulton : Born 1764, Saintfield, County Down, Ulster

We reckoned that when it started getting so cold our clothes froze on us at night it'd kill all the lice we had on us. But it never done it. They got worse. Popjoy said the cooties just dug in closer because they was after the heat from our bodies. Him and the Abenaki Indians he brought, it never seemed to bother.

We got pretty far out front of the others, I guess. Morgan's men, I mean. But they had a lot of trouble back there along the column, I heard. If they had more than us, I'm glad I was where I was at.

Colonel Arnold come up one day. It wasn't raining, I remember that. We'd come to this old Abenaki village where the Jesuits had built a mission and it was all abandoned and in ruins, and Popjoy said these Indians had mostly been killed by the English in the last war or smallpox since.

Colonel Arnold, he looked at the ruins and talked with Morgan, and I heard him say he'd had to stop the rest of the march so they could rest the men and fix their boats, and he said they were trying to get some dugout canoes so they could get rid of those damned bateaux.

So they put us to making brush shelters for the rest of the army when they come up, and then we went right on, and Colonel Morgan was out there yelling and cussing and making everybody move fast. He'd sent Popjoy and the three Indians out ahead to hunt. Bobby was with them.

We'd lost most of our food. The kaigs got wet in the river. There wasn't any way we could keep stuff dry. So kaigs leaked, and when we opened them there was mostly maggots or some kind of squirmy white worms. Alls we had was some salt pork and flour.

You can make a paste and put it on your ramrod. Just flour and water. Hobe Spencer had some salt. Then after you cooked it over a fire, you slathered on another layer. After you done this seven or eight times, you had a long, skinny bread you could eat right off the ramrod. Only trouble was, usually everything was so wet and we was so tired, there wasn't any fires made. We just flopped down and went to sleep all huddled together like a pack of hound dogs.

It was pitiful. We got into swamp then. Or bog. Or something. Standing water. With the river running right through it. And it had started to snow, too. Rain or snow almost every day and splashin through water sometimes waist deep.

Colonel Morgan said we needed to save our moccasins because they wasn't any more than what we carried, so we taken off leggings and moccasins and hung em around our neck, and all day long we'd be splashin around in that water barefoot and bareleg and only this little bitty loincloth on us.

Oh, it was cold. It hurt very bad. It was so cold. Have you ever been so cold that when you come out of the water, snow falling on your bare legs felt warm? God, it was so cold.

Maudine Urie: Born 1760, Belfast

We come to another river that run into the Kennebec. They said it was called Dead River, but it was lively enough. And that's where we run into swamps. It was a kind of spruce bog, and you couldn't hardly walk in it because your feet was always gettin tangled up in limbs under the water. Miles cut his foot real bad.

That was about the time Bobby started making us put up these little shelters each night to keep the rain and snow off of us. He learned how from the Abenakis Popjoy had with him.

You could put up a little hut in a few minutes, with tree limbs, and it helped some. Miles was always so tired, he'd just lay down. Bobby grabbed him one night and shook him like a dog and said if Miles didn't help, then he'd not get inside under cover when we was through makin the shelter.

So Miles helped, and he was so mad and he told me as soon as we got to where they was some fightin, he was gonna shoot Bobby in the back. And I said he wouldn't either, Bobby was our friend and helped us with the calf back in Belfast and ever'thing, and Miles said he didn't care. And they was a couple other sergeants and maybe an officer he was gonna shoot, too.

He was just tired out, that's all. His foot hurt and he was tired out and mad, but he never would have shot Bobby. He was just tired out! I don't think he'd done it.

After Arnold spent a day with us, he went back downriver to the next division coming up. That was Colonel Greene, from Rhode Island. Morgan sent me and Luke Baird with him so's we could be couriers when Arnold wanted to send orders back to the head of the column.

Greene's men was just getting started into the Dead River, and they was in bad shape. They didn't have anything to eat except raw salt pork, and everybody had the flu. One man, I understand, died from dysentery.

Their joints was all swole up because I guess they'd been in the water even more than us, and young men was hobbling around like they was ninety. They was crawling with vermin. And the coughing you could hear in the woods all up and down the river. Anybody tryin to sneak up on them could have found em without much trouble.

Arnold decided to make a hospital there, and we started building jury-rigged shelters for the sick men, and the surgeon was there givin salts and whatever else he had.

So they sent Luke Baird on downriver to the last division, clear at the rear. They said that'd be Colonel Enos of Vermont. And Arnold sent orders for him to come up quick and bring the extra supplies Enos was carrying. They started planning how to get all the sick back downriver without cuttin in on Arnold's troop strength too much.

Luke Baird : Born 1754, Holyhead, Anglesey, Wales

When Colonel Arnold sent me back to hurry up the fourth division, I stayed to dry ground, sometimes a mile or two from the river, and I run most of the way. To keep warm.

Popjoy had told us we hadn't had too much luck with game because we made so much noise we scared everything away. So when I got clear of the river and the column, I watched for a deer or a moose or anything else I could kill and eat.

We still had a little of that Indian scare even if Popjoy did say we wasn't likely to run into hostiles until we got closer to Canada. So I kept my eye out for the red devils. If I'd seen any, I might of shot one of them to roast, so hungry I was.

When I got to this Colonel Enos I found him a sour one, and he acted like it was my fault that he was supposed to hurry along, and he said he'd hurry along as he saw fit.

Full of Vermonters and other New Englanders this division was, for who I lost no love. One of the bastards, a cue from his leader taken, said he was a mind to put his boot in my arse. And I told him I'd be glad to show him where it was, and after he'd had his swing, me and a few dozen of Morgan's riflemen would come back downstream and bloody their God-damned Yankee heads.

This Enos had me stay with him, which was bitter as gall, but it wasn't but for a couple of days. It's hard to remember exactly. The good part was the trailing division still had considerable food, so I ate better than I had in two weeks.

Then he calls a council of war, and he's still a long way from catching up to where Arnold needs some of that food these people got so much of. And at the council of war, this God-damned Enos decides to go back! He's going to turn around and march back down-river to the coast because he says this whole thing is a mistake and he's not going to put his men in any more danger. He's just going to take the supplies Arnold needs and go back to where he can get in out of the rain and eat cooked grub and be warm.

A few of the officers said it was awful, and they took their men on upriver and me with em. But bloody Enos turns tail and scoots, taking about a quarter of Arnold's army with him.

When I got back to where they were trying to take care of all those sick men, making a kind of hospital, and waiting for the supplies from the rear, everyone was callin the place Camp Disaster. It was, too.

And that's even before they heard that Enos had cut and run. The bloody God-damned Vermont son of a bitch. He may have had some

127

good reasons for deserting suffering comrades, but you will skate on ice in hell before you convince me!

Calvin Reed: Born 1753, Holyhead, Londonderry, Ulster

We was glad to be across what our Indians called the Height of Land because it meant now we was going downhill to the Chaudière River which would run us right into the St. Lawrence.

Holy Hoxie, don't ever count unhatched geese. After Height of Land, we had our worst time.

There was water all over the place. The mountains, where we were crossing through, had snow on them now, but not far along their north slopes, there are these stepping-stone lakes, one lower than the other, you see, and water was everywhere, standing. You couldn't find the course of the river a lot of times.

Now it was this here hemlock swamp that beat all. As you come up onto a finger of it, it looks like dark green moss just layin here nice and smooth and firm, and you think, by Hoxie, I'm gonna get to put my moccasins and leggins back on and walk right, and you take the first step onto the stuff and you go right through it and up to your gonads in water. Ice-cold water.

For that part of our trip, we'd been better off if it was later in the year so all this would be ice. But it was just comin onto November. Well, listen, November in a swamp that close to Canada, it'll freeze the brass clapper off the bell, but it won't freeze water solid enough to walk on.

Morgan decided we'd best hold up and wait to help the following division through the stuff, and we did, and they sure as hell needed it. You couldn't find the damn river current, see, so you'd wander off in all directions in the swamp where trees were thick as hops. A few of us and our Indians spent a wild four or five days tryin to find the people who taken off in the wrong direction.

Then we hit real river current, farther along. It was so wild that any boats we had left were shattered on the rocks.

But that hemlock bog or swamp or whatever you call it, that was a damned caution.

Young Bone Trudeau: Born 1741, Sussex County, Delaware

Yesiree, me and Mr. Bobby glad Mr. Popjoy brang them red devils with us. Cause if they was any deer in the woods, they could find it.

After Height of Land, me and the Abenaki we call Ear in deep woods, maybe catch a moose, see? A little snow on the ground, yesiree, and it colder than blue britches.

I see me somethin move in trees, get old rifle ready, and Ear slip up and put he hand on my rifle lock and say, "No, them ours."

Then I see just a few quick move in them trees, yesiree, and it ain't no deer and it ain't no moose. It's red Indians, and I figure crazy Young Bone, you about to shoot our other Abenaki we call Chinaman or that Quiet Water girl, you crazy man. Cause what Young Bone see is men in skin clothes and hair roached black in a string down the back.

But this here ain't Chinaman or Quiet Water. Cause Ear go over and talk to these men a long time, close enough for me to see they ain't no red devils I ever seen before.

So then the talkin finished, and all these others just slide off through the trees and they be gone, and Ear come back and he saz these here is our Indians. Penobscot, he saz. Cousins, he saz.

Nosiree, ain't no red devils cousins of *mine*. So I allow what Ear means is, these red devils cousins of *him*.

Thas fine, thas fine, but I saz to Ear let his cousins know don't come poppin out of the woods too fast on me.

Enoc Fulton

Bobby and Popjoy and the Indians were bringing in more deer on the north side of Height of Land. And we found out that there were

129

friendly Abenaki out in the woods, driving the deer toward our army, so the men in the divisions following us got to shoot some, too.

Sometimes it was hard to find dry wood for a fire or even dry land to build it on, but it didn't matter. We'd eat the meat raw.

We was better off than the ones behind us, I reckon. They was this officer back there, I don't remember his name or what division he was in , but he'd brought this big black dog along. Well, they killed that dog and ate it.

Luke Baird told us about it when he came back up to us from Camp Disaster. And he brought me a rifle he got from one of those sick men who gonna get sent back to the coast by Colonel Arnold. Luke Baird said we'd find me that drum to play later, but for now, I'd better have me a rifle.

One night we'd been helping men from the other divisions through the swamp, and Bobby had us on a long shelf of gray, mossy rock where we made some hemlock limb shelters. And somebody asked where Miles Urie was at and Hobe Spencer said Maudine was afraid Miles had got lost and was back there somewheres looking for him.

Bobby got real mad and wanted to know how long Miles had been missing and which way had Maudine gone, and nobody knew much except that Hobe said she went back the way we'd come. We got fire going and cooked some venison, and Bobby was still stomping up and down the rock and asking if anybody had heard Popjoy say when he'd be back with his Indians, but nobody had.

If an Abenaki, even the girl, had been there, I think Bobby would have struck out looking for Maudine even if it was dark. He wasn't sure of himself enough to do it without an Indian with him.

I didn't blame him for not going back to look. Nobody did. But we kept thinking about that swamp, and we knew some of our men had drowned in it.

They all went to sleep except I didn't. I lay there shiverin and watchin Bobby walking back and forth on that rock, lookin out into the swamp.

The clouds had rolled off and the moon was bright later on, and I guess Bobby saw her coming a ways off. He jumped off that rock and into the swamp, and I figured he'd seen something I hadn't.

Then he was sort of draggin and carryin Maudine up onto the dry ground, and she was saying something real soft I couldn't hear. Then she made a loud little cry, and I heard her say his face was just under the water all calm and white.

I knew then she'd found Miles in the water, dead. And somehow she got back and found us. She was dragging Miles' rifle along with her, and she held onto it until Bobby took it out of her hand. They got into his lean-to, and I seen Bobby wrap his blanket tight around Maudine and his ownself.

Lordy, I was cold and hungry and wide awake. So I taken this hunk of deer meat I'd stuck in my smock pocket to eat the next day, and I ate it right then.

Maudine Urie

I tried to pull him up out of the water. But his legs was all tangled between these hemlock logs under there, and I could feel the bone stickin out of one of his legs under the water when I felt down there tryin to get him out, and I knew he'd broke his leg and just fell in the water and couldn't get out.

His face was just under the water, and it was all white, and it was like he was lookin at me. I kept callin his name, but I knew he wouldn't answer. I knew Miles wouldn't never answer nobody no more.

So I got his rifle out of the water, I guess. I don't remember much then. I just splashed along, and the moon was out, and I never even thought about where I was at or where I was goin. The water was all silver, like a big shiny plate, and the shadows of the trees made black stripes on it. I just kept splashin along. I don't think I ever cried any. Not tears, anyway.

Then I seen Bobby, and he was runnin through the water to get me. And he taken me onto dry ground, and he rolled me in the blanket with him tight next to me, and before long I was warm.

It was the first time I'd been warm for what seemed like a month or two. I'd forgot how it felt to be warm like that.

Before morning, Bobby knew me, and it was all right with him to do that. I didn't have no shame because now my husband was gone and Bobby had always been like another husband anyway. We'd been together all that time since Belfast and raffling that bull calf. He always looked so fine, even after Baltimore, and he'd smile and there was that big gap where he got his teeth knocked out.

I don't think he ever done it with anybody before!

Cranston Shook

What Bobby done with Maudine Urie was their business. One thing about it. Bobby sure treated her better than Miles ever had.

How she found us again, that beats all. I'd not have bet a farthing on anybody doing it. But she did. Hobe Spencer said it was the hand of God that guided Maudine through the swamp and back to us. Maybe so.

Hobe never said if it was God's hand that guided her into Bobby's blanket.

Luke Baird

There were spies. On both sides they was. Sometimes they would come to Arnold. They looked like anybody else. They traveled in twos, mostly they did, not alone. And after I learned about spies, when I seen two strangers hanging about and talking to Arnold, I said to myself, Spies!

Here were we, in the midst of a damned wilderness. The snow or the rain would be falling. The men so hungry some of them were cutting up their moccasins and leggins and eatin them. And then, there would be two men, tattered and thin in the flanks from hard travel, talking with Arnold. Then they'd be gone!

I knew they were spies after two of them had come up and gone and I heard Arnold telling Morgan some of what they'd said.

Oh, I remember this damned time enough of it. What Arnold said to Morgan was, "They know we are coming." He said, "They know we are coming; the British know we are coming!"

How do you like that?

Calvin Reed

Chaudière River. They said it meant "cauldron" in French. It was that, sure enough. It tore our skin right off us nearly before we got down it to the first settlements.

We were still in heavy woods and fightin that river with the few dugout canoes we had. Mostly we walked, and the ground was big rocks and brush and slicks of ice all over the place.

That's where we was on the night when Bobby come back among us after being with Colonel Morgan's party all day, and he said a bunch of Abenaki Indians had come in and told Colonel Arnold some of their boys had gone into Cambridge to get on this expedition, but the Great White General said no. Now they was back and ready to help anyway.

So Colonel Arnold was a little embarrassed because there were spies around who had told him wrong things that made him think all the Abenakis he found would be hostile, and these Indians said hell no, they wanted to help and they was Penobscot Abenaki.

I said, Holy Hoxie, let em help. We need help after all them men got sick and them others was took back to Maine by that Vermont officer.

Yesiree, Ear was right. Them red devils we seen in the woods *was* our Indians, an now Colonel Arnold saz he lak all them boys with the wild hair and the tattoo and the jaybird feather come right along and we shoot the English good.

Ear and Chinaman, they stay with Popjoy an us, but that little girl Nalambigi, she leave. Ear saz she go with big war party cause then she got some other women aroun to gabble with.

It don't matter. We come down off this old mountain now and away from these crazy rivers and bogs, and now theys a road as good as you need for a mule wagon, and theys houses and fields waitin for spring plow an smell like fish. Just lak fields along Kennebec where red devils grow corn. Smell strong fish smell. Cause they puts dead fish in the hole with the seed corn. Fertilize, Bobby says, with fish.

It don't matter now. We close to the English soldiers!

Calvin Reed

Holy Hoxie, those first houses. Little white houses, neat as a lace, and Frenchmen running out, men and women and children. Well, they was Canadians, but they talked French.

We didn't know. We didn't know but what all these Canadians would be shootin at us. But these farmers and village people along the lower Chaudière hated the English much as anybody you'd ever see. That's what Colonel Arnold told us. But a man always waits to see for his ownself when it's something like that.

So here we be, and Colonel Arnold was right. Them good French people brought grub out to us. And Colonel Arnold and Colonel Morgan was right there trying to pay them for it, and most of them wouldn't take money for their grub. It had been a long spell since we'd seen anybody willin to give soldiers anything without money on the line!

As the troops come down the river, Colonel Arnold was gettin billet space for em, so they could have a warm place to sleep, and these French Canadians was puttin us up in their barns and sheds and right in their homes. And feedin us like we was King George's butler!

There was this goose liver you spread on a piece of toasted bread. They was all kinds of fine grub, but I can't get that goose liver out of my mind. We'd sit in some Frenchie's kitchen, warm and dry, and we'd spread that stuff on toasted bread, and that Frenchman and his wife and kids yelling "Pau-Tay, Pau-Tay." And this white goat cheese! They grin, and the kids would yell "Fro-Mash, Fro-Mash." I ain't too fine on that French talk, but my Lord Hoxie, what grub!

One place, there was a Catholic priest and he had us in his rectory or whatever the papists call such places, and he was feedin us just like everybody else, and I asked Hobe Spencer what in the world a good Calvinist like him was doin takin grub from one of the pope's preachers. Hobe didn't say a word. He just kept eatin!

Food wasn't all. Colonel Arnold got a lot of shoes and trousers, too, and some coats. I reckon we taken ever pair of shoes and ever coat between Sartigan and Ste. Marie.

And all the new Indians we had, they was puttin a lot of big canoes in the water, then downriver and toward the St. Lawrence.

Some men got sick, and a few almost died from eatin too much after bein almost starved. But once everybody had a bellyful and felt better about things, we got thinkin about what was downriver. So we went to work on our weapons and got ever'thing clean and all edges sharp.

Luke Baird

Before the whole shebang got down to the big river, Arnold took an advance party to have a look. Bobby was there and me and Morgan and a lot of Abenakis.

We found some timbered high ground behind the houses along the riverbank at Pointe Levi. It was snowing just enough to make things in the distance look gray.

One helluva big river this was, the St. Lawrence. The far shore looked a mile away, maybe more. And there was all kinds of naval ships in the river, two deckers even, with rows of cannons, and I thought about Axel Muir.

Bobby touched my shoulder and he was pointing, and then I saw it. Quebec.

There was this high bluff, and on top was the walls of the city, and behind the walls the spires of churches and other buildings. There were buildings along part of the hill below the city, and at the river-front there, a whole town strung out at the water's edge.

I heard Arnold say that walled top part was called Upper Town and all that stuff at the foot of the bluff was Lower Town. He said there were a lot of smaller towns east of Quebec along the St. Charles River that come into the St. Lawrence right beside of Quebec on the north.

I heard Arnold say some other unwelcome stuff. They had a new general over there named Carleton, and he'd just arrived with some British regulars. Already in the town was some Canadian loyalist troops, some local militia, some British marines, and these Highland troops that was men who'd fought in the last French war then stayed in America and settled in New York and when the trouble started between the colonies and the English, damned if they didn't up and go off to Canada and formed a regiment over there in Quebec.

Damned if I liked the sound of it. Bobby didn't either. And we both knew that all Arnold had left after our march was less than seven hundred men!

Maudine Urie

Bobby was gone almost all the time, even at night. He was up lookin at the big river with Morgan and all them important men and the Indians. But he said once we started across, he'd keep me right beside of him.

Colonel Arnold was tryin to figure out how to get across without the English seein us. They had all these ships goin back and forth lookin for us. Bobby said the English knew we was comin.

One night Morgan got into a mess at the riverbank. One of these English rowboats, a big one, with lots of men in it, was going along our bank of the river, looking for us. So some of the Indians with Morgan decided to shoot at it. The next thing you know, Morgan jumped in the water and he dragged this English officer out of the boat, or maybe he was already in the water, I don't know, but Morgan dragged him onto the bank, and then this warship come along and started shooting cannons with grapeshot but never hit any of our folks.

We heard the cannons shooting, and they sounded like *boom* boom *boom* boom. Far away. Like a big owl hooting in the snow way back in the woods.

I seen that Englishman Morgan got out of their patrol boat. He was so young. He looked scared to death, and he was still wet when I seen him. From the river because it wasn't raining or snowing.

I don't know what happened to him.

Enoc Fulton

There were a lot of canoes. That's how Colonel Arnold got his army across the river. He did it on a dark night and just simply slipped between those British ships.

I was glad I was still with Bobby. We was in one of the first canoes with Morgan and Luke Baird and Popjoy and some Abenakis.

We landed pretty far south of the Quebec bluff, but we hardly got out and sent the canoe back for more troops when we seen this British patrol comin along the riverbank towards us.

Our bunch just kind of fanned out in a little stand of white pine, and the British walked right into us. Everybody shot at once, or pert near so, and we killed three of em, all Englishmen, and the rest of them, mostly Indians, got away.

Morgan wouldn't let our Abenakis scalp the men we'd killed, but I think they slipped back later and did it. Asked Bobby what he thought about it, and he said he didn't see it made any difference one way or the other.

We knew the British behind the walls at Quebec knew we were across the river now. Even if they hadn't heard the shootin, the men who got away would tell em.

It was the first time I ever shot at another man. I don't know if I hit anything. But I aimed to. I thought I'd feel good or bad or something. But I didn't feel anything at all.

I got wonderin how many other people thirteen years old there was in that army fixin to attack Quebec, and if there was, if they was havin as much fun as me.

Luke Baird

Sometimes it ain't best to do a fine job. I reckon that's what I'd done for Arnold, being a courier, so now, as soon as he got the army across the river and ready to attack Quebec, he sends me off upriver so I'll miss it.

Arnold gives me a whole fat package of messages for General Montgomery, who was an American officer who'd occupied Montreal with an army, and him and Arnold was supposed to work together in all this Canada invasion business.

I taken one other rifleman and three Penobscot Abenaki with me. We'd have to stay back a ways from the river because even though Americans were in Montreal, the British still controlled the St. Lawrence with their warships.

Also, we knew the English were using a lot of Ottawa and Huron Indians so we'd have to avoid any of their war parties or patrols.

Hell's fire, I was so disappointed about missing the attack on Quebec, I was wishin we *would* run into some hostiles.

But we didn't.

They was this little road went up the face of that cliff behind Quebec, and we went up it and come out on this flat plain. And there was the rear wall of the city, and we could see the English all along it lookin at us.

We formed up in a long line, Arnold's whole army. They was only about seven hundred of us. And Arnold walked out in front, and we started cheerin—you never heared nothin like it, by Hoxie—cheerin Colonel Arnold.

Morgan had told us that back in the last war, this English army had come to this same place, called the Plain of Abraham, and the British general walked out and kindly laid down a challenge to the French. And the French come out, and then the British blowed hell out of em and won the fight.

So Arnold was tryin the same thing, to get the soldiers in Quebec out from behind those walls. He went up with a white flag. And they just laughed at him. And they said their General Carleton wouldn't talk to no ragged bandit and traitor and if Arnold laid down his arms then he could come in and be hanged.

So Arnold turned around and come back, and he wasn't even back to our line yet when the British started shootin cannon from the walls. We thought we was too far away and we hooted and laughed, and then Bobby started screaming, "Come help him, come help him!"

One of them cannonballs had hit Hobe Spencer and sheared off his right leg, and it was just hangin, danglin there and blood gushin, and Bobby was holding him and yelling, "Help him, help him!"

We dragged Hobe back amongst the houses and there was a surgeon Arnold had up there close to us, and we laid Hobe on top of some barrels and he kept sayin, "Nearer my God to thee, nearer my God to thee."

Bobby held onto Hobe and yellin, "Help him, help him!" And the doctor was tryin to stop it from bleedin, but there was blood gushing out, pump, pump, pump, and there was blood all over the doctor and all over me and Bobby, and he tried to put powder on it and make it burn, but it wouldn't, and Hobe was still sayin, "Nearer my God to thee, nearer my God to thee."

And Bobby still yellin, "Do something, do something!" And Hobe had stopped sayin anything and had started to turn dough white, and the doctor said, "Son, I can't help him."

Hobe died right there on them barrels, all his blood runnin out, and Bobby was yellin, "Those bastards, those God-damned shitabed bastards. I'll kill those bastards!"

We carried Hobe back behind this little settlement where they was a graveyard and we wrapped him in a nice blanket one of the Canadian civilians give us, and Morgan was there and Arnold, and the army chaplain said a good service. He was a Presbyterian, and I knew Hobe would like that.

Popjoy was on one side of Bobby and Young Bone on the other tryin to console him. Maudine was there, too, tryin to console him. But he wasn't gonna be consoled. He said he'd kill those shitabed bastards.

Maudine Urie

I never seen Bobby so mad. He talked awful about the English. I was afraid he'd go crazy and just run out there and up to them walls and try to get inside Quebec.

He didn't, though, thank God, and Colonel Arnold moved the army into the towns around Quebec, and Colonel Morgan's men was put in a place called St. Roch close by the St. Charles River and just about due east of the city.

Back when they first come here, the French sure named a lot of things Saint. Saint this or saint that. Them Catholics do thangs like that, I suppose.

Well, the weather had got better. For a few days it was sunny and warm for November. And we just set, and we waited, making a siege,

140

they said, until General Montgomery come up from Montreal. We had plenty to eat. Some of the soldiers even started getting some meat back on their bones after pert near starvin on the way to Canada.

I hated it, though. I wished we could just up and go home.

Cranston Shook

There was part of the old town of Quebec on the east side that was outside the wall that stood around most of what Arnold called the Upper Town. That was where the British garrison was, behind the wall. There was a gap in the wall on the west side. At the gap the town was built down the steep slope and right to the river's edge. If we assaulted this place, we'd have to do it through that gap.

Arnold said scaling ladders wouldn't work. They had more men than us and could put a lot of soldiers on that wall to kick us down.

If we'd got there with all the army we started with, Morgan said we'd have assaulted that place right off. But with the big bunch that Vermont officer turned back with plus the sick ones we had to leave, we just didn't have enough men until Montgomery got up from Montreal.

So we sat there watching the Englishmen and the Canadians who was helping them. And they watched us when we moved around in St. Roch. They didn't do nothin. We were out of range of their Brown Bess muskets, and we didn't give em any big targets to use cannon on.

Then Morgan moved some of us right in close to the wall where there was some buildings, kindly the suburbs, he said, of St. Roch. And there was an old building the French had built, and it was called the Intendant's Palace.

This building was pretty fancy, of rock and mortar. A sort of head-quarters for the French, I reckon. It was a high building and had a couple of these tower turrets like church bell steeples. From there, you could look right down into the Upper Town and you could see the British sentries on the fire step and the platform behind the wall.

Well, hell, Morgan said, instead of settin on our arse and wearin out our rifles cleaning em, why don't we sneak into those buildings close to the wall, especially the Intendant's Palace, and snipe a few Englishmen?

That's how we paid em back for Hobe, I guess.

Bobby took a team up in the highest turret, and I was one, and Bone and Enoc. Maudine was there, too.

Hell, wherever Bobby went, Maudine wasn't far behind. You could count on that!

Enoc Fulton

Bobby told us to stay well back from the windows so the British wouldn't see us. We was outta range of their muskets, but Bobby said stay hid anyway just to spook em.

There was furniture in this place, all kinds of stuff, so it was being used for something, but all the people were gone from it and we had it to ourselves. We stacked the furniture to make rests for shooting.

"Get the officers," Bobby said, "no matter whether General Washington likes it or not."

That first day, we looked over at the parapet, and there was a tall man who was maybe one of them Highlanders. He had a big woolly black hat and a bloodred coat with a sash that was plaid color. He carried a long staff and wore a sword, and somebody said it looked like a sergeant major from his uniform. Like one they'd seen back in Ulster when there were British regiments in Belfast.

Bobby took the first shot. The sergeant major was standing back from the wall on the catwalk, looking back and forth where troops was at gun ports along the parapet. When the rifle banged, his head snapped back like he'd been slapped and the tall bonnet went sailing, and he melted down into a red puddle without nary another move.

The soldiers didn't know what had happened. They run back and bent over the sergeant major, and they were jabbering. We could hear em. Then Young Bone shot, and another one flopped down right next to the sergeant major.

They knew then where it was coming from. They run back to the parapet and hunkered down behind the wall. Another officer run up to the catwalk, up the stairs from the ground, and he was running back and forth, waving a sword, and the soldiers were pointing in our direction, and the officer ran up to a gun port and waved his sword and was screaming cuss words at us and saying we was a mob of ruffians and filthy barbarians not fit to be called soldiers.

Cranston shot him in the head.

Young Bone Trudeau

Us colony gentlemens was turnin them redcoats into bugs on that ole wall. Yesiree, they runnin round lak bugs an us stompin em. Big ole redcoat officer makin em stick they heads up to see what us fine Rebels doin, an when we see head, we pop it, lak we step on a big bug and he go *pop!* We all go up with Bobby.

Man gets to feel kindly sorry for them sojurs on that wall, we killin em, the others carryin em down off the wall, one after the other, one after the other. They couldn't do nothin. They fume and cuss and wave muskets and make faces, but they can't do nothin.

Now an again the English shoot little cannon at us. It don't make no difference. We shoot, English soldier fall down. They shoot cannon, lots of smoke and birds fly up when it go boom, boom, boom.

They got these little birds in Canada, pretty birds, pretty little birds. They gray with black faces. In winter they stand on windowsill and Young Bone feed them bread crumbs and each day they come and eat, and then boom, boom, boom, they fly up and Young Bone laugh.

Then it got real cold and comin onto Christmas and then past that and New Year comin and enlistments on all us gentlemens runnin out so we can go home and we still poppin the English at that wall.

And one day we hear General Montgomery has come from Montreal and we gone attack this Quebec. And bout that time, too, that

English general gets tired us killing his folks on that wall, and he run some artillery out what they calls Palace Gate and he blows our house down all to Hell. God oh Mighty, them tall towers fall down, and we lucky we get out without none of us fine colony gentlemens get buried under all the rock.

Hope some of them English feed them pretty little birds now, with Young Bone and the colony gentlemens someplace else.

Maudine Urie

I be in Colonel Arnold's hospital. I waren't sick nor nothin. I was there to help with the sick men. Bobby told me to be there while him and the other men was down along the wall shootin at the English.

God in Glory, I loved that Bobby so much sometimes it made my stomach hurt!

They was plenty to keep me busy in that hospital. It was some kind of Catholic place, a school or something, and this priest in a long black gown was always pokin around and it made my skin crawl.

Him and the people who lived there talked French. I knew about the Irish being Catholic. It was some of them killed my paw. So maybe French Catholics is different from Irish Catholics. But I don't trust any of em.

They all got the same pope, ain't they? No matter they talk French or Irish.

Luke Baird

It was me took the message to General Montgomery at Montreal that said a siege wasn't going to work and that Arnold had to attack before the first of the year because a lot of men in his army would be going home after December 31st when their enlistments run out.

Arnold told Montgomery that the garrison at Quebec City could hold out until spring when the river would be free of all ice and the Royal Navy big ships could come back upriver and bring reinforcements of redcoats and besides that blow hell out of our army with their guns. They'd sailed back down to the mouth of the St. Lawrence earlier because moving in that river when there was a lot of ice in it tore hell out of the copper sheathing on their bottoms.

Arnold was a sailor and a soldier, too. So he knew about things like that.

General Montgomery was the nicest Englishman I ever seen. He was a handsome man and always dressed like it was a parade. He'd been a captain in the British army before the war, so now he was a traitor to ole King George and if the British ever caught him, they'd hang him sure.

I reckon this man Aaron Burr thought a lot of Montgomery, too, because he'd asked Arnold if he could be one of Montgomery's aides, so now him and his Golden Thighs Indian wife was with our column when we started along the road downriver toward Quebec.

Calvin Reed

Bobby said it was just a matter of time before that British general inside the walls got tired of us snipin his soldiers and he'd wheel some big cannons out of this gate and take in to blastin us.

Sure enough, one day it happened, and you never seen so much smoke and dust and chunks of rock wall flyin around. Them cannons just, by Hoxie, tore the Intendant's Palace all to smithereens and the other buildings along the wall, too, and we run like scalded cats.

Enoc Fulton got hit so hard on the leg, with a piece of flyin rock, that they thought his leg was broke. Bobby was right beside of him in their horspittle and kept sayin, "You ain't gonna cut off no leg here, you ain't gonna cut off no leg!"

And Colonel Arnold's army surgeon said, "Hell no, stop worryin because they ain't gonna cut off Enoc's leg," but we like to never got Bobby out of there cause he wanted to stay and be sure.

So snipin at Englishmen and Canadian Loyalists come to a halt, but it never made no difference because we was gettin ready to assault the city. After dark on the last day of the year.

Some year it had been, too! 1775. We'll none of us that come up the Kennebec will ever forget that year! As Young Bone Trudeau would say, nosiree!

Enoc Fulton

Everything was all hurry up, hurry up. Some of them old soldiers in the hospital who had fought in the last French war said that was how armies acted. Sit around, sit around, then hurry up, hurry up!

But not me and Maudine. We'd just be sittin there while all the others had the good time.

My leg was still so swoll and sore I couldn't hardly walk. I'd gone along anyway, but Bobby said I'd stay put if he had to tie me with a rope. He said the same thing to Maudine.

Cranston Shook and Young Bone Trudeau was going with Colonel Morgan, and Bobby and Cal Reed was going with Colonel Arnold.

But me and Maudine would just sit on our butts amongst all the men coughin and spittin and ruinin their beds from the diarrhea. That hospital smelled like hell. But the parsnip soup them Catholics brought us was good.

Luke Baird

We come right up onto the Plains of Abraham and then down the cliff to the riverfront. This New York militiaman told me I'd best get my bayonet on my musket, and I told the dumb bastard it warn't no musket, it was a rifle and you don't put bayonets on Pennsylvania rifles, and he says I'd sure as hell need a bayonet where we was goin, and I said not as long as I got this, and showed him my long hafted tomahawk hatchet.

Montgomery had his artillery up, though they wasn't much of it, and he started to shoot. The British started shooting back and they had a lot more than us, and about that time, with the thick smoke beginnin to roll around us, our advance party hit the first street barricade, and the general had the rockets fired up so's they'd bust over the city.

Calvin Reed

Colonel Arnold come out of his quarters, and, by God, he looked fine. He had on this white uniform and a pair of black boots and that little tricorn hat pulled down over his eyes. It was coming on close to midnight, but with the snow on the ground there was a lot of light and nobody had any trouble seeing him.

I expect we'd have put a nice cheer for him, but that's when we heard the cannons start to shoot from the other side of town and we knew the ball had opened sure and sweet, by Hoxie.

We was already scramblin into formation and running down toward the wall. We'd been told. We'd go along the wall to the bottom of the bluff east of the city and then turn right where the wall stopped and go direct into Quebec.

But Colonel Arnold warned us the British had all those houses barricaded and defended with troops and cannons.

General Montgomery, Arnold said, would be coming from the other direction, along the river, and his troops would attack into the city just like us. Colonel Morgan said that was what you'd call a coordinated attack.

As we got started, General Montgomery's boys sent up the sky rockets to let us know it had started. Hell, we knew already.

Ole cranky Luke Baird was down there with General Montgomery's army. I run along, keeping up with Colonel Arnold and

Bobby, and I kept thinkin, I hope ole cranky Luke's all right. I hope ole cranky Luke's all right!

Maudine Urie

We heard this racket, far off, like thunder, and the men said it was artillery. Then I seen these fireballs bustin right over the roofs of Quebec.

It was a shower of fire, all red and white and orange, and makin little pops and crackin and the sparks fallin down into the city.

When I was a little girl in Belfast, I remember they had these little fireballs they shot out over the water from the ships and they called them Roman candles. They was celebratin King George's birthday, and I always liked King George when I was a little girl because when he had a birthday, I could watch them shoot the red fireballs over the water.

But the shower of fire over Quebec was better. It was high in the black sky, but the light from it made the snow below all glimmer and shine.

Then after a while it was all black again, and we could hear a lot more noise from the other side of the city, guns shooting and cannons, and the smoke from the rockets was drifting down on us and it smelled like rotten eggs and spoiled everything.

Luke Baird

We caught hell at the first barricade. The bloody Canadian Loyalists were there, and we butchered one another at point-blank range, and I was right in there with my hatchet. The smoke was thick as soup and gritty on the tongue, and the sweat run off us and froze on our collars.

General Montgomery was there, too, swinging his sword and yellin at his troops to come on, and he busted right through the next barricade of barrels and boxes. They had cannons in windows and muskets all around, and they shot General Montgomery all to pieces and he fell in the snow.

Nobody tried to get to him. Hell, he was dead, we knew that, and the fire from those bastards was like a sheet of hot lead pulled right down in front of us.

Aaron Burr was in command then, and he pulled everybody right back and he didn't even make another single try at that damned second barricade. I was itchin to have a try at it because I figured if we hit it again the damned bloody Canadian militia would break, but Burr ran us right out of there and we didn't stop.

We ended up in a place called Ste. Foy, a couple miles upriver from Quebec, the place where we'd started our final attack from. That God-damned Burr should have tried at least once.

All I could think about was poor General Montgomery back there layin in the snow, shot all to pieces.

I tried to get my mind away from it by cleanin some of the blood off my hatchet.

Calvin Reed

We never got to the bottom of the town. The British was all along the way we was going to get with General Montgomery, with cannons, too, and men with muskets at all the windows and behind all the walls.

It didn't seem like it was hardly started when Colonel Arnold got hit in the left leg. Well, I think it was the left leg. He fell, and we was tryin to get him on his feet, and he pushed ever'body back and him wavin his sword and going right on.

But that wound was bad. Colonel Arnold's white uniform showed ever drop of blood, and there was blood runnin out of the top of his boot, and finally he had to stop and lean against a wall, still wavin his sword.

Somebody yelled, "We better get the colonel back to the surgeon or he might bleed to death," and I expect Bobby remembered Hobe Spencer and how he died with a leg wound, only at least Colonel Arnold's wasn't as bad as Hobe's had been.

Bobby was helpin one of Colonel Arnold's aides, and Colonel Arnold was yelling at all the soldiers running past, and you could hear his voice over the racket of shooting and he was yellin, "On boys, go on, go on, boys. Hurry on, hurry on!" He was yelling, bleedin like a stuck hog but still trying to stay in the fight.

The last I see of that fight as we carried the colonel away was Young Bone Trudeau and Cranston Shook, diving straight along that street, smoke swirlin all around like hell and our boys shoutin and going right at the English with hatchets and a few of Colonel Arnold's troops with bayonets on their muskets, yellin. God Almighty, you could see the bullets knockin chunks out of the walls all around them, and some of them were fallin down.

By Hoxie, it was crazy. Here we was carrying our wounded commander away from the fight and the musket balls whizzin around and hell broke out behind us around Morgan, and my mind floats off and I think, By damn, when these boys gets hit with a bullet, they just drop to ground and don't scream or yelp or say a word. Just drop like a rock.

But as we drag Colonel Arnold along and pass by these soldiers in the snow who has been hit earlier, by now they are carryin on pitiful. Moanin and yellin for water even in this cold. Like the pain waits a while to set in on em. I never knew it done that!

Cranston Shook

We walked right into hell. Smoke too thick for a man to see. Flashes of muzzle blast right in a man's face! You just take one shot with your rifle and then wade in with the hatchet. You hope nobody who's a friend gets in the way because you can't see anything but blurs of something moving. You scale walls and smash through doors and kick boxes and barrels aside, and when the half of your hatchet breaks, you grab some dead man's musket and keep going with the bayonet.

I could hear Morgan bellowing like a bull. I could hear Young Bone Trudeau making some kind of noise, dear Christ, I don't know what it was, like Africa banshees wailing. I could hear men all around cussing like I've never heard cussing before.

You don't know how long this thing goes on. There ain't no time to it. Your bones are weary, and you're bleeding in a dozen places, and the sweat stings your eyes, and your feet are chunks of ice.

Young Bone Trudeau was there close by, but I didn't know it until he grabbed me with both his hands. They were very strong hands. He yelled something, near as I could tell.

"Come, come, English get you here, English get eva'body here, come on, come."

Young Bone Trudeau just simply pulled me out of there, dragged me across men thrashing around on the ground wounded, through snow and rock rubble and out along the river. God, I was still tryin to fight, and he got me up against a wall and starts talkin.

"You come on now. Colonel Morgan gettin his ownself caught by them English and all the other colony gentlemens with him, they gettin caught," he keeps saying over and over. I suppose I just came out of a daze and realized what the hell was happening, so we cut back along the river, under the wall, and back up the hill and stumblin along and finally to the Palace Gate and then all that was left of the Intendant's Palace. It wasn't until he turned me loose and I just dropped down in the snow and kind of sobbed and cried until my breathing got back in kilter.

Then we went on to the hospital, and I knew from the talk around us that everything had gone up the flue. Montgomery's attack had failed, Arnold was wounded, Morgan last seen with the British all around him and his men out of ammunition and exhausted.

All of it. Up the flue!

It was like one of those bad dreams you had when you was a little child. A nightmare. Now there I was, sitting on a broken limber wheel.

The British had let Major Meigs loose long enough to come out of Quebec and pick up all the blanket rolls and personal truck of our men who had been captured in Lower Town. Major Meigs had been captured, too, and he give the British his word that he'd come back if they let him go long enough to get the stuff like soap and extra socks and underpants and letters and books or other personal things.

He told about Colonel Morgan being captured. The British got Colonel Morgan cornered in a hall, like a meeting hall, in Lower Town. All his soldiers were killed around him, and he had his sword in his hand and he was all bloody and he stood with his back against a wall.

Colonel Morgan said if they wanted his sword, they'd have to come and get it. They could have shot him right there, but their officers said they wouldn't just up and shoot a brave man like that. So would he please surrender and give up his sword.

Colonel Morgan said he'd never give up his sword to an enemy, but he'd consider giving it to a priest. So they brought a priest, and Colonel Morgan give the priest his sword and was took prisoner.

When Cranston Shook heard Major Meigs tell the story, he got red in the face and his teeth ground together, and he said if it hadn't been for that damned African, he'd have been where he belonged, beside of his leader. And Bobby told Cranston Shook it was a good thing he hadn't been with Colonel Morgan at the end because them British wouldn't have got some priest to take Cranston's hatchet. Bobby said they'd shot Cranston's arse off right where he stood!

Maudine Urie

That major come in to see Colonel Arnold where we had him propped up on a bed in the hospital. From the time they brought Colonel Arnold in, them Catholic nuns did over him like he was one of their saints or somethin.

Anyway, the major said some Canadian soldier had found this real fancy sword in the snow in Lower Town where they'd had a big fight. Some of the British officers seen it and figured it belonged to somebody important, so they went to where the soldier found it and they was dead bodies all over the place.

Then the major said they found a dead man wearin an officer's uniform, and they drug him indoors and they cleaned the ice off his face. And one of the British officers seen a scar on the dead man's face and said he knew who it was.

It was General Montgomery. And the major said the British wanted Colonel Arnold to have the sword, and the major unwrapped it from a blanket he'd been carrying it in and he give it to Colonel Arnold layin there in the bed.

And the major said them British officers had told him they was going to bury General Montgomery right beside of their own officers who had been kilt.

My Lord, poor Colonel Arnold, so brave and wounded in battle, and he was settin there cryin very hard, holdin General Montgomery's sword in his hands, and the tears just runnin down his face.

That major just ducked his head and run out of the hospital cause I guess he was about to cry, too. I guess all of us around Colonel Arnold's bed that night cried a little, when they brought him his friend's sword.

Poor Colonel Arnold. Nothin ever seemed to go right for him.

Calvin Reed

There wasn't much more to it.

Oh, Colonel Arnold kept the siege on until spring, but nobody ever sent him any reinforcements. So the Loyalists just set behind the walls and waited for the ice to clear the river so the Royal Navy could come. Finally, Colonel Arnold give up and come away.

Wasn't none of us there for any of that, though. By Hoxie, we'd done a share of war, and when our enlistment was up at the end of the year, we cut a swath towards home.

Got back south of the river and overland to the north tip of Lake Champlain, and by God, who appears but Noble Popjoy. Hadn't seen him since before the attack on Lower Town, but there he was. And he had all three Abenakis with him, which is to say, his daughter Quiet Water had come back from wherever it was she went, and was now with her pappy.

I tell you, them Indians can just pop up out of nowhere sometimes.

Anyway, they had two big cargo canoes. Popjoy said they was Huron, the kind they used to bring a ton or two of furs down to Quebec from the deep woods, down the Ottawa River so's to avoid the Mohawks, he said.

Well, we was glad to see that because floatin beats walkin, especially in wintertime.

So we all come home!

Cranston Shook

Except for Bobby.

When we got to where the Mohawk River comes into the Hudson, Bobby turned around and went back north with Popjoy and the three Indians.

There was some fuss with Maudine. But Bobby just finally told her to go on home to Beulah Land and find herself a good Presbyterian farm man and get married and have ten children.

He wasn't a farming-and-raising-children kind of man. We all had seen that. He would go back to Arnold or somebody, and after the war was over, he'd stay somewheres in the wilderness. White water and blue mountain and green spruce and red sunset. That was Bobby.

And we ain't seen him since.

154

Maudine Urie

I knowed all along he'd not marry with me. They was so much rest-less in him. The longer he stayed out in the woods, the more he saw of new places, the more he wanted to see.

I guess I be lovin Bobby to the day I die.

But then all of us does that, don't we?

Chapter 7

They saw Bobby again in time, and when he came Cordelia Muir was breathless anticipating long sessions with him in her kitchen, priming him with huckleberry buckwheat muffins while he talked and she recorded with her goose quill pen.

But Bobby wasn't in the mood for much talking, although he ate plenty of the muffins. It was all she could do, she later complained, to get anything out of him concerning the two things that the Ballymenas wanted most to know about. A woman and a bag of gold coins. More gold coins than any of them had ever seen before in one lump.

When Bobby came, it was seven years after Quebec and two after Yorktown. It was November 1783, only a short time after a peace treaty had been signed in Paris, France, making the thirteen original English colonies the United States of America.

Yesiree, as Young Bone Trudeau would say, colony gentlemens now got a country, and democracy everywhere in this new Republic.

We the undersigned agree to certain Articles of Confederation and perpetual union between the states Newhamp-

shire, Massachusetts-Bay, Rhodeisland, and Providence
Plantation, Connecticut, New York, New Jersey, Pennsyl-
vania, Delaware, Maryland, Virginia, North Carolina,
South Carolina, and Georgia.

Each state retained its sovereignty. The document was pretty em-
phatic about that. What you might call sowing the wind. Because it
sure as hell would reap the whirlwind one day. But . . .

Yesiree, a new country.

Well, snickered Great Britain, not for very long. It will crumble
like a cookie, and then we'll be there to lick up the sugar!

They still had troops in many of the old British forts north of the
Ohio River, along the chain of Great Lakes, forts which were on what
the treaty said was American soil and which were supposed to be vacated by the redcoats.

Well, snickered France, America won't be a country for long. Never
been a successful democracy so big and with so many different interests north to south, east to west. So the whole thing will crumble like
a cookie, and we'll be there to fight the English again for the sugar!

Despite there being a few French aristocrats like Lafayette who
thought the United States grand, the government of fat Louis XVI
hadn't fought beside the Patriots during the war for the love of liberty. Rather taking America's Revolution as a chance to get in another whack at the British.

Well, Spain snickered, too. Surely, Charles III must have thought,
It's going to be a lot easier to get a toe onto the east bank of the Mississippi River from the vast Louisiana Territory now that the east
bank is owned by a weakling little newborn democracy instead of
powerful Great Britain.

As it turned out, foreigners weren't the only ones who gave the
new Republic only a short time before self-destruction. There were
those in the Republic itself.

For example, it soon became clear that New England had a few
brave souls who wanted to take their states out of the Union and
have their own country.

For example, a lot of folk west of the mountains figured they might be better off if they formed up their own country. After all, those original thirteen were mostly seacoast states, with faces and interests toward Europe. West of the mountains, faces and interests were pointed in the exact opposite direction.

But when Bobby came home, the Ballymenas at Beulah Land weren't concerning themselves with such politics. They were too busy plowing and saw-milling and raising barns and children. And watching over their shoulder for the next war party of heathen red devils because although the so-called Revolution was over, some of the tribes along the Ohio were still at it, leaving a trail of black smoke in the sky where farms once stood as they vanished back into the woods in the direction of the Great Lakes.

They were in the commonwealth of Pennsylvania now. Fort Pitt was growing like the weeds along the edges of Silas Fulton's pea patches. There was a real road from Beulah Land to the forks of the river where the Ohio began.

The settlement itself had both grown and shrunk. Grown with the arrival of new people and things, shrunk because of the departure of many of the original Ballymenas. They had a log church now and a log parsonage where Obadiah Reed and his wife Chorine lived, their having arrived in 1778.

Reverend Reed was third cousin to Calvin, who married Maudine Urie in the same year. In fact, that marriage was the first official duty the good Presbyterian divine performed and had been a good job, apparently, because despite Ma Fulton saying Maudine would never bear more children after that stillborn son back in '75, there were at the time of Bobby's return three healthy kids on Calvin Reed's farmstead which was just across the river from Beulah Land in the grove of white birch, the bark of which they were still using to make canoes.

Darrel Stark had a full-blown blacksmith operation going in another of the new structures, also log, and the increasing population in the countryside were patronizing him for horse and mule shoes and other such smithy things. He'd married a German woman whose family had all been killed in a Shawnee raid about ten miles upriver. Stark children were now a traffic hazard in the Beulah Land street.

Well, you'd have to call it a street. There was the blacksmith shop and church on the one hand, side by side more or less, and opposite them the town hall, with the hair still hanging about the door, and the general store that the Maddox family from Fort Pitt had built and been operating for a couple of years.

The Muirs' house was cheek by jowl with the little store, and there Cordelia entertained in the style you'd expect from the wife of a local justice of the peace. Axel Muir had won that office immediately after he'd returned from his own adventure into war when he went with John Rogers Clark to tame the British-led Indians of Illinois country.

Axel Muir was also mayor of Beulah Land. And captain of the local militia company.

"You never know when we might be needed," he said. "The damned British are still in all their forts along the lakes, which they were supposed to get out of, and the Indians are still being goaded and encouraged with English gunpowder and whiskey to burn farms on the north of the Ohio because they just damned well think they'll have all that back in a short time, even if they have to take it by force of arms."

Whether Axel Muir actually knew this or was guessing, nobody knew. But it turned out he was right.

Axel had cause against the British. He'd come back from his duty with the founder of Louisville with a Miami arrowhead in his shoulder, and when Cordelia cut it out, all agreed it looked like metal that had come right straight out of some forge in Liverpool.

All it took to put Axel Muir into one of his towering red rages was for someone to mention the name Hamilton. This Hamilton was a British army officer who had been operating out of some of the Great Lakes forts, and he was known as Hair Buyer. Certainly Hamilton was not the only Englishman who offered Indians bounty money for each Rebel scalp they brought in, but he advertised it more widely and loudly and proudly, and if the settlers along the Ohio could have gotten their hands on him, they surely would have improved on some of the more colorful tortures they attributed to the people they called heathen barbarians.

Other than those, all the other original Ballymenas had moved out onto farms scattered up and down the valley on either side of the settlement. Cranston and Caroline Shook had started a dairy farm, and Luke Baird, after his own stint shooting Indians with John Rogers Clark following the Quebec adventure, had married a Fort Pitt woman of unknown origin.

Luke built a place on the riverbank about a quarter mile from Beulah Land, and there was concerned with making boats—well, canoes—and distilling whiskey from corn mash. He had a natural talent for both endeavors.

As a community, the greatest accomplishment had been obtaining a real brass cannon brought all the way from Philadelphia and purchased with funds provided by the commonwealth of Pennsylvania.

The weapon stood ready near the gate in the old palisade round the original meeting hall, ready to fire an iron ball about the size of Axel Muir's fist at anybody threatening the peace and dignity of the community.

Each day, Cordelia Muir had oatmeal-and-honey cookies for some Ballymena child who'd polish the brass barrel of what she referred to in her journal of events as Our Artillery.

It had been fired twice, in both instances warning outlying folk to get in to the settlement because hostiles had been sighted on the way there. In both cases, it was a false alarm.

This was a rich valley, and as Axel Muir had predicted, anyone who tried had no trouble making a little money in Fort Pitt. Everything from cheese to timber to barley to ham to hops to Luke Baird's whiskey was a cash crop in Beulah Land.

Well, then, there was Young Bone Trudeau. He, like Luke Baird, had not tasted enough war in Canada so went with Axel Muir and the Welshman down the Ohio to offer aid and marksmanship to Clark.

Since returning, he'd taken up residence in Fort Pitt, where he had become successful as a tanner. He had his own business and already had paid back, with interest, the money Axel Muir had loaned him for his start. He was married to an Oneida woman, from that tribe of Iroquois who had gone against their brothers the Mohawks and fought with the Americans during the war.

So Bobby Chesney found Beulah Land when he came walking along the road from Fort Pitt, dressed pretty much as he'd been when he left except maybe the brim of his slouch hat was broader. He carried his rifle casually across his shoulders as though it had become a living part of him. The long fringes on his buckskin jacket and the seams of his leather gaiters swung in time to his long, slender-legged stride.

Behind him, obviously having no trouble keeping up, was a rather comely Indian woman with a baby in a papoose board on her back. Behind her, showing some struggle in keeping up, was Noble Popjoy.

Luke Baird, who was at the blacksmith shop getting a handle put on one of his iron still pots and some barrel hoops mended, saw them first.

"Well, I be outrageous damned," he said. "Here comes Bobby, by God, and look what he got with him!"

Luke dropped all the tools he had in his hands and ran out along the road yelling, "Sergeant Bobby, you old mean son of a bitch Sergeant Bobby," and they actually, two grown men, in broad daylight, and both laughing like hell, hugged.

Everybody greeted Robert Chesney in their own way, according to how distant or close they had been to him.

Axel Muir shook hands with grave countenance, as was fitting for the leader of the community, and said that in view of the fact that this represented the last returning hero of the recent unpleasantness with the British, the cannon should be fired to bring all the Ballymenas in to say greetings.

Cordelia took his face in her hands and kissed him at least twice, all the time exclaiming to everyone as though they didn't know it, "This is our own Robert Chesney, our own Robert Chesney!"

Nadine Spencer, Hobe's widow who was living with the Muirs now, was long past the time for tears over her loss. After he shook her hand, Chesney reached into a pouch on the cradle board, under the baby, and brought out a leather bag bigger than the baby's head, opened it, and took out a handful of large coins.

Axel Muir's eyes popped. He was likely the only one among them who had any idea of the value of such things. These were mostly Spanish gold coins, but there were some French with the head of Louis XIV and a number of what Ballymenas had once, back in Britain, called quid. These were silver with a lion walking on its hind legs, a pound sterling.

Robert Chesney took a number of the English coins and placed them in Nadine Spencer's hand and closed her fingers over them and told some sort of whispered lie about this being a pension from the Continental Congress to the widow of a hero, and that brought the tears.

"They told me," Nadine sobbed, "how you tried to help him at the end."

So that was the second great mystery, the first being the Indian woman. Not what Bobby said to Nadine, but where the hell he'd come by such a treasure as he had in that leather bag at the bottom of the cradle board.

When Cranston and Caroline Shook arrived, they both were warm, but she a little reserved, casting sidelong glances at the Indian woman and the baby and Noble Popjoy, the last of whom she at least acknowledged with a little nod.

"Picked up some extra baggage since we last looked on one another," Cranston said, grinning. Then went directly up to the other two and shook Popjoy's hand and the woman's, too, and said, "Nalambigi, if I recollect the name right."

"You do, you most surely do! My daughter Nalambigi," said Popjoy.

Calvin Reed stood back like a bashful schoolboy, and later

Cordelia said to her husband he was waiting to see what was going to happen when Maudine and Robert Chesney stood face-to-face.

Everybody was waiting. But they were disappointed because not much of anything happened. Maudine held out her hand like a man, and Robert Chesney shook it, and she said, "Hello, Bobby."

"They tell me you've got some real fine young uns," he said. "I'm mighty glad."

"Well, you'll have to come see us, across the river sometime," she said.

Cordelia Muir noted that Maudine looked directly into Robert Chesney's eyes, boldly, as though she might be laying down a challenge, or maybe flaunting what she had now, husband and children and homestead erected like a wall between her and anything that might have happened in Canada. At the very least, Cordelia thought, displaying for Beulah Land that there had been nothing in her past for which Maudine Urie Reed need feel guilty.

Whatever it was seemed a little frosty to Cordelia, and it wasn't surprising that Robert Chesney looked away first. And with more than the usual amount of pink on his cheeks.

Then Calvin Reed stepped forward and gripped Chesney's hand, both of them acting as though it was a duty required because they'd been to Quebec together.

Later, Calvin was heard to say to his cousin Reverend Obadiah Reed that he and Bobby had gone up the Kennebec together, which showed that there was still some pride in it for him.

While all Robert Chesney's old associates from the Canadian invasion greeted him closely, the other Ballymenas stood back, forming a circle of interest but not intimacy, because none of these people were his kin and to most of them their memory was of a rather wild young man who liked whiskey too much and spent most of his time in the woods.

And as it had been a long time ago when Noble Popjoy first came among them, maybe they were a little afraid of this Robert Chesney, veteran now of so much that was to them unknown and foreign.

When Silas Fulton and his tribe arrived, it was a joyful and tearful reunion all in one. Ma Fulton did the crying while all her children except Enoc, who was now a towering young man, stood around staring wide-eyed at a person they couldn't remember but who had been spoken of so many times he was like a knight of Arthur's court returned from his quest for the grail, a story any good Celt told his children.

Silas took Robert Chesney's shoulders in both his hands and said, "Son, we be mighty proud of you."

And Enoc, now over six feet tall and with a fine young beard the color of the carrots he and his father grew, acted like a boy again, wringing Robert Chesney's hand and dashing about to do the same with the Indian woman and Popjoy, bubbling with unashamed delight and shouting things like "snipers in the belfry," which nobody who hadn't been there could possibly understand.

"Sergeant Bobby, Sergeant Bobby," he kept saying.

"Well, no more, I ain't." But Robert Chesney was obviously as happy about this meeting as was Enoc.

And all this while Silas Fulton spoke to Noble Popjoy and to the Indian woman and then studied her as he might a horse he was getting ready to buy. Meanwhile, Ma Fulton had recovered her composure enough to bend to the cradle board leaning against Nalambigi's leg to take out the baby, wide-eyed and with hair the color of burnished copper.

"And lookee here, lookee here, my land, who are you, honey?" Ma Fulton laughed, holding the baby in the sun.

For the first time, the Indian woman spoke. It was a soft voice, but large enough for all to hear, and in English as well polished as any spoken in Beulah Land.

"His name is Benedict Arnold Chesney," she said.

From the moment Nalambigi uttered the name of the man everyone figured was an evil traitor, Axel Muir almost visibly lowered a curtain of frigid incredulity and mistrust between himself and the homecoming hero.

Everybody felt it. Such a thing was impossible to hide. And Axel Muir did nothing to hide it. When Cordelia suggested that Robert Chesney and his people take up residence in the old meeting hall where the bachelors had once lived but which was now used only as a town council hall, Axel Muir roared in his old-fashioned Royal Navy way, and after Cordelia insisted and Chesney and the Indian woman and Popjoy were laying out their pallets near the old pulpit, Axel Muir continued to roar and stalk about the settlement.

After one night, Robert Chesney and his people moved out and took up temporary lodging in Luke Baird's boat shed on the bank of the river.

It was hard for other Ballymenas to explain. It wasn't the Indian woman exactly. Oh, they all hated redskin heathens as much as they ever had, but when Bobby Chesney appeared with Nalambigi, she became *their* redskin heathen.

As with Young Bone Trudeau. They had never had any experience with black Africans, and they certainly had no fondness for such people as a race. But hell, Young Bone had become *their* black African, which made it all right. That meant they could go right on without any fondness for black Africans but with great affection for Young Bone because he was *theirs*!

But somehow, they didn't take to Bobby Chesney's Indian, even if she was theirs.

Maybe it was the bag of money. Where it came from bothered a lot of people, some of them thinking maybe Robert Chesney had become a highwayman or worse. But the real stickler was that they weren't accustomed to having one of their own with that much gold in his pocket.

It was like having a rich Englishman landlord suddenly coming among them, taking advantage of old circumstances to take a place at their table, as it were, where maybe he didn't belong.

And the Indian woman didn't help that part of it any. She had been educated someplace, another part of the mystery they didn't appreciate being kept in the dark about, and she was proud as a six-uddered milk cow and didn't act as if she owed any of them a damned thing even though they'd let her walk right in with her redskin baby papoose heathen.

Calvin Reed's cousin Reverend Obadiah said he knew at first glance this was not a woman missionaries to Indians had saved for Christ, that this was a sure-as-sin pagan even if she might read the King James version as well as he could. He didn't explain how he knew this at first glance, but those who took him at his word probably figured it was divine revelation.

The whole thing was tearing Cordelia apart. She raved at Axel in the confines of their bedchamber, asking how he could allow his people, apparently equating him with Moses or somebody who had "people," to turn against one of their own.

Everybody in the townsite could hear Axel bellowing, "Do not talk of prodigal to me, woman. Do not talk of prodigal."

Perhaps it was fortuitous that Axel Muir had to travel to Fort Pitt at that time to meet with other militia leaders to discuss the continuing problems with Indians along the north shore of the Ohio. He departed with dark grumblings about treachery coming to roost on their own rafters.

It gave Cordelia the opportunity to invite Robert Chesney and Nalambigi to her kitchen for gooseberry pie. He came, but she didn't. Not feeling too good, Robert Chesney told Cordelia she'd said. What she'd said was that she'd rather be drawn and quartered than show up in the kitchen of that bastard Axel Muir who was trying to put a hex on her baby just because of his name.

Knowing the strength of Nalambigi's convictions, Robert Chesney didn't push it, but he came himself. For the issue maybe, or because he enjoyed Cordelia's company, or perhaps he thought there might be a chance to mend fences with Axel.

For whatever reason, he came. And after a while that afternoon, it growing colder outside, the wind whipping under the rough shingle edges with dismal little wailings and the last leaves from the white birch trees across the river blowing along Beulah Land ground like the yellow warblers of September and the sky going gray as it lowered, threatening early snow flurries, and in the warmth and pie crust-smelling kitchen of Cordelia Muir, he told about the woman. Not about the money, but about the woman, Cordelia's goose quills scratching away until early evening when it was finished.

Nobody ever knew how much of Cordelia's journal Axel Muir read. They assumed he read it all. If he was aware of what everyone came to call the Nalambigi Chapter, he never said so in as many words.

Some said he surely knew, and that's why he did what he did. Others said he couldn't have known what Cordelia wrote that night and still flown off the handle. Well, they'd seen Axel Muir fly off the handle plenty, but never so far as to exile one of the original Bally-menas from Beulah Land ground.

"You have to give Axel credit for guts," said Cranston Shook. "Because he sure picked a tough one to try and run off."

No matter the whys and wherefores, the day after Robert Chesney spent the afternoon in the Muir kitchen and Axel come back from Fort Pitt, they met on the riverbank close to Luke Baird's whiskey shed.

It wasn't prearranged. Chesney was already there, looking at the river, staring at the gray water that reflected the dark sky. As though he was deep in thought, according to those who saw him.

A few of those early November snowflakes that look like torn silk had begun to sift down through a windless day when Axel Muir came down the slope of the riverbank and stopped a few steps short of where Chesney stood and acknowledged him with a quick nod. Enough of a nod to make his wide hat brim bounce a little.

The only acknowledging Muir did was to fire his first salvo with all the authority and bombast you'd expect from a former gunnery officer of the Royal Navy.

"Chesney," he said, "the peace and progress of this community is going to be served only when you pull up stakes and move on with all your baggage. Before hard winter sets in, you need to light out."

It was a long time before anything else was said. Robert Chesney looked at Muir and Muir looked back, and there was suddenly as little warmth and welcome in Chesney's expression as in Muir's. Then for a long spell, Chesney turned his head very slowly and looked at the water for a while.

"That woman ain't any more a savage," he said, "than most of the people in this place, I imagine. I brang her, and she got as much right to be here as anybody."

"It ain't the woman," Axel Muir said. "It's the young un."

Chesney looked at Muir again, his eyes hard and not squinted because of wind that had come up and was whipping loose hair into his face but because of anger blowing inside.

"A baby? You're talkin about a baby here?"

"No. I'm talking about his name, and mostly I'm talking about a pappy that would give such a name to him. We won't put up with anybody here suckin English eggs!" Muir's voice was rising as he heated to his subject.

"For a long time, you know, there was English officers in the forts north of here offering their Indians bounty for our hair! They never made a secret of it. They made it known up and down the river," Muir said, and he was beginning to pant.

"So what's that mean here with you and me now?" asked Chesney. "I could tell stories about this British general named Burgoyne who paid bounty for Rebel scalps."

Muir acted as though he hadn't heard, and now he was leaning forward, his face almost touching Robert Chesney's shoulder.

"Some Fort Pitt militiamen surrendered once, white flag, all of it, and soon as they'd laid down their arms, the English turned their backs and let the Delawares butcher all them men."

"They ain't nothin news in that," said Chesney. "War gets to be like that sometimes. Up in New York, some British Ottawas or some such thing killed a lady who warn't only a Loyalist but gonna marry an English army officer the next day. Everybody heared about that."

"I don't care a damn for what happened in New York or if English red devils killed and scalped the wrong woman or any of the rest of that cat dung! What I care is that you come draggin a young un in here named after a sneak and a traitor who sold over to the English! To the *English,* damn their eyes, who's made hell for us since we got here. Now we got to look at somebody carrying that name. Benedict Arnold! And sure as hell everybody's heard about *him*!"

Robert Chesney turned and started away, back toward the whiskey shed, and Muir was ready to follow, his mouth still open for more of it. But then Chesney turned and spoke, louder now against the growing wind.

"Listen, Captain, I don't know what happened when Colonel Arnold was at Philadelphia. I don't know what happened when he was at West Point. I don't know why he sold out to the British, and I ain't sayin that was right. It was wrong, what he done.

"But at Quebec, he got no support. Half his army again him because they wanted some of their own colonial officers commandin. I suspect that Colonel Arnold went heavy into debt payin for thangs the Continental Congress should have paid for.

"The next year, when Burgoyne came down Lake Champlain, that was the last time I seen Colonel Arnold. That was the last time I served with him. And it's because of what he done at Quebec and there in New York that I named my boy for him because I never seen a better, braver man.

"At Saratoga, that hawk-faced General Gates taken Colonel Arnold's command away from him. Then Gates sits on his arse behind his fortifications pert near out of range of any English shot. While the battle went on, that's where he sit, with most of his troops right there in beside of him.

"But Colonel Arnold wouldn't stay relieved. When he seen the chance for us to flank the British on the left, he come riding down and led us. And he got bad wounded doin it, but that flank of the army followed like they'd have followed no other, while Gates sit safe and sound on his arse with all his powder-wig staff officers.

"Now you and all of us heared from the first that the British had the best damned army in the world. Well, at Saratoga, we cleaned their bloody plow. Not the French. Not our friends the Mohawks. But *us*! And the reason we done it was Colonel Arnold.

"That's why I gave my son his name. Because when I served with him, Colonel Arnold wore a damned proud name!"

He started to move off, then stopped and spun around, and his voice was hatchet-blade harsh.

"And that shit-a-bed Gates never even mentioned Colonel Arnold's *name* when he wrote his report on that fight! Well, by God, I mentioned it, and my son will go with it from here on. And if you spindle-brained puff bellies don't like it, you can go out here some-wheres in the woods and piss up a persimmon tree stump!"

That was all. Robert Chesney moved away so fast, Axel Muir was left with his mouth ready to talk some more. There was a moment when Axel was about to follow, to shout some more. But he changed his mind.

Before dawn of the next day, Robert Chesney and the Indian woman Nalambigi, and the baby Benedict Arnold were gone, down-river said Luke Baird, who had sold them one of his big white birch bark canoes for a gold Spanish coin.

Luke Baird reported more, too. He'd been in the whiskey shed when Axel Muir confronted Bobby, he said, and there as well was the Indian woman.

"The whole time they talked," he said, "she sit there watchin through the same winder I was watchin through. And she had Bobby's rifle, rested on a chair back, and it was trained smack on Axel Muir's gut. I tell you true, if Ole Axel had made the least little wrong move, we'd be havin an election around here to vote for a new mayor!"

It took Luke Baird three months to get up enough nerve to tell Cordelia Muir about it, and when he did, she faithfully recorded it in her journal right below the things Robert Chesney had told her about the woman.

Robert Chesney: Born 1753, Thornhill, Dumfries, Scotland

She tagged along. I never paid her no mind. She was just like one of them other Abenakis Popjoy had with him. She went where they went. She done what they done.

Then we was in camp with Washington's army that winter of '79. At Morristown, New Jersey. Worse than the winter before at Valley Forge. That's when General Washington was ravin about men that would profiteer on Patriot suffering. The grub was pretty bad, all right, and damn little of it. Flour half sawdust, full of weevils. Bacon old and rancid.

I come down sick. Fever and consumption and flu. They was a hospital. Looked like an old barn to me. I ended up in what I expect was a chicken coop out back. Half the army was sick. Whoopin and coughin and spittin.

I was clear out of my senses at first. But when I'd come to, she'd be there, wipin my face with a wet rag if I was hot, wrappin me in blanket if I was chilled. Spoonin some kind of hot soup into me, I don't know what it was.

She washed me and cleaned my clothes, and she got the lice off me. And the other varmints. You ain't ever seen as many body varmints as an army can grow. Lice and fleas and mites and God knows what.

Well, she cleaned my clothes of them. She had it all to do over again pert near every day, but she done it.

And then, when I got feelin better, she taught me how to read. Layin right there in that New Jersey chicken coop, this old whale oil lamp stinkin like hell, a red heathen, and a woman to boot, teaches me how to read. If that don't beat all!

Now I ain't taken in to be a schoolteacher. But, by God, I can read as good as most of these yahoos around here.

I guess that done it. I guess that made me decide I wanted her around for all the rest of my time. So I asked her what her name was. I'd clear forgot what Popjoy told me that night on Kennebec.

Nalambigi. No girl now. I knew her. And she was full-growed woman all right. So when spring come and we taken in to scoutin the British in north New Jersey where they had outposts for their army that was still holdin New York, she never trailed with her pappy no more. She trailed with me.

Popjoy was just as happy as a new bug about it. He set a lot of store in that Nalambigi, and now he could rest easy that there was another man to take care of her, him growin old and all, and now she wouldn't face havin to squat at the gate of some fort after her pappy was gone, sellin herself to the soldiers to keep from starvin to death.

So he was glad enough to tell me all about her.

A long time ago, there was a tribe of heathens in New England called the Narragansett. They slowly dwindled away from smallpox or measles or some other sickness, and what was left pretty much scattered around, Popjoy said. They tried to live however they could.

In one way or another, a very young Narragansett girl was taken as an indentured servant or maybe a slave or maybe as part of the family by this white man and his wife who had a farm in the valley of the Connecticut River. Exactly where she come from is anybody's guess.

Well, during the last French war, the Connecticut River was one of the routes the St. Francis Abenakis took to raid into the colonies. St. Francis was in Canada, close to the St. Lawrence. They was always some French army officers and maybe a few soldiers, too, at St. Francis.

One of these raiding parties come down the Connecticut one day and burned out this farm and took this Narragansett girl captive back to St. Francis. She was treated pretty good, Popjoy said, because she was Algonquin like the Abenakis and not one of the Iroquois bunch.

In fact, he said, Abenakis usually treated all women captives pretty good, even white ones.

About this time, British General Amherst sent a raid of his own to St. Francis, only he didn't send but a few of his Indians. What he sent was Robert Rogers and a battalion of rangers, and they pert near wiped out all of the St. Francis Abenakis.

When Rogers left St. Francis, all burning, of course, he brought out a bunch of white women who had been captives of the band, and he also brought out the Narragansett woman because his own Indians told him she wasn't an Abenaki.

While Rogers and what's left of his battalion are trying to get back to the colonies before the French catch them, he sends a party direct across country to Crown Point. He had some sick rangers and a wounded one or two, and he wanted to get the captive women off his hands.

The Narragansett woman was one of the party that cut across to Crown Point. They made it all right, Popjoy said, probably because the French trying to catch Rogers just simply didn't bother with such a small bunch.

And now who do you reckon was at Crown Point, scouting for General Amherst? Noble Popjoy his ownself! Who right off taken great interest in this Narragansett woman, who really wasn't much more than a girl.

That Narragansett woman. Who would soon become the mother of Nalambigi.

Popjoy never said what happened to her. I suspect she died before too long, and Popjoy had to find a place for that girl child. So he taken her to some of the same folks he'd known when he was growin, some Quakers, and they taken her in, and that's where she learned all the thangs she knows. Like readin.

But then he taken her to live among the Penobscot Abenakis, too, so she got to know something about that side of it. That was later, when she begin to bloom out a little, Popjoy said.

When the war was mostly over, Popjoy figured to take his Abenaki friends back to their country, and me and Nalambigi trailed with them. It was a good time, not having to post out sentries ever night to keep the English Indians from sneakin into our camp and takin a mess of our hair.

That's where we was at when little Benedict Arnold was birthed. With the Penobscot. And it's a strange thang, maybe. We was in a summer hunt camp not a day's walk from the place where I'd first seen that woman, when she'd just been a girl and I thought she was a boy and didn't care one way or the other. Not a day's hard walk from the Kennebec.

A little while after the baby was born, me and Nalambigi went to the river and tried to find the place we'd first seen one another. I ain't sure yet if we done it. When you ain't worried about freezin to death or starvin or gettin an Ottawa hatchet in your head, thangs look different.

We'd done our little boy like the Indians do. We give him a baby name, and later we'd give him his growin-up name, and someday he'd give his ownself a grown name. But I'd told her I'd kinda like havin a name for him like my people always done, the same name from start to finish. But we never done anything about it.

But that day when we standin on the banks of that river Colonel Arnold had pert near pulled us along with his own strength, I told her it hadn't ort to be called the Kennebec. It ort to be called the Benedict Arnold River.

Well, Nalambigi said we couldn't hardly name the river that, but it sounded just fine for our little boy. So standin right there on the Kennebec, we named him. Benedict Arnold Chesney.

And I told her if the boy was going to be named that, her being his mother and all, we'd just have to name her Nalambigi Chesney.

She laughed like hell!

Cordelia Muir figured that she'd never know where that bag of money came from because Beulah Land had seen the last of Bobby Chesney.

174

She was right on the second count but wrong on the first because Noble Popjoy knew about the money and he was still at Luke Baird's, comfortably situated and planning to stay, as the majordomo of the birch bark canoe construction business.

"And why not?" asked Luke Baird. "The first bark canoe any of us had ever seen, he made. And still able to make them better than any of us, ain't he?"

And Popjoy, as infirmaries of age stiffened his joints and dimmed his shooting eye, was happy to stay out of the woods except for an occasional trip into the vastness to get drunk and stay that way for a few days without guilt when he sobered up that while in his cups he had howled any number of obscene songs in English, French, and various aboriginal tongues for delighted or appalled or disgusted Ballymenas.

And during all these long terms of living close to fire and shelter, especially in winter, Noble Popjoy was most amenable to suggestions that he visit with the militia captain's wife in her kitchen to sample maple sugar candy or mincemeat tarts.

Cordelia was far from being a fool, and although she had never been on particularly friendly terms with the old scout, as she felt she was with people she'd helped recruit for the Ballymena and Virginia land company, it was clear that the old scout was the only one who might shed light on Bobby Chesney's bag of gold.

Working on that assumption, it was less than a month after the Chesneys departed that she invited Noble Popjoy to sit before her hot cast-iron cookstove, she with goose quill poised.

It was a good day for sitting before a warm cast-iron stove and recalling days gone down.

Axel was out with a party of Ballymena woodcutters so they had the place to themselves. With the whale oil glow there was a silvery light coming through the kitchen window, reflection of gray sky on the ground snow. Glass for that window had only recently come from Fort Pitt.

Now, ice crystals had formed in spiderweb designs around the edges of the pane, making a lacy frame for the view along the slope to the river. They could see two children, heavily bundled in furs, building a snow fort.

Across the Monongahela they could watch the smoke from Calvin Reed's cabin marking a blue trace through the bare birch limbs until the west breeze caught and devoured it. There were crows there in those trees as well, as there usually were in early winter, and their raucous voices made a little ripple of sound to blend with the huffing of the stovepipe above the cast-iron cookstove.

A good day for warm talk, indeed, and maybe best of all, the smell of roasting goose in the room and Noble Popjoy drawing out his tale in hope that he'd still be there at the appropriate time to be invited for supper. He could smell cornbread dressing, too, heavy with sage.

Noble Popjoy: Born 1723, Ohio Valley?

I never seen an army with such a tail on it. When Burgoyne came down Lake Champlain and then along the Hudson to attack Albany, his trains had the usual wagons and carts and horses, but then there was a gaggle of women and two coaches. Regular coaches like ladies ride in, because that's what was ridin in em.

Burgoyne believed in going along in style. He brang his own cook and butler and I don't know what all. His own silver plate and wine glasses and kaigs of good brandy and whiskey. He also brang his mistress. One of the coaches was for her.

Now the Hessians were under this von Riedesel, as much a Squarehead pumpernickel as you'll find. He brang nearly as much personal stuff as Burgoyne. Only he never brang his mistress. He brang his wife and two daughters. Second coach was for them.

The name of Riedesel's woman was Frau Riedesel. I don't recollect ever hearin the name of the English mistress Burgoyne brang.

General Arnold had spies and some of our Indians who watched their column all the way, so we knowed pretty much what troops they was comin with and about these women, too.

At one time or another during this battle, Bobby could have shot all four of em if he wanted. But he never.

Before I neglect to mention it, General Arnold was promoted during the last days he was layin siege to Quebec. About time, too. They should have promoted him right overhead of that damned spineless spider Horatio Gates, who didn't know no more about how to fight a battle than one of these geese around here.

When the British got to the south end of Lake Champlain, they come on by way of roads. They's a lot of heavy timber there so General Arnold had soldiers out ahead of the British, cutting trees to fall acrost their path.

Well, Burgoyne had to keep sendin up his engineer troops to clear a path, and Bobby and some more of the Riflemen would be up in trees a couple hundred yards along the way and they'd shoot the officers who was commandin these engineer troops.

I'll tell you, the English officers was mad as spit about it, but they warn't much they could do except call us bad names.

While Gates was lollygaggin around, General Arnold picked a good place to fight the British and stop em short of Albany. Place called Bemis Heights just south of a farm owned by a family named Freeman.

It was good ground for us, and that's where we fit. Of course, that viper Gates never give General Arnold any credit for what was sure as hell due.

I won't get into the details of that fight except to say on both days, it was General Arnold ridin up and leadin us that beat the British. On the second day, the Riflemen was on the far left, and we begun this flank movement again the British. When General Arnold come up and led us until he was wounded, we just simply raged through them Englishmen!

Bobby and some more of the Riflemen was shinnyin up trees to shoot their leaders. Takes longer to load a rifle than a musket so as the soldiers pushed forwards with their bayonets, the Riflemen would load and then climb up a tree and shoot ahead of the soldiers and load again right up in the tree and get in maybe three shots from one tree.

The Englishmen and the Hessians finally was shot all to hell, and they broke and run back to the road but couldn't run anymore because there was the Hudson River and no way for em to get acrost.

Now this road was the road Burgoyne had been usin all along, so when we cracked that flank and turned it, we was smack-dab acrost Burgoyne's rear. So the only part of his army that we wasn't chewin all to pieces was trapped twixt us and the Continental troops sittin on Bemis Heights in the positions General Arnold had us dig two days before!

Now besides all this, us boys pinnin the British and the Hessians up again the river was fightin right through the middle of Burgoyne's trains. And there ain't nothin as pitiful as a bunch of teamsters and such tryin to defend theirselfs again a hard charge, especially if the charge is a surprise.

I tell you true, it was a grand mess along that river road. Lobster-backs and Squareheads was throwin down their arms and surren-derin, there was wounded men scattered all over the place, dead horses and a small herd of beef cattle stampedin around. Clothes and guns and dishpans and any kind of truck you might mention was scattered around and wagons turned over and flour spillin out of busted barrels and hard crackers dumped like playin cards along the road.

And right in the middle of it, one of those nice coaches with a front wheel shot off it because you see when we done that flankin movement, General Arnold had brought along some artillery, too. It wasn't very big, but it raised hell with some of those wagons.

There for all to see and ponder was powder boxes and bottles of perfume, fancy dresses and fur capes and lacy hats and pink under-pants and chemise. Combs and dainty little hand mirrors and jars of salve and lip rouge and hair nets and two dozen wigs like big wounded ducks.

Well, a bunch of Hessian soldiers dressed in real fancy uniforms was seen runnin from that coach to this house alongside the river, and hustlin along with em were people in dresses, so it was figured that this was the German flock of women and their personal body-guard of special soldiers like you've heared is always lurkin about them high-toned camp folk.

Well, after we'd poked around in the rubble left at the fancy coach, and they warn't any more Lobsterbacks or Germans who wasn't already dead or shot good or surrendered, we meditated on what to do about them fancy soldiers in the house with the women, and I expect folks who lived there and was wonderin why they hadn't gone off to visit Albany that day.

So a couple of our boys started down the slope through some ap-ple trees to this house, and before they went far, the soldiers in the house let go at them with a few musket shots. Our boys was out of range. So they just ambled back to where me and Bobby and a few other Riflemen was layin along a rock wall lookin down at the house.

There warn't any need for us to go down and get ourselfs wounded tryin to gouge them troops out of the house, we figured. They wasn't goin anywheres because we could see all around the place and they was in range of our rifles easy enough.

So we allowed we'd just lay there and catch our breath and watch the house, and maybe the Squareheads there would come out and surrender. We never wanted to shoot at the winders because we knew that women was in there, and we had no great itch to kill em.

So after a while, we seen this one Hessian soldier come out of the house and run down to the river with a little kaig or pot or some-thing, and he squatted at the river a minute, then come runnin back towards the house. All this while, the German soldiers inside the house was bangin away at us with their muskets.

One of Colonel Morgan's junior officers was with us by then. He say the soldier is carryin water back to the house, so they must be out of water in there and them Hessian soldiers will likely be very thirsty like men always are after a big fight, and he say we hadn't ort to let em get any water and maybe they'd elect to come on out and give up.

So before this soldier could get back to the house with this kaig of water, Bobby shot him.

This junior officer of Danny Morgan's said it was too bad to shoot soldiers tryin to get water, but war is war. Or something like that.

As the afternoon wore on, it got a little warm. It was September. So after a while, another soldier made a run for water, and the junior officer touched Bobby's shoulder, and Bobby shot this one before he ever got to the river.

Bobby said he was beginnin to feel like a bushwhacker. Morgan's junior officer said civilians bushwhack one another but soldiers in a battle ambush one another. He said they was a big difference. But he called on another Rifleman to shoot the next two.

Burgoyne was surrenderin his whole army by then, so the people in the house come out with their hands up, and the women come out, too, and I seen Mrs. Pumpernickel. She was huffin and puffin and she looked as mean as a boiled owl, and she was screamin at this junior officer of Morgan's who was with us that somebody ort to take all of us who had been layin along that wall and hang us because she say ever'time she sent a soldier to get water, we shot him in the head.

And Morgan would have been proud of that junior officer because he say to Mrs. Riedesel that she didn't have no business sending soldiers out to where it was dangerous when there was a battle goin on because it was a natural-born duty for enemy soldiers to shoot one another at such a time.

That was about the size of it. I was mighty proud of Bobby and the others for their marksmanship. But them Riflemen by then had come to take good marksmanship as a matter of fact.

That evenin we was at a fire and havin some grub, and we heared General Arnold had been hit in the same leg he'd got wounded at Quebec and the surgeons wanted to cut it off. Right then Bobby was up and ready to go find General Arnold and keep them surgeons away from him, but Colonel Morgan come by and said they hadn't cut it off because General Arnold raise so much cain when they started, they finally determined not to use their saws and knives.

Yeah, that's about the size of it.

Oh, well, yes. The money!

That same evenin when me and Bobby was by ourselfs, he showed me this leather bag with drawstrings and all. He told me he'd found it in all that truck scattered around and inside the wrecked coach the Burgoyne women had been ridin in. He showed me all the money.

He didn't know what to do. I told him I never heared of a soldier offerin back the loot he'd took on a battlefield. He was still a little uneasy about it.

About then, my girl Nalambigi come up and she had some more grub and she had some of Bobby's and my clothes she'd washed, and when she got settled down there with us at the fire, I got thinkin about the money pouch and I got thinkin how my girl Nalambigi and Bobby had already started sharin the same blankets.

So I told Bobby to keep that money as a wedding present from General Burgoyne.

By God, it made sense to Bobby. So he done it!

I hope he and my girl can find something in that money that makes em happy. I never knowed a time when money alone made anybody feel really good. Maybe with Bobby and Nalambigi it'll be different.

Because when Captain Muir ran them off here, he done something else I never thought anybody else could do.

That night before they left, Bobby was gettin his truck together and makin ready to go off, and I come in on him unexpected and he was cryin. He was all by his ownself, and there was tears runnin down his cheeks on account of his havin to leave here, where he'd always called his home.

Goin to Quebec and later at Saratoga and then through all the

181

war, he was always talkin about someday gettin home, where his people was, the only people he ever remembered as kin. And now he'd got run off.

I just acted like I never seen him cryin. And he went on gettin his duffel ready for travel. I knew my girl was ready to go find Captain Muir and gut him with a hatchet, and so now I knew why.

In all my years, I seen many a thang unexpected. But that was the most unexpectedest of all. Seein Bobby cry because he got run off from his home.

Part III

THE

DOWNSTREAMERS

Chapter 8

To All Who Shall See These Presents, Greetings:

Be it known, that I, Campbell Chesney, do swear and affirm that no member of my household family has known of the whereabouts or activity of my brother Hiram Chesney since 1807 until recent date when informed that said brother Hiram Chesney was hanged in St. Charles, Territory of Missouri, in June, 1821, Anno Domini, for the crime of river piracy.

Further, that no member of my household family has profited in any way from larceny, banditry, theft, fraud, or other felonious purpose of aforementioned brother Hiram Chesney.

Further, that I, Campbell Chesney, and all members of my household family, do herewith disclaim any responsibility, fiscal or otherwise, for aforementioned brother Hiram Chesney's business dealings, marriages, mortgages, children born either in or out of wedlock, contracts, promises, or wagers.

Further respondent sayeth not.

Over Notary Public seal signed this date, September 14, a Friday, 1821 Anno Domini and in the 30th year of the Republic, County of Hamilton, State of Ohio. Commission expires, July 1, 1821. Note: Missouri statehood Aug. 1821.

My mother insisted on my executing this document. She insisted on having it published in the *Pittsburgh Gazette* where she had some considerable influence, ensuring that most people in Ohio and Kentucky would read it. And God only knew who else.

When I made it known, after considerable screwing up of nerve, that I thought the whole idea foolish, Mother drew herself up to her full height and fixed me with what we children had come to call the Red Savage Glare that we believed would ignite dry leaves at fifty paces.

At those times, no matter what style Philadelphia clothes she was wearing, having had such things shipped down the Ohio to her, Mother looked every bit what she was, a three-quarter-blood Penobscot-Abenaki-Erie Indian.

Also, it was a sure signal that someone had, to her mind, been thwarting her progress toward her major goal in life, which was to Beat the White Man at His Own Game.

Only Mother knew what that meant. But it had always seemed to me that her path toward this rather uncertain objective she planned to pass directly over my humiliated body because as with the affidavit, a lot of what she did in the name of her personal victories somehow appeared to be designed to infuriate me.

Which may make sense if you consider that maybe Mother counted me as foremost among the White Men whom she was about to Beat at His Own Game.

I have no idea. I have spent half of my life trying to figure out what my mother was up to. It was so difficult, I told myself, because she was an Indian. Well, one-quarter white, but that quarter was French and I could never figure out Frenchmen, either.

There was something competitive about it. Like a turkey shoot. I suppose that's why I continued to jab at her when I should have kept my mouth shut. It was maddening. But actually, it added considerable spice to my life.

"I don't see why we should advertise that we've got a criminal in the family," I said.

"We are not doing that," Mother said with the disdain in her voice intended to indicate that her opponent of the moment was either drunk or crazy. "What we did was let everyone know that *we* are not criminals. And that there is no use anybody coming around here making claims on us for something Hiram did."

It seemed to me silly to make excuses for something nobody had accused us of yet, and she said we had ensured that nobody did accuse us.

"Nobody is going to come around here trying to prize any money out of this family," I said. "People along the river know better than to try."

"Oh yes, oh yes, you talk like you'd be dangerous to them. Listen to me, don't be a fool. When your pap and I were fighting to get the fine Republic we got now, it was all right to shoot a Mohawk or Englishman when you seen one. But you go shooting somebody now, you be tried and end up like brother Hiram!"

Mother prided herself in her English grammar. It was all part of Beating the White Man at His Own Game. But when she got irritated or angry, she often slipped into Pap's wilderness speech. This was when she was most dangerous.

"It's then that you learn to duck in a hurry," my sister Clariese always said. Of course, she never had to duck. Clariese was Mother's joy. When she was a little girl, and obviously Mother's favorite, we boys figured it would pass as we all grew older and Mother would stop treating Clariese as if she was Queen of the May. But down all the years, it never changed.

"You're just like Hiram, and you could get in his trouble, too," she said. "You be careful, or you end up like all this other bad-smell border ruffian trash good people hang now and then."

"All right," I said. I knew it was dangerous, but I had to gouge her a little anyway. "You ought to know all about border ruffians, living with Pap all these years."

I could almost feel the heat from her glinting black eyes. Although I was a good head taller than Mother, at that moment she held herself so defiantly it seemed I was looking up at her.

"Your pap is a Scot. From across the waters," she said in her snake-hiss voice, as we children called it. "No ruffian, either. Now you go out from my house and see if your wife got any supper fit to eat for you, and when you come back sometime, don't you let me hear you talk bad about your pap, boy! Not ever!"

Well, that was about the way it usually ended. And she loved to call me "boy" at some point because she knew it irritated. Me, who was running most of her business enterprises by then and thirty-two years old.

Mother was better educated than Pap when they first met. She'd been schooled by Quakers as a girl, and she taught Pap to read in English. She spoke French, too, which she learned from her father, and I don't know how many Indian tongues.

It didn't bother Pap. He rather enjoyed the idea of having what he called a red savage heathen for a wife who was more learned than himself and most of the white people he associated with along the river.

Pap made a joke of washing some of Mother's red savage heathenism away in the blood of the lamb. When there was a Presbyterian church established in the area, he took her there for the first few

Sundays. Then he let her find her own way because he was no churchgoer. But she kept at it, a part, I suppose, of that beating the white man, etc., etc.

Pap laughed about that, too. He said our mother had turned out to be a better Presbyterian than most of the Presbyterians were, and in fact a better Christian than most Christians were. He never said it to Mother. She made no bones about it. She might go to the white man's church, but she was no Christian.

I don't know what she was. Except for being a genius at business enterprise.

Pap had a sack of gold, but Mother controlled it. That was fine with Pap. She established a profitable life in a settled homestead, and he was allowed to roam as he pleased, going out into the woods whenever he felt the urge, or sometimes going off for long periods to see one of the little wars that were always popping up here and there.

It was an arrangement both enjoyed and at which they prospered and continued to love one another with a fierce, burning kind of loyalty.

When Pap got home after a stay in the tall timber, as he called it, or after one of his little wars, he and Mother would retire to their privacy as often as possible over a few-day period and then things would return to normal, Mother busy as Ben Franklin and Pap lying around her fire cleaning weapons and telling us wilderness stories. As soon as we were old enough to listen.

This story has gotten ahead of itself, so best we start where stories are supposed to start, at the first. At least, as much of the first as they ever told us children about. Like that sack of gold. We never did know where it came from.

When we were persistent in asking, Mother would smile, which by the way was a glorious treat for us because she was beautiful then, big white teeth and bow-shaped lips and those, high, high cheekbones.

So she would smile when we asked about the money and say it was a wedding present from a British general. Then maybe she'd wink and say, "How you like *that* for a red savage heathen? Pretty good, huh?"

Pap brought Mother downriver in 1788. But she wasn't exactly a bride. They lost a child during the winter spent at Fort Pitt.

I was about eight years old before I found out about it. Rummaging in one of our sheds I found an old Indian cradle board. I took it to Mother and asked if it had been mine. She said she had used it for me and for Hiram as well, but Pap had made it for a little baby boy born to them before they came to the Ohio Valley.

She let me worry with that for a couple of hours and then told me about my older brother.

"Don't say anything to your pap about it," she warned.

"Why not?"

"He thinks the child dying was his fault," she said.

I suppose I looked horrified, thinking that my pap had done some horrible deed that caused a baby's death. But Mother shook her head.

"It wasn't his fault. He thought he'd brought bad luck with the child's name. But it was measles, a white man's disease brought from across the big waters."

"What was his name?"

"Your pap named him Benedict Arnold, a brave man we knew during the Revolution. Pap said afterwards he should have known better. All things connected with that name had turned out bad luck. But the child died of measles. I knew he would."

"How did you know?"

"I dreamed he would be buried still a babe," she said. Matter-of-fact, she said it. "I dreamed it on the day he was born."

As I grew older, I wondered what Mother had dreamed on the day I was born. But I was too proud to ask. I think she expected me to. It was one of my small victories in our little war with each other.

So they came downstream and Pap found a high plateau on a great north bend of the Ohio, and there they stopped and built a small longhouse, and with all the supplies they had brought from Fort Pitt and the meat and berries from a summer's hunting and gathering, wintered without hardship.

It was a hardwood forest area. There were butternut hickory, the usual profusion of oaks, walnut, and hornbeam in the sharp hills on all sides of the plateau and willow and birch along the streams. There were two smaller creeks flowing south into the Ohio, one on either side of the plateau, and they came to be called Great Miami and Little Miami.

South of the river was Kentucky. The topography there was much the same. There was a small stream called Licking Creek, and in later years Pap would take us hunting there.

Throughout the area were these long, low mounds, grass covered. Mother said her pap had told her these were the burial mounds of an ancient people that lived there. Mother told us, as we grew to a destructive age, say five or six, never to dig or otherwise harm those mounds.

She needn't have bothered with any warning after telling us what the mounds were. They scared hell out of us, and we stayed well clear of them. Even as a grown man, being around one of those things always gave me a little gooseflesh up the back.

They were in wonderful isolation for over a year. It was a time when hostile Indians were not presenting any problem in that area and traffic on the river was still less than occasional.

It was the year I was born, in October, and that event seemed to change many things. There was a sudden flood of people looking for land, coming on any kind of vessel that would float. Some headed for the Mississippi and maybe even St. Louis and homesteads west of the river. That was all Spanish territory, west of the Mississippi.

In later years, Mother had a favorite story she told of a missionary of some persuasion deciding to stop and build a mission on the same plateau where Pap and Mother were enlarging their buildings.

"It was one of the few times I've seen your pap mad as a snake,"

Mother would say, with just the hint of a smile. "This preacher asked Pap, 'How long have you had the squaw?' Pap didn't say anything for a while, and I thought he hadn't heard.

"Then he looked at the preacher and he said, 'Now I know why you're so ugly! Anybody whose job is askin that kind of question is bound to get ugly. And let me give you some advice, friend, out here on the frontier we don't much cotton to a man sticking his nose into our business. And if they wasn't a lot of immigrants today, stoppin here for a while before goin on downriver, keepin me to my best behavior, with a question like the one you just asked, you'd likely be crow bait hangin in a tree by now.'"

"Next morning, when that batch of immigrants had gone, the preacher had gone with em."

Then Mother would chuckle, sort of to herself, shake her head, and mutter, "Yes sir, crow bait."

During early winter of the year of my birth, two groups of immigrants arrived who stayed. There were about eighty of them, all told. They had title to land they'd bought from General Rufus Putnam, who had established a town upriver that he called Marietta. They named the settlement on our plateau Losantiville.

Mother pointed out to Pap that they'd best establish some land claims of their own. He said he was about ready to move on, maybe as far as Spanish territory beyond the Mississippi.

That's when Mother established the relationship that would last their life long. She told him he could do what he wanted, but this plateau above the Ohio was her home from now on, and he could go elsewhere if he wanted or he could make it his home, too, and gad about from *there* all he wanted, hunting or seeing about wars or whatever.

Pap decided the plateau above the Ohio was his home, too, but he accepted the offer of being able to move about as he pleased.

"But this General Putnam, I never got on well with," Pap said. "He was close to General Washington and didn't care much for Indians, like General Washington, and I always had a gaggle of red savages with me."

"He'll like you better now, with only one red savage tagging along, instead of a gaggle," Mother said.

So the following spring, we were in a dugout canoe, Pap and Mother paddling and poling up the Ohio to see General Putnam. Me, I was at midship on the cradle board, staring up into a brassy blue sky.

As we went, clouds of yellow butterflies would sometimes come out to the canoe for an inspection, and sometimes one landed on my nose. Telling about it, Mother would laugh.

"You didn't cry once. Big yellow butterfly on your tiny nose, and you didn't cry. As good as any Penobscot baby."

I think maybe on that canoe trip, with a yellow butterfly on my nose, Mother was more proud of me than for anything else I've ever done since.

It's something to irritate, which Mother probably knew. A man's finest moment lying helpless in a canoe with a butterfly on his nose!

The Republic under the Articles of Confederation didn't last long. There was only one house in the Congress, and there was no executive at all. Nobody knew who was supposed to do what, and there wasn't much hope of putting up a united front before foreign pressures. And there were plenty of those.

So they got together and wrote the Constitution.

But the Confederation Congress did two things that affected just about everybody, including the Chesneys. They passed the Northwest Ordinance and the Land Ordinance.

The Northwest Ordinance dealt with all the land between the Appalachian Mountains and the Mississippi east to west, and the Canadian border and the Ohio River north to south. They called this the Northwest Territory.

The law specified that this area would eventually become no more than five states. Future boundaries of states were drawn, and Congress appointed a governor and judges for each of those territories.

When there were six thousand people within the future bound-aries of a state, the people could elect a legislature. Then, after the legislature made provision for state offices and a state constitution, they could petition the federal Congress for statehood.

Most states came into the Union under that system even after the Confederation Congress ceased to exist.

When I was born, Ohio was one of those territories, and as yet there had been no states admitted from the Northwest Territory.

The Land Ordinance dealt with disposition of the public domain. Or land.

When the thirteen colonies became America, each of them ceded to the central government all the western lands they had claimed under original charter from the English king. This in-cluded the Northwest Territory and was a huge load of real estate. In Ohio Territory alone, there were about forty-one thousand square miles.

The central government planned to sell this land and use the rev-enues thus generated to run the government. It superimposed on the map a grid system so land could be recognized and sold for clear title.

The earth's surface would be surveyed, and the basic unit of land would be the township, a rectangle six miles on a side, and divided into thirty-six equal sections of six hundred forty acres each.

Four sections in each township would be retained by the central government for post offices and that sort of thing, and one section would be set aside for public schools, which it was expected the states would operate.

Nothing smaller than a section could be sold, and no price smaller than a dollar an acre could be charged.

Well, it was a good idea except that there were few farmers or small businessmen or craftsmen who had ever seen six hundred forty dollars at one time in their life. Which meant somebody with a lot of capital would have to buy the land and then resell it, and they could charge any damned thing they could get.

In later years, as a grown man, I got into at least four whopper fistfights for suggesting that Congress had passed the law that way knowing the big beneficiaries would be bankers and land speculators.

I don't know if I was right. But everybody knows that in those early years of the Republic, in fact as long as the public land lasted, land speculation was a favorite get-rich-quick business for a lot of people. There was nothing crooked about it. It was just there.

It didn't take long for the central government people to figure out that the land wasn't bringing in enough money to run the government. And that's where General Rufus Putnam came forward.

Putnam and a number of friends capitalized a land company and called it the Ohio Company. Then Putnam went to Congress, where he certainly had some friends from the Revolution, and said he'd buy a great hunk of the public domain north of the Ohio River if the central government would sell him the land at a reasonable price so he might expect a little profit. They said fine.

The Ohio Company in 1787 bought one and a half million acres. At nine cents an acre!

So when Mother and Pap went to visit the general at Marietta, they could expect to buy some land at a reasonable cost if Putnam was so inclined.

And he was. On first look at my mother, he became enthralled. I won't say he fell madly in love with her, but it was a reasonable facsimile thereof. He could hardly believe that this stunning woman, he said, was the same person as that dirty little girl he'd seen during the Revolution tagging around after Sergeant Bobby Chesney.

But of course, it was, and mother bought fifty thousand acres from him, with Spanish and English and Dutch gold coins from the leather pouch Pap handed her.

It was prime farm and timber and settlement land. A number of those acres would one day be a part of the city of Cincinnati.

Mother fluttered her eyelashes, and the general sold her the whole thing for ten cents an acre!

Congress decided to tax whiskey. They needed more money, and whiskey was a commodity widely distributed and enthusiastically consumed. In some parts of the country, it was a medium of exchange, like money.

In eastern Pennsylvania, settlers relied on their stills to survive. There was an uproar over this tax. In fact, there was a revolution. A couple of tax collectors were given coats of tar and feathers, and the moonshiners armed themselves and said they'd not pay.

By now, the central government had an executive in accordance with the new Constitution, and his name was George Washington. He was not kindly disposed to anybody who disrupted the Republic he had fought so hard to create.

The whiskey rebels suddenly found themselves confronted with a large body of troops who were serious about shooting somebody, so the rebellion fell apart and everybody went home and started distilling whiskey again.

Perhaps she had suggestions from her friend upstream, but whether or not that was true, Mother leaped at an opportunity in the whiskey tax business.

Passing the word to the growing community at Cincinnati and its hinterland, she let it be known that she would take all the whiskey made, at a nominal fee, pay the taxes herself, and market the product. At the same time, she began to think of a distillery of her own located on Little Miami Creek, where, of course, she owned a lot of property.

That's how my mother became one of the founders of a Cincinnati distillery, the first of many that would make the city famous for its quality spirits.

Not many people knew it was Mother. This was part of her genius. The use of silent partnerships. She'd find a white man she figured would be acceptable and well received in the community, and he'd put up there as though he owned and operated the business.

I have no idea how much tax Mother paid on her whiskey, but it had to be considerably less than the individual moonshiners had done. Soon, she had a product recognizable in its distinctive bottle. She even established her own glassworks.

None of this enterprise was disadvantaged by the fact that Mother's friend General Putnam had been appointed as one of the judges for the Northwest Territory.

The general came downriver often to visit Mother, and to hold court almost incidentally. But he was never her lover. It was more like the adoration of a loyal subject to his Wilderness Princess in an operetta, and the general knew the part he was supposed to play.

Then there was the tannery and shoe factory. General Putnam was instrumental, I am sure, in obtaining a contract order for militia shoes for Mother before she even had a shoe shop, much less a full-blown factory.

But with more immigrants coming almost every day, there was no problem in finding cobblers, and when Mother needed equipment and machinery for any of her endeavors, it seemed that shipment along the river was expeditious.

None of this was hampered when President Washington appointed General Putnam surveyor general of the United States of America!

So all horizons seemed opened to her. Mother started a business that manufactured these little stick matches with sulphur heads that were a boon to people in the area until then dependent on a flint-and-steel fire starter to initiate a flame in the kitchen stove.

There was a small industry producing playing cards. Many of Mother's customers in that effort were people who could read nothing except playing cards.

There was constant movement of real estate, at profit. Having as a close friend the surveyor general of the United States of America did no harm there.

In all my years, I have been amused when I hear people, usually white men, saying that Indians are not smart enough to engage in

American-style commerce or business or mercantilism or whatever you wish to call it. The same men, by the way, who also say that women of any stripe are incapable of dealing with property and finance.

The central government established a national bank in 1791, but Mother scoffed at the idea.

"It's the child of Alexander Hamilton," she said. "And it's some of his highborn white man friends who have this bank, and the Republic deposits our money there, and the banker friends of Hamilton can loan it out and take the interest themselves. The bank doesn't belong to us. It belongs to the friends of Hamilton, who make a profit on our sweat."

I recall laughing at the idea of my mother sweating, then I was ashamed because I knew she had been to Quebec and a lot of other places during the Revolution, with Pap, and not only sweat but maybe bled a little.

Anyway, she was right about the bank, and it would be in my old age that it became a real people's national bank under President Andrew Jackson.

Mother knew what she was doing and took a vicious pride in it. She never did it when Pap was around, but often after she had made a particularly good business transaction, she would grin at me with a mischievous glint in her eye and speak with a particular gloating in her tone.

"How do you like that," Mother would say, "for a red savage heathen?"

Memories of my mother are so full of her dealings with General Putnam and all her business ventures, that I forget sometimes the rest of it.

She loved that point of land on the high plateau above the river. She made a fine homesite of it, too, over the years. Going, with the help of hired hands mostly, from longhouse to log cabin to log house to shiplap siding and stone and mortar.

There was a flowering dogwood tree in what Mother liked to call her front dance ground, a flat slab of ground perhaps twenty feet on a side, and she loved to sit there in the evenings during autumn when the geese and ducks were on their way down the Ohio flyway to the Mississippi where they would wing on southward.

At dusk, sometimes the echelons of geese would fly so low over the water their reflections were cast on the surface. Sometimes even though Mother sat in deep dusk, the geese would be flying so high they were still in the sunlight, fiery bright specks in the purple darkening sky.

Sometimes, she would rise from her bed and go to stand under the dogwood tree and listen to the sound of the geese honking overhead. It was as though the birds were a call from the northern forests, reminding Mother of her ancient heritage.

It was a time she wanted alone. When I was a very young boy, a few times I would wake and go out to her, feeling somehow that I could share whatever it was she had found in the dusk above the river.

Without turning her head, she would know I was there and would speak, softly but firmly.

"Go back to bed."

Mother was protective of her children, but she maintained a distance from us. It wasn't cold, but it was definite.

There was Hiram, two years younger than myself, then our sister Clariese, and even though she was obviously Mother's favorite, there was no cuddling or kissing.

Finally, there was Gance, three years younger than Clariese. It was as though he was from a different world.

When Gance was old enough to hold a rifle, Pap took him on a hunt south of the river into Kentucky, which was a state by then. They were back at home quicker than anyone expected.

It seemed that Pap had killed a deer. When he hung the deer to a tree limb, head up, and ran his knife along the underbelly hide and the entrails plopped out in a gush of blood, Gance got sick and threw up. And for almost a month, he wouldn't eat meat.

Pap felt terrible about that. He told Mother he'd have neck-shot that deer so there wouldn't be so much blood in the body cavity, but he didn't know Gance would react as he did to a little gore.

Years later, Gance admitted to me it hadn't been the blood that had sickened him. It had been the guts.

Pap was always more affectionate than Mother. I've heard that the Scots-Irish were undemonstrative, but I can recall that even as I grew to be a stout boy of ten or twelve, he often took occasion to hug me and kiss my cheek.

Maybe it was because he saw much less of us than Mother did, what with his roaming all over the Ohio Valley, looking for somebody to legally shoot, as Mother said, only half in jest.

It was during one of Pap's long absences from home that Mother's father, Noble Popjoy, came down the river to find us because he was dying and apparently wanted to do so as far away from civilization as he could get.

This was a curious old man. He looked like wrinkled leather, his skin not much different from the smock and leggings and moccasins he wore. Hiram said he looked like a river bum, but not where Mother could hear him.

The old man scared Gance half out of his wits, and my youngest brother would not stay in the room alone with his grandfather.

It was all uneventful. His dying was pretty much taken for granted by Mother and himself, as though it were as common as supper each evening. Maybe it was.

When the day came, Mother brought two of her tannery roust-abouts to the house with a wagon and two mules. She wrapped the body of a man I had trouble thinking of as my grandfather in one of her best blankets, and the bundle was loaded in the wagon, and we all of us boarded the wagon and headed north out of Cincinnati.

It didn't take long to arrive in some wild wooded country. There'd been some Indian depravations recently not far from there, and Hiram kept Gance in a constant state of terror whispering to him about being scalped.

We drove off the road finally and into a grove of sycamore. It was summer and the woods were full of bird calls, each one of which Hiram told Gance was a hostile redskin making signals to his friends waiting with hatchets.

Mother's hired men dug a grave and then were sent back to the wagon, and we stood beside the hole where the men had lowered the wrapped body, and for a long time Mother looked into the grave. She was holding her father's rifle, and I wondered why, thinking it was the Indian scare.

Then Mother dropped the rifle into the grave and said something in one of her Indian languages and repeated it in English for our benefit, I suppose.

"For any Mohawks or Englishmen you might see."

Then she marched back to the wagon and her men.

"Go cover him so he can start his journey."

On the way home, Clariese, who was the only one who had nerve enough to do it, asked the question we all had in mind.

"What journey, Mother?"

"To the place of dreams, where there is always deer to hunt and corn growing, and it never gets cold, and all of his friends are there to help him fight his enemies."

"You mean there are enemies there?" I was bold enough to ask.

Mother stared at me as though I had lost my mind.

"Of course. Everybody's there!"

So Mother took her pap back to where he'd come from and buried him in the wilderness, unmarked except by the tall sycamores over his rest. And for me, the memory of my grandfather would not be the image of his face or the texture of rough skin on his fingertips as he touched my face or the scratching tone of his old voice. My memory of him would be only of my mother dropping the rifle into the grave as the whistle of a hunting hawk came down through the trees to the grave site as though it were part of the sunlight filtered through the sycamore branches.

It was astonishing. Within two miles, you could go from deep-woods wilderness to a growing town called Cincinnati. As good a town as there was along that old Ohio, Pap said. If you like towns, Pap said.

Well, you might wonder what happened to that first name we had. Losantiville. Pap told me the men got together about two years after they'd originally named it and decided Losantiville didn't have much ring to it.

So Pap said they decided to name their town in honor of a group of fine gentlemen from the Revolution. Washington and Jefferson and Madison and a lot of other people who really amounted to something. It was a club. Something like the Freemasons, Pap said.

The club was named from some old Greek who had done something wonderful that Pap didn't know about, but anyway, he said everybody decided this old Greek must have been something fine because all those great men had named their club for him. The Society of Cincinnati.

So they named their town for him, too. Well, actually, maybe they named the town after the club that was named after the Greek.

Cincinnati.

So Mother, in her home in Cincinnati, above the Ohio, which she improved so often that in my memory it seemed a constant happening.

There were no naked logs now. Everything had been covered with sawed lumber from the mill on Great Miami Creek. And each addition was of stone, and there was glass in all the windows, shipped from the East because Mother's glassworks did only bottles and jugs.

People passing on the river at sunset could look up and see the flash of orange fire reflected in those windows. And in all weather, during daylight the house stood shining in its coat of whitewash like a Greek temple on the high bluff above the Ohio at the edge of the growing settlement of Cincinnati.

And the passersby would say, "That's the house of Nalambigi Chesney. She's the friend of General Putnam."

And if they passed in the night, maybe Mother would be there unseen above them, on her river promontory, nostrils flared, gazing across the Ohio into the darkness, into Kentucky, listening for the bark of foxes or the murmur of whippoorwills. Or for something else only she could hear.

Then at last, turning back into bed in the white man's house she had built, there maybe to dream one of those dreams of hers that explained or prophesied, or only painted brilliant images across her mind.

My mother's house had many rooms. I did not know them all.

Chapter 9

At the time, I supposed that President Washington did a passable job. It was only later I began to understand he'd done a difficult job very well indeed. The thing was, he had to shoot from the hip, as Pap said, because nobody had ever done the job before, so there were no precedents to guide him.

My mother would have none of what she called wicked words spoken against Washington in her house.

"He and your pap and I fought to make the Republic," she often said to me. "And I will not allow anyone to say a bad thing about him."

She was like a reformed drunk, fanatic in her newfound perceptions. Coming from a race of people who never had a talent for organization of various parts into a unified whole, witness the failure of Tecumseh, now that she was part of just such an arrangement, she defended it and all who had a part in creating it like a religious zealot on the stump for his particular path to salvation.

But many folk in the Ohio Valley weren't too happy with him. He was too patty-cake, they said, with Alexander Hamilton, who was overly friendly to the English. In the Ohio Valley people generally hated the English with a roaring passion.

Well, people west of the mountains and north of the Ohio River had reason to hate the British. According to the Fort Pitt newspaper, more than twelve hundred settlers had been scalped by various hostiles in just a few years, and everybody was convinced the English were increasing the heat again to keep the tribes constantly stirred up.

After a few years of relative peace, when the only hostile raids were local affairs, it had come round once more to the situation that had existed along that border for over a century: tribes promised steady trade by whichever white man controlled Canada in return for cooperation in making the Ohio Valley unhealthy for trespassers.

First, it had been French-instigated atrocities against British settlers. Then British against American. Now, too, there was an added incentive that tribal leaders were beginning to understand. That Americans were not traders but settlers who came with women and kids and hogs and plows.

"It had to happen," Mother said. "It's been too quiet too long. The damned English will not treat us as a real Republic until we fight again."

It was thirteen years after the Treaty of Paris, when Britain had agreed to leave American soil. Yet there they were, more than a thousand redcoat regulars in forts strung like beads across the Great Lakes area.

Mother could reel off the names of those forts like one of her red savage chants. And why not. She had a vested interest in settlers. They were prospective customers.

Mackinac, Detroit, Fort Erie, Fort Niagara, Oswego, Dutchman's Point, Fort Miami on the Maumee River off the western tip of Lake Erie.

All of those on American real estate. All of those with regular British garrisons. All of those with the trade goods Indians wanted. Needed. Guns, hatchets, powder, and lead. Whiskey. Well, the British used rum now.

Pap was almost as unhappy with the situation as was Mother. He said he was getting damned tired of going on a nice deer hunt and having to worry all the time that some Shawnee was going to slip up behind him and bury an ax in his brain.

I always figured Pap said that just to please Mother. Actually, I think Pap enjoyed the prospect of hunting in a forest where there was constant hazard. It was something I never understood. At home, he was sloth and sleeping. In the woods, he enjoyed walking on the knife edge of danger.

Finally, to everyone's relief, President Washington said he'd had enough, and so he sent the army to put down the Indian menace. Unfortunately, there wasn't any army to speak of, and the commanding general was one Josiah Harmar who had managed to get through the Revolution without falling down a well.

The ragtag troops, about three hundred regulars and over a thousand militia volunteers, along with their general, arrived in Cincinnati in 1790 and built Fort Washington as a staging depot for operations toward the north.

And in the north, there were Shawnees, Delawares, Ottawas, Miamis, Ojibways, and God only knew what else, led by a Miami chief named Little Turtle, and they were waiting, with a lot of their white friends. And maybe while they waited, they were laughing, too.

For our new Republic, the whole thing was a disaster!

Pap had the bit in his teeth. He couldn't wait to join up with old Harmar so he could get out in the woods and whack some hostiles. Everybody knew where Harmar and his little army were headed. The Maumee River and Fort Miami.

But Pap waited until Fort Washington was built. It was about two miles from Mother's front door and, like her front door, overlooked the Ohio River. Pap waited because he wasn't at all interested in getting his hands blistered with a hammer and saw building blockhouses.

Most of this I got later from Mother or Pap. There are some memories of it, but I was only seven years old.

When the last log was laid and the last dowel seated, Pap got all his woods gear together, kissed Mother good-bye, and went to war. General Harmar was drilling his army now in the outskirts of Cincinnati.

Three days later, Pap was back, cussing and stomping around. Mother asked him if General Harmar didn't want him to scout for the army, and Pap said hell yes, but Harmar was so drunk all the time it would be a fool's journey to lay in with him.

So Pap took himself out of the war. Mother was truly astonished that Pap would pass up a chance to go off and shoot somebody. But she assumed Pap knew what he was doing.

After an overly long preparation, Harmar marched off into the north woods with his army. The citizens of Cincinnati stood at the roadside and waved to them and gave them cornbread muffins to put in their haversacks. The soldiers looked pretty ragged, even the regulars in their knee britches and gaiters and tricorn hats.

It was September, and the persimmons were showing bright orange in the sunlight, waiting for the first frost before they would be edible, and the corn stalks were already turning brown in the slash-and-burn Indian fields scattered through the forest.

In a couple of weeks, the army was back in Cincinnati. Well, what was left of it was back, straggling in whipped and forlorn, Harmar reeling in his saddle.

Little Turtle and his Indians, along with a sizable contingent of Canadian Tories and a few British regular officers, had led the little army into the deep woods, like a bird feigning a broken wing to lead a snake away from the nest, and then ambushed them.

Mother said the ones who got out were lucky. She figured if the hostiles hadn't been spending so much time pausing to take hair and weapons from the first batch of dead and wounded, nobody at all would have made it back.

As the stories of survivors were later patched together, it turned out she was right.

In Philadelphia, which had replaced New York as the capital city, President Washington likely turned eastern Pennsylvania and most of New Jersey blue with his language.

When he had recovered sufficient breath to issue orders, he sent a dispatch to Arthur St. Clair, authorizing him to recruit fourteen hundred men and wipe out the threat. St. Clair at that time was governor of the Northwest Territory.

So Pap started through his routine once more, making ready to charge off to war. This time, Mother intervened.

"That St. Clair," she said. "He has many friends at Detroit."

"Detroit? The English are at Detroit."

"This is what I say to you," and Mother's eyes were glinting. "St. Clair is enough Tory so that if we caught him back when we were fighting with Danny Morgan, we'd have put a tar-and-feather suit on him and burned his barn!"

"How do you know?" Pap asked, well aware that it was the kind of thing Mother *would* know from various of her business associates.

"Stay at home for this war," she said.

And he did. Along with the rest of Cincinnati, Pap watched as St. Clair collected troops and supplies at Fort Washington and began drilling them. And drilling them. And drilling them. Dispatch riders arrived on lathered horses with messages from President Washington asking why there was no word from the Northwest Territory about St. Clair engaging and whipping the hostiles. Whereupon St. Clair drilled his troops some more.

Finally, St. Clair started crawling north. It was another fall, only late enough in the year so that the persimmons had been frostbitten and were fit to eat. It was about the only ration they got, as it turned out.

As he moved, St. Clair built forts. On the Wabash River, he found Little Turtle. Or more accurately, Little Turtle found him.

Once more, the citizens of Cincinnati had to observe the spectacle of a routed army coming home. In fact, if it hadn't been for one of those forts St. Clair had built on the way out giving them a place to hide on the way back, it would have been worse.

"My God Almighty," Pap said. "They lost six hundred dead and almost as many wounded! That's more than we had killed in some of the big battles during the Revolution!"

It turned out that St. Clair being slightly pro-British didn't have anything to do with the disaster. As Pap said, he was the kind of general who didn't know piss from rainwater and just got himself out-thought and out-fought.

By this time, President Washington must have been close to apoplexy. But now, he made a decision that prompted Pap and a lot of other old soldiers to say, "Now we'll see about those red hellions."

The president assigned the job to the Legion, which was a force of about a thousand regular infantrymen plus some supporting cavalry, and soon it would be enlarged to about three thousand and trained like a real army at Fort Washington.

But the best part, the old soldiers said, was who commanded the Legion. A tough, no-nonsense, disciplinarian who drank too much by President Washington's standards, Pap said, but who never lost control of a battlefield.

A man solid in body and spirit, he didn't suffer fools or slovenly soldiers, and he insisted on men who could shoot and scoot in the woods, Pap said. He was hell to serve under. But you knew when the guns started, there were few officers around who could better call the tune.

His name was Wayne. A Pennsylvanian, he had a good record in the War of Independence, and President Washington knew him well and always thought he was too harsh with his troops. But he was the only officer left wearing the uniform of the United States Army who might get the job done.

The men in the Legion called him Mad Anthony.

To the last of his days, Pap enjoyed talking about that campaign. Maybe it was because General Wayne made Pap chief of scouts. It was a position more exalted than any he'd held during the Revolution.

At the time, the United States had a peace conference going on at Sandusky, but the tribes were in no mood to talk much. So in the spring of 1794, President Washington cut Mad Anthony loose. Pap said the general had been straining at the leash.

They moved cautiously north, Pap scouting ahead all the way. General Wayne built a couple of forts as they went, and there were a few skirmishes. All along, Pap had cut Indian sign so he could tell General Wayne that Little Turtle was watching every move the Legion made.

As the Legion drew near the Maumee, the hostiles decided it was time to bust this bunch just as they'd done the other two American columns before it. And the Legion was headed directly toward Fort Miami, one of those forts on American soil garrisoned by British troops.

The Americans didn't know it yet, but Little Turtle had taken a good look at the advancing column and suggested maybe it would be good to make peace. All the Indians could see was more glorious victories. So another Miami named Turkey Foot became their war chief.

Just a few miles from the western tip of Lake Erie, there was a long ridge where a tornado a few years before had felled all the trees. The big logs lay along the hill like piles of Mother's matchsticks, Pap said. It was a natural fort, and from his scouting, Pap was able to tell General Wayne exactly where the Indians were waiting behind those breastworks.

There were a great many Canadian militiamen with the Indian army, and Pap said maybe a few British officers.

One thing was sure, a lot of redcoat regulars were nearby. Because almost within sight of the ridge was Fort Miami, and a gaggle of Royal Army soldiers inside were at the palisades, watching expectantly for what reckoned would be yet another American debacle.

General Wayne brought up his troops and went into a line to assault the ridge. Most of the troops lay hidden behind bushes and tree stumps. Another group, with the cavalry, moved out of sight to one flank of the hill, Pap guiding them.

A charge was ordered, a few soldiers ran toward the felled trees, and the Indians and their friends whooped and began firing. Immediately, the advancing Americans turned and ran back, and the Indians, figuring it was another rout, jumped up from their positions and followed, waving hatchets and thinking about all those scalps, Pap said.

But once they were well clear of all that fallen timber, General Wayne's main body rose up in their front. After a volley that ripped the hostiles, Wayne's men charged with bayonets.

Pap always said the best way to fight Indians was to surprise them, and these were surprised. Also badly hurt and very frustrated. They turned and made for their ridge of fallen timbers.

Before they could secure themselves behind the fallen trees, Pap's group from the flank was into their position, which surprised and hurt them even more. From here on, it was a footrace.

As surviving Indians and Canadian militia ran toward the British fort, the Legion was among them, shooting, clubbing, hatcheting them to the ground. Pap said maybe as many as half the enemy force got to the fort.

That's when they got the biggest surprise of all. Seeing how things were going, the British commander inside the fort ordered the gate closed, so the retreating Indians and militia were caught against the outside of the palisades where riflemen of the Legion calmly moved up and began to shoot them as they tried to get inside the fort.

In complete panic now, the remaining hostiles ran north into the woods, Pap and his friends following, killing more of them as they went.

"The Englishmen just set in their fort," Pap said. "And watched us butcher their friends. They didn't come out, and we didn't try to go in. The general said we wasn't at war with England."

"Not yet," Mother said grimly.

The Legion re-formed and began a search through the forests at the toe of Lake Erie and along the Maumee, burning sprouting Indian corn, because Mad Anthony Wayne had come in the spring, not the fall as the others had.

Over the next few days, they found many villages that had been deserted in panic, and they burned them all. And they were still running down warriors, shooting them like fear-crazed hares, Pap said.

In that June, Pap said the smoke of fires lifted like wisps of a widow's veil up through the leaves that were so new they looked like fresh-washed lettuce. And on the ground, when they caught anybody, the sprouting cloudberry blooms were splattered with a darker, liquid red.

"I seen many a Shawnee or Ottawa those few days, disemboweled and layin like he was takin a nap in a patch of skunk cabbage," Pap said. "I don't think I ever seen so much skunk cabbage as they was along the Maumee that year."

At the time, Mother was as rapturous as any of the victorious soldiers. For different reasons, of course. The drubbing Mad Anthony Wayne had given the Ohio Valley Indians made some pretty good ripples in Whitehall, I guess, so Mr. John Jay, who was there trying to get a treaty with the English to let up on raiding American shipping, had some success.

Not as much as a lot of people, including my mother, would have liked. But for a while, General Putnam said, the British navy stopped boarding our merchant ships and taking sailors off to serve in their navy or else confiscating cargo they claimed was war material the French might get. The British at the time being in and out of war constantly with France as a part of the European reaction to the French Revolution.

And in the Northwest Territory, the Battle of Fallen Timbers wasn't lost on the tribes. Before long, they all came in for a treaty and ceded all of what would soon be the state of Ohio to the United States.

The British didn't pull out of the forts on American soil. But there was a noticeable decrease in Indian activity, meaning maybe the redcoats had backed off inciting tribes against us.

"But not for long," Mother said.

Well, a long time later, a lot of missionaries and others said the Americans stole the land from the Indians and we ought to be ashamed of ourselves. It's the only time I ever heard my mother swear, I mean really cuss.

"Horse dung! Those people know all about conquest. They's did plenty of it their ownselfs. Winner gets the territory. If they is one thing in this world they understand, it's damned sure that. Winner gets the hunting ground!"

You can see how angry she was, with all those errors in grammar. And you can see, too, that Mother didn't have much loyalty to race, but only to culture. Like all her red ancestors believed, a captive white who became part of the tribe was considered as much Indian as the bloods. No matter he was of another race.

Years later, when Mother was confronted with the idea, she admitted it.

"Of course," she said. "A Huron could hate a Mohawk worse than he hated any white man. And not only were Huron and Mohawk the same race, they were both Iroquois!"

But there was a darker side to it maybe, if you want to call it that. By the time of the Battle of Fallen Timbers, you can see that Mother was really making progress in beating the white man at his own game! Well, at least joining him at his own game.

It wasn't the only time Mother showed that streak of resistance to racial loyalty. There was what we called the Tecumseh Incident.

Tecumseh, a Shawnee chief, didn't have very good luck in either war or diplomacy, as it turned out. His father was killed fighting for the British in the Revolution. His brother was killed at Fallen Timbers. And while he was trying to get all the tribes to form some sort of alliance to fight the Americans, his number-two man got Tecumseh's band into a battle that shouldn't have been fought, lost it, and destroyed any chance for Tecumseh's alliance.

So Tecumseh went on tour, as it were, denouncing war and learning English and Roman history and such things, I suppose, from his white lady mentor whose name was Rebeca Galloway. As you might expect, some rather off-color comments were passed about Rebeca Galloway in the taverns along the Ohio River.

Well, Rebeca Galloway came to Cincinnati with the chief, and naturally, the first place they visited was the house of the Native

Princess of Hamilton County. They were served coffee, and Mother said Tecumseh put seven teaspoonfuls of brown sugar in his cup.

There was another man in the party, obviously a half blood, and he seemed a kind of Shawnee preacher whose job it was to further the wishes and desires of the chief. Standing behind Mother's chair through all this, I was aware that he spoke English as well as any American preacher I'd ever heard, and he was dressed as though he'd raided General Putnam's wardrobe.

I recall Tecumseh as looking rather tall sitting in my mother's best rocking chair. And odd. He was attired in good broadcloth and linen, which looked strangely out of place because his hair was still roached.

After some polite conversation on weather and crops, Rebeca Galloway indicated that the second man in her party had something of importance to say.

"We have an enemy who fights well," he began, "and we call him warrior and we torture him unto death, and if he is brave, we call him a valiant chief, and to honor him we eat of his flesh and drink of his blood so we might have his courage.

"The Black Robes told us long ago you had a man who spoke well, and you called him prophet and you tortured him unto death, and he was brave so you called him God, and to honor him you eat of his flesh and drink of his blood so you might have his spirit.

"Where is the great difference in us?"

For a long moment, there was a deadly silence, and my mother's neck had gone stiff. I was behind her so I couldn't see her face, but I knew her eyes had the glint that meant danger. Suddenly, she rose from her chair, and her voice snapped like a whip.

"Why do you come into my house and ask me that? Am I the one who must decide that our grandmothers were only a mask with a Black Robe's story underneath?"

The visit was over. And everybody in the room knew it. Rebeca Galloway quickly led her charges out, dropping words of farewell behind like little sheep turds, Mother said later.

"I thought it was a pretty good speech," I said.

"You are an eight-year-old child," she said. "Go find your little sister. Go play with Hiram. But stay out of the root cellar. I know how many apples are in those baskets so don't try to steal one."

That night I heard her say to Pap, "Tecumseh loves the English. He and his family love the English. Before that, they loved the French. Then the French were gone. Now, I would rather have three rattlesnakes in my house than those three I had today, who love the English so much. They have fought alongside the English every time, since the French left. The three cups they drank from, I broke them as soon as they were gone!"

Pap thought it was funny as hell. I heard them in their room that night, and he was still joshing her and Mother was scolding him. But she was laughing, too.

"Yesiree, as an old African friend of mine used to say," Pap said, shaking his head and laughing. "Your mother bit that Galloway woman and run off the Shawnee high muck-dee-muck! Don't ever come up crosswise with your mother, boys."

They were good years along the river. In recall, there are a few bright or painful or simply memorable days. Like shards of glass from a broken windowpane glinting a warning of cut feet to passing barefoot urchins playing on the polished kitchen floor.

There were too many confusing things happening for a twelve-year-old boy to make head or tail of it. It was many years before I could. None too well then, maybe.

John Adams was elected our second president. And the source of all our problems, according to Mother, was still the war between the English and the French. Once more, both those countries were stopping our ships on the high seas, and if a captain was lucky enough to escape that, he'd still have the Barbary pirates to worry about.

"Those damned Spaniards, those damned Spaniards," Mother would mutter, and when she did that, I knew she'd had word that the Mississippi was closed again to American commerce.

Everybody was talking about war. Some wanted to fight Britain, some wanted to fight France. There may have been a few who wanted to fight Spain, I don't know.

"You better hope we don't start a war with anybody," Pap said. "After gettin a close look at some of the raggedy-ass soldiers they've got in this Republic, you know we ain't ready to fight nobody cept maybe a few poor ignorant savages."

I guess Pap knew that would get a rise.

"Ignorant savages?" Mother snapped. "Do you mean the same ignorant savages that whipped Harmar and St. Clair to a frazzle and sent them home like cut dogs?!"

"Well, Harmar and St. Clair, that's raggedy-ass, too. Anthony Wayne ain't big enough to go around to all the places we'd need him if we was to fit the British or the French. So it's best not to calculate our takin them on."

"Oh, we'll take on the English. Not now, maybe. But someday, and before long."

"You seem mighty sure about that."

"I am sure. I dreamed it would happen."

There was a new thing called political parties. The Republicans, who were Jeffersonians. And the Federalists, who were behind John Adams and Hamilton. At least, as near as Pap could figure out in terms he could use explaining it to me. The Republicans liked the French. The Federalists liked the English.

Then we had word from Europe that as a part of their revolution in France, they'd cut off their king's head. And it wasn't long before we heard they'd cut off their queen's head, too.

"God Almighty," Pap shouted. "I ain't ever been much to tag around after kings, but cuttin off their heads? And that queen, why I heared she was a pretty little thing."

They had a woodcut picture of a guillotine in the Pittsburgh newspaper, and when Pap explained how the contraption worked, it made my flesh crawl.

Well, the French whacking off their own king's head, and his queen's in the bargain, threw a bucket of cold water on the Republicans' love for France.

And as the war in Europe heated up, the British playing hell with our ships at sea and obviously itching to get back into the Ohio Valley didn't set too well on the stomachs of the Federalists, either.

It was a trying time. Pap and Mother, especially Mother, couldn't get away from worry about it all, but Hiram and I could.

It was in that time that we made a wonderful friend. Her name was Judith Dwyer, a widow lady who had come down the river from the East after her husband died and left her a considerable inheritance which she used to start an inn and tavern. Pap said she was Irish and hated the English even more than our mother did.

Once established, Judith Dwyer made a brown sugar brittle each Wednesday which she sold in her tavern, a penny for a small waxed bag full of the crunchy confection. Candy was uncommon along the river that far west, so naturally Hiram and I made arrangements to have our share of Judith Dwyer's without having to bother our mother about the penny.

It was Hiram's idea, and a good one. On Tuesday nights we set trotlines along the riverbanks and before dawn on Wednesday were up and checking them. Hiram would start at one end of our set and I at the other, collecting the catch and meeting halfway.

He always had more fish than I did. It took a while, but eventually I figured out that he was taking fish from any line he found, no matter who set them.

I never mentioned this little theft of fish to our mother, even in that year far in the future when we heard that Hiram had been hanged for doing the same sort of thing with furs but on a more ambitious scale.

Anyway, he always had enough fish to select a large mess of the best ones and throw the others into somebody's hog pen. On presentation of these fish at the back door of Judith Dwyer's tavern, her black slave woman would give us two sacks of the brown sugar brit-

217

tle, and we'd go back to the river and find a quiet spot on the bank and eat the candy. All of it.

There's never been much pride in telling that story because Hiram and I were so selfish. At least I recall once suggesting we share.

"Let's save a couple pieces for Pap and Mother," I said, mouth full and teeth crunching brittle.

"Not enough," Hiram said, mouth full too. "Besides, it'd just make Pap's teeth hurt. You know how he's always talkin bout how he got the toothache."

"Yeah, I forgot about that."

Thus comes the death of good intentions.

There was a sign hanging over the door just inside Judith Dwyer's taproom.

Jefferson and Liberty, Hurray!
Adams and Constitution, Be Damned!

When she heard of it, Mother said, "Well, I see we've got another Federalist in town."

"With the one you're talkin about, what's the difference?" Pap asked. "She can't vote, and she ain't got a man to tell him how to vote, either."

"I like part of her sign. But not all."

"I didn't expect you'd cotton very much to that damning the Constitution bit of it."

There were a few hectic days as a result of Judith Dwyer's sign, and Pap wouldn't even try to explain it, and Mother would only snort and say something like "Damned British lover New England pipsqueak Adams."

All I could get from this was that Mother didn't much care for John Adams. I knew that already. So I had to wait for time and wisdom, both of which are damned slow for a twelve-year-old.

Somebody that Pap called a jake-leg law appeared from upriver. He even had a badge. I heard on the street that he was one of the most purple-faced Federalists in the Ohio Territory. Everybody called him Spooner. He wore knee britches and silk stockings, but at least his wig wasn't powdered.

Spooner marched into the tavern and tore down Judith Dwyer's sign. He informed her that under the laws of the Republic, specifically the Alien and Sedition Act, if she put it up again, he'd come back and arrest her and carry her off to Pittsburgh for trial because her sign obviously libeled the president of the United States, which aforementioned law expressly prohibited.

As he went back down the hill to his boat, this Spooner received the honors of the town. It was midsummer so considerable numbers of ripe vegetables were at hand, like tomatoes. Many of these, especially the more-than-ripe ones, were showered down by hooting men, women, and children. I got off a couple of good ones myself. Hiram was throwing rocks. Our own town constable caught him at it and told him he should be ashamed of himself.

Before the red-dripping Spooner was out of sight up the Ohio, Judith Dwyer's sign was up again. Only now, instead of hanging by the door inside, it was hanging by the door outside.

Nobody figured Spooner for any gumption at all, but they were wrong. He waited until October, when there were no more tomatoes, and returned.

Somebody spotted him coming up the bluff from the river, and the call went ahead to Judith Dwyer's tavern. By the time Spooner got there, the door was locked. He banged on it for a while, with no response. He began to shout threats about arrests and jail and the pillory, at which point the shutters directly above his head opened and somebody leaned out with a large white chamber pot and dumped its considerable contents on Spooner's head.

This time, on his walk back down the hill to his boat, a damp Spooner did not suffer thrown vegetables but only the verbal missiles that hurt most, derisive laughter.

It was the last anybody in our settlement ever heard of Spooner.

Somebody suggested to Mother that surely it had not been Judith

Dwyer who had handled the chamber pot on that day, for ladies do not comport themselves by throwing the contents of chamber pots on gentlemen who wear knee britches and long broadcloth coats.

Mother smiled. Soon, she invited Judith Dwyer to her house for sassafras tea. Judith Dwyer arrived with a large quantity of brown sugar brittle.

Pap was awake half the night with toothache until finally he was so drunk from taking his toothache medicine that he fell into a noisy slumber. We could hear it all over the house.

But there was something else from Judith Dwyer. In the year that George Washington died, she brought to our settlement a divine treat.

There was an icehouse on the Little Miami. A man named Perkins cut ice from ponds and river in winter, packed it in sawdust, and had ice to sell through most of the summer.

So on this July afternoon, Judith Dwyer asked Hiram and me to go to Mr. Perkins's icehouse and bring back two large tow sacks full of ice, all we could carry. When we returned with the ice, Judith Dwyer and her slave girl Mobe were in the tavern kitchen with a contraption that had a large tin bucket, gears and wheels, a crank, and all of that fitted into a wooden tub.

Judith Dwyer mixed a lot of good things together. I could smell the vanilla. She poured the mixture into the bucket and put the lid on and put the bucket in the tub, and Mobe began chipping ice into the tub, putting in salt with the ice and packing it all down. The crank was still sticking up above the whole business, and after they had the ice packed and covered with burlap, Judith Dwyer showed me and Hiram how to crank it.

We did turnabout on the crank, and finally it got very hard to do, and after almost an hour, I suppose, Judith Dwyer had us stop. She opened the tin can and spooned out two bowls of this white, fluffy-looking pudding and told us to eat.

It was overwhelming. So delicious and cold. As we ate, Judith Dwyer talked.

It was a food invented in Italy, she said. Now it was going all over the world because people liked it. Judith Dwyer had a friend in the city of New York who sent the machine by way of New Orleans, and it had been held up at the mouth of the Mississippi because the Spaniards had the river closed for a while, but then the way was cleared and altogether it had only taken four months to get to us.

She said it was called ice cream.

When General Putnam bought all that land from the government, it held out the section in the township where we lived on our Cincinnati plateau. As soon as we had a territorial legislature, it sold part of that section to finance building a school and hiring a teacher.

My mother was involved with it in a rather large way, but as with her silent partnerships in business, out of sight behind the scenes.

She had heard Presbyterians were very strong on mission schools and education in general, so she asked the general to find us a schoolmaster who was a Presbyterian. Not only did he do that, but the one he found had a wife who was almost as well educated as anyone could hope for, so the two of them were our teachers in the big log schoolhouse.

In most of the frontier settlements teachers were boarded in someone's home, shifted around from time to time so one family didn't carry the complete burden. But in our township, our schoolmaster was a preacher as well, and his wife did sewing or baking or just about anything else you might want. So they were pretty self-sufficient.

I didn't mind lessons, but Hiram was in constant, noisy rebellion against them. What a relief summer was, when we could spend so much time on the river. Just to get some peace from Hiram.

We came to love that river, the Ohio. We didn't think of it as a great highway to the West, even though that's what it had become. To us, it was just simply joy of life.

My brother Hiram and I often stayed among the rushes near the mouth of Little Miami Creek in summer dusk and listened for loons calling from the Kentucky side. The lonely cry coming across the water that still shown like a ribbon of shining gray silk always had the power to make gooseflesh pop up on my arms. It still does.

Sometimes, after she was old enough to walk, we'd take our sister with us. I had to watch her. Hiram refused, saying if she fell in the river, it would serve her right for always whining after us.

We fished. And once we caught a snapping turtle with a huge, vicious mouth, and we dragged him still alive up the bluff to our yard. Mother cut off the head with a two-bitted ax, all the while lecturing us about staying clear of snapping turtles. She said a turtle like that could bite off little Clariese's arm.

After that, Hiram and I made a habit of slipping away, leaving Clariese behind. Then came Gance, and Hiram refused to watch him, too.

But that turtle. He was a monster. Mother fed us delicious white turtle meat for three days, and the soup was enough to make a grown man cry, Pap said. Hiram cleaned the shell and gave it as a gift to Clariese. To keep her from screaming to Mother about us boys leaving her behind all the time. She used that turtle shell for a bathtub until she was twelve years old.

Duck flyaway time was the best of all. The river was wide enough all along so that in spring and fall, when the birds were migrating, there was always a lot of still water at certain points along the bank, and Hiram and me knew them every one.

Pap bought an old British Brown Bess musket from some passing pilgrim. He gave it to me for a bird gun. The thing was a .75 caliber so it would hold plenty of small shot for close-range duck shooting. For geese, you had to load it with buckshot.

Some evenings, we'd come home with a tow sack full of birds and our shoulders aching from that rearing, kicking old mule of a gun. Pap always helped us clean them, if he was home, and Mother could make a duck or a goose into something any European king would have slobbered over.

If we didn't feel like fishing or shooting, we could go belly-down on one of the high bluffs above the Ohio and pretend we were painted hostile savages taking potshots at the flatboats and dugouts and rafts and keelboats that were moving up and down the river.

"Someday," Hiram said, "we'll get us one of those boats and go down the river all the way to where the Spaniards are."

We didn't know it at the time, but in 1799, when we marked the death of George Washington, it was the end of something that had started in 1607 when the first English-speaking people came to settle in what they would call Virginia.

Now that was finished. And there was the start of something new.

It was no sudden thing, like hail in summer. It didn't come with cannon fire or the raising of a flag or a band playing. That's why we didn't know it at the time, or wouldn't even have recognized it had we known.

It was a change in direction, yet so smooth and natural that it took any number of years to realize our course had shifted.

You might think of a man who stood on a promontory along the coast of Massachusetts and looked out across the Atlantic toward Europe, looked out toward the land that sent him forth, the land that continued for two hundred years to be his contact with kinfolk, the land by which he measured all his hopes and aspirations and from which he expected to be forthcoming the rules that made all things work.

Then the end of the century. Washington dead. The man turned, walked up to a high peak of the Allegheny Mountains in Pennsylvania.

He looked along the Ohio River and saw beyond, to the valley of the Mississippi, and beyond to the long sweep of the Missouri and on beyond to the Shining Mountains.

He was no longer looking east.

He was looking west!

Of course, there were a few, like Pap and the people he came over with, who were looking west from the beginning. So there wasn't any change for them.

Well, there was a change. Instead of being alone, now suddenly a great many people moved to catch up.

Maybe Pap's kind were surprised to see the rest of the nation now joining the original band in reaching out all the way to the Pacific.

And my mother would probably have said to them, "We've been headed in that direction all along, and now that you've stopped thinking us fools, and now that some of you who've tried to stop us have changed your minds, and now that you've decided to get in the canoe with us, next you'll be making claims that moving this Republic west was your idea from the start."

So 1799. George Washington dead. And finally people began to wonder what would have happened to us in the dark days of the Revolution without him. What we would have done during the dark years of the new nation without him. A greedy Europe snapping at our heels, Barbary pirates snapping at our heels, hostiles along our borders snapping at our heels. Sometimes snapping at our own heels.

Well, everybody was still snapping at our heels. But it was different. And maybe Mother said it best. "Every year we get stronger. Every year, the Republic grows more sons!"

So 1799. The patriarch dead. A new direction.

And Hiram and I had discovered ice cream.

Chapter 10

The Republic had a new president and a new capital city.

Thomas Jefferson and Aaron Burr received the same number of electoral votes so the issue was decided in the House of Representatives. Jefferson won because Alexander Hamilton used his influence to swing votes away from Burr.

When the news of all this reached us, Mother laughed about it.

"It's no feather in Hamilton's hat," she said. "He'd help Old Nick himself to keep Burr from getting anything."

We had no say in that election because Ohio wasn't a state yet. But Mother and a lot of others expected the Northwest Territory to get more attention now that Jefferson was in office.

Mostly, they were disappointed. At least at first, then things blew open with a bang.

The new capital was the city of Washington.

Travelers coming down the river who had seen it were unanimous: Why did the central government move out of Philadelphia?

The great old Pennsylvania City, they said, was a fine town, with cobbled streets and fine ladies-wear shops and brick homes, churches, and public buildings.

The city of Washington was a small town in the woods. And swamps, they said. Streets were seas of mud. There was one decent tavern in the whole place and not half a dozen boardinghouses. Already, they said, members of the government took every available opportunity to cross the Potomac to enjoy the local ales and white clam chowder at Alexandria.

Shortly after the turn of the century, General Putnam came from Washington to see to his business interests in the territory and naturally visited my mother. He said that a few weeks before he left office, President John Adams moved to Washington City and occupied the partly finished presidential residence, called the White House because it was covered with a coat of whitewash, and that Abigail, his wife, was so disgusted with her surroundings she was ready to turn around and go back to Philadelphia before she'd unpacked her valise.

My mother laughed about that, too.

"Those pipsqueak politicians," she said. "Now they get a taste of frontier living, with hogs passing in the street beneath their windows. Good! It will make them work harder to build their city. Look at us here, in the wilds of Ohio, and already we have a shoe factory with three employees and a volunteer fire brigade and fine docks on the river!"

It was like Mother, to be more of a booster for our town than any of the white men who lived there. Part of beating them at their own game.

America had a postal service before it was America. The same system continued after the Revolution. It was pretty good, I suppose, on the eastern seaboard. Along the Ohio, we had a natural highway so letters and parcels and newspapers and all manner of things could be sent. The river. That, and the good intentions of passing travelers, made for a reliable exchange of information, at least for that time, provided you were prepared to wait weeks or sometimes months for whatever it was you were expecting.

Some of us would live to see such things as the magnetic tele-graphic. But at the front end of the new nineteenth century, such a device was nowhere to be found.

Even for those of us who lived then, it was hard in later years to realize the changes that came, large and small, and so many hardly noted at the time.

Sometimes, afterward, when I thought about my mother and my-self, it was a shock to recall how primitive our lives were and how quickly change can come.

We were still so young. And easily amazed. As when we heard, al-most a decade into the new century, that they were lighting the by-ways of London with gas streetlamps. And that a man named Fulton had navigated the Hudson River in a ship using the power of a steam engine.

Morphine was yet to be isolated from opium, but it would be before the war with the British that Mother had dreamed was com-ing. We were yet to have a gauge to measure how hard the wind was blowing.

Britain was yet a few years away from outlawing slavery. Eli Whit-ney had just discovered a way to make interchangeable parts for firearms. We heard there were sixty thousand people living in the city of New York, and none of us believed it.

Everywhere in polite society, women were demanding fur coats and men wanted hats made from the felt produced from the beaver. The great textile mills of New England and Europe were still a decade away from demanding cotton, cotton, and more cotton, so that fiber was still a cash crop in a distant second place to sugar in the New World.

And all the men were still wearing pigtails beneath the flat, up-turned back brim of their tricorn hats. And along the Ohio, we'd still be pigtailing our hair a long time after such a thing went out of fash-ion in the East.

It infuriated Mother that it took so long for her to find out what was happening in other places because she said a lot of that would someday affect us.

"Well," Pap said. "You can't change what's happenin in all them far places you worry about. I can recollect when you didn't know what was happenin beyond the next bend in the shoreline of the lake we might be paddlin along."

When Pap said something like that, Mother would usually look at him. Just simply look at him, with no change in her expression. Then slowly, her eyes still on Pap's reddening face, she would take her clay pipe from her apron pocket, pack it with tobacco, and light it with one of the matches her employees made in a small shed by the river.

I may not have mentioned it. Mother smoked that pipe a great deal as she grew older. I think she used it as a screen between herself and all the rest of us when all she wanted was to look, not talk.

I mentioned that to Pap once when we were hunting turkey along Licking Creek in Kentucky, and he laughed.

"Your mother can say more words with a look than a politician can say during a whole session of the legislature," he said.

Perhaps I also failed to mention that Mother's match works, the shed on the river, had to be rebuilt six times that I can recall. It was always catching fire. And when it did, it was always one hell of a fire, and the whole riverfront smelled like sulphur for two days.

About that smoking. Maybe I waited so long to mention it because I was always a little embarrassed about my own mother with a pipe in her mouth. I would think that such a thing really marked her as a barbarian. Then I'd be ashamed of myself.

Mother and Pap smoked Indian leaf rather than the better-cured Virginia-style tobacco. It had a particular odor. When I was very young, lying in the dark, and one of them would come near, I never knew which it was unless they spoke because they smelled the same to me.

228

We knew what had happened after the French Revolution. Before, the French had a king, not too different from the one we had before our own Revolution. Afterward, they had a dictator. Napoleon.

Then there was a long spell when we didn't know what was happening until, as Mother said, it started affecting us. As with Napoleon. He wanted to get France back into North America, and part of that was asking Spain to return the Louisiana Territory to France. And King Charles IV did. The king probably figured it was all right because France had ceded Louisiana to Spain after the Seven Years War to keep Great Britain from getting it, and besides, not many people were in a position to say no to Napoleon when he asked for something.

Napoleon probably asked for Florida as well, but the Spanish monarch said Ponce de León had claimed Florida for Spain in 1513, and after almost three hundred years, you get sort of attached to a piece of property. Or something like that.

We didn't know the French were no more inclined to open the Mississippi to our trade than the Spaniards had been.

We didn't really have time to find out because before we could, Napoleon changed his mind and instead of getting France back into North America, he sold the Louisiana Territory to President Jefferson.

Well, not to President Jefferson personally, but to the United States.

Mother was delighted because it meant an open Mississippi all the way to the Gulf of Mexico. Pap said he didn't care one way or the other.

"Those as wanted to go west of the Mississip before, they went. They'll do now also. It don't make any bother whoever owns it."

But the next big news from the West changed Pap's mind, and he became overnight an enthusiastic Republican simply because Jefferson had grabbed the ram by the gonads, as he said, and bought all that unknown country whether the Congress or the Constitution said he could do it or not.

Because that next news was about Lewis and Clark. Pap may not have known or cared much about trade to Europe through the Gulf, but Lewis and Clark meant moving to far wilderness full of wild beasts and Indians, and that Pap understood as well as any man ever did.

Pap came in one evening after having spent most of the afternoon in Dwyer's taproom. I was fifteen but certainly old enough to perceive that Pap was more than moderately drunk.

He collected his family in what Mother now called her sitting room. There was Mother, myself, Hiram, Clariese, who was ten, and five-year-old Gance.

Pap said that Captain Meriwether Lewis and William Clark, another army officer, were organizing an expedition under orders from President Jefferson to advance up the Missouri River to its source and to explore on beyond that to the western sea. To the Pacific.

Much of that country they would traverse was unmapped, and almost everything about it was unknown. He himself, Pap said, would go to the city of St. Louis where the expedition was fitting out, and join Captain Lewis.

All seriousness evaporated then, and Pap laughed and shouted and danced about the room and sang a song he'd learned while serving with Morgan's Riflemen during the Revolution.

The whole thing delighted me and Hiram and Clariese, but the performance scared hell out of little Gance, who ran crying to his mother. She had been sitting there smoking her pipe, listening to it all, watching Pap with a bright wistfulness as though she might like to accompany him.

Now, she lay her pipe aside, told Gance to hush, and led Pap away to his bed. Pap was still singing and shouting that Sergeant Bobby was on the loose again.

Next day was dark with low clouds. Mother helped Pap get all his wilderness gear in shape. The day after that, still gloomy, he took a boat downriver to the West. We did not go to the riverbank but said our good-byes on Mother's promontory, then watched and waved as the keelboat he had taken passage on slowly pulled away and into the stream.

I recollect my mother's last words to him that day.

"Don't let the English catch you," she said. "If they do, they will give you to one of their savage tribes or else take you back to Nova Scotia and put you in one of their filthy prison hulks that float off the shore near Halifax."

For a moment, Pap had a confused expression on his face. Then he laughed.

"Sweet old girl," he said. "We're not going out to fight Englishmen. We're going out to discover new rivers!"

"The English are always lurking about waiting to do their work," she said. "And remember, after Fallen Timbers, there were English officers who offered their Indians a lot of money for your hair."

On that day, Mother stood on her promontory in the gray mist a long time after the rest of us had gone indoors. Her eyes were bright, but there was a grim turn to her fine lips.

"This time," she said when she came in to the fire herself, "your Pap will be gone for many moons."

For almost a week, I sensed a despondency in Mother I had never felt before when Pap was off in the woods. I finally decided it was because this time, he was going toward something foreign to her.

She knew the north woods and the tribes there. From Maine along the St. Lawrence and the Great Lakes. She was one of them. Regardless of the many, many differences among them from tribe to tribe, they had one thing in common which she understood. They were canoe people.

Now Pap was going to a place where Mother had heard all the tribes were horse people. She wasn't sure exactly how that worked.

Before, she could picture him in her mind, could almost feel herself with him. In dense forests and along many rivers, and among

231

tribesmen she knew. Now he was off to a place mostly treeless, with few streams, and the people moved about on horses.

I think Mother felt that on this trip, Pap was truly alone. That her spirit was not beside him. I wondered what she might have dreamed of him going on that long journey to the western ocean.

If she had dreams, she never confided in me.

It was good that Pap was away that summer of 1803.

I was working in the shoe shop. Mother said I ought to learn how to do something besides hunt in the woods. There was another boy my age who worked there, one of the three regular employees. His name was Otto and his father was foreman of the shop, a good German worker who had some time before changed the family name from Schwartz to Black.

Mr. Black had fought in the Revolution, a young cannoneer in the battery once commanded by Alexander Hamilton. Had Mother known that before she hired him, she might not have done so, her disposition toward Hamilton being as it was, but once Black had been in the shop for a few weeks, nothing could have budged my mother's fierce loyalty toward him because he knew shoes and how to make them.

He often regaled me with stories of his service as a boy in one of the artillery regiments of Frederick II of Prussia during the Seven Years War in Europe. It was after that war when he immigrated to America.

Mr. Black's language was a great mystery, indeed. I've heard many old Miami or Illinois Indian men who hang about our waterfront in summer in their pitiful tattered hide clothes, speaking in a drunken babble of English that was easier to understand than was Mr. Black's.

Afterward, when Otto and I took our hourly rest to smoke pipes behind the shop and throw rocks at dogs passing in the alley, he would give me his translation of what his father had said.

I had no illusions as to why I was working in Mother's shoe shop.

It wasn't to learn a trade. It was to render periodic reports on the conduct of Otto Black. Because Otto Black had been hanging about our house since early spring, especially on Sundays, making outrageous calf eyes at my sister Clariese.

Clariese was a large girl, and a pretty one. Certainly she was old enough to have boys notice her, and before long she would be old enough to have parents, especially mothers, scouting about for favorable mates.

Mother had seen, in the various societies where she had lived, marriages for convenience, lust, and even for love. She had also seen marriages contracted for by parents of both parties at a distance from the actual wedding date.

My mother favored contracts for marriages, as in any other business enterprise.

It was always amusing to me when I heard people speak of Indian promiscuity. Let them get old enough to tell the difference between boy and girl, these experts said, they were into the bushes. As the girls became squaws, they said, not only was unfettered fornication accomplished as often as possible, but they made jokes about it afterward.

Unfortunately, these whites who said such things probably got all their knowledge of Indian morals from observing the unfortunate women from almost any tribe who stayed at forts where there were soldiers, or towns where there were river men, or any place else where there was a ready market for their prostitution, a last resort they were sometimes forced to as the only way to feed themselves or their children.

From what Pap had told me, I knew of differences in the tribes as to how they viewed carnal affairs. Some were very loose and easy, Pap said, and some were strict as Puritan preachers in Massachusetts Bay.

My mother, from heritage or training or whatever it was, strongly inclined toward the latter.

Thus I was detailed, without Mother putting it in those exact terms, as a moral monitor over Otto Black. Each day as she ladled out my supper in her kitchen, she would ask questions about Otto, casually yet often to the point.

"Is he like most of those riverfront boys?" she might ask. "Saying wicked things about ladies?"

"Oh, no," I'd say, watching my food very carefully so my eyes remained downcast. "He thinks you're a nice lady."

"I'm not talking about me," she snapped. "I'm talking about young girls. Little girls."

"I never heard him say anything."

"He's never said a word about your sister?"

"He says he thinks she's pretty."

"Ah ha!"

I didn't know what that meant. But I knew one reason Mother was being so protective of Clariese with older boys.

It was because of my brother Hiram and Judith Dwyer's slave Mobe.

It happened in a chicken coop behind Judith Dwyer's inn. For Hiram, it was a case of new exploration and adventure. For Mobe, it had to be polishing up old tricks or some such thing. She was almost thirty.

Mobe had been with the Dwyer family all her life, her mother before her purchased in New York by Mr. Dwyer from a Martinique plantation owner in the North with his wife or mistress or somebody, looking for business with colonial smugglers interested in buying sugar. It was one of those periods when the English had outlawed direct trading between any of their colonies with French or Spanish possessions in the West Indies.

Judith Dwyer, in telling this tale, said to make a long story short, which she always failed to do, the Martinique man sold her husband a pregnant slave girl, the babe was Mobe, and later Mr. Dwyer died from eating oysters out of season, after which Mobe's mother ran away, then Judith received a large inheritance and the British were most helpful, this being during the Revolution in the city of New York and of course the British occupied the city of New York throughout the entire war.

Now Judith Dwyer had used her husband's money, earned mostly with smuggling on the New England coast, and had a nice tavern and inn and caught her slave girl and my brother Hiram in compromising positions in a chicken coop.

I was never sure what compromising position meant and maybe Judith Dwyer didn't know either, but what she saw in that chicken coop she figured was nasty. So she sent Hiram packing in a hurry and gave Mobe a good face slapping and then headed straight up the hill to my mother's house.

Part of it I heard. Judith Dwyer told Mother the whole story, and from the next room I supposed Mother was sitting in a rocking chair Pap had made her, beside her window that overlooks the river. When Mother spoke, it was in that quiet, dangerous tone that I had to strain to catch through the wall.

"It seems untidy to me that you're accusing my son of inventing all these things which a boy his age doesn't know anything about, with a woman old enough to be his mother, who knows all about it and a lot more besides."

Judith Dwyer left the house in a huff, yelling that Hiram was no longer welcome in or near her property. I slipped out of the house and headed down the bluff for the river. Better to let Mother cool her temper awhile before she had a chance to talk to me, which I knew she would, thinking that my being the oldest, maybe I'd put the idea into Hiram's head.

Well, she surprised me once more. She didn't say a word to me or Hiram about it except to say that she wanted us to stay away from the tavern and inn for a while.

About a week later I heard them talking and she said something, and I heard Hiram say, "Aw, she's just a slave."

"Yes," Mother said, and her voice bit him. "And my mother was a

235

slave, too, a red Indian slave to a white man. So her being a slave got nothing to do with it."

So maybe Mother figured Hiram had acted like boys are supposed to act. Which I guess is true.

But when it came to her daughter Clariese, it was different. Hence, when Otto Black started making those calf eyes at my sister, Mother must have recalled what boys might do in chicken coops and didn't like what she saw in her head so set me to spying on Otto Black's motives.

Of course, the first chance I had, I asked Hiram what had happened. We were on the riverbank cleaning some blue perch. Behind us prowling up and down were half a dozen cats, and now and then we'd throw them a handful of fish guts.

"That nigger asked me in there to help her collect eggs," he said, giggling. "She grabbed me and had me half undressed before I knew what was happ'nin."

After a little while, Hiram looked out across the surface of the river, and he had a dreamy look deep in his eyes, like maybe he was contemplating one of life's great mysteries. Which it turned out he was.

"You know," he said, as though he might be talking to himself, "she got this flat little chest. Flat as mine. But on there is two big pump knots. You recollect last summer when we found those wild huckleberries in the woods up Little Miami Creek? Purple and plump, the size of your fingernail? Well, that's what they looked like. Two ripe huckleberries on her chest."

"You gonna tell me now you tried to eat one of em?"

My brother thought it was so funny he almost fell in the river laughing.

It was in this time that we heard of Alexander Hamilton being killed in a duel with Aaron Burr. I heard Mother discussing it with some of her friends, but other than the fact that it seemed strange for a vice president of Mother's beloved Republic to be on some New Jersey sandbar killing a man like Hamilton, I didn't give it much thought, and it was only years later that I knew it had been over some sort of political quarrel in New York state.

Despite a general dislike of Hamilton in our part of the country, everybody thought the whole affair mighty bad. Mother said it was no way to be rid of someone you disliked.

"After all's said and done with," she said, "Hamilton did fight bravely in the same war as your pap and I to make this fine Republic."

There was something about Aaron Burr that made my mother uncomfortable. Just the mention of his name could bring on a whole day of irritability. Because of that, Burr was a man I despised before I ever saw him or knew anything about him. When Mother was very cranky with me, I'd say to myself, She must be thinking about that Burr man who had a Penobscot Abenaki Indian wife at one time.

Mother took every opportunity to say something cutting about Burr and the Indian woman he'd taken to Quebec. For some reason, she resented the idea, which I thought strange in view of her having taken a white man husband. But with Mother, you never had to worry about a lack of contradictions.

And so now, there came a Mr. Creigor McCallum. I was not at all interested in Mr. Creigor McCallum and the fact that he was from New Orleans and had stopped in Cincinnati to talk with my mother about a venture in the manufacture of shoes.

Nor was I at all interested in the strip of hide Mr. Creigor McCallum brought, which he had said came from a bayou alligator, of which he said Louisiana had an abundance, both alligators and bayous, and that boots made from this kind of leather would be handsome and might be expected to develop large profits.

However, I was intensely, almost frantically interested in something else he brought. His daughter, Sarah.

From the moment I walked into my mother's sitting room and saw her standing beside the chair in which her father sat, I was lightheaded. Nothing had ever affected me like the sight of her wide blue eyes and the cornsilk curls of hair spiraling down from all round the lace trim of her bonnet.

Mr. Creigor McCallum introduced her, adding she was twelve years old and already a lady, and Mother said I was her eldest son, and this astonishing creature walked across the room and smiled and curtsied. I had never been so embarrassed and at the same time delighted as Mother told me "Make a leg, Campbell," and I bowed as General Putnam had taught Hiram and I to do when we were hardly out of the cradle.

"How do you do?" said this Sarah McCallum in a tiny voice that rang in my ear as though it were the most delicate Christmas bell west of Philadelphia.

"All right, I reckon," I blurted. "How's yourself?"

The child turned her head slightly, her eyes still on me, and said, "Very well, thank you, sir."

At that moment, standing awkwardly in my mother's house, I knew that I would risk whatever was necessary, welcome whatever pain I need endure, slay all the dragons who might come before me just to have that face with its teasing little smile a part of all the years left in my life.

It startled my mother when I took so willingly to the suggestion by Creigor McCallum that I accompany his daughter to the kitchen so that as they discussed making shoes from alligator hides, Sarah could introduce me to the wonders of pecan pie.

They had brought a large bag full of the nuts, shaped like tiny brown watermelons, and as I watched enthralled beside my mother's cast-iron stove, the astonishing girl made a pie right before my eyes.

From dough to shelling the nuts to mixing the sorghum filler to placing the pans, two of them, in the oven. All the while, Sarah was talking faster than Judith Dwyer in her bell-tone voice as I stoked the fire in the stove, making it hot enough to roast a hog, it seemed to me.

I can't recall saying a single word. I do recall the sounds issuing from her pink, moist mouth, not any of the words, just the sounds. And I recall at least twice when our hands touched.

Well, I do recall one word she said often. *Pecan.* How she pronounced it: p-*Khan!* Like a little French girl in a little French kitchen speaking a little French word: p-*Khan.*

P-*Khan!*

Of course, I knew she wasn't French. She was a Scot, like my pap. But that word had a spell to it. For all my life after the day spent making pies in my mother's kitchen, I was ready to fight anyone who pronounced it *pee-can,* as though it were a chamber pot under your bed at night. It was an insult to my delicate, lovely Sarah.

The pies were delicious, of course, but it wasn't until later, when Mother made one from the recipe Sarah left with her, that I realized it. On the night we ate Sarah's pies, I was incapable of tasting anything.

Creigor McCallum returned from their lodgings next day for a final word with Mother, but the bastard didn't bring Sarah, saying she was packing their baggage for the trip home. I was ready to run down the hill to Judith Dwyer's inn, violating Mother's current ruling that we not go near there, but McCallum stayed only a few moments, speaking with Mother on her promontory briefly, then away.

It was raining so hard that day that I wasn't even able to wave to their keelboat as it passed beneath the bluff and on toward the Mississippi.

I retired to the stalls in Mother's new horse barn and lay in the hay and contemplated the prospect of suffering the agony of a broken heart for the rest of eternity.

It was still raining when Hiram came in giggling and winking at me. He had not been unaware of my behavior at supper the night before and now decided it was time for a bit of teasing.

"Mother thinks Otto Black is making calf eyes at Clariese," he snickered. "Until you showed her what calf eyes are when the calf's sick with glanders or something."

"Why don't you shut your big mouth," I mumbled.

"Now I tell you, Campbell, that towhead girl, I bet she got some *real* huckleberries on her titties. If she and her pap ever come back, I'm gonna get her sweet little butt in the chicken coop and . . ."

I don't know what he was about to say. He never finished it because that's when I hit him with my fist, right across the front teeth. I was a fury. I hit his face until he was bleeding, and it wasn't until later I realized he was hitting back because I was bleeding as bad as he was.

We might have gone right on hitting and scratching and gouging and kicking and biting except that we stumbled, lurched, and crawled outside where we could be seen from the house.

I'll tell you what I believed. I believed Mother saw us a long time before she stopped it. I believed she just let us fight, like Hiram said, noting my condition the night before and my forlorn face on this morning, and maybe she figured a good scrap might clear my head.

It was only when Hiram and I started calling each other some of the choice obscenities you could hear every day on the riverfront that Mother ran out into the rain and grabbed us and dragged us onto the back galley and made us sit there most of the afternoon so we wouldn't bleed on her clean, swept sand floors.

Maybe the fight did help clear my head. At least, the day never came again when I was so hip deep in gummy, gooey, reason-shattering love. Maybe it made me take a deep breath and get things in perspective enough anyway to recollect the nature of Mother's expression after Creigor McCallum's short talk to her on the promontory.

She looked grim.

Before I slept that night, nursing a swollen lip and an aching jawbone, I guessed that the New Orleans Scot had more to talk about than swamp alligators. I sensed Aaron Burr intruding on that conversation.

It turned out I was right.

Chapter 11

January of 1805 was a dismal time. There were the usual snowfalls and wintery blasts of cold air down from the Great Lakes and Canada. But it was more than the weather.

Hiram was sullen and hateful, still nursing a grudge about the fight we'd had and I suspect waiting for a chance to bushwhack me.

Mother was morose, sitting for long hours beside her river-view window looking down on the dreary gray landscape and sometimes saying aloud that she knew Pap needed her and she should have gone with him. Feeling low.

Even with Ohio now a state, just like Kentucky and Tennessee and Vermont and all those early ones on the East Coast. I knew she'd been waiting anxiously for our part of the country to have equal standing with those original thirteen, the damned English colonies she called them, yet now that it had happened and we had a legislature and elections for governor and sheriffs and all the trappings, her spirits were too low to be reached.

The intensity of Mother's feeling about our statehood and frequent eastern opposition to it was obvious in what Clariese called the paste-up wall. From time to time, Mother would tear an item from the Fort Pitt newspaper and paste it to her kitchen wall near the wood box. These were items she felt confirmed easterners' low opinion of us out here in the Northwest Territory, and often she would stand at her stove preparing a meal and reread the clips and hiss like an ill-tempered snake.

One such report was a statement of the New York politician Gouverneur Morris. When asked if states west of the mountains should be admitted with equal status to the original thirteen, he said no!

"The interior would not be able to furnish men equally enlightened to share in administration of our common interests," he said. "The busy haunts of men, not the remote wilderness, is the proper school of political talents!"

This item had the honor of being more hissed than all the others combined.

So when Mr. G. Morris and all the other eastern naysayers were rebuked and western states were allowed into the Union as equal partners, it should have brightened Mother's eyes. It didn't, which was a measure of her melancholy in that time.

I felt a warm kinship with Mother then. I wouldn't think of mentioning it, of course. But there she was, despondent that her love was away, and there I was, my love away, too, in New Orleans or some such damned place, making pecan pies, I supposed, while her pap waved a hunk of big lizard skin over her head, shouting all the while about boots, boots, boots.

Love. A strange thing. Maybe because the word was not uttered in our house that I can recall except when Pap said "I love pork chops" or something like that. So we didn't talk about it. We just had it. Like an unmentionable disease.

The only one who was constantly delighted was Clariese. Every time Otto Black came mooning around, which was almost every evening. It made the rest of us sick. Well, not Mother.

I assumed that none of my reports on Otto had been destructive so Mother could reconcile herself to Otto Black, employee, soon becoming Otto Black, son-in-law, without too much resistance.

Then we got the big, fat letter from Pap. That should have made Mother happy, but it had the opposite effect.

A keelboat master brought the thing up the bluff to her, and she immediately closeted herself and was out of sight for two hours, reading and rereading. Well, it was pretty long. You could see that from the size of the package. It was hard to imagine Pap composing such a document.

Finally she appeared, looking grim, and lay the letter on the kitchen table and said I could read it, and the other children, too, if they wanted.

Then she returned to her room, and we didn't see her again until suppertime. That night she fed us cold meat from a venison haunch one of the town hunters had brought to us a couple of days previously; I'd cooked the whole thing over an open fire in the rear of the barn for just this kind of occasion when Mother didn't feel up to cooking.

Clariese never cooked anything. She was the only one of us who could get out of doing any chore around the place. Even little Gance was responsible for keeping the wood box filled.

But the letter. It wasn't easy reading. After Pap died, I took the letter and had it transcribed with all his unique spellings. Sometimes he spelled the same word differently within the space of a few lines. As for proper names, most of the tribal names became known to me over the years, and I substituted those for Pap's version.

Also, I paragraphed in certain places so the writing would make easier reading. Pap used not a single paragraph in the entire manuscript. Capitals scattered without rhyme or reason; no period in all of it. My God, for somebody like Pap, writing must have been a great adventure full of quicksand and briar patches.

Even with changes I made, reading it years later, it still has the odor and essence of Pap about it, like one of his buckskin woods jackets just hung on a wall peg outside Mother's bedroom door in the first moments of his return from the deep wilderness.

His words made me see his face in my mind, a big grin showing off that outlandish gap between his front teeth.

ole gurl, here i be in Saint Lewis they sent me back here from thair winter camp becuz cap Clark sez my laigs is so Bad now with roomatiz i aint no use to the expodeshun no more all that wade around in cold Water when we was on the way to Quebec and some since has caught up and the ole Bones has turned again me so here I be in general Wilkinson's Hous in Saint Lewis generul Wilkinson is governor around here and still a general in the army and he was with ole hawk face Gates at saratoga which same makes him a piss Ant but anyway now he is all rite I expect so he is Lettin me stay here with his man Mendez who is a spanyard and becuz i be with Lewis and Clark at first and they ast me all these things about it generul Wilkerson when he be here and Mendez all the time When generul Wilkerson aint

Cap Lewis and Cap Clark was enlistin men for their Scout when i got here Me and cap Clark recollected times we Fit the Shawnee and Miami with Mad Anthony Wayne and he is a smart man and a Frontier man and a dam good soldier and cap Lewis is even Smarter I reckon but he be hard to talk to sometimes and acts like he got belly ache a lot or something but he be one dam Fine soldier too and both of them officers is brave enough to bite a two edge ax on a frosty Mournin

cap Lewis got a big Black dog he calls Scammon and i guess he is Welsh from his name I mean cap Lewis not the dog cap Clark is Red headed and he got a slave named York who made me recall Young Bone Trudeau because he is strong and friendly and mighty Handy to have on the river

they was formin up a Regular army company with all the discipline and drill you would xpec and they called that the Detachment and then they Hired a red savage lingo man to help them talk to tribes we would meet and a hunter and they hired me on as a Hunter too and by early may we was ready cap clark got the boats in the Water just acrost the Missip From Saint Lewis we pick up cap Lewis on far side he be in town for Biznes it took ten days to shake out the Kinks and get into the Mouth of the Missouri above Saint Lewis with 27 Regular army men and three of us scouts and York and the dog in a nice big Keel boat with three swivel cannons and about three dugout Canoes cap Lewis called perogs and Three horses we took in the keel boat or rode along the banks Whichever Worked but one died right off of scours or something

That Missouri is a snake of a river twist and turn so Brown water like a Boilin pot snags and sand bars hid and banks all cave in and Heavy Hardwood timber close on each bank Skeeters bad and lotsa water mockasin snakes try to come right in the boat with you and it rained all the time cap Lewis Writin in his big book in boat cabin cap Clark done some writin but he was mostly Just tryin to get the boats up that Dam River

one of the Men who knowed the river sez maybe when we on the Missouri before she Heads North we might see some Osage and they was big powerful men but we never seen any but I expect They seen us

we come out of the Hardwood jungle at the mouth of the Kansa River and there was not many Trees the Missouri turned due north Here we started seein traders comin Downstream with their fur catch of the Winter they was scruffy Lookin men with Big beards and the first one i seen i figured was a hairy Beest he had two squaws with him and a boy cap Lewis and cap clark talked with Him a long time about tribes and what was Happening on the River

there was bufler now in the Praire and trees of any Size got scarser and scarser me and Other hunter out on the bank each day gettin meet and they was plenty we seen a lot of Red savages here, Otos and some Missouri and we found out there warnt many Missouri left and We seen Pawnees who are supposed to be mean Indians but cap Lewis and cap Clark stands right up to them and these people live mostly on Bufler Meet

we found out the smal pocks had killed a lot of Indians out here at diffrunt Times and they got the Usual wars with each other that kills a few

there Is The same thang Happening along this river that was done on the St. Lawrence the Tribes are fightin each other all the Time to see who will control the fur trade so first one outfit then another Closes the river and wont let nobody go up or down past them so they can control it a tribe called Arikaras far upstream Who was supposed to be the bad ones for a long time but now a new bunch is comin Down from the lake country run out of there from wars with the Chippewas and these are called the meanest savages on the Missouri and keepin the River closd to everybody they remind me of the Mohawks and are called Sioux

this country Here can make a mans eye go to sleep when its wide opun from all the flat land like you was in a dish plat and lookin in All direkshuns and sometimes you cant tell where the sky starts and the land stops you get to starin acrost the country and Heat waves wrinkle thangs and the sun crinkles up a mans eyes and makes me feel like i ant nuthin but a spek of Dust blowed by the wind that never stops and you thank its all flat and right in front of you there comes up a whole herd of bufler that was hid in a swale and They might just as easy be Hostile savages right on top of you before you know it

i be along the bank on Horsback after meet for us and see more of the land than them Men who is always on that dam keelboat all the tribes we see cap lewis and cap clark Talk to them and one of the Things President Jefferson said he wanted was to Have peace out here so cap Lewis and Cap Clark are tryin to get a council together somewheres and the tribes are sendin out Word to everybody to come its across the river from Where the Platte comes in from the west

Cap Lewis sez all these tribes has been tradin with one another for a long time trade goods Has moved backards and forth and even the Sioux trade with other tribes for a While Then fight them for a while and steal their horses and women all the time cap Lewis sez

we seen Kickapoos down south clos to mouth of the Kansa and sinse then we seen Omaha and Poncas and Aribara but the ones we are waitin for is the Sioux some of these tribes like to fight the Sioux and they all do some-times but some of Them are afraid of the Sioux because they are Feerce fighters and theys so many of them

cap clark sez these people we see now are planes tribes they all ride Horses and they Have more dogs than you ever seen and they fix their Hair all kind of ways they live in what they call teepee Poles set together like a cone and buffalo Hides laid over them none of them has any guns yet maybe a few but guns is one of the big thangs they want from fur traid and want Whiskey and guzzle it down fast to get drunk and have visions

cap lewis sez We Aint gonna give these Indians much Whiskey only sometimes like a special thang if they be good and cooberade

it was July when we come to the mouth of the Platte the water was Dark brown just across the river was High cliffs and we had this meeting there with many of chiefs So cap Lewis named the place Council Bluff where we spent some time Talking with Indians and hearing more about the Sioux closing the river another hundurd mile or so to the north

Time to tell some other thangs besides about red savage tribes the Game was all over the place so we et very nice and we had one man Die of the stomach colic and we had a man deserted and cap Lewis and cap Clark sent me and another man back downriver to catch him His name was Reed and I wondered if he was related to any of them Reeds I come from Ulster with

we cotched Reed short of the Mouth of the Kansa he Had two Otos with him and they run like scalded cats when we come up With our rifles ready to shoot they was on a sand bar butcherin a Calf buffalo Reed never offered much fight to speek of except once he tried to get a hatchet to swing on us with so we tole him if he dint behave his self we was gonna brake his arms

We et most of the calf Reed had been dresin And Reed et his fare shair the Otos never come bak

Cap Lewis held a court martial with cap Clark and three of the men sittin in judgement and they Could have shot Reed for desertion but they didnt they give Him three times Along the gaunlet so all the regular army enlisted men made two lines but us Hunters couldn't be in it and Reed Run along between the lines three times and the men was Swingin these heavy leather belts at him and they tuckered Him out real good by the time he run along the Gaunlet three times after that Reed was sent back to Saint Lewis with a passing trapper without no pay or any rifle or anything else and Dam lucky cap lewis didn't have him Shot

they had your ole Sargent Bobby a vetern horse rider by then out on Hunts like a regular genrul or somethang but now was When I had to help getting the keel boat along so I waded a lot of cold water and started the Rumatiz in my knees an ankals sos i cudnt hardly walk no more

We come to a river they called the James and seen our first Sioux they was Yankton Sioux and pretty meek according to What we'd Heerd they was and after a good talk and a lot of notes made in the Books, cap Lewis said we'd go on then at Bad River we seen the Teton Sioux and these were the mean ones they was a lot of them and they was riding Horses and making a real show for us

ever trader we'd seen and Most of the tribesmen said these was the savages who Pushed them around and Kept the river closed and bullied everybody so cap Lewis had a few chiefs on Boat and talked and gave them some Presents and some whiskey when cap Clark went in one of our dugouts to take the chiefs back to the bank, a bunch of the braves grabbed the boat and said the presents from the White Father was cheap and the English had always give them Better truck and they taken the mistooken notion they could Bully cap Clark he whipped out His sword and the soldiers with him up with their pieces all Fire locks Cocked so the Sioux backed off and said they was just joshin

next Day cap Lewis went on the Bank and talked and gave some more presents and the Sioux started Shovin and kickin up a fuss again and cap Lewis Whipped out his saber and cap Clark lit a match and was pointin the swivel guns at the Sioux and everybody knew them guns was loaded with Scrap arn and cap clark sent a dugout with twelve soldiers ashore and they come onto the bank with their weapuns ready and moved rite at them Sioux and them Sioux backed down again and cap Lewis got on the boat and Come back

so they Backed down again and cap Lewis sez to send two chiefs out to the boat and They did and cap Lewis sez We was going upstream and the cheifs sez they wouldn't allow that and cap Lewis sez if Anybody tried to stop us the first Sioux to go to their spirit Land Would be the

chiefs on that boat So they backed down again and cap
Lewis Told them they better stop making war on everybody and tryin to close the River or the Great Father
would send a whole bunch of people even meaner than
Him and cap Clark and the chiefs sez they would sure do
everything and was Lyin in their teeth but anyway We
Went upriver and the Sioux found out they was men they
couldn't Bamboozle and bully

you could sure tell the word about us backin down the
Sioux went ahead of us up that River all the Tribes we seen
after that was bowin and Scrapin and the ones who was
worst enemies of the Sioux almost Fell all over theirselfs
tryin to do nice things for us and puttin on Shows with
their dances and hors ridin tricks

It was comin on the end of Septembur so we went as
fast as we Could at the Grand River or the Heart i forget
which we seen the Arikara or Rees who sez they heerd
we'd made Women out of the Sioux this was the bunch
Who had been closing the river to Traders but seemed
pretty tame now but said they and their cousins the Crows
were fightin the Sioux all the time

then we come to the mouth of the Knife River and
where the Missouri bends back due west and there was the
Mandan towns they was big friendly Indians and light skin
and lived in log and Mud domed houses big as a Mohawk
long house only shaped round like a Wheel and they had
palisades and Had been having a Good time fighting the
Sioux but they was far outnumbered they Said the Sioux
had only a short time Ago started coming down from the
northeast close to Lake Superior and Crossing the river
and going out onto the planes

this was a different kind of place we been in the last
month no trees xcept on streem lines wind Here like a knif
even in just October plenty to Eat and Everybody busy
building Winter camp and a lot of Indians and trappers in

cap Lewis and cap Clarks hut all the time them talkin and writen talkin and writen here they was a trapper with two Indian women his Name Charbonay and he sez he been all the way up the Missouri and to the rock Mountains Beyond

Cap Lewis and cap Clark hired this Charbonay so Him and his Wives part of expadishun now One of his wifes was a Shoshone a tribe of the Rock mountains and her Name was Sacajawea

well that little woman remined me of you ole gurl when you was with that pack of mighty mean men going to Quebec and them other times and I sure hope this Sacajawea is as good luck for cap Lewis and cap Clark as you was for me

i was not long for it then and my legs got so bad i had to come back and i come With this Mendez who had been doggin our party all along and said he was a Spanyard trader he was the one Taken me to Generul Wilkinson and now is stayin here along with me and him and wilkinson talk a blue streek when they get together

cap lewis had me brang a bunch of what he called specimens back to Saint lewis in two sacks to send on to president jefferson they was plants and some small game hides and leaves and that kind of truck that president jefferson tole cap 1 to collect on his way

the generul and Mendez sure ask a lot of questions and they say the Spanyards in Sante Fe are interested in what cap Lewis and cap Clark is doin and I even heerd One say maybe they better write the Spanyards and have them send out a Bunch of soldiers to turn back cap Lewis and cap Clark which i took as mighty strange

Generul Wilkinson comes in to me and sez him and Aaron Burr the vice president is About to form up a new Country of everything west of the Appalacians and all down into Texas because it is all too big for one government to Handle and that president Jefferson knows all about it and thanks its alrite already Have troops and boats and truck at this Ballestero Island and I wondered if that is the same ballestero we know about and he sez the British are in on their plan and so is the Spanyards and all think it is a fine idea

You are the one who knows politics ole gurl but this sure sounds strange to me you Might want to send Campbell up the Ohio to see about this Ballestero Island thang and before i forget the Generul sez they are still Gettin up money for this new country and likely he'll Come by to see you because he sez everybody Knows you are a fine citizen of Cincinnati

well that about whips the Dog so will quit i ought to be home in early summer meantimes I am eatin like a lard class hawg give my greeting to children if you send Campbell on that airund be sure he's bought hisself a good Pennsylvania rifle Rob't Chesney Decembur 7 1804

It was easy to see why my mother looked so grim after she'd read Pap's letter with that mention of Aaron Burr. For almost three days, our house was deadly quiet, and I knew Mother was thinking and maybe not very happy thoughts, so we all stayed clear of her.

I was almost seventeen years old, which in that time was considered the start of manhood, so it was easy to find business at the shoe shop or Mother's little land office she'd established with a man named Carter Purcell, a surveyor and friend of General Putnam who Mother had hired to run her still active real estate sales enterprise.

Carter Purcell said the distribution of land was so important that half our laws dealt with real estate in one way or another, so learning that trade was as good a place as any to start being an adult male in the new state of Ohio.

I became rather expert in reading plats and locating tracts Mother still owned, even the ones a considerable distance out in the woods.

Many times Carter Purcell was out of the land office with his surveying equipment verifying property lines on sales so I was left alone to show any prospective customers the maps and charts we kept laid out on plank-sawhorse tables in the office.

The government had established a land office in Cincinnati by then, and we were next door to it. There were many times when the people there gave us first option on a particularly good piece of property when it became available through new surveys or mortgage foreclosures or public land where squatters had been run off by the sheriff. We got this kind of treatment because of Mother's special relationship with General Putnam, who had organized the local government sale of land and put his own people in its land office.

We did a brisk business buying as well as selling. The money came out of the leather pouch Pap had first used to carry that English gold. The gold was long since gone, but now it was replaced by new coin or letters of credit or notes issued by one bank or the other. Now and then, I'd see that pouch when Mother brought it out to her sitting room table, but I had no idea where she hid it in her bedroom. If indeed her bedroom was where she did hide it. She may have carried it around under a smock or skirt or some such thing that ladies wear.

There were any number of state banks scattered around Ohio, but Mother would never trust her money to any of them.

It was on a cold February day about a week after we got Pap's letter when Clariese came for me at the land office. She was red-faced from the cold but also because she'd run all the way, and she said Mother wanted me at her house, and right now.

I started to complain that I was alone there, Carter Purcell being upriver for one reason or another, but Clariese said I'd better fan it up the bluff because there were two men there to see Mother and she was staying back in her kitchen and making them wait until I got there. And that one of the men sitting right now in my mother's house was Aaron Burr!

There was snow on the ground, and I fell twice running up the bluff.

There was not much of that afternoon left that I recall clearly. Aaron Burr was a frail man, it seemed to me, darkly handsome perhaps, but with lips a little too elaborately etched like a cupid's bow beneath a rather prominent nose. His eyes were memorable, black and darting, never still.

His companion, General James Wilkinson, was a great blob of a man, red cheeked, red lipped, red eyed, and sending out waves of whiskey fumes into all corners of my mother's house.

They both wore black, shin-length boots, cloaks with high collars, which they had not removed when Mother and I came into the room, and tricorn hats which they had removed as they entered and were greeted by my sister while Mother hid in the kitchen.

I recollect that at the time I wondered what they must have thought, no sooner my sister ushering them inside than she disappeared and they were alone until she had had time to get me from town and likely my mother peeking at them through a curtain that hangs across the kitchen door.

Mother sat. The rest of us stood, me behind Mother's chair, Burr and the general before her, doing their leg dragging and bowing, and I thought the general wheezing and puffing a little more than was necessary as he slapped his hat, which had a white plume, against his leg.

They dropped the horrible news on us immediately, there really being no other way they could have done it.

"Mrs. Chesney," Aaron Burr said. "We come on grievous assignment with unfortunate tidings."

"Your husband was a hero of the Revolution," General Wilkinson said. "I knew him and treasure our mutual accomplishments in the Great and Glorious Cause!"

I knew something was coming that would turn the room cold, and

Mother did, too. She rose slowly, until she was at her full height, taller than either of the men before her. Her voice was icy.

"I did not know you treasured him," she said. "Why are you here now? What are these unfortunate tidings?"

Both men started to speak, then stopped and looked quickly at one another, then started again, and the general was obviously embarrassed. Burr cleared his throat and patted a white lace handkerchief against his lips, and I saw his long fingers and thought of them holding the pistol that had killed Alexander Hamilton.

"Mrs. Chesney," Aaron Burr said, "I most humbly regret to report that your husband has passed on to his great reward."

"His *what*?" Mother snapped loud enough to make General Wilkinson jump.

"He is dead, Mrs. Chesney," Aaron Burr said, and I heard Clariese behind me gasp.

"He was a guest in my home in St. Louis," said General Wilkinson. "A terrible sickness contracted undoubtedly on the absurd scout of the Missouri River ordered by the president overtook him, and in the still of the night he was taken with a wild delirium and rushed from my house and to the river and ran onto the ice and the ice gave way beneath his weight and he disappeared into the flowing stream.

"My trusted servant ran after him, but in your husband's fevered madness he was too fast to be caught up to and was gone beneath the ice."

"You have my most profound sympathy, Mrs. Chesney," said Burr.

"My trusted servant did all . . ." General Wilkinson did not complete his sentence but stared at my mother's face.

Then she turned, and I saw her eyes and knew why the general had stopped. I had never seen such a fire of hatred as burned in my mother's eyes. When she spoke to me I am sure no one in that room except myself heard her words.

"Get these white men out of my house."

And she walked slowly past me, past Clariese and into her bedroom and shut the door. Clariese gave a short sob and turned and rushed from the room, and I heard from the kitchen a yelp of disbelief from Hiram and then the broken sobs of Gance and knew Clariese had blurted out the terrible news.

In those moments after Mother left the room, my world seemed shattered with the dreadful news the two men had brought, and my memory of what took place came from a blur of images mixed and changing places as the years went down.

Recalling it, I somehow had the distinct impression that I was shooing chickens from the room, as indeed I had often actually done, arms outstretched on either side, making some sort of clucking sound but in fact, I expect, explaining that under the circumstances we were not fit to entertain.

They went willingly enough, but talking with each step, and fragments of their words returned to me at various times over the succeeding weeks. Aaron Burr was saying something about the grand design for a new republic west of the mountains. Wilkinson was saying something about the scheme needing funds and everyone knowing the Chesneys would be willing and able to support such a cause.

Hard as it had been for me to credit what Pap had written, I now realized that these people were in fact making plans to have every state west of the Appalachian Mountains break away from the United States and form the core of a new confederacy that would reach to New Orleans and maybe all the way to Texas.

It was money they wanted, of course, and laying on a thick coating of soft soap, telling me how much value a young man like me would be. I recall, too, the general saying that I was now man of the family and this was good because my mother, being a woman, could not possibly understand such matters as new empires and the proper use of money in obtaining them.

Later, when my grief and disbelief with Pap's dying had passed, I had to laugh at that and was amazed at myself, even under the circumstances, for not having said something to the effect that my mother in such matters could likely teach them a few things.

Incidentally, I never mentioned that part of it to Mother, even though she later insisted that I remember everything and tell her. It was better, I thought, for everybody's safety, if she were not informed that Aaron Burr and his puffing, red-faced whiskey soak Wilkinson thought her less than any white man in affairs of money.

Anyway, I drove the chickens from the room and saw them off down the bluff in the snow, General Wilkinson still talking furiously, leaning toward Burr and waving his plumed hat about. Burr walked as though about to leap over a wide ditch, each stamp of his booted feet against the ground throwing up plumes of dirty snow.

Once during that dismal afternoon, Clariese went into my mother's room. None of us boys had the nerve to go near. Mother came out after almost an hour, dry-eyed and with a purpose, it seemed, and told us to hitch our team to the sleigh.

We had bought a pair of Kentucky horses and a small hack that Mother used to get about Cincinnati and the countryside during good weather and a small sleigh for snow seasons. Hiram and I went to the barn and took Gance with us to occupy him and maybe stop his continued blubbering.

That didn't work out too well. One of the horses bit him on the butt and he wailed like a wounded bear cub, so we sent him back inside where our sister could deal with him.

We drew the team and sleigh up close behind the house, and Mother was there almost at once and with the musket in her hands and told me to drive and told Hiram to stoke the kitchen stove fire under a pot of rabbit stew made the day before.

That musket. Taking Pap's advice in one respect at least, Mother had sent me to Able Steinhartz, the best gunsmith in Cincinnati, to buy a weapon. He had a shop along the river, sitting on property he had bought from my mother, and he was doing a wonderful business selling firearms to people traveling down the river toward the west.

"For hunting, is it?" Mr. Steinhartz asked.

"No," I said. "For personal protection."

"Gut," he said and brought out a weapon he had refitted and sawed off. It was a British Brown Bess flintlock with a barrel only twenty inches long and a bore of .79 inches so that you could load it with a pumpkin ball and half a dozen double aught buckshot or leave out the ball and tamp in a full dozen buckshot pellets.

"No charge," he said. "But my gift to your fine mama, and I throw in a bag of buckshot, too. Campbell, you load him with buckshot, but then don't you shoot him at no roof or next time it rain, you gonna have roof that leaks like hell!"

So Mother and I drove out along the Great Miami River road, her with the gun between her legs, each of us bundled in hair-on deerskin robes. We passed beyond the last of the buildings in the settlement and then into the country where there were a number of homesteads on the east side of the river along the road. On the far bank there was an unending wall of timber, mostly hardwood and bare branches now. There were many crows there fussing at the cold weather, and flitting overhead were what seemed hundreds of smaller blackbirds, the kind that enjoyed darting behind a crow in flight and pecking at the larger bird's head.

I let the team trot. Mother seemed in no great hurry. She said nothing until after we'd been on the road almost an hour and were beyond the last of the recently cleared fields and log houses and barns. It was getting dark when she told me to pull off into a stand of red cedar close by the river.

Once more without speaking, Mother handed me the musket and got out of the sleigh and walked down toward the Miami. She was soon out of sight among the low cedars. I had been sitting for what seemed a long time when I heard a moaning sound at first quiet as a whisper of wind through the evergreen needles.

Soon, the sound increased in volume, and I had the musket up because at first I thought it a wounded wolf or some such thing, and then I realized it was my mother.

I had never heard an aboriginal death song. It sent the gooseflesh up my back as the quavering notes hung in the cold, darkening air, without words, without substance almost, as though it was part of the snow and darkening shadows under the cedars. There was no rhythm to it, and even though at first it seemed discordant, very quickly there was some kind of vibrant, warm throb like blood pumping from a heart, each echo of it part and parcel of this whole wilderness, indistinguishable from it.

Soon, she was back, but even as she came into the sleigh and pulled a robe across her knees, I still seemed able to hear the sound of her chant back there beside the river, and as I whipped the horses out onto the road, we slowly left the sound behind, the quavering notes growing fainter, fainter in the darkness.

I shivered, not from cold. If I turned this rig around, I thought, I would hear the sound again as I drove back to the spot, growing stronger, stronger as we drew near. I shivered again. Because it was there, still, even though unheard. My mother had left it, that awful, dreadful, beautiful sound, like a gravestone, and it would always be there. I snorted, thinking how absurd such an idea was. Absurd!

As we rode back into the town, my mother spoke only once. And that, I expect, more to herself than to me, or maybe to whatever gods it had been to which she had made her chant.

"It wasn't right. Something did not feel right."

Well, maybe it wasn't right to my mother. But to me there was an unearthly sensation. For the first time in all my memory, there was what I imagined a surge of the Iroquoian-Erie and the Algonquian-Penobscot-Abenaki blood of my ancestry making fire in my belly.

By God, I kept thinking, I'm a red savage heathen barbarian. Just like her!

I had never felt closer to my mother. Nor have I since.

It has always been amusing to me, the way some folk spend

leisure time slicing up their heritage like a pie, so much of this, so much of that. Yet I have done a great deal of that myself.

I supposed always that I was one-quarter Abenaki, one-eighth Erie, one-eighth French, and one-half Ulster Scot. Only three-eighths American Indian to five-eighths European white.

Then why was it that after the trip we made to the edge of the wilderness outside Cincinnati so my mother could sing a death song, I was always blaming or crediting anything I did to the influence of my Indian bloodlines?

Nobody I ever knew could explain where Shawn Ballestero got all his money. But there was surely considerable of it, enough anyway for him to buy an island in the Ohio River near the mouth of the Little Kanawha that flowed north into the big river from Virginia. It had been named Ballestero Island, appropriately enough, and was about ten minutes downstream from the settlement of Marietta, where General Rufus Putnam had established his first Ohio Company land office.

That spring when Otto Black and I paddled upriver to get the lay of the land, as Pap would have said, we passed the island in a driving rain and saw little of it, but I guessed that it was more than a mile long and of substantial girth. Mother had suggested we visit General Putnam's office in Marietta before putting in an appearance at the island.

All of the people we found in the Ohio Company's office were strangers to me but of course they knew of my mother, and therefore we were accorded polite hospitality. Which meant a supper of hot pork loin roast with apple sauce and a chance to dry out before going back downstream. And a fat feather tick on a straw pallet, which Otto Black and I shared, unfortunately.

I say unfortunately because Otto Black was one of those people who combined sleep with a constant agitated motion somewhat like a cedar log caught in the raging water of a creek in spring flood.

Throughout the night, I was wakened by an arm slung across my face or a leg flopped across my butt.

It came to me that maybe I should warn Clariese about what she was getting herself into when she married this man. The thought of that made me chuckle so hard and long that Otto Black woke, sputtering and clawing around in the bedclothes for his pistol.

This pistol business. I had been against any armaments for this journey, but Mother insisted. At first, she wanted me to take the sawed-off Brown Bess, and I raised such a smell she relented, at least to the extent that I wouldn't look like a bear hunter as Otto and I made our way up and down the river.

So the next day I came home from the land office to find Able Steinhartz, the gunsmith, waiting with my mother in her sitting room. He had two beautiful weapons which he called the new Harpers Ferry pistols, flint firelocks, rifled bores of caliber .59 inches.

"Big enough for buckshot, too, you need it," he said.

Hiram and I shot the pistols that afternoon, blowing large holes in the side of the barn until Mother made us stop. Hiram was furious when I took both pistols on my trip, one in my own belt, one for Otto Black.

There was more than that, too. Mother dressed me out as a gentleman land speculator, I suppose. A high-crown narrow-brim leather hat, short coat, linen shirt, doeskin trousers and shin-length boots with the tops turned down. I felt as fancy as Aaron Burr himself, a comparison I certainly didn't make to my mother.

Thus accoutred, and even with a squire, Otto Black, I went forth like a knight in shining armor I thought, on the first quest my mother ever assigned me. To wit: find out what the hell was going on at Ballestero Island.

When we left Marietta, the sun was breaking through the clouds and it was a shining day. Foliage along both banks was thick from all the recent rain. It was glassy bright in the sunlight, and there was a scattering of flowering trees like the dogwood, the white blossoms still clinging in many places. It was a little late in the season for what some locals called bunchberry, but the larger flowering dogwood were in their prime.

Compared to the rest of the shoreline, Ballestero Island presented a pretty ugly face because of all the tents and log shacks and piles of what looked like lumber but turned out to be river rafts. There were a number of jury-rigged docks jutting out a short way into the river and evidence that a couple of them had been crumpled in a spring flood.

The claptrap appearance of the landing area was nothing like the other side of the island, where Ballestero had his big log house and where General Wilkinson and Aaron Burr stayed when they were visiting the place.

We had no opportunity to see if that were true so had to take the word of the man who met us at the dock, a burly, bearded man named Bertis Shoat. The beard looked out of place because most men in these parts still went clean-shaven in that time.

Mr. Shoat seemed to be the majordomo of this place and the greeter and the police force and the revenue collector and anything else required. Most of all, he seemed to be the man responsible for finding out in detail the business of anybody landing on the island.

He was friendly enough, but there was a cast about his eyes I didn't like, and I saw Otto Black holding a hand under his coat where I knew he carried the Harpers Ferry pistol.

There was a tent with the sides rolled up and under it slab lumber tables and benches and behind it a line of ovens and cook pots hung above open fireplaces formed with rocks and two wagons with all sorts of kitchen truck seeming to hang out of all sides.

There was a very fat man as bearded as Mr. Shoat and obscenely naked from the waist up, shouting orders to a number of black African slaves, I assumed, and they were just as naked as the white man. They all moved about the fires and pots and stacks of chopped wood preparing a meal, I assumed, although the only odor I could detect was that of a great many fish who had died a long time ago.

I also assumed the language this fat cook and his black Africans were using to communicate was supposed to be French, although it sounded only marginally like the speech between my mother and her father when he had come to Cincinnati to die.

At any rate, Mr. Shoat seated us under this tent, and one of the black slaves brought a large jug and three tin cups, and as he began his routine of questions, our host poured a generous quantity of amber-colored liquid into each cup, drank from one, slammed the cup down on the rough table, and exclaimed on the wonder of Kentucky whiskey.

Not wanting to offend, Otto Black and I did likewise, thereby nearly scalding any capability of speech from our throats. It didn't matter much because Mr. Shoat did a great deal of the talking himself.

When Mr. Shoat became aware of who we were, his mood went from a rather suspicious expansiveness to that of a secret ally including us in a glorious conspiracy.

"Aw yes, Mrs. Chesney," he said. "What will be her contribution to our cause?"

"That will depend on what news we brang to her of your progress here."

Whereupon Mr. Shoat described how men and arms were being collected here and in other places, locations which he was not at liberty to reveal. At Ballestero Island, as we could see, many rafts were being built which would float the expeditionary army down the Ohio and Mississippi to New Orleans, which would be taken without much trouble, there being few United States troops there and General Wilkinson being in command of those that were, and the British being in such accord with the movement that their squadron in the Caribbean would be standing by to assist, and the Spanish and French residents of Lower Louisiana being fully aware and in support, as well as the residents of Upper Louisiana, or Missouri Territory, where General Wilkinson not only was commander of all United States troops there but was territorial governor as well.

"Is Mr. Jefferson going to stand by and watch all this with any degree of calm?" I asked.

"Oh my," Mr. Shoat said and laughed and took another drink from his tin cup. "You know what Mr. Burr says."

"What does Mr. Burr say?" Otto Black asked and took another drink from his tin cup.

"Mr. Burr says that with a good regiment behind him, and we already have more than a few good regiments, he can run the president and the Congress besides right out into the Atlantic Ocean!" said Mr. Shoat, and he laughed some more and then lowered his voice and winked. "But everybody knows the president is well aware of what is happening here and is well disposed toward us because he knows what *we* know, that the country is too large to be a democracy and that no republic can be effective in trying to govern such vast spaces and such different peoples."

"I hadn't heard what kind of government Mr. Burr might be thinking about," I said.

At once, Mr. Shoat resumed his suspicious attitude, squinting at me, his lips working without words, and color coming to his cheeks.

"It's a thing my mother would be interested in knowing before she invests," I quickly added, and the comment regained some lost ground. But he was still a little suspicious, I suspected.

"Before she invests," Otto Black blurted and took another drink.

So with some hesitation, Mr. Shoat started talking about a confederacy of separate provinces that would elect a leader, Mr. Burr of course, much as they did in the Holy Roman Empire.

I didn't know much about the Holy Roman Empire except that in the newspaper out of what was now being called Pittsburgh I recalled something about Napoleon abolishing it. Well, one other thing. I knew that its leader was called an emperor.

Emperor Aaron Burr! I could imagine the expression on my mother's face when she heard *that*.

There were other tidbits. General Wilkinson was on the island at this time but indisposed, and I said there was no need to disturb him, and Mr. Shoat giggled and said General Wilkinson refused to be disturbed anyway when he was having a bout with Kentucky whiskey and Virginia trollops, both of which were imported on a regular basis for General Wilkinson's pleasure.

Making polite excuses, we departed. Mr. Shoat instructed one of the Africans to assist me in getting Otto Black back to our dugout and then he disappeared quickly in the direction of the south side of the island, and I guessed he was going directly to General Wilkinson, despite Kentucky whiskey and Virginia harlot, to inform him that maybe they had Mrs. Chesney of Cincinnati on the hook for a large donation.

Well, it was perfectly obvious they'd been getting a considerable amount of money from someplace. I'd seen enough cut lumber on that island to build a small town, and I assumed all the people I saw were being paid, and thinking back I recalled seeing plenty of rifles or muskets in stacks before some of the tents and cabins.

I had little time to think of it at the moment. I had to handle that damned bulky oak log dugout by myself. Otto Black was lying in the bow, head hanging over the side, moaning and puking.

"Those lying English swine!"

"Mother, they're not English. One is the highest-ranking officer in the army of the United States and the other was only recently vice president of the Republic."

"Have I borne a son who is so addled that he thinks what these people are up to is something President Jefferson knows about and agrees with?"

"All right," I said, "it must be that they are surely lying. And they are traitors. But they aren't Englishmen."

"They are in cahoots with the English. You said they told you so."

"Well, this Shoat told me so. And with the Spaniards, too, which makes sense because the Spaniards are not too happy I guess with Mexico being cheek by jowl with our Louisiana Territory. They'd feel safer if it was just a bunch of separate provinces, as Shoat called them."

"Being in cahoots with the English makes just as much sense," Mother said. "The English want to see a weak Republic south of the St. Lawrence and the Lakes. General Putnam has told me the English do not even recognize President Jefferson's purchase of Louisiana."

"All right. And Mr. Jefferson doesn't know about all this as they say he does, because if he did he would be throwing a cat hissy fit! But Wilkinson and Burr are not English, they are Americans, which makes it worse."

"It makes them traitors!" she said.

"That's the right word."

"Then we've got to stop it, don't we?"

My God! Maybe losing Pap and now this Burr business have set Mother's mind off its proper course. In that instant, sitting there in our kitchen drinking sassafras tea, just the two of us, the horrible thought went through my mind that now Mother was going to send me and Otto Black off with those new pistols to assassinate an army general and a former vice president of the Republic.

Calmly considering it later, I did not find the prospect of shooting either of those two, or both of them, at all distasteful. In fact, there was a certain pleasure to be found in it. My red savage bloodline, I figured.

But at the moment, in my mother's kitchen, it was a momentously terrifying idea. But her next words set all that aside.

"We'll write a letter," she said.

"A letter? Who to?"

"Yes. A letter. To President Jefferson."

"What?" I gasped. That was almost as bizarre as the assassination idea. "He won't pay any attention to a letter from us. He doesn't know us."

"He won't know it's from us. It'll be one of those, how do you call it? *Anonymous.* Sure! An anonymous letter."

"To the *president*?"

"Yes. Get some paper and the quill, and there's ink on top of the kitchen safe. We'll write it and have General Putnam get it into the right hands," she said, and her eyes danced with excitement, as though she might be stalking game.

I guess she was.

For the Eyes of President Thomas Jefferson

Your Excellency:

The purpose of this letter is to acquaint you with a dastardly undertaking designed in its various parts to sever the states west of the Mountains from the Union, to create an independent country of the Louisiana Territory, to seize and hold New Orleans, to attack Mexico with the purpose of taking Texas from Spain to be a part of the aforementioned independent country, all with the connivance of certain Spanish and English citizens of this country. [Do we have to put in *English*? Put it in!]

Men, material, boats, arms, and ammunition are now being assembled along the Ohio River, and the writer thereof has been personally solicited for funds to further this cause.

The plan is to move this military force down the rivers to New Orleans and once that city falls to invite or force, as the case might be, the Purchase and Texas and perhaps Mexico to join the conspiracy for the formation of an empire.

The man leading this treason is former Vice President Aaron Burr. He is in this part of the country frequently to further his ends for he intends to be Emperor of the new country, made at the expense of our Union. [We don't

know if he'd call himself an emperor, maybe just president. Write *Emperor.* It sounds nastier.]

Your Obedient Servant and Citizen of Cincinnati and
always faithful to our beloved Republic. [We shouldn't say
Cincinnati because it makes it easy to find out who wrote
this thing if we do. All right, do it how you want and let me
see it.]

Your Obedient Servant

A Citizen of the Republic [All right? All right.]

The next day, as though on cue, General Putnam appeared for
one of his visits. After we all had a nice visit in Mother's sitting room,
she and the general went into the kitchen alone and we could hear
their low voices but not the words. When he came out, he looked
grim, and I knew Mother had given him his marching orders. To wit:
get this letter into the hands of Thomas Jefferson.

He was hardly out of sight when Mother grabbed my arm and led
me back to the kitchen and sat me down and placed a quill and ink
and paper on the table and told me to write a second letter, even
more strongly worded.

"What for?"

"If President Jefferson doesn't do something with that letter we
sent, we'll send one by somebody he can't ignore."

"Who?"

"Those two horses in our barn. Do you remember when I bought
them, the man who brought them here?"

"Yes, I remember him."

"Do you know where he is now? He's Joseph Daveiss, the United
States attorney for the district of Kentucky. I don't like him very
much, but he'll do a favor for me, especially if it might put a feather
in his cap.

"The next letter, we'll send to *him,* and he'll either have to prosecute somebody or take it to Mr. Jefferson."

Mother turned and marched out of the room, back straight, head up. At the door she paused long enough to look back at me, and there was that glint of mischief in her eyes.

"Pretty good for a red savage barbarian, don't you reckon? Your mouth's hanging open. Close it and write the letter."

Two days later one of the infamous Ohio Valley tornadoes ripped along the river, a black funnel cloud roaring from west to east. It knocked down a number of structures in Cincinnati, but most of the force was on the Kentucky side and a whole shantytown of buildings there was blown away before our eyes as we watched from Mother's promontory.

I was shocked to see that she was terrified of this storm. She clung to one of the huge oak posts holding up the porch roof, and her eyes were glassy as she watched the path of the swirling winds. It was a long time before she stopped shaking.

And it made me gleefully happy to see her trembling.

Well, for a moment, anyway. Then I was ashamed of myself and tried to think of a way to comfort her but couldn't.

My only defense was that I'd never seen my mother afraid of anything before.

There is no recollection of ever having seen her afraid of anything again, either.

Chapter 12

It was the time when Clariese Chesney became Clariese Chesney Black and moved with her husband Otto into a small log-and-clapboard-and-cedar-shingle house behind the shoe shop, a house built on my mother's property and with her money and sold to Otto Black, house and land on which it stood, for a total of eight hundred and fifty dollars, secured by promissory note held by my mother, payments to be made semi-annually at the rate of one hundred dollars plus eight percent interest compounded or on demand.

Mother included the on-demand stipulation so she'd have a club to hold over Otto's head in case she might feel, at some future date, the need to redirect Otto's conduct if he fell into what she perceived as unwholesome or extravagant habits harmful to her daughter's happiness and peace of mind.

"You don't need that," I said. "He works for you anyway. You could just threaten to fire him from his job if he doesn't blow his nose the way you think he ought to."

"Two clubs better than one," she said. "And don't think you're getting big enough to act the smart aleck with me. Sometimes, when you use all those smart-aleck white man's words, I am sorry I taught you to read. I am sorry the Quakers and the Jesuits and the Presbyterian missionaries taught any of us red savage heathen how to read and how to talk this smart-aleck English language."

"Mother, you speak this white man's English smart-aleck language better than any white man smart-aleck Englishman I know."

"I'm warning you! I'm warning you! Here I be in grief still over your pap, and you want to play with me."

"No, I don't want to do that," I said. "But if you are still grieving, when are you going to slash your arms with a knife the way red heathen savages are supposed to do?"

"I'm warning you. You know my people don't slash their arms when they grieve."

"Mother, how would I know that? You're the only one of your people I've ever known."

"Don't talk to me like those same people aren't your kin as well as mine. Well, I'll tell you this, the next time I go to the woods to speak with my gods, I'm taking Hiram or Gance."

"Don't take Gance. It would scare him to death."

I thought there was a hint of smiling in her eyes then. It seemed to me that Mother had begun to rather enjoy these little verbal sword fights we had, although she'd never have called them that nor admitted she enjoyed them.

Anyway, a wedding, and Otto Black wasn't interested in conditions. He was so goofy over my sister he would have agreed to anything just to have her.

It was a nice wedding, performed by the circuit rider Methodist parson in Cincinnati. Mother'd been attending his sermons for some time, having discovered certain things about the Presbyterians she disliked. The Methodists were a little looser, she said. They didn't much care what you believed so long as you attended services and sang loud and could read the white man's Bible.

She could do all of it, except that reading a Bible would require borrowing somebody else's copy because so far as I know, she never had one in her house.

Back in 1801 there had been a big outdoor religious revival meeting held in a place called Cane Ridge, Kentucky, not far south of
Cincinnati. Soon, these camp meetings were popping up all over. In
later years, they would call it the Great Reawakening.

The Cane Ridge thing had been Methodist, best as I can recall.
The Methodists were better at this revival business than anybody
else because they had a national and state and territorial organization. There was a bishop in Baltimore who was head of the whole
shebang.

It operated a lot like land speculation. Only instead of selling
land, the revivalists were selling salvation. Before long, churches
started sprouting in towns because local boosters, like my mother,
realized a town needed some religion if it was ever going to amount
to anything.

You could usually bet that the first three actual church structures
in a settlement were going to be Baptist, Presbyterian, and Methodist. And usually the Methodist church was built before there was a
resident preacher. When a circuit rider was not close by, services
were conducted by a layman of the congregation.

Later experience taught me that sometimes you could figure on
who had first settled a town by the place of its churches. If the town
was dominated by New England or New York Yankees, a church or a
cluster of churches would occupy the choice locations. In places
where the early folk were mainly Virginians, the central location was
marked by the courthouse.

Then there was another kind of town, like ours, where the important interest was business, so the central position was held by the
mercantile store, the overland coach depot, the land office, and later,
the post office.

Well, the wedding.

There was some dancing afterward on Mother's front-yard
promontory, it being nice weather with honeysuckle in bloom and
the scent of it overpowering the odor of spilled whiskey.

Otto was serious enough about it that he stayed relatively sober.
Hiram got drunk as a keelboat captain, which Mother overlooked,

but she was irritated that Hiram got little brother Gance drunk, too. Gance was eleven at the time.

Gunsmith Able Steinhartz roasted a pig, German style, which took two days, and Judith Dwyer, over her snit with Mother by now, brought a tub of potato salad, and Carter Purcell of the land office, his wife did a pot of chickpeas and venison. Everyone got plenty to eat and plenty of beer to drink, there already being a nice brewery in Cincinnati established just the year before by a man named Gunter, who was cousin to Able Steinhartz.

We had quite a little community of Germans in the town by then, and Mother liked them because they were clean and industrious and minded their own business. Any suggestion to her that the English had been Germans a long time ago and that their royal family still was sent Mother into a tirade about me making up fairy tales just to irritate her.

It was the time of less happy things, too.

The Aaron Burr people were still operating along the river, building up their expedition openly it seemed, and nobody doing anything about it. Most people in the Ohio Valley liked Burr, as I've said, maybe mostly because he had always been Alexander Hamilton's enemy. At the same time, as also noted, they were not too happy about the way it all ended on that New Jersey shore.

It made Mother furious that our letter to the president had brought no action. We had what we called Letter Number Two written and waiting, but thus far I'd been able to dissuade Mother from sending it to the U.S. attorney for Kentucky. The whole business made me feel foolish, even though I despised what Burr and Wilkinson were trying to do.

Now, because the Republic was trying to stay neutral in the continuing war between Britain and Napoleon, and both navies hampering and harassing our ships at sea, President Jefferson imposed an embargo on many things our people were selling to various overseas markets. The idea being to suggest the United States was really neutral and would deal with none of the belligerents.

Obviously, that was as popular as skunks in the kitchen, but like it or not, the only way to do much business anymore was through smugglers. Money was tight. Even the land boom had cooled down to an ember. All the way round, most of our people began developing a decided dislike for President Jefferson.

Jefferson's embargo didn't hurt Mother's many businesses much. So long as immigrants came. In 1802 the central government had authorized a national road. You could now load out a wagon in Maryland, drive it across the mountains and then all the way to the east bank of the Mississippi River at St. Louis without having to cut a single tree to make passageway.

Well, that was the plan, but it wouldn't be a fact for another ten years. Even so, a lot of people were westering overland on what they called the National Road.

The trace passed just north of Cincinnati. Anybody traveling that route paused and came into Cincinnati to resupply before passing on to Indiana Territory or the Grand Prairie in Illinois Territory.

Most still used the river all the way, but some came west to our town and left the river to go on overland.

Whichever way they chose, they all spent money in Cincinnati, and even in depression, the town grew.

We saw many kinds of people in those years. There were Episcopalians from old Virginia. Unitarians from New England. There were Catholics from Maryland. Quakers from eastern Pennsylvania. Many German sects from who knows where. The Moravians and Amish. And there were some Congregationalists and Baptists. Some Dunkards and Shakers.

A few of them stayed in Cincinnati to become craftsmen or merchants or laborers. By the time Clariese was married, we had half a dozen Catholic Irish and two Jews, a Swede, maybe a dozen freedmen blacks, and up the river from the south, we had a Creole family, and a Louisiana-born Spaniard.

All that in addition to the old settlers, who included a lot of Scots-Irish and Germans whose families had been in the country since before the Revolution.

"Where did all these people come from?" Mother asked. "Why don't they go on to St. Louis."

Even a good business in leather goods and matches couldn't brighten Mother's disposition. Her mood was mostly murderous at best. People in the town avoided her when she drove the team and buggy down the bluff road to see to her various enterprises. Nothing could be as stony as my mother's high-boned face when she set what appeared to be a permanent frown on it.

Then Hiram ran away from home. He was old enough to leave home and strike out on his own, but he did it by stealth, slipping away during the night, taking only a few of his clothes and one of the Harpers Ferry pistols.

Your guess is as good as mine as to why. He'd had a boil under his tail for a long time.

Now, surprisingly, Mother seemed deeply saddened by it. She didn't lose her temper, rave and rant, whip her horses too much. While he was home, Hiram could have been a stick of furniture for all the attention he got, but he'd been working in the shoe shop for a long time, seemed satisfied, and Mother hadn't been gouging him about anything.

But now that he was gone, she was saddened. I could tell from her face. A kind of despondency replacing the normal rage over the Burr thing.

And I knew she was saddened from what she said. Only once did she mention it, after supper one evening before she went to bed.

"Now he's by his ownself. Now he'll find how bad it can be out there when you're alone."

Maybe one of those Penobscot gods was whispering to her that she would never see Hiram again.

Then a wonderful thing happened.

Well, I thought it was wonderful. Mother didn't. It made her grumpier than ever. But at least, maybe it helped the pain for Hiram.

On a bright fall Sunday, Mother and I were sitting on her promontory discussing the establishment of a gunpowder works in Cincinnati, I saw coming up the bluff from town a tall man who looked familiar.

I only glanced at him once, and then all my attention was on the small figure hurrying along beside him.

It was Sarah McCallum!

Memory can be slippery ground. Just when I thought each detail of an important hour was forever fixed in my head, it shifted and changed and took on different colors. Each time called up, the image changed a little, unnoticed, until finally, what I took as truth was only the most recent version of what I suspected was true.

My first two meetings with Sarah McCallum were like that, and later I often wanted to ask somebody what she said, what I said. But there was no one to ask except her, and too much pride was involved for me to admit that with the passage of a relatively short time, I couldn't keep any of it straight because I was so fuzzy headed simply by being near her.

Oh, there were a few images real enough. Her father with a distraught expression drawing my mother into the house to speak with her and Mother going only reluctantly.

And my taking Sarah's hand, *taking* it, not just a casual touching as had happened when we made those pecan pies in Mother's kitchen. *Taking* it and drawing her to the far side of the promontory porch, to the log bench there, where one could sit and look across the river into Kentucky and see the sugar maples gone scarlet along a ridge, like a bright ribbon of silk lying on a carpet of the yellow and burnished brown leaves of the other hardwoods.

And talking, babbling more like it, about anything that came into my head, about the geese soon flying along this river toward the Mississippi and sitting in the dark and hearing them overhead.

And about the sounds of fox dogs racing in the timbered hills across the Ohio, their voices coming ghostly and making hair rise along the arms.

And about all the times I thought of pecan pie. And about anything that came to mind, as though afraid if I stopped for a single second, she might vanish.

Babbled like a fool, holding her hand in mine, until she said, "You're hurting my hand, Mr. Chesney," and I drew back as I might from a hot stove, and all the words rushing up stopped in my throat like a logjam in a flooded river, and I realized finally what a fool I was acting. She said, "I'm so sorry about your father, Mr. Chesney. We heard he'd passed on.

"That's why we're here," she said, looking as though she might burst into tears as she gazed out across the river toward Kentucky without seeing any of it, I suspect.

"Father does what they say, now. Going up and down these old rivers trying to get more money for Mr. Burr."

That brought me back to reality.

"General Wilkinson said now that she's in mourning, your mother would be distraught and likely more easily persuaded to contribute," Sarah said. "That's all he does, send Father on these errands for money, and Father has become so frantic.

"He sold everything he had in New Orleans and General Wilkinson used the money to collect all the things he needs for Mr. Burr's army, and all because Mr. Burr promised my father that he'd be made a high government official in Mr. Burr's country when they conquer Texas and maybe Mexico and of course all this here."

She waved her hand toward the river as she said it.

"He thinks my mother will give money to Burr because Pap is dead?" I asked. "Good Lord, my mother wouldn't give Aaron Burr a bucket if his house was burning. Don't they know that yet?"

"I don't know what they know. It's so frightening. We'll go back up the river now to that Ballestero Island place with all the flies and mud and dreadful, swearing men, dirty and hairy and always looking at me. Just like those people General Wilkinson hired to sail our keelboat up and down the river. Father doesn't even own the boat anymore. So it's not even our boat now, it belongs to Mr. Burr, and we have to pay him to use it, to raise money for his cause."

"You have no home where you can stay?" I asked.

"Father sold it. The boat is the only home we have until Mr. Burr gets his country, and then he's promised my father a home and servants and power in Mr. Burr's capital in Texas or New Orleans.

"Oh, there's one of those tiny, dirty log huts at the island that belongs to us, I suppose, but it's hardly a home."

"These people are actually serious about this new nation, aren't they?"

"Mr. Chesney, there are so many of them in it, and I can't make heads or tails of it. Father has met with General Wilkinson at the Spanish intendant's mansion at New Orleans. And with an English businessman living there. All in the dark of night and slipping about the city in a coach with the blinds drawn and whispers and passing packages back and forth.

"We don't even have money to buy me a dress, and I've been wearing these tacky things so long."

Until then, I had paid no attention, but now I saw that the cuffs of her shirtwaist were frayed and a button was missing from the front of the broadcloth bodice that so wonderfully emphasized the curve of her breasts.

"My father has a hole in the soles of his boots, and to buy new ones, he has to go like a beggar to the general."

She gave a start and her eyes widened, and I heard her father calling to her from the far side of the house. I knew the conference with my mother was finished and Creigor McCallum had emerged from the sitting room of my mother, and I knew without being told or seeing his face that he had been disappointed in any endeavor to squeeze money out of my mother, and made that discovery in an astonishingly short time.

Sarah's sudden movement was like a trap trigger for me, and I leaped up with her, took her shoulders in my hands, and holding her well away from my body, kissed her on the mouth.

278

She shoved me back, gasping, her face turning crimson and her eyes wide.

"Mr. Chesney!" she said and started to say more when the surprise on her face turned to a hot anger. "You can't do that! Why do you think you can do that?"

I started to apologize with excuses about her beauty or being carried away or some such thing, but no word got out of my mouth before she hit me. It was a hard, popping slap, and I could almost feel the red mark of her palm on my cheek.

It was a reflex, of course, nothing more, but my right hand drew back in a fist, and she stood there staring straight into my eyes, and she didn't know it was only a reflex but waited for my return blow, daring me to hit her, her chin thrust out.

"Oh, for God's sweet sake," I muttered and dropped my hands to my side. "Your father's calling you. Go on now."

And she did. Whirling as haughty as my mother might have done, she started toward the corner of the house. Then stopped and stood for what seemed the longest time. Then turned, and there was some different shine in her eyes, but I had no time to analyze it.

In a few quick, running steps, she was before me and reached up with both arms, taking my face between her hands and kissing me very hard.

Before I could react, before I could come uprooted from the spot where my feet were planted, she had turned and was gone, running around the house toward the sound of her father's voice which by now was retreating down the bluff road.

The emotions that spun through my head that day! For all my life, I suspected that I would never walk onto that promontory porch again without remembering the firm softness of her hands on my face, and the urgent, demanding hunger of her mouth.

Well, maybe the urgent hunger was all mine, not hers at all. But wherever it burned, for me it was a very hot fire indeed.

Everything was suddenly brought back into focus with my mother's voice, loud and strident.

"Campbell, get in here!"

But it was all right for Mother to break that spell. Because it would always be on call. Just think the words: *Sarah McCallum.* On my mother's promontory porch. Scarlet maples across the river. Smell of wood smoke drifting up from evening fires in town set against the fall chill. And warm lips.

Just the thought of those, and the thunder would crash silently through my entire being.

There was no stopping it now, and I no longer wanted to stop it. That second letter had to be sent.

Mother called in Otto Black and Gance and me. She told us where to go and what to do. She armed us as she might a band of river pirates, gunsmith Able Steinhartz giggling and nodding and saying "ya, ya, ya" as he supplied each of us with large bore pistols good for buckshot, two sawed-off muskets with the same capability, and a fine Pennsylvania rifle.

"You keep the buckshot pellet in pistols and muskets," he said. "Then you don't have to aim so good when you shoot."

"What in hell's name are we expected to shoot?" I asked. "We're only going to Lexington."

"She'll find somebody," Gance said, meaning Mother.

When we came back home carrying all the ordnance, I asked Mother if she was sending us to deliver a letter or to fight the British army.

"With the English close by in Canada," she said, "you don't know where they might pop up from behind a bush, them and their savage friends the Ottawas."

"I thought Pap and Mad Anthony Wayne killed all the Ottawas at Fallen Timbers."

"All right," she snapped. "Then Ojibway or Miami or Kickapoo. Maybe one of them. They understand buckshot!"

"Mother, we're going in the opposite direction from . . ." I stopped. The expression on her face said stop, so I did.

We rowed a skiff across the Ohio in early morning, and it was cold and there was a mist rising from the river because the water was still warm as summer. We had tried to outfit ourselves like hunters so the firearms we carried wouldn't be so out of place, but we wore more broadcloth and wool than we did buckskin so we were the object of a lot of curious stares as we went to Covington's only stable and rented horses.

There was a fair road all the way but it was about eighty miles, so that meant two nights either sleeping in the open or trying to find a tavern with beds to let. We had blanket rolls and saddlebags with corn muffins and dried apples and planned to go it like true pioneers.

The first night we went to our blankets hungry and then very nearly froze stiff, or thought we did, and determined to forget the pioneers and find an inn for the second night.

The inn was at a place called Sadieville, or some such thing, and the ham and boiled potatoes were edible. All three of us had to sleep in one bed. After that experience, we determined that we'd go back to blankets in the woods.

I was astonished that Gance seemed to enjoy all of this, at least more than Otto and I, and I expect it was because in the Sadieville bed he'd been the man in the middle so didn't wake half a dozen times in the night with frost on his butt as Otto and I did because the man on the far side of the bed had pulled too much of the cover to himself.

We found Mr. Joseph Daveiss in Frankfort, a small detour that added a day to our sojourn. He was a small, bouncing man, acting as though the little courthouse was not large enough to hold him, and he seemed delighted with the letter and said he had a few names he wanted to add to the list of rogues. It was some time before I found out what that meant.

We did better in our accommodations on the way home and managed to avoid a single night in the open.

All along the way, a great many people looked at us with considerable suspicion, what with the weapons we had about our persons. Soon we began to swagger a little, having a secret laugh about all the terrible stories some of these people would tell that night around the supper table about the highwaymen they'd seen.

Back at Covington in midafternoon, we found a small traveling circus with a trained bear and we watched too long, Otto and Gance enjoying the spectacle more if accompanied by generous sips of Kentucky whiskey Otto had bought in a brown jug. By evening they were both drunk, and rather than facing Mother with that kind of evidence that I was unfit to supervise even a bloodless expedition, I took a room in one of the taverns and we slept south of the river one more night.

We rented a room with two beds, and I insisted on one for myself alone, but it was a terrible night. Before retiring, Otto Black exposed us to various German marching songs his father had taught him, and all the while he smoked these black cigars they were now making in Conestoga, Pennsylvania, and naturally called Stogies. The odor of those cigars permeated the room like some sort of wicked, satanic incense, the last thing in my nostrils when I finally fell asleep and the first one when I woke up in the morning.

It was raining, and going back across the river we were thoroughly soaked. But when we dripped into my mother's kitchen to report, she didn't seem to mind, interested only in hearing all the details of the mission, which I gave her exact and complete. Well, I left out the brown jug of Kentucky whiskey.

Now Letter Number Two was on the way to President Jefferson. We hoped. We hoped he would find it as interesting as all the things Lewis and Clark had brought back from their journey. The expedition had returned to St. Louis by now, but the wonders of their discoveries were far from our minds.

It was three weeks after our return from Frankfort. We had just received the news by word of mouth passed along the river that Aaron Burr had been arrested.

I had never seen my mother so happy. She even giggled twice

when Gance made what I supposed she regarded as funny statements. They were not so funny that I can recall what they were, but I remember the giggles.

In fact, she was so spent with the frustration and anger and waiting in all this Burr business that she went to bed early that evening.

We would have to wait again before we learned any of the details of the arrest, but at least the conspiracy had been discovered and understood for what it was and stopped in time.

If Mother was overjoyed, I was only a little less so, but for me there was a hard knot of apprehension at the center. It kept repeating itself in my head. What had happened to General Wilkinson? What had happened to Creigor McCallum? And most of all, what had happened to Sarah McCallum?

It could have driven me out of my mind had I pondered on it, so I forced myself to do other things that evening with the rather hollow reassurance that our next news would come quickly and be complete.

There was now a craftsman in Cincinnati who produced the finest candles anyone had ever seen. On this night, I had a row of them across Mother's kitchen table, and I was reading by the excellent light a book I had taken in trade at our shoe shop some months before.

Often migrants had things to barter, in order to save cash, and although Mother frowned on it, I sometimes came across things I liked. This book was one of those, and I had it from a man and wife who came from the Carolinas and were going to Illinois Territory. The book had been written by somebody named Walter Scott and entitled *The Lady of the Last Minstrel.* A compelling poem indeed.

It was a book I could never forget, not because of what Mr. Scott had written but because of what happened as I held it there before me in my mother's kitchen.

Her blue eyes sought the west afar,
For lovers love the Western Star.

I had just read those lines when the candle flames before me wavered with cold air passing through the room, and I supposed Gance had opened an outside door. I started to complain, turning toward the source of the sharp gust of air.

There were two buckskin-clad men standing in the doorway, their eyes shining in the candlelight, and their fur hats with hanging squirrel tails along each cheek, and over their shoulders hair-on buffalo robes. One held a musket, and I could see paint on his face, yellow. The other one was heavily bearded, a coppery beard streaked with white. Behind those two were the indistinct forms of two others with blankets over their heads.

I knocked my chair over as I leaped up, ready to spring to the kitchen bread safe where Mother kept a loaded Harpers Ferry pistol.

There was a loud cackle, what I assumed was supposed to be a laugh, and the man standing slightly ahead of the other, the bearded one, took a further step into the room. His beard opened in a wide, open-mouth smile, and I saw the gaping space between his front teeth.

"My God," I whispered. "My God!"

"Well, ole boy," he shouted, throwing out his arms. "Here be ole Sergeant Bobby back from the Lewis and Clark expedition!"

He stood there grinning at me, his arms still spread as behind him the others came into the room, bringing that strong odor of woodsmoke and cooked meat with them, and for an instant I was rooted to the floor like an idiot.

But only for an instant.

"Mother," I bellowed. "Get out here. Pap's come home again."

I charged across the room, and we were both laughing as I banged into him, and we hugged violently, if such a thing was possible, and almost fell to the floor. Over Pap's shoulder I could see the three Indians, two of them women, I realized now, watching without expression as Pap and I held each other close as bark to a tree.

By God! It was Pap all right, and he smelled like he'd been denned with wolves for six months.

What a story Pap had to tell. The only problem was, he seemed pretty reluctant to tell it. He got the expected treatment from Mother during his first days back. King on a throne, bring him soup and cornbread and buttermilk when he wanted it. She scrubbed him down in a big kitchen bathtub we'd had for only a month, out of Philadelphia, and then the next day scrubbed him down again.

"They sure drug me out of that ole river" was about all he'd say until Mother began to get short-tempered with him.

"They" were the three Indians who'd brought him home.

The man's name was a tongue twister, even for Pap, who called him Snake. He was a Fox, and Pap said the Fox and Sauk tribes in league with one another were about as bad as Indians got if you were their enemy.

They'd fought the mighty Chippewa and Sioux to a standstill, Pap said, even though they were always outnumbered.

"Lucky for me," Pap said, "Ole Snake was downriver from St. Louis in a winter fishin camp and him and the two women pulled me out of the Mississip, yesiree, after that Spaniard son of a bitch of Wilkinson's throwed me in the water upstream. That son of a bitch Mendez."

The women in question were Winnebagos, captured or traded for or outright bought at some time or another by Ole Snake or by his brother or daddy or somebody and given to Ole Snake as a gift.

Snake wore a strange warlock. His head was clean-shaven except for a patch at the very base of his skull, and from it thick hair hung halfway down his back. He always wore paint. The only special occasion he needed to get out his paint pots was waking up each morning. So far as I could tell, he spoke no single word of English, and Pap spoke to him in some tribal lingo and Mother spoke to him in French.

The two women were flat faced, light skinned. You'd have to look close to see they were Indians if you caught them without their hide clothes on.

Mother wasn't at all cordial with any of them. She gave Ole Snake a little money as a reward for saving her husband, then informed him in her most ringing French that he and his squaws would be fed as long as they wanted to stay, but they'd sleep in the barn with the horses, and maybe when they departed she'd give them a new rifle and a big jug of whiskey.

"I won't have any of that smelly bunch of savage heathen in my house," Mother told me defiantly.

"Fine," I said. "You won't get any argument out of me about it. Since you got so accustomed to using soap on yourself, you got every right to have all things around you smell clean. That's what civilization is."

"You better look out," she said, waggling a finger at me. "Now that I took care of that traitor Burr, I've plenty of time to see to your proper upbringing."

"Upbringing? Everybody in Ohio knows I'm already up about as far as I'm gonna get brought," I said. "And don't take all the credit for gettin Aaron Burr. Maybe there were a few others told Mr. Jefferson about him, too."

"It was me," Mother said, jabbing herself in the chest with her fingers. "Me! I got Aaron Burr!"

Snake seemed perfectly at home with a dictatorial matriarch. Pap said that among Foxes, women carried a lot of heavy weight. Well, I said, maybe Ole Snake had known women as hard as my mother, but neither one of those Winnebagos would come close to fitting such a mold. In fact, they both acted as though they were scared to death of Mother.

"Can you blame em?" Gance asked.

Mother made a project of shaving Pap's beard, but he put his foot down on that so she had to be satisfied with trimming it only. Pap said you could tell men from the East and men from beyond the Mississip. Easterners were still clean-shaven like they were during the Revolution, but westerners mostly wore face hair.

"Out there on the prairie," Pap said, "you got to be able to see

286

right quick if a man walkin up to your fire is a red savage heathen so you can get the old Betsy ready to shoot. Man with face hair, that ain't no savage red heathen. They can't grow no big beard like us white men."

And he winked at Mother and I think pinched her bottom. She sniffed.

"Them white men grow beards because they're too lazy to use a razor," she said. "And too scared to pull out whiskers one by one with a muscle shell tweezer."

It was good to hear Pap and Mother joshing each other. It was Old Times. But Pap kept the beard.

All this while, people were coming to the house to see for themselves that Pap had come back from the dead. Judith Dwyer brought a gooseberry pan pie. Pap's old cronies from the riverfront tavern came, too. Mother monitored the gift jugs they brought, assigning most to the root cellar.

It was very strange. Pap seemed not at all happy that these people were coming. He'd always been a happy drinker and good mixer, and we tried to reason it out but had no luck except to suppose it had something to do with what had happened to him.

So finally Mother hit on a strategy to loosen Pap's tongue.

One night at the supper table, after the grub was dispensed with, Mother went to the root cellar we had under the back of the house and brought up a two-gallon crock jug of whiskey.

Usually Mother had an ill word for whiskey and anybody too fond of it, but now here she was, pouring Pap a tin cup brim full, and smiling and saying as how it was snowing to beat the dickens maybe it'd help his stiff joints if he helped himself to a few jolts.

Pap didn't need a second invitation. I saw Gance get a glassy look in his eye and he was licking his lips, looking at Pap drink, like an old dog sitting beside the table watching you eat pork chops. Little bastard, not even fifteen years old yet.

Of course, my mother saw the look in my eyes, and she gave me a wink, one of the few winks she ever gave me, and I knew immediately what was happening here.

"Can't ask a man to drink by his ownself," I said. "Get another cup down, and I'll join Pap to celebrate his coming home."

I had her there. I was old enough to be drinking if I wanted, and if I did now, it couldn't do anything but help Pap have a few extra ones. So Mother got me a tin cup, glaring at me, and I sipped and smacked my lips while she tried to set fire to my shirt with her look, Gance about to fall off his chair watching me calmly sip what he knew I didn't much like and him about to die for a single snort denied even a sniff.

Well, Mother and me playing little games was foolish maybe, considering that we were into a serious undertaking. But it worked. Within less than an hour, Pap was mellow enough to talk about anything.

"Ole Wilkinson was in an out," Pap said. "I was sick with more than roomatiz. My innards had took on strange water too long, I expect, so I wasn't in condition for a while to pay much attention. All I knew was Mendez the Spaniard had took me to Wilkinson's house on the waterfront at St. Louis."

As Pap came out of his misery enough to understand what was going on around him, he wondered why Wilkinson was so interested in his welfare. But as his health improved, he began to realize, as he told us in his letter, that these people were trying to find out all they could about the Lewis and Clark expedition.

"Why, for Lord's sake?" Pap said. "I didn't know nothin about what Captain Lewis and Captain Clark was doin except find a route to the western ocean."

Pap said there was a lot of coming and going in the Wilkinson house because he was acting governor of Upper Louisiana, or Missouri. But a lot of that traffic was decidedly Spanish, and there was much talk about this new country Aaron Burr was going to pull together.

"Finally, I'd got well pretty much," Pap said. "And they'd stopped asking about the expedition. I got the notion they was wonderin how the hell to get rid of me now that they knew I couldn't tell them anything."

One day Mendez and the woman he had with him were outside chopping firewood, and Pap started nosing around some of the papers on Wilkinson's desk. He found a letter that pretty much confirmed his suspicions about all that interest in the Lewis and Clark mission.

"It was an official piece of paper, like parchment, and even a seal, all in Spanish, and I figured it was from Spain's intendant at New Orleans.

"My Spanish ain't all that good," he said and reached across the table to squeeze Mother's arm. "I sure wished for you then, ole girl, sos you could decipher the thang. All the words was long as General Washington's leg, too."

There was enough there that Pap understood it was a letter that had accompanied a payment in gold to Wilkinson for information he had supplied about United States defenses along the border of Spanish Florida.

In another, longer letter, somebody was expressing appreciation for somebody's recommendations, Pap assumed General Wilkinson's, that Spanish troops ought to march up and stop the Lewis and Clark expedition because the whole thing looked as though it might have the purpose of establishing forts from which to launch an attack on Santa Fe or Texas.

"I got the feelin the Spanish governor at Santa Fe was about to wet his pants thinkin about the Americans joinin up with the Comanches to wipe out all of the people in the northern provinces of New Spain," Pap said and laughed. "From what I hear about the Comanches, they don't need much help from anybody if they ever decided to do such a thing."

Well, while Pap is doing all this recreational reading, Mendez and his woman come in and catch him at it. Now this woman, as Pap described her, was an Oto, and she weighed about fourteen stone, or two hundred pounds, and she was a deaf mute.

"If a man's got a taste for Oto squaws, it's better to have a deaf and dumb one, else they'll sure talk your arm off," Pap said. "But when Mendez seen what I was lookin at, he went wild tempered and slashed me with one of them Basque clasp knifes and opened me up pretty good."

We'd seen that scar when Mother bathed Pap in the kitchen tub, a red and ugly gash that started at Pap's shoulder blade and went down his left arm almost to his elbow. Added to that, the Oto woman hit him across the head with a stick of stove wood.

"I wasn't out of my senses complete, but I seen there wasn't much use to fight without no weapon, so I just fell down and played possum," Pap said. "I hoped they'd not gut me completely, and they didn't. They figured I was dead or near to it, so the woman picked me up like a sack and they carried me down to the river. It was dark of night."

They threw him into the Mississippi from the end of a boat dock. It was a long way from the current so ice had formed there, and Pap went right through it into a flow that even close to shore was enough to carry him along.

"I tell you, it was cold. That water woke me quick, all right," he said. "Black as pitch, too. I swum along under the ice and found air pockets where I could breathe. Ice on running water always has these ice pockets between the water and the ice. That's the way turtles breathe when a river freezes over. So I was swimming back toward what I thought was shore, findin them air pockets to catch my breath."

Looking for one of those breathing spaces, Pap came up at one point and found a hole in the ice, and as his head popped clear of the water, he saw dark figures along the bank.

"It was Ole Snake and some of his friends," Pap said. "They carried me to their fishing camp back in the woods and put me in a bark shack, and there was a fire, and they got me dry and started spoonin the vilest stuff I ever tasted into my mouth."

The Fox band was doing some winter fishing for turtles along the big river south of St. Louis. It was the edge of Osage country, Pap said, and the Foxes and Osages were enemies from so long ago nobody could recall it ever being any other way.

But these Foxes were a tough bunch and besides that figured the Osages would all be in winter camps a lot farther west. So they were cutting holes in the ice, and those big river snapping turtles would come up for air, and they'd put loop rope on the turtles' necks and drag them in.

Knowing how dangerous a big snapper could be for fingers and hands, I had to admire the Fox method of catching them.

"It was a spell for healing after what that spade-beard, gold-earring Spaniard done to me. The Foxes made a fine job of it, though. By the time I got well enough to travel, I got thinking maybe it wasn't so good to be seen along the river because if somebody did and told Mendez about it, he'd be after me to finish the job he'd started with that Basque knife for I knew too much about his boss Wilkinson to let me wander around free to talk about it."

So that was why Pap was a little uncomfortable about all the locals coming to see him. They'd be telling up and down the river about Pap coming back from the dead, and Mendez or one of his cohorts might come nosing around with the idea of maybe eliminating a serious witness against the general.

"But Pap," said Gance. "They arrested Aaron Burr and it all fell through, so you don't have to worry about it now."

"He does," Mother said, and her voice was grim. "It's dangerous for that fat pig Wilkinson to have somebody like your pap around who can tell what those weasels were doing against our Republic that we fit for, me and your pap."

Mother's voice rose as she talked, and her face worked with fury. Pap tried to calm her, stroking her arm as he might a Canadian lynx, ready to jump back if the claws came in his direction.

"Damned English-loving white man savage trash," Mother shouted. "And throwing my wounded man in the ice water."

She stopped and looked around the table at all the upturned

faces, the wide eyes, and she was suddenly embarrassed with her outbreak.

"Come to bed, you Sergeant Bobby," she said, her voice still strident. She spun and was gone almost instantly. I never understood how my mother could disappear from a room so quickly.

So now we had it. After Pap and Mother were out of the room, I pushed the jug over to Gance.

"All right, big man. Have your drink."

He did, right from the jug, and I wondered where he'd learned that. Taking the jug down from his lip, he sputtered and coughed, and I laughed because it was funny Gance drinking like a river raftman, and in the candle shine I could see the sprouting of a light fuzz on his chin.

"That bastard Spaniard. You think he'll come here?"

I shrugged. My younger brother stared at me, and somehow I began to see some of the fire in his eyes that I thought was a quality of my mother's eyes alone. Gance wasn't dark skinned and his hair was not a raven black, but he had our mother's Indian eyes.

"Well, I'm loading a pistol with buckshot!" he said.

"You'll find about four pistols in this house already loaded with buckshot," I said. "Don't you know your mother well enough to appreciate that? She's always ready in case the damned English come to get her."

"I'm not joshin," he said, and he was so serious, so grown-up serious for a fourteen-year-old, that I sensed a new kind of Gance here before me. Big for his age, no doubt, strong as a bull, no doubt, but I still thought of him as a baby brother who puked when he saw deer guts. Maybe it was time to think otherwise.

"It's serious. I know. We'll do whatever we can to protect Pap. He keeps improving his health, he won't need much help in that department soon."

"Well, I mean I'm going to have a loaded pistol by my bed from now on," he said. "And I'm going to have a loaded pistol under my smock when I go to town."

An expression of indecision and doubt crossed his face.

"You think Mother would allow that?"

Now I did laugh.

"You bet. She'd be delighted you'll be ready for any invasion. I've been hearing you shooting some out behind the horse shed. Can you hit anything?"

Now there was no indecision or doubt. He grinned wickedly and his eyes sparkled, just like Mother's, I thought.

"I can clip a cat's whisker at twenty paces."

I laughed again at the arrogance maybe, or because I had the sense he was close to speaking true.

"If you're such a deadeye, why the buckshot?"

Unfazed, Gance lifted his arms in a gesture of complete confidence, and he was grinning still.

"Hell, big brother, in the dark, buckshot's better!"

I went to bed with the uneasy feeling that Gance was excited with Pap's story, his blood running hot. Which was only natural. This family, I thought, has had its fair share of violent stories, but Gance is only now coming of age when he can appreciate what danger is about.

In the dark, hearing my brother breathing across the room, I reached down to the box beside my bed to feel the pistol there. It had been there a long time, since Pap left for the Lewis and Clark expedition. Buckshot loaded.

All right, I thought, me and Gance are brothers under the skin after all. Then I wasn't sure. It was difficult to get the whole business out of mind. It always ended a little unsettling.

Because no matter how I turned it, Gance sounded like a man itching to butcher somebody!

Chapter 13

Rufus Putnam warned Mother that with her businesses expanding, what with the new gunpowder mill we were building, the time had come to be very careful about whom we hired to do the work. There was an element among the local folk who were not beneath setting fire to your barn if you took on laborers of whom they disapproved, he said.

The initial purpose of General Putnam's visit was to have his annual summer supper with us. It was a thing that had grown over the years between Mother and General Putnam, in the spirit of a holiday the two old friends had become accustomed to and allowed the rest of us to join.

Gance had shot a bag of upland birds two days before, and we'd cured half a dozen hams the past winter, so we feasted on cold sliced ham, woodchuck with cornbread dressing, cranberries, and fried Indian corn. General Putnam had brought a green cheese and a bottle of Madeira.

There'd been a big spring flyover of Canada geese that year and

Gance had brought in a number of them, and for General Putnam's feed, as Pap called it, we had the greatest treat of all, braunschweiger that Able Steinhartz had made for us with those goose livers.

It all had to do with freedmen, General Putnam began. Black Africans who were not slaves, free for one reason or another.

The old Northwest Ordinance that had created the territories along the north shore of the Ohio River and beyond had barred slavery. So when Ohio became a state, it was written right into the constitution. No slavery.

But it was soon obvious that this was no concession to virtue. Some legislators who met for the first time under that constitution began to think of ways to keep Africans out of Ohio.

For Africans who were slaves in Ohio at the time, they simply lived out their lives as slaves. Even though many slave owners freed slaves now and then, I knew of no single instance where state authorities actually forced such a thing because there was this overpowering sanctity that attached to private property, to include slaves.

Nobody worried too much about blacks considered native colored folk. They had already set themselves into the pattern of things. But a lot of slaves were being freed now in Virginia and Maryland and Kentucky because their owners could see no economic value in having big work gangs of slaves in those places, what with worn-out land plus new ideas of diversified crops.

These freedmen had to go someplace. A few were likely absorbed locally on patches of farm ground nobody else wanted, but the great majority had to go looking for a way of life, and our local folk figured many of them would be coming to Ohio. That's when restrictive immigration laws began.

No matter how much lip service some people gave to the bad character of African slavery, and there were fewer of those than you might imagine, almost nobody wanted the Africans.

Some were pretty blunt about it. They figured Africans were at a lower notch on the scale of human kind than the white man, so they didn't want any truck with them. A surprising number of those had never been close enough to a black to hear the sound of his voice.

But there was another, more logical reason our locals wanted to keep blacks away. They'd likely work cheaper than whites, and the worst scene imaginable was black craftsmen and mechanics and laborers flooding the job market.

Many men I knew complained that if we just let any and all niggers sashay in here, our own white folks would be reduced to catching fish in the river to put grub in the bellies of their children, and how the hell do you pay the debt you owe the government for your land if all you got to pay it with is fish?

They'd cut their eyes down then and add, "Or how would we pay off them mortgages your mama holds on us?"

That was the kind of thing the general was warning Mother about.

"There are places in the East where they have begun to employ children to make shoes," General Putnam said. "And if there were a lot of children around here, you could probably do that, too, and nobody would lift an eyebrow. Although I am sure you would never do so.

"But you start hiring a work gang of blacks, your new powder mill is going to have a tendency late at night to blow up quite unexpectedly from time to time."

That attitude was more or less official. Because despite the no-slavery clause in the Ohio constitution, laws designed to discourage black immigration began to go on the book shortly after statehood in 1803.

One such law I recall required that any man, woman, or child of African descent who desired to become a citizen of Ohio must post a bond of five hundred dollars to ensure good deportment.

Well, we weren't alone. Most of the old Northwest Territory states had the same kind of thing when it came their time. It was depressing.

"Who among those people would have five hundred dollars?" Gance asked. "None, that's who. So why not just say, 'We won't let niggers come here.' "

But on that same visit, when General Putnam advised Mother to take great care in hiring, he had something more important to tell us. He had all the Aaron Burr news.

"The president was in receipt of a letter from Mr. Daveiss of Kentucky," General Putnam began.

"Ah ha," Mother said and glared at me in triumph.

"Daveiss told of Aaron Burr's scheming and planning along the Ohio and elsewhere. He accused General Wilkinson of being in league with Burr, and he added a few of his own personal enemies, like Henry Clay, a rising young politician in Kentucky. But the president was unconvinced."

"He was unconvinced?" Mother almost shouted.

I couldn't bring myself to look at her and gloat. And besides, my mother is not a pleasant sight when she feels slighted.

"Unconvinced," General Putnam continued. "But there were others telling him the same thing, and apparently General Wilkinson heard there were what he called slanders against him, so he decided it was best to jump Burr's ship while the jumping was still good.

"Wilkinson sent a long letter to President Jefferson detailing Burr's plan, putting in about everything, I suppose, except, of course, that he himself had been part and parcel of the plan from the start, and certainly nothing about his having been in the pay of Spain for many years."

"That slimy son of a bitch," Pap said. But he was calm and peaceful, sitting there smoking his pipe with Clariese beside him pouring when his cup was empty.

"It was then that the president sent out his warning to all agencies of the central government and local law enforcement people as well that Burr should be arrested on sight," General Putnam said.

"As I understand it, Burr was somewhere in Mississippi Territory with part of his army, which had floated right past your promontory some weeks before," General Putnam said, smiling at Mother. "Burr gave himself up to local authorities, but a grand jury there failed to find evidence enough that he was trying to destroy the Union and released him."

"That man must be slicker than a green swamp frog," said Otto Black.

"That he is, that he is," General Putnam said. "But somebody had the presence of mind to arrest him again, and this time he was taken to New Orleans and brought by naval vessel to Richmond. There, the grand jury thought evidence pointed to Burr undertaking disunion. They indicted him for treason."

"Were there others arrested?" I asked.

"Yes, I don't know who or even how many, but there were," he said. "Some of those were released in Louisiana, and some were brought with Burr to Virginia."

"Where is Wilkinson all this time?" Pap asked.

"Why, going about his duties as the highest-ranking man in the army," General Putnam said, laughing. "He would have gone to St. Louis, I suspect, except that President Jefferson had replaced him as acting governor of Louisiana. With your friend Meriwether Lewis, Sergeant Bobby."

"Yes," Pap said and chuckled in a way that left no doubt he enjoyed this part of the telling. "Meriwether Lewis, governor. And Captain Clark superintendent of all tribes west of the Mississippi. Two good men, them two, General."

"Without doubt," said the general.

"But Wilkinson?" Mother asked.

"He finally appeared in Richmond and was almost indicted by that same grand jury, but was not."

"Damnation and go to hell, he should have been," Pap said, and now he was becoming almost as intense as Mother, who through this whole thing leaned across the table, watching General Putnam's lips as though seeing the words was as important as hearing them.

"The president and many others besides could not bring themselves to believe that Wilkinson was involved in a scheme to dismember the Union," said Putnam. "He had fought in the Revolution.

He was general at about twenty-four, I believe. He was aide to Gates at Saratoga."

Pap snorted on that one. And almost strangled on a drink half down. After a fit of violent coughing, Clariese pounding him on the back, he wiped his eyes and took another drink.

"Wilkinson with Gates," he said. "The buzzard eatin on the skunk. You can hang the both of them for all of me, by Gawd!"

"So Wilkinson got out by the skin of his teeth," said the general. "I heard that seven members of a sixteen-member grand jury voted for a true bill against Wilkinson. It's closer than I'd want to come, nine to seven against an indictment."

"So now, Wilkinson's just out there being a good soldier," I said.

"Apparently so," General Putnam said. "In the southern department near Spanish Florida, I believe. But the trial."

The most unbelievable part was yet to come. The chief justice of the Supreme Court sat before the petit jury to try Burr's treason. And that was John Marshall, one of President Jefferson's bitterest political enemies. And Marshall found that unless witnesses could place Burr in person on Ballestero Island with the armed group there, no treason had occurred, and the prosecution failed to produce such a witness.

Under those circumstances, General Putnam said, the jury acquitted, and Burr walked free.

"And now," the general said, "Aaron Burr is in Europe, and I understand going back and forth between England and France with various schemes to destroy our Republic."

It was so stunning that nobody could speak for a long time.

Finally, Mother spoke only loud enough for me to hear. "Damned English!"

I didn't know what that meant.

A little good, a lot of bad, that's what life brings, Mother said. The good was that Aaron Burr was out of the country, but everything else was pretty bad. Sarah McCallum was on my mind as never before.

I had hoped General Putnam might know something about the fate of the McCallums, but he didn't. I asked him pointedly that evening as I escorted him back down the bluff to the town.

It seemed a fair time to mention my distress to Mother. This thing was ripping my insides anyway, and there had to be some relief. Where else would I turn?

She was making off to her bed one night, Pap already there, and I could hear him singing softly, some old song from the days of the Revolution. She was wearing a long flannel nightgown, a garment she had come to enjoy, I suppose a fragment of that white man's game at which she was still determined to beat him. I had no notion how far she need go before finally admitting she'd accomplished her aim.

I explained my distress, rather awkwardly, I'm sure. She said nothing for a long time, gazing into my face, and now I was rather proud to see she had to look up instead of down. Finally, she lifted one hand and her fingertips touched my cheek for an instant, and she turned away with an expression on her face I'd never seen before.

"You must do what you know needs doing," she said and turned at her door. "You know that your pap is a danger to this English dog Wilkinson. So you know that your Sarah McCallum is even more dangerous to him because they know many things more than Pap does.

"For now, my little Campbell, you must wait, because there is nothing more you can do. Sometime, maybe soon, you will know which devil to burn.

"But then will be like now. Your mother cannot help you. Only your own strong spirit can help you."

And she turned into her room.

Well, that did a lot of good, didn't it? But maybe that look in her eye meant something. Maybe one of her gods had whispered "soon, son, soon." Maybe soon, she'd said.

I had never wanted so desperately to know about my mother's god or spirit or medicine or power. Whatever it was she had, from

300

whence she heard those whispers, if indeed she ever heard any whispers at all.

And I'm convinced she did.

Ole Snake, the Fox Indian, was still with us. The two women were long since gone. Either Ole Snake ran them off, or they grew tired of Mother's obvious disdain for them.

Whichever it was, when they left they took a sack of shelled corn, a cast-iron skillet, and one of the sawed-off muskets.

And the next day Able Steinhartz complained that somebody had stolen a shoat from his pigpen and left moccasin tracks all over the barn lot.

"Mrs. Chesney," he asked, "you think them English is sending Ottawas down here now to steal pigs?"

But Ole Snake stayed. There was some sort of agreement between him and Mother. He was helpful with Pap. A lot of help was required. Pap's joints were constantly swollen and he could hardly walk, and his breathing was labored, and he couldn't keep grub down the way he once could.

The things Wilkinson's people had done to him, and the effort to escape them had taken more toll on him than anyone had suspected.

Mother didn't treat the Fox as a guest in the house. In fact, he was seldom allowed inside the house. She made loud remarks concerning the inferior character of all western Indians as opposed to her own people, who had come from the Maine woods or similar northeastern piney forest and lake country. After she said such things in a language Ole Snake could understand, she'd translate into English so none of us could miss her meaning.

Ole Snake didn't seem to mind. It struck me that this man was not the sort to take lightly being so badgered and made light of until finally I realized he was staying because he enjoyed being near my mother.

It wasn't an easy thing to accept, at my age. To find that my own mother was attractive enough to turn a man's head. Whether it was love or lust or whatever Ole Snake might have thought it was, it being there at all was a hard pill to swallow, especially with the certain knowledge that Mother was well aware of what was happening.

General Putnam had been around since my earliest memory, so the thought of his affection for Mother never really entered my mind. But here was a still-wild Indian who roached his hair and wore paint on his face and sometimes smelled like a freshly skinned bear making moon eyes at my mother and her not running him off with one of the sawed-off muskets the man's squaws had left us.

But she didn't.

So there he was, day after day, helping Pap move around in the woodlot or leaning against the horse stalls with his hooded black eyes watching Gance and I come and go, or squatting on the end of the rear porch eating meat Mother gave him and sounding like a wolf cracking bones in the den.

Ole Snake carried a quiver with bow and arrows almost everywhere he went. This was no bow such as northeast woodland Indians used. It was much shorter and with a double curve.

"Them western savages," Pap said, "they reinforce the wood on their bows with horn. You take strips of horn, that's buffalo horn, and soak it until it's soft then shape it onto the bow, inside curve, outside curve. You stick it in place with hoof glue and wrap it with sinew. When she dries, you got a bow that will drive an arrow right smack through a one-inch plank!

"Besides which, it's short enough to use when you're horseback."

The arrows were vaned with owl feathers, Pap said, because owl feathers don't go soft and spongy when they get bloody like goose or turkey feathers will.

"Buzzard feathers," Pap said. "They work good, too."

All of that aside, with his hanging about and watching Mother constantly, I came to resent Ole Snake. I came to resent him right up to the time the Spaniard came looking for Pap.

We were at the riverfront, Gance and myself, talking with Stanislas Lewicki, Cincinnati's biggest river freight man. He had everything from the best sail-driven keelboats to barges to dugout canoes going up and down the Ohio and south on the Mississippi to New Orleans, carrying the trade that brought such things as glass windows and Spanish lace and bolts of linen and took away such things as hogs and shoes and lumber and playing cards.

We were expecting various materials we needed for the new gunpowder mill to arrive from Pittsburgh, but this was not the day for it apparently. So we were sitting on empty barrels in the shade of a Lewicki shed lazily smoking pipes and talking, sipping from a bucket of Judith Dwyer's beer, swatting at blue belly flies, and trying to recall any past summer when the river had been so low.

"We need some good pumpernickel wurst with this beer," Lewicki said. There were two German taverns in town by now, and pumpernickel was Lewicki's term for anything German, whether it be man, beast, or structure. And food, whether it was sour rye bread or not.

Lewicki had come to North America during the Revolution, a Pole who said he was a friend of the great Pulaski. I doubted that he was, but it made for a good story. He'd learned the river trade along the Vistula, which he said was the grandpapa of all rivers, which I also doubted.

I was almost asleep when I became aware that Gance, next to me, had suddenly sat bolt-upright on his keg.

"Who was he?" my brother asked.

Lewicki was squatting on the ground, facing us. His eyes were close together, pale blue, accented somehow by the red woolen stocking cap he wore winter and summer, the forward roll pulled down so far on his face it hid his eyebrows.

"Hell, we don know, we don ask. He just this little man, gotta good keelboat, crew about six men, stop here for couple kaigs whiskey, and we talk, me and this little man. Two his people go up to Judith's and buy couple kaigs, and they come and everybody get back on keelboat and go upriver, set sails and go with that summer wind blow from the west, you know?"

"Yes, I know, Mr. Lewicki, but what did you say he asked about?"

"About your papa, he asked. I tell him, sure I know Sergeant Bobby, everybody know Sergeant Bobby; he just come back from Lewis and Clark sick, and your mama nurse him to make him well up in her house."

I wasn't napping now. Mr. Lewicki squatted there, blinking at us, and I saw he wasn't going to say anything more until we primed him a little.

"All right," I said. "What did he want to know?"

"He wanted to know where Sergeant Bobby live. He good friend of Sergeant Bobby from the Revolution and coming back down the river soon and want to have visit with Sergeant Bobby maybe, you know?"

"What did you tell him?" Gance almost shouted, and Lewicki's eyes widened and he looked offended.

"What was true, I tell him," Lewicki said. "That Sergeant Bobby in house on the bluff, you mama's house up there, that's what I tell him. He's old friend from the Revolution."

"That was all?" I asked.

"Sure, what else is all?"

"What did he look like, this man?"

Lewicki shrugged elaborately. "Just a little man, you know, had this black spade beard. Had a gold ring in his ear like them gypsies in my old country wear."

He burst out laughing.

"What's funny?" Gance said.

"That little man, he had on his keelboat, she never get off but I see her sure, a big, big squaw, I mean she big like enough to fill you mama's barn, I tell you. When they leave, we all laugh we think about that little man bouncing up and down on that big, big squaw, like you got a cork on a fish line, you know?"

"How long ago was this?" I asked.

He held up his fingers. "Two," he said. "Two days."

"And he went upriver?"

"Sure, upriver. They goin back to Ballestero, you could bet."

Gance and I were both off our barrels now, tensed to start something, I wasn't sure what, as soon as we had all we could squeeze out of Lewicki.

"Why do you figure that?"

"Hell, three of them men on his crew, they in that bunch rafted down the river last year with the Aaron Burr bunch from Ballestero." He laughed again. "Now with ole Burr gone, I guess they workin for the little man. But I bet they goin to Ballestero. Hell, I even remember that fancy keelboat in the bunch that went past with Burr's crowd, you know?"

I grabbed Gance by the arm. "Come on, boy, we better make it up the bluff before dark."

"Sure, all right," Stanislas Lewicki shouted after us. "You come back tomorrow, maybe you get that stuff in, you know, maybe we get another bucket beer, maybe some good pumpernickel wienerwurst, too, you know."

All the way up the bluff road, as we hurried along, Gance kept whispering to himself. "It's him, it's him. That son of a bitch! It's him, scoutin out where Pap's at."

Gance was so hot to get this Spaniard Mendez, he always thought that was the only reason we went back to the island. There was another reason, in fact the main reason, but I kept it to myself. When I told Mother Gance and I had some business upriver that might keep us away for a fortnight, I'm sure she knew I was playing a hunch.

"Take the red savage," she said. It was already dark then, and Pap was in his bed, which was for the best. I didn't want him excited and insisting on coming along.

"You mean Ole Snake?" I asked incredulously. "Who's going to talk to him? Neither one of us speak French or any of those tribal jargons you use on him."

"You talk natural," she said. "He'll know."

So it ended as a three-man expedition, armed to the boot heels. Only none of us wore boots. We wore moccasins. We dressed top to bottom for the woods, including fringed smocks and leggings. Rabbit felt, soft-brim slouch hats. Well, Snake wore his shaved head with trailing scalp lock.

We were a really tough-looking bunch, I suppose. I knew Mother was proud of the impression we might make on any innocent bystander.

"Watch out for the damned English," she said.

For armaments, Snake and I carried sawed-off muskets, Gance a Pennsylvania rifle. The Fox had his short bow, of course, and between us, Gance and I had three Harpers Ferry pistols. Buckshot loaded. And each of us with the requisite hatchet and hunting knife.

Instead of fighting against the current of the river, even though it was summer low-water soft now, I decided to go overland. Besides, that way we could take a straight-line course east across the long southward bend of the Ohio between Cincinnati and Ballestero, cutting off many miles. Horses would likely be faster than going upstream against the flow, even at low water.

Mother owned five horses now. So we could ride away from our house without alerting townsmen that we were going east. Even though it was nighttime, we'd be seen if we pushed off with a boat. Horseback, going out of yard into forest, so to speak, we might be four, five days gone before anybody missed us.

Hezakiah Stewart was our regular Methodist circuit rider. He had his headquarters in Marietta, and sometimes to cover the backwoods country, he'd make a swing north and come into our town along the Sandusky Trace which started on Lake Erie and ended almost at my mother's chicken coop.

He was a fascinating old bird and I'd spent a lot of time talking with him, and now those conversations paid back interest.

There was a route that was part road, part wagon trace, part pig trail that led from Cincinnati eastward to Chillicothe. Just short of there, we could veer off across the valley of the Scioto, cross the ridges to Hocking River, and along that to Hockingport on the Ohio just downstream from Ballestero Island.

Hezzie Stewart said by that route it was about sixteen leagues from Mother's backyard to the town on the Ohio that stood just around a bend from the island. So fifty miles and on good horses, rested and grain fed along the way, you could figure three days travel, or less, depending on how rough the ridgelines were between the Scioto and the Hocking.

"And," Hezzie said, "a few good taverns along the way where if you decided to sleep the night inside, mostly you don't have to sleep with no more than one or two of the proprietor's young uns in the same bed with you."

We'd sleep in the woods, weather being summertime. Unless it rained. But the taverns meant we needn't take any huge larder of grub.

So like a band of desperate highwaymen, we set off in the middle of the night, Mother watching us from her back porch with folded arms, a lantern beside her casting an orange glare up along the solid planes of her face.

The horses were cranky and hard to control at first, since they were unaccustomed to work in the middle of the night. But a gentle attention to their flanks with leather quirts and with proper oaths and common cussing, they began to understand the need for good manners and were soon going forward without any fuss, likely enjoying the cool darkness and the sounds of night birds.

By dawn, we were into Highland County, almost twenty miles from Mother's door.

We found one of Hezzie Stewart's taverns and had a breakfast of cold hasenpfeffer, a rabbit stew the German settlers make. We found a lot of hasenpfeffer on that journey, cold, hot, and all ways in between. I began to believe that had it not been for the lowly rabbit, half the pioneers in southern Ohio would have starved to death.

Ole Snake said not a word but seemed to understand anything we might say by way of instructions. Some of the tavern keepers who served us along the way, and a couple of horseback riders we met, gave him a close inspection, but seeing he wore no black paint on his face and was in our company, they treated him like they would treat anyone.

They were all accustomed to Indians. Even those carrying guns.

Since we had started, Snake had not applied any fresh paint to his face, and when we'd begun the few stripes of yellow across his cheeks were two days old. Before long, it was hard to tell he was wearing any paint at all.

So we were on our first war party together, Gance and I. And nevermore would I think of him as a *little* brother.

Chapter 14

Hockingport wasn't much of a town. But it provided all we needed in the person of Jubal Cretch, proprietor of the only inn and tavern, a log structure ostentatiously named the River Bend Arms.

Unlike tavern keepers in the backcountry, who could sometimes be suspicious and closemouthed, Jubal Cretch was more the typical river inn host, garrulous and open faced as one of Judith Dwyer's pumpkin pies.

It didn't hurt that I had a small poke of gold coins to buy whatever we wanted. Like many men in his position, Mr. Cretch assumed that anyone who paid hard money for his services expected plenty of conversation to go with it.

I wasn't sure exactly how to go about what I intended, and in later years Gance would say our short visit with Mr. Cretch was a reconnaissance of possibilities. At the time, I suspect he thought it was more like stumbling along in the manner of a blind mule.

Anyway, we explained ourselves as travelers from upper Ohio going to see General Putnam at Marietta and had decided to take a boat from Hockingport. Mr. Cretch would keep our horses until we returned, for a small feeding fee, and further would rent us a large skiff which he said was seaworthy and with the river being so low and the current so sluggish, would present no problem rowing upstream the few miles to our destination.

Having a casual sip of hard spirits in the cool of Mr. Cretch's keg room, with Ole Snake outside squatted against the wall with a bucket of warm beer, I mentioned that we'd heard there was a famous old rich man around these parts who had been involved with the Burr conspiracy.

This was the only invitation Jubal Cretch needed to launch into a full-blown account of the whole episode, and it was our first real trial in this adventure. To sit calmly and listen when there was so much more on our minds.

"Oh, yes sir, Mr. Campbell," he said, addressing me with what I had told him was my surname. "That island just upstream, you'll row right past it; a regular garrison of armed men gathered there, but gone now."

It was important. It meant we were not facing an armed camp. After the Burr trial, there was a general exodus from the island, and now only three or four people lived there. In addition to old man Ballestero and his household.

Trying to sound only casually interested, I said, "I expect those people still living there are some of the men recruited as soldiers for Burr's undertakings."

"Well, I don't reckon so," said Mr. Cretch. "Just old Ballestero's majordomo, don't know his name but they say he comes from St. Louis, and then this McCall or McClacken or some such thing who was one of Mr. Burr's solicitors. Him and his daughter run up and down the river trying to raise money for their enterprise. They say he collected a small fortune. Man from New Orleans originally, I understand."

Gance was sitting across the crude plank table from me, so we were not touching. But I could feel him go tense with Cretch's words, and I knew that now my brother understood the real mission of our expedition.

A short distance upstream from Hockingport, the river made a sharp bend due east. Here was a straight stretch of considerable distance, and it was in this length of the Ohio where Ballestero Island lay, a long, narrow strip of land shaped like a canoe with a point fore and aft and about three miles end to end.

We took our time rowing along that stretch of river, staying close in to the north bank, seeing all we could of the island as we went past. The island was close to the far shore of the river so we figured anybody there who noticed us at all would pay little attention to three small figures in a small skiff on a big, heavily traveled river.

The sun was blazing down on us, and the gnats were very insistent about biting our eyelids, and with the water so low, there was the constant odor of fish in our nostrils. Somewhere on the near side of the river there was a meadowlark making a joyful racket all out of whack with how we were feeling, sweat running down our faces and the damp crotch of our woolen pants beginning to chaff.

Ole Snake chose that time to take out his little pots of paint and start doing his face. It was a well-rehearsed ritual because he didn't use any hand mirror as I'd heard Pap say a lot of them did when they put on paint.

The paint smelled worse than the dead fish along the riverbank, but there was no heat in my irritation because all the while, as his fingers worked across his cheeks, Ole Snake never took his eyes off that island across the river and I suspected he was seeing more than Gance and I.

It was somewhat good to know that regardless of his inability to communicate with us, he knew enough to understand that we were coming close to some kind of resolution.

It was extremely nerve-racking, nonetheless. Because most of what Snake daubed on his cheeks and his bald pate was black. And anybody even close to an Indian frontier at that time knew they all used black for war. And death.

Anyway, the island.

There were more trees on it than I had remembered from my first visit. The Ballestero house, which was supposed to be rather fine, was on the far side, but a cluster of other buildings we could see through the trees indicated an approximate location.

There were a few log cabins, more like huts, and I shuddered recalling that Sarah McCallum mentioned one of these as the only home they had after her father sold his New Orleans holdings.

Along the north bank, there was a scattering of lumber and rope and broken barrels and other trash from raft building, all left to rot in the sun. There were some dilapidated sheds. The dock there had nothing tied to it, and in fact there was no boat of any kind in sight along the entire length of the island.

I assumed there was a dock on the far side.

We passed along the entire length of the island by late afternoon, and we saw only one human figure, a woman it appeared to be, well back in the trees, carrying something. Perhaps a bucket of water. But we saw no one else.

A good sign indeed.

Maybe Ole Snake thought so, too. He had begun to sing a low chant under his breath, barely audible, and he took the short bow from the quiver and started to string it as Gance and I turned the boat in toward the easternmost point of land on Ballestero Island.

After we'd secured the skiff under an overhang of young willows, we moved along a gravel shore on the south side of the island. There was no evidence that anyone had seen us. Much of this end of the island was covered with a second growth of sycamore and black locust, and with it becoming deep dusk, the trees offered good cover.

There was a path, well worn, that led from what appeared to have been an old dock area, looking long since abandoned, up the slight slope toward the higher spine of the island. I led the way into it but moved only about thirty feet and stopped, waving the other two up beside me.

I could hear a dog barking, far away. Across the river in a settlement called Parkersburg, Virginia. At least, I hoped the dog was there and not waiting for us farther along the island.

Nobody had spoken since we beached the skiff. That was good. But Gance and Snake were alert and looking about in all directions. The Fox seemed to be sniffing, like a hunting dog.

Now I waved them forward again. We went slowly, the shadows under the trees growing darker. Then Ole Snake, moving just behind me, touched my arm and pointed through the woods toward the main channel of the Ohio.

There, shining weakly through the tree trunks, was a light. It looked about a quarter mile away, but there was no telling in these trees and with dark of night on us now.

We moved off the path and into what appeared to be a tangle of wild grapes, the vines climbing and clutching the trunks of a half dozen beech trees. Here, it was very dark. I could hear Gance panting, and I knew it wasn't from exertion. My own breath was heaving in and out of a tight chest, too.

"All right," I whispered. "We'll leave Snake here, with the long guns."

"What? Leave the long guns? What are you fixin to do, anyway?" Gance panted.

"I don't know," I said. And it was true. I didn't know what I was going to do. "But check your two pistols for priming, hide em under your smock, and leave the long guns here."

Mumbling in weak protest, Gance began to check his pistols, lifting the frizzen, blowing out the old primer powder, putting in a pinch of fresh powder from his horn, closing the frizzen to hold the new primer in the pan, and slipping the pistol under his smock. The same with the second gun as I made hand talk with Snake, who seemed to know what I was saying before I did.

Snake took the muskets and the rifle and leaned them against a small rock outcrop, then moved a few paces farther back into the grapevine. About all I could see of him was his gleaming eyes, what with his black face paint and the growing darkness.

"Come on," I whispered to Gance.

"What's he gonna do?"

"Cover our road out of here, I hope."

"Listen, I've been thinking, if whoever they be know Pap's come home and figure he's told everybody what happened to him, you and me better damned well hope these people really believe we're the Campbell brothers." Gance was gasping now. "Or somebody. Because if they suspect who we *really* are, we're gonna end up fish food in that river!"

"I know that," I whispered harshly. "Now shut up."

We were moving through the trees slowly, still on the path. We could see the light off to our right. The dog I'd heard had stopped barking.

"What the hell are we doing, anyway? Don't you think it'd work better if I knew, too?"

"It'd work even better if I knew," I said. "Now shut up and keep your eyes open."

"Jesus Christ!" Gance said.

I stopped suddenly and turned to him, and he bumped into me before he realized I was standing still.

"Have you joined somebody's Christian church?"

"What does that mean?"

"If you haven't, that's a strange kind of oath-making you're doin!"

"Come on, let's get this done, whatever it is."

I was amazed at myself. Slipping through those trees toward what had to be Ballestero's house, I was trying to pinch off a throat full of giggles. The more Gance snorted and complained, albeit very quietly, the funnier it became.

Then suddenly, we were out of the trees, and directly before us, not fifty paces away, there was the dark looming form of a very large

314

house, single storied but sprawled like a black spider among the trunks of a walnut grove. At such a time, why would we notice the smell of cooking bacon?

Beyond the house, where there were lighted windows glowing orange, was the pale surface of the Ohio's south channel. To our right, the trees had been cleared and there were a number of small cabins, log I assumed, but it was too dark to tell.

Only one of these smaller structures was lighted. We could see a window and an open door.

"Come on," I said and plunged ahead toward the big house, making for what I perceived as a front porch facing the river and on the side away from the other cabins in the grove.

That's when the dog ran out. He was barking in a froth of excitement but was afraid, no watchdog, because he circled us and tried coming at our backs until Gance leveled a kick at him along with a few harsh words, and barked like the dog was barking.

The dog understood a threat when he heard one. With a last growl, he turned back toward the rear of the house and disappeared there. Somebody shouted in the darkness, but I couldn't make out any of the words.

I was on the porch in two long strides and frankly very glad to hear Gance directly behind me. The door was open and lamplight flooded out, and I stopped and swept off my hat.

"Hello the house," I shouted. And without giving it a second thought, launched my plan. "Mrs. Robert Chesney's sons from Cincinnati here to see Mr. Ballestero."

"Jesus Christ!" Gance moaned, and I saw he had both hands under his smock where the pistols were hidden.

Almost at once a small, bowlegged man appeared in the doorway, and the lamplight behind him made a halo of the powdered wig he wore. It was the first powdered wig I'd seen in that Ohio Valley country since my childhood.

"Who is it?" he shouted in a high, crackling voice. "Who is come here?"

I repeated who we were and asked if we had the honor to address Mr. Shawn Ballestero.

"You do, you do," he shouted, leaning forward to peer at us. He was wearing knee breeches, silk stockings, and buckle shoes and a long waistcoat, in the style of the Revolution. "Sons of Mrs. Chesney, are you? Well, I've heard of her. Come in, come in, you're in time for supper!"

Somewhat tentatively, Gance and I moved into the room, and it was a large one, elaborately furnished with most expensive rug and table and chairs and a glass-front dish closet and another matching one with racks of wine bottles. Over the center table, a long rectangular affair with a white linen cloth, hung an ornate chandelier with four lighted whale oil lamps with clear crystal globes.

"Thank you, sir," I said, and as he turned to move behind his table, I nudged Gance and he took off his hat.

"Yes, yes, just in time to take supper with me, not many visitors now," Mr. B. shouted. He had a narrow, deeply lined face, florid, clean-shaven, and I assumed Irish.

"Solomon," he shouted. "Two visiting gentlemen for supper."

On the far side of the room, at the door I figured led into the kitchen, I saw the faces of two very old Africans, slaves I supposed, at least once slaves, the man Solomon and a woman. And there were others there, too, but I more or less sensed rather than saw them.

Mr. B. indicated two chairs at the table, facing that door, and we seated ourselves, Gance to my left, and at once he pulled his chair close to the table and thrust his hands under the hanging edge of the linen tablecloth.

"More bacon and fish in the pan, Daisy; more settings, Solomon," Mr. B. shouted, and I realized shouting was his normal way of discourse.

He took a seat opposite Gance and I, smiling his ruddy smile, and the old black man came in and began to lay out places. It was sterling and the china was creamy bone, and I knew then the stories I'd heard of how rich Ballestero was were indeed true. I had never in my life sat down to a meal with such expensive equipment, and never did afterward.

I noted that as Solomon's long black fingers laid out our plate and silver, he laid out three additional places, two at the table's end next to me, one at the opposite end immediately to Gance's left.

"Yes, we have so little company here," Mr. B. said, and now Solomon had brought a number of bottles and had begun to fill glasses, crystal glasses of the same high quality as the rest of the setting. "A little sip as we wait. And Solomon, run tell the others that we have guests, bid them come sup with us."

It was exceedingly uncomfortable, the whole business, but lucky for us that Mr. B. was so engaged in his own conversation that he failed to take notice of it.

Our host had launched into a discussion of politics, not unusual in any way, and he seemed intent on making the point that we would soon be saved from the Serpent of Hades when the presidential elections would be held and Thomas Jefferson turned out of office.

"He is a godless man," Ballestero shouted. "He is known to have said that the teachings of Jesus are worthy of any man's strivings, yet he has also said that Christ is not divine and we do not come to the Kingdom through Him!

"He is a Deist, his followers say, who believes that God is evident through reason and not revelation," Mr. B. shouted, his face flame red. "Balderdash! He is an atheist, sirs, I tell you he is a godless atheist! Along with all those others who claim Deism, like Madison and even John Adams, who is a Unitarian. All Unitarians are damned atheists, too, you know!"

I was ready next to be subjected to the beauty of Irish Catholicism, but it didn't happen. Because the other guests had arrived, coming through the door behind Mr. B.

The man was short, wiry, dressed all in black except for a white linen shirt and blue cravat, his eyes were darkly piercing, and he was watching me from the moment he entered the room. He wore a black spade beard, and in his left ear was a golden ring.

And entering the room immediately behind him was Creigor Mc-Callum and his daughter, Sarah!

It was the most difficult supper I ever had to sit through, each bite of grub sticking in my throat until a second painful swallow sent it on its way.

There was no fancy food on the fine tableware. Bacon and fried fish, green beans swimming in grease, stewed tomatoes, and butter-milk biscuits. Half a dozen different wines which our host sampled without system, as though he might be searching in vain for some soothing syrup for his overworked voice box.

Behind him from time to time I saw one or the other of the old Africans passing back and forth, and there was another man there, a white man, whom I saw only twice and fleetingly, with a heavy growth of black beard and wearing a billed military-style cap of some sort.

It was astonishing that Gance sat there eating like a starved woodyard dog, having sat back down again after rising to shake hands with Mr. Mendez when introductions were made by our host. The thought crossed my mind that my brother was determined to stuff all the food possible into his gut just in case this might be his last meal.

Yet I knew the kind of self-control it had taken for him to calmly shake hands with this Spaniard who had made every effort to kill Pap, for it was the same with me. And now to sit under that man's intense and obviously hostile gaze.

Creigor McCallum had shown a kind of startled irritation when he'd walked in and seen us, like maybe we'd interrupted something important. He called me by my first name as we shook hands. His memory surprised me.

And Sarah. Well, when she first came through that door and saw me, her eyes and mouth opened wide but she said no single word, and I very nearly had to bend forward to take her hand and speak a

318

greeting to her. Her palm was icy cold and moist. At table, she watched me as closely as did Mendez. I tried to reassure her with my own gaze.

So mostly, it was the rich old Irishman talking, at least until he ran out, temporarily I was sure, of good Jeffersonians to berate. Then he leaned across the table toward me and asked what brought us to his shore.

"Sir, our mother had heard that Mr. McCallum was living here on the island," I said. "I'm sure you know that he visited her on two occasions. Earlier this year and last year as well."

Mendez spoke for the first time, and I was surprised at the low, almost gentle quality of his voice.

"Mr. McCallum and his daughter have been guests in my home on this island for some time," Mendez said. "How did your mother know he was here?"

"Someone passing on the river mentioned it, I suppose."

"Well, yes, Mr. McCallum visited your mother on Mr. Burr's behalf," our host said, and his cackling laugh coming suddenly, made Sarah give a start. "And I seem to recall your mother sent him off without a farthing."

"Mother doesn't concern herself with politics," I said. "But she is good at business enterprise, and one reason is that she is very tight-fisted with her money."

Mr. Ballestero seemed about to explode with laughter, his face turning an even brighter shade of red as he sputtered and roared and pounded the table.

"Yes, by God, tightfisted with the money, that's right, that's the way to be, heh Mendez?"

I cast a quick glance at Mendez, and there was the brief show of a smile on his face. But it was quickly gone.

At the other end of the table, nearer me, McCallum and Sarah were immobile as stone, their eyes wide, their mouths making only the slightest movements of chewing. I needed nothing other than that picture of them to know beyond doubt that they were not here on this island as happy guests or contented cabin owners or bosom friends to our host and the man he'd introduced as his farm manager, Mendez.

In fact, throughout all of this, I noted that Sarah avoided looking directly at Mendez or Mr. B. at all, rather painfully focusing on me or on Gance and his dexterity with his left hand, the right being still under the hanging tablecloth.

"And so my mother wanted to extend an invitation to Mr. McCallum to visit her again," I said. "Mr. McCallum mentioned an undertaking of making shoes with alligator hide, and Mother thinks it might be a good time to investigate such a thing further."

Creigor McCallum opened his mouth, I thought to speak, but Mendez cut him off with the quiet voice that may have been soft but now took on sharp edges.

"Mr. McCallum is not well," he said. "Mr. McCallum never leaves the island. We are concerned with his health."

"That's correct," Mr. B. said, nodding so violently his wig appeared ready to fall into his plate. "But you tell dear Mrs. Chesney we would welcome her here. Isn't that right, Esteban?"

"Yes," said Mendez, and he looked at me. "Your father as well."

I heard McCallum catch his breath so I knew he was probably aware in some way of the connection between Mendez and Pap. But most apparent to me at that tense moment was Gance, deliberately placing his fork on his plate and moving his left hand under the tablecloth.

"I had thought Mr. McCallum looked in fine health," I said.

It was, as Pap would have said, grabbing the wolf by the ears, and Gance had a perfect sense of what was happening because I heard a soft snick of metal under the tablecloth and knew he had cocked the hammer on one of his pistols.

"Appearances can be deceiving, sir," Mendez said. "Perhaps your mother would allow me to represent Mr. McCallum if you would take me to her."

God, I couldn't believe it. Mendez apparently assumed that Pap hadn't told us what happened at Wilkinson's house in St. Louis, or else having told us, made no connection between that and anybody at Ballestero Island.

So now he had the gigantic gall to be asking me to escort him into my mother's house so he could destroy Pap and any chance he would ever have of testifying against General Wilkinson or Ballestero.

Such bravado infuriated me, and in that instant I wanted to let this Spanish bastard know where he stood with us.

"Mr. Mendez," I said. "Surely after your shenanigans in St. Louis, do you really think I or anybody else could guaranty your life if you ever stepped into my mother's house!"

For a single instant, there wasn't a sound, even from the kitchen. And it was McCallum who broke the silence; pushing back his chair, pulling Sarah to her feet beside him, he spoke with quavering voice.

"Mr. Chesney, I'll go back to Cincinnati with you now!"

"Now wait," Mr. Ballestero wailed, but his man Mendez was already up, kicking back his chair and coming round the table toward Gance.

"No, Shawn, they'll destroy us," he shouted, and from somewhere he'd produced what I suppose was the same Basque knife Pap had seen, and the long blade Pap had felt gleamed in the chandelier lamplight.

Gance was half rising, half backing away from Mendez, and I saw his pistol was hung under the tablecloth when he shot, the room vibrating with the shock of the sound and the linen covering Gance's hand shredded and set blazing with the muzzle blast and Mendez gasping as though a mule had kicked him in the belly and with an expression of surprised amazement on his face going backward against his chair and the glass front of the china closet behind him shattering with the impact of stray buckshot that had missed his chest.

Sarah began a long, low crying, not so much a scream as crying, and Ballestero was shouting, his wig fallen onto the table, his arms thrashing about knocking over wine bottles. The man with the black beard was in the kitchen doorway with a short-barreled blunderbuss, and now Gance had the second pistol free of the tablecloth and shot the bearded man in the face, the shot passing so close over Ballestero's head that the old man caught his breath like a baby does when you blow hard into its mouth. Across the room now roiling with powder smoke and smelling of sulphur we could barely see the man with the dark beard flopping backward into the kitchen where Daisy and Solomon were calling on their Lord.

By then, I had Sarah by one arm, her father had the other, we were both shouting, and she was still yelling and so was the old Irishman, and the last thing I saw in the murky room as we pushed through the door was my brother bending to the floor to get his hat.

"Follow me," I gasped and leaped off the porch and started for the far south side of the walnut grove, where our path led back to where the skiff waited. I hoped.

There were shouts behind us, and I heard men's voices, not Solomon's. We could still hear him wailing as we entered the deeper woods, and toward the Ohio's channel, I saw a large dark shape running along the shore, in the same direction we were taking. Hair trailed out far behind, and I remembered Pap's story of the big Indian woman Mendez had with him.

Pulling my own pistol from beneath my shirt, I aimed in that general direction hoping to scare her off, but the pistol clicked, the powder dashed from the pan at some point in this mad scramble. No matter; she was already gone behind a stand of willows ahead of us. She'd been out of range anyway.

I pulled up the McCallums once we were well into the trees, and Gance caught up to us. We were all puffing and blowing like bloated dray horses.

"I don't think anybody else is comin," he panted but kept watching the path behind us. "Damn. Damn!"

"Are you all right?" I whispered to Sarah. Her father still held her other arm, but I got the feeling she was leading him more than the other way round.

"Yes, Campbell," she said and pressed for a moment against my chest. "Thank God you came to us."

"Mr. Chesney, I don't know if I can run any more," said McCallum.

"You better be able," Gance said, turning and taking McCallum's coat lapel and pulling him along the path. "Where did we hide those damned long guns?"

We ran on, stumbling, falling sometimes, and there was a moon out now, full and bright, which had been well up at nightfall but we had been so intent on moving to the big house we hadn't even noted it. Now it was making the landscape bright, a very bad thing indeed for us, the hunted now.

The trees seemed to thin. There was more moonlight coming through the canopy, and our faces were dappled in black and white. We were breathing hard, and Mr. McCallum's air made a harsh rasping sound in his throat.

"Sweet Jesus, please," he said, and Gance stopped suddenly but not because of McCallum's difficulty.

"By damn, Campbell, look what we got now!" Gance said.

There in the path before us, not fifty paces away, was the Indian woman. It had to be the one Pap had told us about, the one in St. Louis who'd carried him and dumped him in the river. She'd beat us to this spot on the path and now stood between us and our boat. She was monstrously big, standing in full moonlight and looking toward us, and I even thought I could see the shine in her eyes.

"Find a club," I gasped, scrambling around on the ground. "Find something."

Only McCallum remained standing, bent, blowing hard, the others of us scratching about through last fall's dead leaves, trying to find a tree limb, a large stone, anything.

Gance heard it when I did. A sharp twang, as though somebody had plucked one of the wires in Judith Dwyer's harpsichord. We paused in our search for a club, on our knees, looking in the moonlight toward the huge woman. Then it came again, that strange sound like a metal wind suddenly released for just an instant.

The Indian woman took a step toward us. Then another. And then, like a hardwood tree that had been burned through at the base, fell sideways and struck the forest floor so violently I said the island shook in the telling of it later.

Ole Snake was there, coming from somewhere out of the woods, the short bow in his hand and already another arrow slotted. He waved us up and on, and ten yards short of where the woman lay was the wild-grapevine cache of weapons we'd left on the way in.

We walked now to allow McCallum better breathing. It was terribly difficult running through those woods with three empty pistols. But now we had two muskets and a rifle and a Fox Indian who may have been more deadly with the bow than all the firearms among us.

As we passed the fallen Indian woman, lying in the bright moonlight, Sarah looked down at her in horror.

Still clutched in one of her hands was a pole ax. Her dead eyes were like milky white marbles in the moonlight. There were two arrows in her chest, both buried to the vane.

While we'd retrieved our weapons in the grapevines, Ole Snake had gone ahead, so he'd passed the woman first before moving on toward our skiff. But I saw that brief as it was, he'd had enough time to take his trophy. The woman had been scalped.

It was only a small patch of hair taken from the back of her head and had not distorted or given her disklike, flat face a mutilated look. Had the woman survived the arrows, she could have gone on with her life without anyone ever knowing an enemy warrior had taken her hair.

I made no effort to point any of this out to Sarah. But a few steps farther along, she threw up anyway.

It has always been a mystery to me that my most vivid memory of that night at Ballestero Island was not the violence and blood and death, but Gance's reaction to it.

Certainly, I don't know what would have happened to us had Gance not been so furiously aggressive, part of it motivated no doubt by what these people had done to Pap and part of it pure survival instinct.

Whatever it was, once we were safe, away in the skiff, Gance went into what was almost like a trance, staring fixedly at the water as Snake and I rowed furiously for the far shore and then downstream to Hockingport.

I remembered the time Hiram and I had teased him for his faint heart when he'd vomited at the sight of intestines as Pap dressed a deer. Yet here he was, the sudden, vicious killer, and I watched and wondered if he was about to be sick again.

But before we were well on the way down that moonlit river, he was at an oar himself and no trace of guilt or remorse on his face. I attributed it to the boundless resilience of youth.

Years later, when the shock of proximity was no longer a concern, I asked Gance if he ever thought of that night at Ballestero. A distant gleam came to his eyes, those eyes so much like our mother's, and he grinned.

"Yes," he said. "I think of it as the night of stomping on scorpions."

Then he laughed and shook his head.

"But you know, Campbell, I've never since been able to eat stewed tomatoes."

When we'd gone to Ballestero Island together, Gance had been fifteen years old.

Our journey home was memorable only in that Sarah McCallum was at first almost hysterical with relief to be rescued from what she had apparently perceived as a situation life threatening to her father and to her.

Not a bad perception, either, because it was pretty clear to Gance and me that Esteban Mendez had no intention of allowing either of them off that island.

Her father was incapable of comforting her. We were afraid he might collapse and die on us. From the moment Ole Snake got him into the skiff until we were long back in Cincinnati, he seemed in trouble with his breathing, his speech was mostly incoherent, and he could hardly take a drink of water without assistance.

So the task of consoling Sarah until she regained some shred of her composure and self-control fell to me. Which was one of the more pleasant experiences of my life to that time.

It consisted of stroking her hair and holding her close in my arms and whispering encouragement into her tiny ear and that sort of thing.

All of which Gance observed with a wide grin that indicated he assigned all sorts of wicked intent to my actions. I was frankly enjoying the whole business so much that I didn't bother to refute him.

My euphoria ended in Cincinnati.

Happy enough to see us back safe, Mother wasn't so happy that she was going to take another woman into her house, so from the first night the McCallums were established in one of a number of small houses Mother had been financing on the last of her lots in what could be called the town.

"He can pay for it when he starts making a wage," she said, and later I realized she already had a place for him in her shoemaking endeavor. "Why not? He came in here the first time talking shoes, didn't he?"

Mother wanted only the most general details of the trip, and likely all she really wanted to know was whether we'd found Mendez and what we'd done with him. We told her that, of course, and at the end of it she actually smiled and laid her hand on Gance's shoulder.

"You are a fine red savage heathen, aren't you?" she said.

There wasn't much bright in her life. Pap was in such ill health that he was in bed most of the time now.

He lay there as we told him about Ballestero Island and about the big squaw Ole Snake had killed, Ole Snake at the moment where he'd been since we returned. In the horse barn where he did nothing but eat and sleep for three days.

Gance gave Pap the Basque knife. Until that moment I'd no idea Gance came away from the island with it. But I recalled his bending for his hat after the shooting, and he'd taken the knife at the same time.

Pap was delighted with it, of course, and praised Gance as though he was a big hero of the Revolution or some such thing, and Gance became embarrassed about it and blushed and kept saying, "Campbell did most of it, Campbell did most of it."

And the day Mother told Gance he was a fine red savage heathen, she said to me, "You, too."

But she said it when nobody else was near enough to hear her. It was good to be back in the old jousting arena. What did I care? I was seeing Sarah every day, and delighting in how wonderfully she and my sister Clariese were getting on and having secret delight in picking out a small house somewhere close to Mother's house. A house to buy.

We heard some wild rumors along the riverfront about a shooting upriver at Ballestero Island, but when the local sheriff rowed over to see about it, the old man there ran him off and told him to mind his own business.

There was an election. Jemy Madison, a friend of Mr. Jefferson, was going to be the next president.

"He'll do all right," Mother said, "so long as he keeps an eye on the damned English!"

It was really criminal that somebody like my mother had no voice in selecting a president. Or a representative or sheriff or any other elected official. It was criminal she could not vote because she appreciated the process of government better than the vast majority of those who could.

It wasn't because she had so much Indian blood in her veins that she was denied the franchise. It was because she was a woman.

Pap died in November of 1809. In his sleep. Mother was convinced it came when he heard the bad news.

She had warned against telling him, but one of his old tavern friends was visiting one day and informed him that somewhere along the Natchez Trace, Meriwether Lewis had been murdered.

Nobody seemed to know the details. The leader of the Great Expedition had been drinking too much over the past year and according to close associates in St. Louis, was despondent. He was traveling toward Virginia when it happened, maybe on the way to visit his old mentor Thomas Jefferson who had just come home after serving eight years as president of the United States.

He was found close by an inn where he'd spent the night. He had been robbed and shot twice, once in the chest, once in the head.

It was a terrible thing for Pap to hear. He raved about getting well and leaving his bed and going down there to Tennessee or wherever it was and finding the dastardly scoundrel who had done such a thing to a man so brave and resourceful in the service of the Republic.

It was a last surge of Pap's massive energy. But now it was all an illusion.

So Pap went in his sleep, without much pain, we supposed. Mother put us all out of her house while she bathed him and dressed him in woods gear and wrapped him in a thick quilt.

It was a considerable funeral procession to the forest this time. There was a wagon with four gravediggers and Pap, the buggy with Mother and me, and a second wagon with Otto and Clariese, Gance and the McCallums, Ole Snake walking along behind the whole cavalcade.

I was surprised she allowed the McCallums to come with us. It was her final approval, of Sarah as a member of the family, or at least soon to be when I had a house for us to move into.

We had to go about four miles before we were clear of the town and close-in cabins and barns. It was farther than we had brought her own pap when we buried him, but in the same general area along the east bank of the Great Miami River.

It was cold, and there was a wind and low-flying clouds. The trees had lost most of their leaves, and the green cedars stood out in sharp contrast to the gray of surrounding hardwoods. Somewhere above us there was a hunting hawk making his sharp little cry, and he seemed to follow us all the way.

We stayed in the wagons until the four men had a grave dug. It didn't take them long because the surface of the soil here was mostly soft leaf mound.

Otto and I carried the long bundle to the grave, and it weighed so little you might suspect no body was inside. Gance walked beside us with the Pennsylvania rifle that Mother had specifically asked him to bring, Pap's big hunting knife, and his pipe-tomahawk hatchet.

It was a shallow hole, and Otto and I got into it and lowered Pap's body. When we scrambled out, Mother had Gance help her down, then she took from him the rifle and knife and hatchet and lay them on the rolled blanket.

She said something then, but I couldn't catch the words.

She sent us all back to the wagons to wait, and we were shivering in the cold wind when finally she and her gravediggers reappeared.

On the way back to town, Mother and I in the buggy leading, it was a long time before either of us spoke. Finally, I did.

"I expected to hear you do another chant," I said.

"I sang his song before, when I thought he was dead," she said. "One death song is enough for any man, even your Pap."

"It was hard for me to hear what you said in the grave."

"It was meant for your pap, not for you. So I spoke in Abenaki, the language I taught him," she said. And there was almost some sound of triumph in her voice. "I gave him his weapons and told him."

"Told him what, to watch out for the Mohawks and the English?"

"No. I didn't have to tell him that. He knew. I said to him, 'Here are the things. For your journey up the Kennebec.'"

A small chill went along my back. I supposed because it had begun to snow.

Part IV

THE ENGLISH AGAIN

Chapter 15

Ole Snake had decided to stay.

From the first, he had thought he'd return to his home country along the Wisconsin River in what the white man now called the far northwest part of the Illinois Territory. At first, he'd thought he would go once he'd brought Two Gap Tooth back to his people, Two Gap Tooth being what Robert Chesney was called among the Fox Indians.

Then Ole Snake saw the Woman. Two Gap Tooth's Woman. So he decided to stay a little while. Just to look at her from time to time and think the things a man sometimes thinks when he looks upon a handsome woman.

There was never any secret plan to steal the Woman. Not that Ole Snake wouldn't have liked to steal her. But it would be very lethal. Two Gap Tooth was sick but could be dangerous still. And his two sons were even more ruthless, especially the younger one, Ole Snake reckoned.

And all three of these people would be angry if Ole Snake did something they didn't like, and stealing the Woman was definitely something they wouldn't like.

But when Two Gap Tooth died and they put him in the earth, Ole Snake decided he wanted to stay a little longer. Looking at the Woman had become a habit hard to break.

And with Two Gap Tooth gone, it was only logical that some other man appear to service the handsome Woman. Ole Snake reckoned he was that man.

Because he'd spent so much time looking at her, Ole Snake knew this Woman was bold and direct. He therefore decided that if he was to take the place of Two Gap Tooth, he must be bold and direct as well.

Selecting a day when no one else was around, Ole Snake presented himself to her in her kitchen as she stood at the white man's cooking stove. When she noticed him inside her house she turned to confront him and say something, and at that moment Ole Snake pulled aside his loincloth to show the strength and dimension of his longing for her.

Ole Snake was never sure of the sequence of events during the next few seconds. He was later painfully aware that he had been struck on his head just above the left ear with a cast-iron skillet. He recalled sprawling on the floor where he found himself looking into the muzzle of a cocked pistol.

Scrambling to his feet, Ole Snake walked out of the kitchen in some haste but with as much dignity as he could summon under the circumstances. He was cursed and reviled and struck across the back twice more with the skillet before he could get to the door.

At his horse barn quarters, Ole Snake prepared to take his gear and make a quick departure in the direction of the far Wisconsin River, but pride forced him to remain and take whatever the handsome Woman thought appropriate and to do so without any more of the embarrassment suffered in her kitchen, but standing like a true warrior, on his feet with weapons in his hand.

But nothing happened. After three days, Ole Snake decided the Woman had not disclosed to anybody his display of masculine endowments. For a moment, it was so humiliating that she was simply ignoring it that he almost bolted for Illinois Territory then and there.

No woman had ever viewed what Ole Snake had shown this Woman without an appropriate display of admiration or even awe. And she was simply ignoring it, as though it were nothing more than some sort of irritation not to be taken seriously. Like a wood tick. Or a bluebottle fly.

In some perverse way, it made Ole Snake want even more to stay close enough to observe the Woman from time to time, even though now he knew there was no chance of stealing her and taking her to the land of his people where she could take care of his household and dominate his other wives while he himself lay around and smoked or sometimes went out to fight the Osage or the Kickapoo.

But he needed to attach himself to somebody, as he had done to Two Gap Tooth. To be his special friend. His special ally.

Because Ole Snake knew that living in the white man's world, as he more or less was doing now, a white man friend or ally was good and in fact essential if one was to avoid other white men posing serious questions as to what the hell he was doing there. Especially when some of the British army people to the north were selling guns and whiskey to various tribesmen and encouraging them to go south and have a good time burning houses and killing Americans.

Of course, Ole Snake had never had any love for the English and had no intention of making trouble for Americans as one of the Sauk chiefs in his home country was always advocating. A man named Black Sparrow Hawk, whom the white man called Black Hawk.

Therefore, with Two Gap Tooth gone, another Chesney was required as a special friend.

The older son, Campbell. He was too interested in that little white woman they had taken from the island in the river. And he was always going about in the town, seeing to the various things people were doing who worked for his mother, the Woman.

So it would be the younger son. It would be Gance. He enjoyed shooting and the woods and traveling about and having plenty of whiskey to drink. Ole Snake knew this kind of man, a man who had

335

grown from a shy, timid boy into a roaring bull of a man. Well, not yet a roaring bull. But with all the character of his father, Two Gap Tooth, already popping up here and there.

Ole Snake reckoned his age about twice that of the younger son. Ole Snake had found his medicine, hence become a man, at some indeterminate point in his life, but assumed about the twelfth summer, and since then had seen the seasons pass about twenty times, making him somewhere near thirty years old.

That meant at the time they went to the island and took the little white woman for the older son, Gance had been about half of Ole Snake's age.

A good separation. They could do things together, like hunt and fish, but Ole Snake had enough age to act as an older uncle, maybe, and teach the younger son many things.

And of course, the younger son, Gance could teach Ole Snake the white man's language, which was the language spoken by his mother, the Woman, when she was not cursing Ole Snake in French or one of many tribal dialects, some of which he knew, some of which he didn't.

Yes, Ole Snake reckoned, it was good. Him and the younger son of the Woman. A fine pair. He'd work on that.

Ole Snake watched the older son, Campbell, trying to figure out what would make anybody so crazy. Except for the little white woman, of course, who only had to pass by and the older son would begin to behave like a camp dog struck in the head with a stick of firewood.

That part of Campbell's craziness was understandable. Ole Snake had seen it plenty of times. Especially among certain young Menominees, although maybe that didn't count because Ole Snake always figured a lot of young Menominees were crazy without getting hit in the head with a stick of firewood.

And building that new lodge near Little Miami River on the far side of town, a house, the older son called it. All day getting into a sweat. Yelling at men carrying cut trees and lumber. Carrying windowpane glass sent to him from a place called Pittsburgh, carrying it himself all the way to where they were building the house because he didn't trust anybody else to carry it.

Ole Snake had never believed in carrying much of anything except weapons. Maybe a little food and whiskey, but carrying that only so long as it took to find a nice place to sit down and consume it.

But the house was understandable too, because when it was done, the oldest son had married the little white woman they'd stolen from the island in the river and they'd moved into the new house, along with the woman's father.

Ole Snake had been at the wedding. At least, he'd been at the horse barn behind the Woman's house when the wedding took place. He had been pleasantly drunk throughout most of the singing and dancing and other white man foolishness associated with weddings. More celebrating, Ole Snake figured, than was necessary even for a good scalp dance after a successful raid on the Assiniboine.

It was a good idea. The older son wanted a woman, and he would be a fool to bring another woman into the big Woman's house. Maybe Indians could do that. But white women always seemed to have trouble getting along together if they had to cook in the same lodge.

Besides, the Woman was probably getting tired of having her oldest son underfoot all the time.

So Campbell getting his own house was good. Now he had a house, and the Woman had a house. They could get through a day now and then without insulting each other.

That was something Ole Snake couldn't comprehend. That Campbell would insult the Woman. It was obscene. Not because she was his mother. But because she was the *Woman*!

But once he was in his new house over there on the Little Miami, Campbell started doing the really crazy thing. He became the Pig Man.

Gance had done a pretty good job teaching Ole Snake how to talk and listen to the English language. They spent a lot of time together south of the river, in Kentucky, hunting turkey or deer.

When they killed a deer, Ole Snake would cure the hide and Gance would sell it on the Cincinnati riverfront. Then they'd take the money and sit in Judith Dwyer's tavern sipping warm beer or, if they really got serious, some of that locally distilled clear liquid the Germans made and called steinhager.

Steinhager almost blew the top of Ole Snake's head off, but he enjoyed all the various colors that flashed through his mind after a few jolts of it.

At first, Ole Snake sat outside in the alley while Gance was inside. Then one day Gance said, To hell with this, and took Ole Snake right into the taproom.

There were half a dozen white men in the room and they muttered and spit, and one finally came over and told Gance to get his family Indian out of where white men were trying to enjoy their libations.

Ole Snake was ready to leave. But Gance put his hand on Ole Snake's arm and said to the man, "This here is my own good brother, and the only way he goes out of here is when you try to put me out."

Gance was already a little drunk. They'd been along the river, shooting a few turtles with one of the Woman's pistols, and the pistol was still in Gance's belt.

The man and all the other white men in the tavern looked at Ole Snake. Then they looked at the pistol. Then they looked at Gance's face. And the man said, "Well, I guess it's alright for the red heathen to drink a little beer if he doesn't bother nobody."

So Gance said, "It's not this Indian who's about to bother somebody."

So the white man went back and joined his friends and they laughed a lot, and one of them shouted, "Alright, Chesney, this one time, because he helped your daddy."

No one ever got serious about running the Indian out of the place after that, although Ole Snake never would have thought of going in there unless Gance was with him.

Gance had taken some of his pap's clothes and given them to Ole

Snake. Woolen trousers and a broadcloth coat and some linen shirts. He still wore his moccasins, though, and he would have nothing to do with a hat. He still had his hair in that scalp-lock-down-the-back fashion, which really stood out now that pigtails for white men had pretty much gone out of fashion east of the Mississippi.

Sometimes, Ole Snake wondered if the Woman had approved of her son taking Two Gap Tooth's clothes. Maybe so. But even if she had, and even though she saw Ole Snake wearing the stuff every day, it didn't signal near enough approval to give him any ideas about going into her kitchen again and drawing back his loincloth.

At the Woman's house, Gance sometimes brought Ole Snake into the kitchen, and they'd eat together. But never when the Woman was there. Ole Snake could always tell if the Woman had just departed because at those times, the smell of her would be very strong.

The Woman never asked her youngest son to do chores of any kind, as she'd done when he was younger, Ole Snake supposed. Once he heard her say, "You're just like your pap, wandering around in those dark woods all the time."

And Gance had said to his mother that he'd always do anything she wanted him to do, and the Woman had laughed and said, "No, it is good to have a man around the house who is so undependable and wants to do nothing but eat and hunt because it reminds me of your pap."

Ole Snake got the feeling that when he'd been a young child, Gance had been afraid of a lot of things and now that he was coming into his manhood, he was proving how he didn't give a damn. Proving it to himself more than anybody else.

Ole Snake had known a lot of his own people who did that. Some of the little pipsqueaks before they came into their medicine arrived at manhood with the bang of a cannon. He figured Gance was like that.

It was all fine with Ole Snake, and being around Gance so much, he sure learned that English language pretty good, too.

So when Campbell got really crazy and became the Pig Man, Ole

Snake knew all about it because he'd heard the brothers talking in the dark at the horse barn one night after he and Gance had eaten some roasted bear ribs somebody had brought the Woman. The older son had come up the bluff to tell his mother about his plan and so afterward stopped at the barn and told Gance, too.

"A lot of these settlers out along the Little Miami came here from the mountains in Virginia or Tennessee," Campbell said. "They let their hogs range in the woods and then hunt em down and slaughter when they want meat."

And Gance said, "Or try to sell them."

Those woods-ranging hogs were a hard, tough lot, and Campbell said that's why he was going to do it. Gance asked, "Do what?" and Campbell told him.

"I'll contract for a few shoats from a couple of those people, not many to start with. When a sow farrows, out in the woods, and the settler finds the pigs, he'll hold out until they're weaned then shoot the sow for himself and bring in the farrow, and I'll pen em and feed em corn. Keep em in a lantern-lit shed and stuff the food down em, day and night. All they'll do is eat and shit, and then I'll slaughter em.

"I'll have a big smokehouse for hams, shoulders, and bacon. I'll sell some fresh, like to Judith, but most of what I don't smoke I'll grind and make sausage. Before you know it, I'll be shipping cured meat and sausage all up and down this river!"

"Where'd you learn to do all that?" Gance asked. "You never as much as raised a rabbit before."

"Not me. A bunch of Germans and Poles. Gustus Staufer is gonna run it for me. Oh, and we'll sell the hides to Mother's shoe shop."

"What in hell's name brought all this on?"

"By God, I aim to make my own way. I got off the bluff so now I'll get out of her match works and shoe shop and distillery and land office."

"And the new gunpowder mill."

"Yeah. That, too. But by God, you wait. This town's gonna be the jewel of the Ohio for meat processing before I'm finished. And hell,

Gance, half the people comin downriver now are Germans from eastern Pennsylvania or else right from the old country, and they know how to make that sausage."

"What's she say?"

Ole Snake knew Gance was talking now about his mother, the Woman.

"She's givin me a loan to get started right. I had some saved, but hell, she's fillin it up, Gance, she's fillin it up."

"Yeah," Gance said. "You always was her favorite."

They both laughed. Ole Snake didn't know what the joke was, but he laughed too, until the older son glared at him over the lantern sitting on the floor between them.

Ole Snake was aware of a noticeable increase in river traffic that year. He heard Gance talking with Carter Purcell, the land office man, so he understood that business and travel and everything was good because President Madison had let the old embargo on European goods expire.

Maybe President Madison had done it in hopes the English would cancel those old Orders in Council that had caused President Jefferson to put on the embargo in the first place. It was under those Orders in Council that the British navy stopped American ships anyplace they pleased and sent boarding parties to carry off any sailors they claimed were British deserters.

It turned out the British left the Orders in Council in effect. So under threat of their big guns, British navy ships continued to stop American merchantmen whenever they felt like it.

Any talk about the English interested Ole Snake because he enjoyed watching the Woman get angry. And when the American embargo on English goods was lifted and the Brits kept right on stopping American ships, she threw a tantrum Ole Snake held in dear memory for years.

Part of it was the Woman running out into the night screaming oaths in Abenaki or something nobody else could understand, and shooting off a musket in the direction of the river, and they said later that every dog on that side of Cincinnati ran for the Little Miami looking for someplace to hide.

Gance said all those ships being hindered at sea didn't have much effect on his mother's businesses or her life, either, but she saw that as just another indication that the English, with troops still in forts on American soil around the Great Lakes, were selling arms to the Indians and guiding them on bloody raids into the Ohio Valley.

Almost everybody believed the same thing. So whether it was happening or not, everybody thought it was, and it made Ole Snake uncomfortable when local citizens glared at him like he'd been out slaughtering settlers' wives.

After news from the north, from around the lakes, came to them that another settler or town had been buried and butchered, Ole Snake would stay inside the horse barn for a few days.

He had to hide more and more frequently. Because the English savages, as everybody called them, were beginning to get serious again, and always, it seemed, when a few of the raiders were shot and they dropped equipment behind to be found, here it was: a good Manchester-made musket and fine-quality gunpowder, the kind only the English and Germans could make.

"Damned dirty English dogs," the Woman would scream from her kitchen, and Ole Snake could hear it all the way out there in the horse barn, and nod, and think, What a fine Woman!

Sometimes in summer, Gance and Snake went to a place on the Little Miami upstream from where Campbell had his smokehouses and hog pens and lie on a high ridge above the stream and watch a ceremony that Ole Snake came to associate with a certain white man god who, as best he could figure, lived in the water there.

Gance had explained it as best he could, but progress in learning English was not yet adequate enough to allow Ole Snake any more than a fragmentary understanding of what was going on, so he had to fill in the gaps from his own imagination.

There would be a gathering of white men and women and children beside the river, and a few of them would be wearing what appeared to be a white dress over their regular clothes.

Standing about waist deep in the river was a white man, a bald-headed white man, wearing the same kind of dress. This white man did a lot of shouting and waving of arms, and often, as he shouted, the people on the bank would yell a loud "A-Men!"

Then two men, older men like the one standing in the river and doing all the shouting, would take the arms of a man or woman or child who was standing on the bank wearing one of those dresses and lead that person out into the river.

Sometimes, the one being led out into the river didn't look too happy about it. The people on the bank would be singing and shouting "A-Men" some more, and then the bald-headed man would grab the one just led out from the bank and thrust this one backward into the water until he or she was completely submerged.

But the bald-headed man always changed his mind about drowning the one he was holding and would pull up the person just in time. The people on the bank would yell "A-Men," and the bald-headed man would release the one he'd been holding, and this one, spitting and sputtering and gasping, would be helped back onto the bank. And a new person wearing one of those dresses over regular clothes would be grabbed and dragged into the river.

After he saw this exercise the first time, Ole Snake asked Gance why the bald-headed man always changed his mind about drowning the sacrificial victim and why all those other people gathered to watch when they knew damned well the bald-headed man would change his mind right at the last minute.

It took Gance the better part of a day to explain what was happening, and even then Ole Snake's mind was cloudy, except to have it confirmed that white men sometimes did things that defied all explanation.

Even Ole Snake's friends, the Chesneys, seemed to confirm his low rating of white people's reason.

The Woman's daughter and her husband, the shoemaker, had a little girl. As near as Ole Snake could figure, that made the Woman grandmother to the little girl, so the Woman should have been teaching the child from the start about not crying all the time and later how to keep a lodge clean and later still how to cook and later still how to make a man happy.

But as far as Ole Snake could see, and as always he observed the Woman very closely, she didn't try to teach the child anything at all. In fact, the Woman acted as though she didn't care whether or not the daughter brought the child when she came to visit.

Then Campbell and the little woman they'd stolen from that island in the river had a little boy and they named him Campbell.

Ole Snake thought it was crazy the way white people gave sons their father's names because names were all tied up with medicine and power, and everybody knew each boy had to come into his own medicine and power when he got old enough to hunt and marry and fight the Ojibway.

And then, the silliest thing of all, after they gave the boy his father's name, they called the child something else, like Junior, as though everybody was ashamed of the father's name and wouldn't call it, or else if they did were afraid their gods would be upset about it like the gods got upset when a man died and you spoke his name again after he was dead.

And the Woman, who had married a white man and then lived among white men for so long sometimes she acted as crazy as they did. Because now she had a grandson, which was supposed to be a great joy, but she didn't pay any more attention to this Junior than she did to the little girl.

Campbell and the little woman they'd stolen on the island in the river would come up the bluff a lot of times in the evening when there wasn't snow on the ground, and sometimes when there was, and bring the baby, but Ole Snake could hear them in the kitchen and they never talked about the baby. They always talked about something the Woman and Campbell could argue about.

"I hear your old friend Tecumseh is going around talking to a lot of red savage heathen up near Lake Erie."

"Yes, and I expect he's still got that female missionary tagging along with him warming his bed at night."

"Well, even though that's likely not true, it is true that he's doing a lot of talking to the tribes about not hacking wounded men to pieces and not torturing prisoners."

"Those people don't listen to Tecumseh. They listen to the English because it is the English, not Tecumseh, who bring them guns and whiskey. And if the English say hack and torture, their friends the Ottawa will hack and torture."

"I thought Pap and Mad Anthony Wayne killed all the Ottawas in one of those battles they were always talking about."

"Don't rub that the wrong way, boy! You're always saying that. And can't you make the baby stop crying?"

Or maybe it was a conversation about things Ole Snake didn't comprehend at all.

"The newspaper says the New England states are doing good business now that the embargo has been lifted."

"I never read this newspaper they've got here now."

"I don't know why not. They usually have everything in there, every week, that the Pittsburgh newspaper has."

"That's an Englishman who runs it. He was saying things about *poor* King George going mad. So his son the Prince of Wales had to do the king's work. *Poor* King George! That's the man your pap and I fought to make this Republic."

"Well, certain parts of this Republic, like New England, are doing a lot of good business with those same Englishmen you fought."

"I know that! The New England states did business with the English during the Revolution. The New England states do business with the English even while the English soldiers stay in *our* forts, on American soil, and stir up Indians who slaughter *our* settlers."

"Not everybody sees it like you do, Mother."

"Not everybody knows them like I do. My people fought against them once with the French. I fought against them, and your pap, too, during the Revolution."

"Mother, New Englanders were some of the best troops and leaders in the Revolution. I didn't fight that war, but remember, you sent me to this local school, and that good Presbyterian parson told us all about the Revolution and there were not any more Loyalists in New England than in other places."

"You're treading on dangerous ground, boy!"

Or maybe something nobody could really understand.

"Mother, I read they took a census."

"What's that?"

"They count everybody. And they say that in your glorious Republic now, there are more than seven million people. It's 1810, and there are more than seven million people living in the various states."

"I don't believe that. Nobody counted me. Whoever said that don't even know I'm here!"

Listening outside, Ole Snake grunted. That Woman! She was right. Nobody had counted Ole Snake, either.

Then he thought, Maybe they didn't want to count me and the Woman; maybe they don't *want* to know we're here.

Chapter 16

It was the same year Campbell Chesney decided to run for the federal Congress when Pieter Groot and his wife Willimena came down the river from the East. He'd come to take a job as master shipwright in Stanislas Lewicki's boatyard. And within a fortnight, she was working for the widow Chesney in her big house on the bluff.

From the name, you'd expect them to be Dutch. They were from New York, too, and there were a lot of Dutchmen in New York. And a lot of those knew how to build ships and boats.

But at first glance, it was obvious Pieter Groot was not really Dutch. His skin was the color of weak coffee, his hair bronze-red, his eyes a yellowish gray. All of which told you he was a considerable distance from Africa but that his line in America had started a long time ago in a slave ship from the Ivory Coast or some such place, and had since been considerably bisected by one or various strands of blond hair.

So one could use a term for him common in the territory of Orleans, about to become the state of Louisiana, by the way. *Mulatto.*

People north of the Ohio usually said *Negro* or *colored* or *nigger.* No matter the degree of cross-pollination.

The first Pieter Groot had been a Netherlands shipbuilder in New Amsterdam at the time the colony was taken from the Dutch by the English in 1664 and renamed New York. He had owned a single African slave, whom he freed by last will and testament. Since then, to honor that emancipation, the eldest son of each succeeding generation was given the name of the old Dutchman who had effected their freedom.

So when the latest Pieter Groot arrived in Cincinnati, he came free and he could boast a lineage in America that stretched back farther than that of most whites and a century and a half of that not enslaved.

No matter. He still had to pay the five-hundred-dollar bond required of all immigrant people of color. Well, actually, Stanislas Lewicki paid it but not without great screeching and swearing and gnashing of teeth.

Lewicki wouldn't pay the bond on Willimena, whose background was completely unknown, and besides that she wasn't a skilled boatbuilder. And no mulatto, either, but very black.

Willimena's bond was paid by the Widow Chesney, who did even more screeching and swearing and gnashing of teeth than Lewicki had done.

Some of the people along the riverfront said the reason Campbell was going to run for the Congress was to somehow get Ohio's people-of-color bonding law repealed and his mother's money refunded.

Like a lot of things said about politicians either in office or trying to get in, it wasn't true, but it made for good conversation in Judith Dwyer's or in one of the many other saloons that now decorated the Cincinnati riverfront.

In fact, Campbell Chesney was running for office on an issue close to his mother's heart. The English. Only he was taking a stand against another war with Great Britain, which wasn't exactly her idea of the Republic's proper reaction to Royal Navy seizures of

American ships at sea and redcoat soldiers along the American side of the Canadian border.

"You're doing it just to make Mother mad," Gance said. "You don't really believe such a thing."

"I do," Campbell said, and his face got red and he shouted, which was what most always happened now when he began discussing politics. "We aren't ready for war. Too many people want to start blowing things up just because we aren't gettin on too well with the English. It'll all take care of itself if we let it."

"Pap is spinning in his grave," Gance said.

"Pap was from another generation," Campbell said. "Now we need to get away from all that Glorious Revolution talk and learn to get along with people."

"Hell, Campbell, that Revolution generation, they're the ones Mother says is kitty-cat-lickin around the English and letting them bully us and treat us like no-account relatives cause they know those coots won't do anything about it."

Even so, Campbell did a lot of lying awake at night in his bed beside Sarah, listening to her father snoring from the next room, and grinding his teeth because he wasn't so sure but what Gance was right. Maybe he *was* doing it to spite his mother.

Stanislas Lewicki believed that when he paid a bond on somebody to come into the state, that somebody owed him at least eight or ten hours work a day. For which he'd pay a good wage, of course.

So when, within two months of his beginning to cut frames and lay keels and shingle sheathing for a river keelboat being built in Lewicki's yard, Pieter Groot started spending as much time doing hammer-and-saw work on the bluff at Widow Chesney's as he did in the boatyard, Lewicki was naturally irritated.

It seemed that the Widow Chesney had taken such a shine to her new housemaid Willimena Groot that she would not hear of her and her husband living in that rat-trap shack on the riverfront near the boatyard, Willimena having to walk up the bluff each day, fair weather or foul. So she decided to build extra rooms onto her house where the couple could live.

Besides, Gance and Ole Snake both showed considerable interest in the new man because of his color and the way he talked and the stories he could tell of building ships in New York big enough to carry cannons with barrels longer than the bar in Judith Dwyer's taproom.

And sometimes, when Pieter Groot was supposed to be in the boatyard, Lewicki heard he wasn't even working on that new room at the widow's but out in the woods on the Kentucky side of the river hunting turkey or deer or some such thing with the widow's good-for-nothing son and that shave-head red savage they kept in the barn up there on the bluff.

Which was true, because Gance figured that to pay back Pieter Groot for all the good stories he told about things Gance had never heard of, it was only right that Gance take Pieter Groot to the woods and show him things that Pieter Groot had never heard of. Well, had never done anyway, like shoot a Kentucky gobbler.

Tried beyond his patience, Stanislas Lewicki stormed up the bluff to the Widow Chesney's house and told her that the next time the circuit court was in session, he aimed to sue her for taking away a worker he'd paid bond on, and she told him Pieter Groot was tired of working on his little river vessels instead of ships that went out onto the high seas, like he'd done in New York, and she'd pay Stanislas Lewicki the bond on the spot in gold.

Stanislas Lewicki figured he'd never get a better deal, especially if he went to law and had to hire one of the string-tie attorneys who had begun to gather in Cincinnati like woodpeckers on a dead oak snag.

So Nalambigi Chesney paid Stanislas Lewicki five hundred dollars, and they sat on the promontory porch and drank sassafras tea and ate venison pemmican with brown sugar melted on it and talked about what blackhearted bastards the English were, all the while her younger son standing in shadows, sort of at Stanislas Lewicki's back according to his story of it, fingering a pistol in his belt.

"I never been so happy to get free of a place since me and Count Pulaski got caught by a bunch of British dragoons in a New Jersey tavern just after the battle of Trenton," Lewicki recalled. "That damned young son of hers looks like he could be a real crosspatch if he wanted to be, and them two others always hangin around don't appear too benevolent either."

The two others being Ole Snake and Pieter Groot.

"Well, them three has kindly banded together and don't do much that I can see except work a little on that new room at the widow's house," said Carter Purcell, the land office agent.

"They go out and wander around in the woods all the time," said Able Steinhartz. "With Campbell at his own business, the widow'd be hard put for a man to run that powder mill if it wasn't for Campbell's father-in-law."

Sometimes people called the three young men bucks, as though they were an Indian band. But they played soft pedal on that theme because no telling what the widow might do if she thought folks were saying bad things about her youngest and his boon companions.

And a few of them thought Nalambigi Chesney, no matter how she had proven herself in the white man's world, was reverting a little to her red savage lineage and was a wee mite proud of those three because they were the tribe's free spirits and protectors and reckless warriors.

Pieter Groot fit himself right into that mold. Maybe because after all his life knowing what was called freedom, with Gance and the Indian he was learning what real freedom was: doing what they damn well pleased, working when they wanted, drinking when they got thirsty, going to the deep timber when they got an itch to, and simply refusing to allow the word *responsibility* to enter their lexicon.

Plus having good women to feed them and a dry place to sleep. And no law to make them loyal to anyone or anything not of their own choosing.

They were not the first men, white or black, nor would they be the last, who found red savage heathen life almost irresistible for an adult male.

Nobody paid much attention to Gance Chesney and his two cronies. There were more serious things to consider. News came like summer lightning, rolling downriver from the British navy's predations on American ships or south from the Canadian line where more and more frequently columns of black smoke marked an Indian raid.

Gus Staufer at the Campbell Chesney meat house welcomed a cousin named Manfried Oldenburg direct from Bavaria who said that when he passed through Philadelphia the news was all about an English man-o-war that had stopped a ship flying the Stars and Stripes just off Sandy Hook at New York, for God's sake, and had taken away three men who were American citizens.

"Dem Gott dum Englanders," Gus shouted, banging his butcher's block with a stein of pilsner. "Dey simbly vant to fight!"

Every traveler from the north said large bands of Winnebagos, Potawatomis, Delawares, and who knew how many others were coming to the Wabash to join forces with the Shawnees.

Meanwhile, newspapers along the Ohio were reporting that Tecumseh was traveling all around, even into Creek and Cherokee country far to the south, whipping up support for an Indian Confederation.

"You wait," said Judith Dwyer, "the first thing you know, the British and their red friends will be on the banks of the river at New Orleans. And we'll have the Mississippi closed to our boats again."

And it wasn't all that far-fetched. Spanish Florida had a long panhandle that *did* come to the east bank of the river above New Orleans, and everybody figured Spain was so busy putting down priest-led revolutions in Mexico that anybody could take the Florida panhandle, and there was a rumor that the British had a big naval and expeditionary force waiting in Jamaica or some such place.

Well, Americans in west Florida had a little revolt and occupied the Spanish province capital at Baton Rouge and asked the United States to annex them.

That's when President Madison turned anguish into joy in the valley of the Ohio. And a lot of other places. He said to Congress that we'd sure better annex the western tip of Spanish Florida. Just in case!

Congress agreed. So Territory of Orleans militia moved in, the Stars and Stripes was raised over what had been a part of New Spain, and now that banner flew on both sides of the river from as far north as anybody figured it was important to the Gulf of Mexico.

Now, everybody said, strutting a little, if the damned English want west Florida, they'll have to deal with *us* instead of those poor Spaniards trying to whip all the rebellious priests in Mexico.

To make it even better, it was about this time that the territory of Orleans became the state of Louisiana. And something nobody knew then, but their grandchildren would know, the future capital of Louisiana was a city located originally in that western tip of Florida which America simply seized from the Spaniards. Baton Rouge!

To make it better still, the king of Spain, who was powerless to stop America from stealing some of his real estate, was Joseph Napoleon, brother of the big Napoleon, whose navy had always been a bully on the high seas second only to the bloody British.

To put a cap on it, as Creigor McCallum said, at about that time, Cincinnati saw its first steamboat. A little side-wheeler, she had been built in Pittsburgh, christened the *New Orleans,* and was passing down the Ohio to the Mississippi where she would begin a regular run between the city for which she was named and Natchez.

It would be a long while before they saw another steamboat, but it was a harbinger of great days to come.

So everybody who could got pretty drunk on the first weekend after all of these grand things happened. The Widow Chesney sat on her promontory porch in the dark, listening to the riotous celebrants below in the town, and hoped that her youngest son would get back up the bluff without too many broken bones or criminal charges lodged against him.

It all passed with no serious damage to people or property, and everybody got back to waiting with dread for the next bad news from the East or the Great Lakes region.

There was simply too much Indian activity along the Canadian line for President Madison to ignore. People there were frightened out of their wits when there was any suggestion that a confederation of Indian tribes was in the offing. They'd tasted the results of a few wild raids, mostly by drunken young bucks, and the thought of any kind of coordinated hostility was terrifying.

So Jemy Madison did a second thing to endear himself. He commissioned William Henry Harrison, governor of Indiana Territory, to do something about Tecumseh. Whether there was any real threat to Ohio Valley settlers or not. And of course, Jemy Madison believed there was, as did William Henry Harrison.

Autumn had come on gloriously that year, with enough cold snaps to start leaves turning by mid-October. But the days were still warm and even after sundown there was no real chill in the air, and everything seemed safe and secure with the peaceful sound of waterfowl flying south, their muted voices as much a part of the night sky as the stars.

Everyone on the bluff was in bed except for Gance and his cohorts. And Otto Black was with them as they sat with backs against the wall of the horse barn and smoked clay pipes and drank German beer and watched the shooting stars. It was a good month for meteors in Ohio.

And it was a good time, too, for Gance to begin his appreciation of Pieter Groot, and the New York Dutch black's wisdom, if youth had such a thing, concerning problems now extant in this Ohio Valley.

Gance had all his short life been most guided by his mother, then in descending order, memory of father, older brother, Presbyterian teacher, and riverfront toughs.

Perhaps his most powerful quality had always been to know which guidance to apply in any specific situation.

But whatever it was, and him unaware of it anyway, the best part on this night was sitting against the wall and listening to the sound of Pieter Groot, whom Gance knew was older by a wide space yet who took him, Gance, as a kind of ship's captain. For whatever reason, nobody ever knew.

"If old Tecumseh gets all that red bunch together against us, it will be hell to pay on Sunday," Otto said.

"I remember Tecumseh," said Gance. "He came here to visit Mother once. I was a sprout, and he scared hell out of me. I remember Mother yelled at the man with him."

"They'll be hell to pay on Sunday," said Otto.

"Not necessarily so," said Pieter Groot in that fine New York dialect that so fascinated Gance Chesney. And in the dark when he couldn't see the color of Pieter Groot's skin, Gance always had the weird sensation of being spoken to by the best of the Presbyterian teachers in the local school.

"Well, they say he's got em all hoopin and hollerin and talkin in redskin tongues and jumpin around like a Baptist revival meetin," said Otto Black. "And they all stopped drinkin whiskey!"

Ole Snake understood enough of that to grunt with disapproval.

"Perhaps congregated, men will abstain," said Pieter Groot. "To please a well-respected shaman. But it's not congregated in village that you worry about the young bucks. It's when they go out of the towns and feel a powerful need to strengthen their medicine. Then a monstrous thirst comes on them. And to slack it turns the wolf loose."

"Well, they say Tecumseh has been trying to get his people to stop butchering folks they take captive," said Gance.

"I have no doubt Tecumseh is a good man," Pieter Groot said. "I have no doubt he is a great leader. And a great orator. And his people will be caught up in his ardor for a while. But they have lived too long the life he tries suddenly to change.

"You do not tame a robin redbreast by saying it is safer to eat the seeds of sunflowers inside a cage instead of going about hunting for bugs and spiders and worms. The robin redbreast, he leaves you to hunt bugs and spiders and worms. Where the Cooper's hawk finds him and kills him.

"Now that robin redbreast likely knows all about the Cooper's hawk. He likely knows you have been right to say it is safer to stay in a cage and eat the seeds of sunflowers than to hunt the things he really likes to eat. But even knowing all these things, he will one day leave you and your seeds of sunflowers and take his chance with the Cooper's hawk. Because he is a robin redbreast, and nothing you can do will change him."

"Oh," Otto Black said, a little belligerence edging his voice. "When'd you get to know ole Tecumseh so good?"

Pieter Groot laughed, and Gance could see his white teeth shining in the darkness.

"I don't know your ole Tecumseh at all," he said. "But I know what everybody in New York knows. The Iroquois had a fine confederation until the Revolution. Then they split apart on the question of which side to take.

"There was a man named Joseph Brant. Thayendanegea was his real name, to the best of my knowledge. I didn't know him, either, but I knew people who did, in the valley of the Mohawk.

"Well, sir, Mr. Joseph Brant was a shaman like your Tecumseh. The English took him to Whitehall, and he met the king. He held together the Iroquois Nations against the French, and they fought for Great Britain.

"By the time of the Revolution, he was famous. All his tribesmen knew him and respected him. But two of the Nations, the Oneida and the Tuscarora, decided to fight for the Americans. Mr. Joseph Brant preached and threatened and explained how it was less dangerous to fight with the British instead of against them.

"It didn't matter. The Onondaga, the Cayuga, the Seneca, and Joseph Brant's Mohawks fought as they always had, with the English, but even after years of being with the redcoats, two of the Six Nations pulled away and Joseph Brant couldn't hold them.

"They are not of a mind to make lasting confederations and unions. It is like the seed of the sunflower. They die on it. And they soon lust for the old way. For freedom.

"Not even Tecumseh can change that in such a short time."

Ole Snake grunted again. And Gance laughed.

"You understand that, Snake? You know his words?" Gance asked.

"Aw, for hell's sake, Gance, even I don't understand half what this New York sailor is talkin about," Otto said. "Ole Snake is just digestin that grub we et."

"Aw, yes, that," Gance sighed.

For supper, Willimena had made what she called a Dutch carbonnade. Lean pork and chicken floured and simmered in beer with slices of onion and whole peppercorns.

"I pert near busted myself on that beer stew," Otto said.

"But now Snake, did you hear ole Pete here? Did you get any of that?"

"Sure," said Ole Snake. "Tecum home, they stop drink whiskey. Tecum go away, they start drink whiskey some more. Tecum home, they sing like Christian. Tecum go away, they paint face black some more."

"Mr. Snake, you have it perfectly," said Pieter Groot and laughed what Gance thought of in the darkness as a shining laugh.

And Ole Snake did have it perfectly.

Cincinnati Intelligencer Saturday, November 9, 1811

GREAT VICTORY

SAVAGES ON WABASH ROUTED

Gen Harrison Triumphant
Tecumseh Arrived Too Late
Many Indian Casualties
A Jubilant Frontier

Our latest courier from the north informs that Gen W. H. Harrison, Gov of Indiana Territory, with his troops, marched up the Wabash River to Prophetstown where his command was fallen upon by the Shawnees and other savages. Our brave soldiers recovered from the surprise attack and inflicted many casualties on the Indians.

The tribesmen were scattered and ran off and their town was burned wherein were many winter supplies of clothing, weapons, and food.

Gen Harrison marched his troops back downriver toward Vincennes, proclaiming many hostile bands now badly beaten.

Yet another rider informs that Tecumseh was not on the scene, but the hotheads of the tribe made the attack despite Tecumseh's instructions not to do so in his absence to the south where he was attempting to recruit other bands to his cause. When he returned, all he found was a burned Shawnee town and a scattered band.

It is now reported that Tecumseh will repair to Amherstburg to confer with Sir George Prevost and join formally with Britain.

The sense is ever keener here that we must have war in order to annex Canada and hence wipe out the source of our Indian problem.

More details in next week's edition.

The name of the Shawnee town destroyed was Tippecanoe.

"Tecum gone," Ole Snake said. "They put on black paint some more, sure."

With additional reports, the popular jubilation at such a vast victory cooled a little. William Henry Harrison had lost about sixty-five men. Which was probably more than the Shawnees lost. And that item about Tecumseh going to visit Canada's governor general had ominous overtones.

So Tippecanoe peaked the westerners' urge for war with Britain, and the blood banner was held highest, waved most enthusiastically by the speaker of the house in Congress, Henry Clay. Of Kentucky, of course, and a great hero along the Ohio. Because he stands up stout against them eastern elites, people said.

And it was at this precise time of rising fury against the English that Campbell Chesney began making little speeches here and there in his run for the Congress. One of his recurrent themes was: we need to stay out of war with Britain, and it's foolish to think anybody in Canada *wants* to become a citizen of our Republic.

Late one evening, with the cold wind coming harsh along the Ohio from the west, Gance Chesney stood with his mother on her porch promontory and they looked down at the lights along the riverfront, and their breathing made clouds of vapor, quickly whipped away.

She put her hand on his shoulder and spoke softly, but the deep resonance of her voice carried her words easily through the wind to him.

"Try to talk with him," she said.

"He won't listen to me about politics, Mother," Gance said. "You might be able to. You talk to him."

"I'm afraid to talk to him," she said, still gripping her youngest son's shoulder. "Our tempers are so hot, and on this English thing, I'm afraid we'll say things we'll be sorry for."

"Well, I'll try. If you want me to try, I'll try."

"Yes, I want you to try," she said. "There is more of your father in you than in any of my other children; maybe that will cause him to listen. He's *got* to listen. This English business. Has he lost his mind?"

But as fate or whatever it was would have it, there was no time left for discussion.

It was Otto Black who came running up from the town, breathless and wild-eyed as he burst into the kitchen where Nalambigi Chesney and her son were having a supper of roast duck and succotash. Otto still wore his heavy leather cobbler's apron, but he had thrown on a knee-length coat against the cold.

"Papa says you better come," he panted, vapor and saliva spray coming from his mouth in a heavy moist cloud across Nalambigi Chesney's table.

"Stop breathing all over my grub," she shouted, leaping up. "What are you talking about? Come where?"

"Not you, ma'am. Gance," Otto gasped. "Down at Crock and Bottle Tavern, Campbell's got hisself into a real mess."

"Mess? What mess?" she was shouting, but Gance was already away from the table, grabbing a coat from the rack near the door, then from the kitchen bread safe, a pistol.

"Oh God, ma'am, about all this politics and Henry Clay."

"Pete," Gance shouted as he dashed for the door that Otto had left standing open. Before he reached it, Pieter Groot was coming from the rooms behind the kitchen where he and his wife lived and had obviously heard all the shouting. He, too, was drawing on a long winter coat.

"Gance. Gance?" his mother called. He only gave her a quick look as he ran out into the night, Pieter Groot behind him and then Otto Black. She heard him shout once as he passed the barn.

"Snake!"

She went to slam the door shut, felt the cold nip of night air against her face, and she shuddered and said aloud, "Damned English. It's the damned English! I know it."

All her dreams for so long had been of men in red coats and black gaiters and they caught a running man, hanged him in a tree head down, and squealing like drunken swine danced about hitting the hanged man's head with long poles.

In her dream, she had never seen the face of the man in the tree, but she knew it was her eldest son.

And she knew that since her talk with Gance, he'd had no chance to dissuade his older brother from the stupid preaching of peace when everybody wanted war. So she knew what was happening as she heard their footsteps fading down the bluff. Not the details, but she knew.

To give her hands work, she took two more of the pistols from her bedroom trunk and going back to the kitchen, sat down at the table, pushed plates of partly eaten duck and corn aside, and began to reload and prime both weapons.

And as she worked, she reached out to join her own medicine to the power of her dead husband, and she spoke words that she had not spoken since the night before the English had surrendered at Yorktown, when the two of them had been fighting for the Republic yet unborn and each night furiously, savagely loving one another in sweat and mud and blood and unburned cannon powder.

And she spoke aloud. Because it comforted her and besides, it made her forget the mourning wind that blew through the rough edges of the cedar shingles her husband had put on this house with his own hands.

PERSONAL AND PRIVATE:
The Continuation of my Life's Journal
Rufus Putnam

On the Occasion of Interview with Ancel McCracken, Sheriff of Hamilton County, State of Ohio. It Being a Monday. November 18, Anno Domini 1811.

In Regard to Various Occurrences in the Town of Cincinnati on the River Involving Sons of Mrs. Robert Nalambigi Chesney, Old and Deare Friend and Comrade in Arms During the Recent War Against Tyranny and Tax Oppression.

There Being One Additional Witness to This Exchange, Oscar Wieser, Trusted Clerk, Who Can Verify in All Detail What Follows.

RP: On the night in question, how did the disquietude come to attention, Sheriff?

AM: Why, Judge, I was just along River Street from the Crock and Bottle, at Ben Unger's meat market. I was there takin him a poke of the wife's goose eggs that he sells to pilgrims on the river. So I heard Hawley Stitchel yellin they was about to panfry one of them In'yun- and nigger-lovin Chesney boys down at Daget's saloon.

RP: May I assume Hawley Stitchel was drunk?

AM: It was past sunset so we'd be safe to assumption that Hawley was more than moderately boiled.

RP: So you went to Daget's Crock and Bottle.

AM: At a dead run. Inside, they was likely about a dozen men, all on their feet. Behind his bar planks was Chester Daget with a bung starter, wavin it around, and yellin, "Not close to the bottles, no fightin close to the bottles." They had young Campbell up on a table at the far corner of the room, or I expect he got on the table his ownself, and they was ringed all around him and some had bottles and Corliss Hooten had a lumber hatchet, and young Campbell had lost his hat and his hair was down in his face and his nose was bleeding and he had his fists up ready for a fight.

RP: What were they saying?

AM: Why, Judge, they was giving that young man what for because he'd been sayin we was foolish to start a war with the British. They was callin him English lapdog and a shame to his daddy's memory and his mama ought to spank him for turnin into a lickspittle British.

But they was a few, like Bedford Croft and Densmore Korkendale, who was sayin more serious, dangerous things.

RP: How more dangerous things, Sheriff?

AM: Why, Judge, they was sayin how somebody likely come give him a coat of T and F some night.

RP: Meaning Tar and Feathers, I assume.

AM: That'd be a sure certain assume, Judge. And they was somebody talkin about smokehouses burnin, you know, young Chesney's got that pig business up the Little Miami.

RP: Were these men all drunk?

AM: Judge, from my experience of such occurrences, it's safe to reckon about half of em was half drunk and the other half was whole drunk.

RP: So continue, Sheriff McCracken.

AM: I hardly get into the door and start up along that tap-room towards where they got young Chesney on the table, and everybody yellin, and some of the boys are takin swings at young Chesney's legs and he's swinging back and he's yellin, too, about a bunch of damned fools too stupid to know what's good for em, which don't help their disposition none, and I'm tryin to get up there when the back door must have let in the new bunch.

This was when I pert near got trampled to death cause most of them tryin to attack young Chesney begin to evacuate the premises, and this howling, screeching horde from the rear, all of em swinging ax handles, comin right behind em, and if Campbell Chesney hadn't got to me right quick, I think one of this new bunch would have brained me. They'd laid a few licks on the others, which had caused the quick exodus, you see.

RP: Now, Sheriff, just a minute. This new bunch you call them. Am I to assume this is young Gance Chesney and assorted friends?

AM: Assorted is right. There was Otto Black, you know him, his papa anyway runs the shoe factory, and there was this freedman nigger, him and his wife works for the widow, and there's this In'yun, wearin a coat looks like it come out of the Revolution and his head shaved and a scalp lock a foot long down the back of his head and a mess of old paint on his face that I don't think he freshened up in a week, and all three was howlin like a den of wolves, with young Otto Black kindly taggin along behind and lookin pretty scared and sick.

RP: Nobody was seriously injured, I take it.

AM: No, Judge, they was a few hats knocked crazy and a few scalps with welts and minor cuts, but nobody laid out. The taproom got cleared of everybody real sudden, though.

RP: Except for the Chesney contingent.

AM: Yes sir, that contingent was still there, and of course me and Chester Daget who was still hollerin behind the plank bar until I told him to hush. The rest was all in the street, and I could still hear Corliss Hooten and Bedford Croft cussin and sayin the time was nigh to sweep the county clean of English-loving fainthearts and best to start with the in-laws first, the biggest English lover of them all.
    So I told . . .

RP: Excuse me, Sheriff, but what was that? The in-laws business?

AM: Why, Judge, the little lady Campbell brang back to Cincinnati from New Orleans to marry with, her papa. Everybody knowed he'd been goin up and down the river tryin to raise money for the Burr conspiracy.

RP: How would that make him an English lover, I wonder?

AM: Why, Judge, everybody knowed ole Aaron Burr had told the British about his plan, and they was lickin their chops and ready to help him.

RP: Well, I wasn't aware that such a thing was necessarily true. But no matter. Go on.

AM: Well, let's see. Yeah. I told them men in the street to go on home and sober up, and I told Campbell Chesney to get his people out by the back way and up the bluff and him back to his own home and to stay out of riverfront taprooms when he felt the need to instruct folks about us and the British.

RP: And what did Campbell say?

AM: He never said anything to me, Judge, him and his brother was goin at it like cats and dogs, yellin at one another, and young Gance sayin Campbell was crazy and Campbell sayin why didn't Gance and their mother mind their own business.

RP: Their mother was mentioned?

AM: Oh you bet your life, Judge, Campbell was yellin about his mama sendin Gance and the boys downtown to save him when it wasn't any of her business and he could take care of his ownself, and Gance was yellin how it didn't look to him like Campbell was doin such a good job of takin care of his self. They left, still yellin at one another, and if it hadn't been for that nigger Dutchman gettin between em, I think they'd have gone right at one another and it might have got bad because Gance still had an ax handle in his hand.

RP: Where did those ax handles come from, Sheriff?

AM: Alvie Loomis, he's got the little lumberyard down by the river and he's always got thangs like ax handles and hoe handles and poleax handles in these barrels outside his place, and them boys just grabbed one as they run by and then into that alley behind the Crock and Bottle.

RP: Tell me about the ham picnic, Sheriff.

AM: Well, Campbell had some placards printed at the newspaper shop. He was offerin the town a feed of ham at the meadow up the slope behind his pigpens, just like a summer Methodist revival meetin, and nobody had ever seen anything like this, so they showed up, most of them. It was like a kind Providence was lookin out for him because it was a warm day, not shirtsleeve warm, you understand, and a man could see his breath, but it wasn't bone-chill cold like it ort to have been for that time of year and they come and they brang their women and their yung uns, and Campbell had plank-and-sawhorse tables and his smokehouse work crew had sliced up a mess of ham, and while folks ate it, standin around tryin to pretend it was colder than it was, Campbell, he give a speech.

RP: This was a Sunday, wasn't it? After the various services at the churches. Have I got it right?

AM: You have, Judge, an it was a pretty strange picnic. All that bunch of Gance Chesney's was there and . . .

RP: Did they have their ax handles?

AM: No. No Judge, they never. In fact, they give them back to Alvie the night they taken em, before they went home.

So anyway, I was there and expectin some trouble because young Chesney started hurrahin the crowd about how we didn't have no business gettin into a war with England and that if we just stood pat a while, thangs would get to be all right.

It was downright spooky, Judge. That crowd just kept chawin on their ham and watching Campbell, and it was like when a mean dog ain't barkin or makin any fuss, he's only just lookin at you and you know that in a minute he'll just walk right up and bite you. The eyes of them people just kindly turned yellow like a mean dog's eyes'll turn right before he walks right up and bites you.

RP: Was there any shouting amongst them? Anyone refuting the things Campbell was saying?

AM: No sir. No sir. Not a single time. And that's what made it seem mean and strange because you knowed, standin there, that most of the people in that crowd didn't like nary a thing Campbell was sayin.

RP: I assume most of them were sober, this being Sunday.

AM: That's a good assume, Judge. Didn't stay thataway, though. Finally, Chesney finished, and everybody went off their own way, and Gance and his crew was watchin em ever step like they'd been watchin while Campbell spoken his speech.

RP: Allow me to intrude here, Sheriff, and ask. Was the Widow Chesney there to hear her son speak?

AM: Oh no, Judge, and nobody was surprised because it was well known that the widow never took no stock in what Campbell said, like when he was givin Henry Clay hell.

RP: The widow especially liked Henry Clay, you mean?

AM: Well, Judge, nobody really knowed who the widow liked or didn't like, but they surely knew she was hellbent again' the English.

RP: Now, was Mr. McCallum at this picnic? Or his daughter, Campbell Chesney's wife?

AM: McCallum was never, that I know of, around when young Campbell was in public. Of course, he went home at night to Campbell and his daughter's house. But Campbell's wife, she was there. And Judge, she looked scared, too, little ole bitty thang like she was holdin her breath ever time her husband said something.

RP: All right. Sorry for the interruption. Go on.

AM: It's all right, Judge, you can interruption any time. Well, being fall of the year, it got dark pretty soon, and I went along the river and the taverns was doing a right smart business for a Sunday night. Bedford Croft got so drunk he fell in the street, and I got him up and home to his wife Thelma and she acted spooked as a cat caught in the lightnin.

Well, when the riverfront closed down, it was late, and everybody just seemed to kindly fade into the night, but there was still that fever in the air although a wind had come up blowin from the west and it turned cold as a witch.

I was right well relieved that the day had ended, Judge, and I was home and asleep in bed when my Iva gouged me awake and said they was something on fire up the Little Miami River. I never even got my trousers on before I was awake enough to know what it was.

RP: Campbell Chesney's house.

AM: Yes sir, Judge, yes sir!

When I got there, the place was gone, Judge, a fire like you never seen, like somebody'd put turpentine and pitch under all the eaves. Young Chesney's wife had her papa out, and little Junior, well away from the heat. McCallum was crazy with fright, I reckon, carryin on pitiful, and she was tryin to console him, and young Chesney was runnin in and out of the house tryin to save thangs. If I hadn't stopped him, I think he'd gone right on until it caved in on him.

RP: You saw no one else near, someone who might have been carrying a firebrand?

AM: Oh mercy sakes, Judge, wasn't no doubt in my mind it was a set fire, but whoever done it was a long time away from there and I reckoned at the time half the town might of been there settin fire to that house of young Chesney's with some of them matches his mother sells from her little match factory.

Now, I hadn't hardly got there til other folks started comin, to help. There was Old Man Black and his wife Anna, Otto's mama, and there was Judith Dwyer and her nigger slave girl, and there was Gance Chesney and that Pieter Groot. By God, Judge, I wouldn't have believed it, right there, damned if Gance and his big brother almost got into a fistfight again, like they wasn't enough trouble with the house burnin down.

RP: What were the boys angry with one another about, could you tell?

AM: Anybody with ears could tell. Gance was screamin in his brother's face about all his silly peace talk, and Campbell was callin his brother a fool like everybody else who couldn't think of any way to settle their problems except with bayonets. Same argument they'd had before, Judge. Young Chesney callin his little brother a damned Henry Clay War Hawk!

RP: Was the widow there?

AM: At the fire? No, Judge, she wasn't. You know if she hada been, she'd have kept them boys apart and scalded their butts for all their sass. But that Dutch nigger Groot was there, and if it hadn't been for him, they'd have gone at it hammer and forge, you can bet.

RP: Well, now Sheriff, what was it I heard about somebody being wounded?

AM: Oh, that. Well, later, after everybody had watched the last roof rafters cave in and the little missy had her papa and babe off up the bluff to the widow's house, and after young Chesney and Gance and Groot had gone up there, too, the rest of us walked back into town, and there was people up all along the way, watchin, eyes all shiny, you know how they be sometimes, but Judge, not one of them people made a bucket brigade and not one of our firemen showed up and of course, no fire wagon came.

Anyway, back in town I saw the Crock and Bottle had a light and I went over there after I sent my missus home, and Chester Daget was sellin liquor, and half a dozen men had Densmore Korkendale laid out on a table and his breeches had been cut off him and there was as fine a red savage arrow in the left cheek of his ass as you ever seen.

RP: I imagine these men were tolerably drunk.

AM: Judge, you could imagine them more than tolerable. Ole Densmore was squealin like one of young Chesney's hogs, naked rear end sticking up and blood all over the place, and Corliss Hooten and the others yellin at one another and every last one of them with a knife or a razor in his hand to cut that arrowhead out once they pulled out the shaft. It's God wonder, Judge, that they never cut off each other's hands.

So I run em all off and did the work myself, me and Daget, and ole Densmore Korkendale wakin the whole of old Cincinnati with his bellowin, and while we pulled out the shaft and cut in for the arrowhead, I got a real strong whiff of turpentine off ole Densmore's clothes.

RP: But you arrested no one?

AM: Been no use, Judge. You couldn't have found anybody who set that fire admit to seein somebody else there cause that'd put *them* there, too, wouldn't it? And once the circuit court got into session next spring, I doubt you'd be able to find twelve men anywhere in this end of Ohio who'd convict anybody for settin fire to a peace lover's house. Even the ones who agreed with him would be afraid of the others.

But of course, Chester Daget kept sayin I'd have to arrest the Chesney Indian that came back with Sergeant Bobby from St. Louis and been here ever since. So the next morning I went up the bluff, and I was dreadin it.

The Widow Chesney had me in and give me a cup of venison broth for breakfast and told me that because the local law wasn't doin its job, meanin me, her youngest son had told their Fox Indian friend to stay at her oldest son's house the night before and sleep on the porch to protect him from people who didn't believe in the Constitution of the Republic, which says a man's entitled to his own opinions without havin to worry about a bunch of river scum burnin down his house just because they don't agree with him.

But so many ruffians come, the Fox Indian couldn't hold them off and only managed to shoot one in the ass with his bow and arrow and then was so disturbed about doing such a thang that he'd just tooken off to walk back

to the Wisconsin country before somebody could catch
him and hang him.

And the widow said if I was finished with my broth, I
could get the hell out of her house and don't come back.
And tell all the town ruffians who'd burned her son's house
that if they came near *her* house, they'd get buckshot and
ball and not some innocent savage's bow and arrow and
not just in the ass, either.

Excuse me, Judge, did I say something funny?

RP: No, no, Sheriff McCracken. Now, let's see, Campbell
and his family stayed on the bluff again after this, is that
the way of it?

AM: Well, yes, they moved into one end of the horse barn
which was fixed up better than most houses in Cincinnati.
But the father-in-law, Sarah Chesney's papa, he was at the
riverfront two days later, bag and baggage, and bought hisself a keelboat ride to St. Louis and then was goin on to
New Orleans. Where he used to have business, you know?

Sarah and the baby were there, all tearful with her
papa leavin, and Gance and Pieter Groot come with him to
the river and I know damned well they both had a brace of
loaded pistols under their waistcoats. Because there was
some people who figured Creigor McCallum was the root
of young Chesney's trouble, what with being part of the
Burr thing and with English connections everybody
allowed.

RP: And that remains the arrangement, with Campbell
and his family on the bluff?

AM: It does. Young Chesney don't come down to the rest
of town much. Gance, of course, he goes where he wants
to go with that Dutch nigger, but now the Indian don't follow along, too.

RP: The Indian never returned, then?

AM: No, Judge, and everybody says good riddance, but I really couldn't see he ever done much harm except puncture Densmore Korkendale's butt. Now, it's just Gance and this Pieter Groot.

Young Campbell, he goes to work ever day, walks past that burned house, the logs black and charred, his first home, where he taken his new wife, where his son was born. They say he don't look at it, just walks right on past to his hog business.

Young Chesney don't take his pork to market now. Gus Staufer, his majordomo at the pens, does it. Good meat, Judge. Them Germans knows how to cure pork all right.

So Chesney stays pretty much on the bluff, except now and again people see him goin out north along the Miami with a rifle, to hunt, I guess.

RP: Sheriff, when Campbell Chesney came back home with the woman, with Sarah, do you know where he'd gone to get her?

AM: I don't reckon anybody knew. She come from New Orleans, everybody knew that. She come by Cincinnati twice that everybody knows of, with her papa. But alls we know is the two boys and that Indian, not long after Sergeant Bobby died, taken out someplace, and about three weeks maybe, they was back.

RP: You never heard anybody suggest where they might have gone?

AM: Oh, I think everybody figured they went down to Louisville maybe. They didn't go by the river, in a boat I mean. Tell you the truth, Judge, nobody much give a damn. Right after that, young Chesney taken this wild hair to get elected to Congress or something and started talkin the way people didn't like, sayin we was fools to want a war with the English and all the time knowin his mama, the widow, hated the English as bad as anybody. It was peculiar, Judge.

RP: Very well, Sheriff, I appreciate you coming by. I have here a letter I'd like you to take to the Widow Chesney when you're back in Cincinnati.

AM: Well, I'm not sure I'd be too welcome up there yet, Judge.

RP: You take this. She sees my name on it, she'll let you in her house and I'll bet feed you some pemmican with honey! That's a treat. Tell her I'm sorry it's been so long since I've been downriver. Damned gout and other things. Tell her maybe next spring.

AM: All right, Judge. I'll do it. It's just a little strange up there on the bluff since the fire, and young Chesney back under her wing so you might say, and all the time him doin that damned fool preachin we knew his mama didn't like, and it got him in this trouble.

That business about us being fools to want a war. Can you imagine that, Judge?

RP: Yes, I can, Sheriff. I'll tell you something you needn't repeat to anyone. I think what the widow dislikes most is that she realizes Campbell may be right. But she's too proud and bullheaded to admit it. As I say, repeat not what I've just said. Most especially to Nalambigi Chesney.

AM: Judge, you know good and well nobody in his right senses would ever say something like that to her, even if he had a long runnin start.

Excuse me, Judge. Did I say something funny?

Chapter 17

Nalambigi Chesney had decided not to say anything about it, Gance figured. She was set against it, but she didn't mention it.

Not to Gance, not to Willimena Groot.

Campbell Chesney was building another house right on the foundations of the old burned-out one. With the whole town watching, he was stubbornly refusing to accept what any normal man would have taken as a public referendum that he shouldn't hold the views he did and still be free to live where he damn well pleased.

Even provided, naturally, that he could pay in cash money or accepted credit for his choice.

And after Gance and Pieter Groot talked about it for a while, they decided that even though Campbell's mother might disagree violently with Campbell's opinion, she so admired the idea of standing firm for principle, regardless of odds, that she simply couldn't shout against it, even knowing how dangerous it was for her son or anybody else, in this western part of the Republic.

Oh yes. Dangerous. News from western Pennsylvania or some

such place, that a man had been badly beaten, two more tarred and feathered, and one shot dead on the back stoop of his house. All because they took a public stand against war with Great Britain.

The fourth day Campbell made the walk from the bluff to the site of his burned-out home, he was challenged on the path that led from the valley of the Miami up to his hog pens by Bedford Croft and Corliss Hooten, who apparently had lost sight of the fact that this man they were stopping and calling vile names had the blood of Nalambigi and Sergeant Bobby Chesney flowing in his veins.

Campbell Chesney was carrying a D-handle shovel, a pick mattock, and a claw hammer. When he was blocked in his passage, he dropped everything except the shovel, without any conscious thought of choosing that particular weapon, and with one jab, as though he were using it as a bayonet, very nearly decapitated Bedford Croft and did in fact break his jaw in two places.

Corliss Hooten decided in the instant that the better part of valor here was to start screaming for mercy, figuring, everyone later supposed, that he couldn't outrun Campbell and his best chance of survival was to plead a case of mistaken identity or some such thing.

It worked, because all Campbell did was tell Corliss Hooten to get cracking and help his moaning partner Bedford Croft back down the hill and into town where they both belonged. And so Corliss did as he was told, and old Doc Claudes Insel patched up Bedford Croft as best he could, and nobody even bothered to file a charge of assault with Sheriff McCracken against Campbell.

So the work went along uninterrupted.

Campbell wasn't doing it alone. While he supervised his mostly black or indentured people cleaning up the char and laying in new floor and studs, just above the house site each day after the encounter with Bedford and Corliss, there were Gance and Pieter Groot, Gance with a Pennsylvania long rifle.

And before long, Pieter Groot there with Campbell doing the sawing and nailing and planing and shingling. Even though Gance remained on the hill each day, not so much to protect anybody as to stay clear of manual labor.

"Just like his pap," said the widow, with some acid of reproach in her tone but a lot more of admiration.

After the first little spasm, nobody from the town bothered them. Not so much because of the threat of Gance's marksmanship, almost as good, they said, as his pap's, Old Sergeant Bobby, but because it was breath-holding time.

Breath-holding until the war that was now certain, they all figured.

Besides, there was other intelligence coming by way of the two newspapers they read. Other intelligence, as the newspapers themselves called it, that held their attention for a moment. Or word-of-mouth news from the travelers on the river. Or letters some received through the ever improving postal service.

"You hear about those two crazy men?" asked gunsmith Able Steinhartz. "Blowed up a hot air balloon in St. Louis and rode it through the skies all the way to Canada!"

"What for?" asked Densmore Korkendale.

"Well, I don't know what for," Steinhartz said. "They just done it. Wouldn't you like to fly in the air from St. Louis to Canada, Densmore?"

"God, no!"

And Chester Daget, of the Crock and Bottle, with a business mind start to finish, saying, "They's this John Jacob Astor, formed up a fur company and founded hisself a town called Astoria in the Oregon Territory. I heared a man knows trappin from Michilimack-inac say, you can walk along that western sea coast and just hit them seals on the head with a club and have some of the best furs they buyin in China. By God, I ort to go out yonder and join up with Mr. Astor."

"Take a bath first, Chester," said Carter Purcell.

"Mr. John Jacob Astor don't give a penny's worth of damn iffen you take a bath or not!"

The big thing was, nobody in the Ohio Valley knew what was happening. Except maybe a few like Rufus Putnam and William Henry Harrison. And them only a long time after it happened.

The French had issued a paper called the Berlin and Milan Decrees. The British had issued a paper called the Orders in Council dealing with shipping.

It was under authority of these two documents that the French navy and the British navy had been stopping American merchant ships and taking off sailors, saying they were deserters, or else cargo, saying it was headed to the war effort of their enemy.

And as usual, France and Great Britain were the enemies involved here.

Then Napoleon whispered that he was rescinding the Berlin and Milan Decrees. Thus saying or implying that because the French were such great sports about it, the English ought to be great sports, too, and rescind the Orders in Council. Everybody agreed and waited for Britain to rescind their Orders in Council.

But they didn't.

What nobody in America knew was that Napoleon had lied. He hadn't rescinded the Berlin and Milan Decrees. But unaware that Napoleon had lied, Americans got upset further still that Whitehall kept the Orders in Council in force while France had been so good about the whole thing.

Well, Napoleon probably got what he wanted out of it. Because President Madison asked Congress to give approval to fight and Congress said "of course," so on June 19, 1812, President Madison proclaimed that a state of war now existed between Great Britain and the United States of America.

And Britain rescinded the Orders in Council. Not because of Napoleon's lie. Not because of America's declaration of war. But because the British felt it was creating too much friction with America when they had their hands full on the continent, with France.

In fact, cross-Atlantic communications being what they were, the British didn't yet know that, when they abandoned one of the central issues that had created so much distress, they were already at war with the United States.

A change in what was happening on the high seas may not have mattered. The fire had already started along the Canadian border, and with Henry Clay and his War Hawks in pretty solid control of Congress, somebody was going to insist on some shooting in the old Northwest Territory where English troops still occupied forts on ground that had been American by treaty since the Revolution.

And every time an Indian with an English-made hatchet in his hand showed up, people began to remember how northern tribesmen had burned and raped and looted and murdered in the Ohio Valley for more than six score years.

There were a lot of old Northwest Territory kinfolk sleeping in that bloody ground!

Having been Washington's surveyor general, Rufus Putnam's advice was often sought. At this time, he was in Washington City conferring with those government officials concerned with establishing a survey system in the Louisiana Territory.

Or rather in what was now Missouri Territory.

He wrote a letter to Nalambigi Chesney, and she received it in less than two weeks, a near miracle everybody figured.

In the letter, Putnam said this war was getting off to a bad start what with all that confusion about Decrees and Orders in Council, and the central government completely ignorant about running a war, and the old national bank now disestablished and therefore no organized system for raising needed money and getting loans and pooling resources and coordinating state input to the tax base.

"You've got to have taxes to make war," he wrote.

He wrote something else that sent the widow into one of her furies.

379

"The New England states are so opposed to this war that the governors of Mass. and Conn. have already told the president they will not supply troops. They fear the war will destroy their trade relations with the English and the English sugar islands and with Canada, but I suspect it will instead create a lot of new rich men there from trading with those very people.

"There is talk now among them about holding a convention to address the possibility of their secession from the Union!

"It is a great irony, is it not, that in the very birthplace of the Revolution (Lexington and Concord), there are men now seriously speaking in public about dissolving the Republic we fought for!"

Nalambigi Chesney threw her best sugar bowl against a wall, screaming vile oaths against the bloody English.

Nobody except Willimena went inside her house for two days. Gance and Pieter Groot slept in the loft of the horse barn.

On the second afternoon, Little Campbell Junior waddled up toward the house of his Gran-Gran, which is what he called her, and one of Nalambigi's geese attacked the child, honking furiously, wings flailing, and Sarah ran up the hill in time to see white feathers flying and the goose retreating in a headlong dash for safety, the red savage heathen close behind swinging a wooden water bucket and the child screeching in terror.

Sarah snatched up her child and stood staring pop-eyed at her mother-in-law, who was snorting and stamping and slashing at the air with the bucket. Then stopped and fixed that deadly gaze on Sarah and took a few deep breaths before saying as calmly as though she were serving sassafras tea to Judith Dwyer and the rest of the Methodist Ladies Aid Society: "Please take your son back to your house before my goose pecks his nose off!"

And as she hurried back along the slope to the temporary home she was making until Campbell got the new one built at the smokehouses, she heard the widow roar.

"Gance! Pieter! Get down out of that loft right now and catch that damned bird with the black marked neck. We're going to have roast goose tomorrow night."

And stalking back to her house, she muttered to herself but loud enough for Willimena, watching from the kitchen, to hear, "No bird is going to flog a child of this tribe and get away with it!"

Then stopped and thought a moment, whirled around to face the horse barn once more just as her son and the New Yorker emerged, brushing hay off their clothes.

"I am naming that goose with the black mark on her neck," she shouted. "I am naming her New England. And between now and sunset, you kill her and pluck her, and tomorrow Willimena cooks her and we all eat her. And I get the *heart*! Do you hear me, boy?"

"Yes ma'am."

"Pieter, go down there and tell Sarah and my other useless son that we all eat at my house tomorrow night. And tell them I will not abide any talk of how New England won the Revolution all by their own selves!"

"Yes ma'am."

She started for her kitchen once more, stopped, turned, and pointed her finger like a pistol.

"Tell them we are going to *eat* New England!"

Well, for the peace of mind of all the folks of the old Northwest Territory, it was probably just as well that communications were slow and the tidings of conflict were as disjointed and incomprehensible as the beginning of this war had been.

Anything that happened on the high seas, and there was a lot of that, was of passing interest. But what really mattered to them was the subjugation of Canada, an avowed war aim of the United States, and hence an end to troubles of the past regarding red savage heathens periodically coming south to raise hell in the neighborhoods.

"When we annex Canada," said Judith Dwyer, matter of factly, "our anxieties will be vanished and we can get on with settling our western territories."

It was a common theme. Liberty, ownership of private property, mobility, already the staples of the federation, would be enhanced. Just annex Canada!

But as always happened, simple objectives described in taprooms turned out to be pretty complex on the ground.

"We'll do it," said Sheriff McCracken, already organizing the local militia. "Just bang right into Canada, where all them folks is just dyin to be citizens of the United States."

To begin this whirlwind conquest, Michilimackinac at the northern peak of Lake Huron surrendered to the British. In less than a month, Fort Dearborn or Chicago surrendered to the British, some of the garrison taken prisoner, many more massacred when the English officers lost control of their Indian allies.

"Wait til I get my hands on some of them redskin bastards," said Densmore Korkendale. And a lot of others were saying the same.

At Detroit, the British told General Hull they didn't think they could control their Indians if there was fighting. So Hull surrendered Detroit. General Hopkins marched north through Illinois Territory. To retake Detroit. But after a short distance, his militia decided they'd marched far enough and turned around and went back home.

"Where in hell are we getting all these generals?" asked Otto Black.

"Oh for General Washington," Nalambigi Chesney wailed, but General Washington was not there, even in her dreams, nor Danny Morgan nor Benedict Arnold nor Mad Anthony Wayne.

Well, at the far end of Lake Erie, General Rensselaer attacked across the Niagara to take Queenston. The British and their Indians counterattacked. The militia reserves refused to cross and sat on the American side of the river watching Rensselaer's force being cut to pieces on the other bank.

The following month, somebody named Alex Smyth made a night attack across the Niagara. He got his force as far as midstream before he changed his mind, turned around, and rowed back to the American side.

To the east, an American column moved from Plattsburg to take

Montreal. They proceeded for twenty miles, and the militia refused to go any farther. They marched back to Plattsburg.

"Where is William Henry Harrison?" shouted Carter Purcell.

Well, Harrison was organizing a three-pronged attack aimed at Detroit. One prong was mauled at Raisin River where the British couldn't control their allies again, so a great many wounded Americans were massacred on the ground where they lay.

Another prong got caught on the Maumee where the British couldn't control their allies yet again. So it was the hatchet and knife for wounded men.

The third prong at least got into Canada. They took York, capital of the Province of Ontario, and the troops had a wonderful time burning government buildings and private homes, turning families out into a bitter cold April night. Then they came back home.

And on brief visits, the Americans burned a couple more Canadian cities, and the British army burned Blackrock and Buffalo while their still uncontrolled allies were out in the surrounding countryside burning farms and killing livestock and shooting citizens.

Fat General Wilkinson turned up leading a column against Montreal, was reluctant to do much fighting, and was dismissed.

It was a moment of delight for Nalambigi Chesney.

Then the British burned Washington but were turned away from Baltimore, both of which Northwest Territory old settlers considered a part of the eastern theater of operations along with the sea battles, and they weren't too interested.

Then a young professional officer named Winfield Scott said the valor of New England troops was the best he'd ever seen, after actually leading some in an American victory.

When she heard that, Nalambigi Chesney killed another goose. She named this one Winfield Scott. She ate the heart, too. After Willimena Groot had roasted the goose, of course.

That was how it was, and soon people were no longer waiting to hear news of great victories. In fact, they came to dread news in any form expecting surely it would detail American blundering, slaughter of wounded men, senseless torching of towns, and who knew what all.

There was no longer any talk of how the Canadians would rush to become citizens of the United States. Because of that, they developed a sincere hatred of Canadians.

And instead of the red savage heathen problem getting better, it was getting worse. And they knew now that Tecumseh was right there in the middle of it, him and his people and a lot of other pickup tribes fighting alongside the redcoats.

Oh, there were some battles won, at the east end of Lake Erie and elsewhere, but any celebration of such oddities was subdued in the murky despondency of general confusion and aimlessness of the Canada venture.

In the midst of all this fiasco, Nalambigi Chesney went almost crazy wanting to do something. Her sons were sure that if she'd been maybe five years younger, she'd have taken a Pennsylvania rifle and marched north to join somebody.

One might think under those circumstances, she would be encouraging her sons to fight. But she didn't. She was running about the same course she always had with their father. If they wanted to go, they could. If not, that was all right, too.

Nobody expected Campbell to go, what with his feelings about the war being stupid in the first place. He stayed right there in Cincinnati, living in his new house and working the hog business, turning out more and more of the best hams and bacons on the river.

But everybody kept eyeing Gance and Pieter Groot. They figured these two were bound to load up on woods gear and be gone some morning. But each morning, they were there. Working sometimes in the Chesney Gunpowder Works. Sometimes just doing what they'd always done. Hunting, fishing, eating, and getting drunk in Judith Dwyer's taproom.

Some of the locals marched off to join William Henry Harrison. Corliss Hooten and Densmore Korkendale and Bedford Croft and some others. There was still talk of retaking Detroit.

Sheriff McCracken snorted at that.

"The British control Lake Erie," he said. "As long as they do, any army we've got stickin its nose between Lake Erie and Lake Huron is gonna get fizzled and scalped!"

"Correct! Which proves our sheriff should be something in this war a lot higher up than commander of local militia. He's got a few brains, anyway," said Judith Dwyer, who had learned her tactics listening to traveling military men over the years who paused in her saloon to take on large quantities of famous Cincinnati German beer.

But finally, in August of 1813, Nalambigi Chesney had had enough of noninvolvement.

"Boy," she said to Gance. "Load a strong little wagon with barrels of our best gunpowder."

"Our best gunpowder?" he asked. "Well, it's all the same. Eighty percent potassium nitrate, ten percent sulphur, and ten percent charcoal."

"All right, all right," she said impatiently. "Don't spout them long words of Pieter Groot at me; just do what I say. Then take it north and find somebody to use it against the English."

"*What!* Mother, that's crazy!"

"Don't start talkin like your older brother. Get at it. Plan to take Pieter with you."

"But who will I take it to?" Gance asked. "You want us to just wander around up north until we find somebody who might be fightin the English?"

"It's better than just sittin here not helping."

"Oh, and what if we run into a bunch of English soldiers?"

"Kill as many as you can and then blow up the powder and run into the woods."

"Just run into the woods?" He was incredulous. "That's how your plan calls for us being saved from the British. Just run into the woods!"

"Listen, boy, I know you," she said. "Just like your pap. You're so good in the woods, with that rifle, a whole regiment of the English couldn't catch you."

He could do nothing but stare.

"Well!"

"All right. All right."

So what the family would later call the Powder Trek began for Gance and Pieter Groot. And they took a boy from the powder mill, Claven Sadowski. And they took two long rifles. And they left their clay pipes at home because they would be riding on twenty thirty-pound casks of black powder. Up the north road out of Cincinnati, toward Lake Erie. Toward the war.

Chapter 18

Gunner's Mate Theolonius Parker stood facing his gape-jawed recruits, his back to the sparkling sunny blue of a small bay where it was protected from the wider waters of Lake Erie by a hook-shaped spit.

Lying at anchor in the bay was a flotilla of ships where men could be seen on the two largest of them in reefing drills, filling deck-level bulwark ready-racks with solid shot, rolling and heaving gun trucks into position at the ports and securing the lashings, tightening ratlines, practicing with halyards the hoist and trim of the yards.

The explicit commands of ship's petty officers came across the unruffled surface of the bay in harsh, staccato throbs of sound, strident with an urgency that seemed out of place this calm afternoon. The foliage of peach leaf willow on the spit was a low blue-green, only a faintly ragged boundary between Prussian blue water and topaz blue sky.

Adding to the illusion of serenity were the lake birds. Breeding and nesting were finished by now for most of them, but they sailed and dipped aimlessly for a while along the lakeshores before flying south for winter. There were grebes with white striped heads and bitterns and snowy egrets, whose white feathers glistened in the sunlight.

Most prominent of the birds were the herring gulls, who nested in these lake regions, long soaring wings gray with black tips. About four dozen of them now wheeled about the vessels in the bay, being the most excellent of beggars or scavengers or maybe both and knowing exactly from whence came the slops.

"Now hear you this, lads," Gunner's Mate Parker roared, and all his recruits jumped. They sat in a tight line along what appeared to be a giant spar which lay athwart a wooden jetty pointing directly into the bay. From beneath it came the gurgle of water around pilings. "Here you be now on a grand mission, lads, to serve as seamen, a noble calling, and assist His Excellence Commodore Oliver Hazard Perry launch a stroke again the God-damned bloody British!"

As he spoke, Gunner's Mate Parker bobbed his head up and down like a pecking bird. Some might have wondered how the little black leather naval brim-hat stayed in place on a head of what appeared to be unruly and thickly curling yellow hair. He wore a swallow-tailed blue coat with brass buttons on a collar so high it almost hid the fact that his right ear was nothing but a stump of gnarled flesh, the better part of it having been bitten off by a Barbary pirate.

"Oh and young lads, there is more than honor alone in being a sailorman. There are the doxies," and he leered a lecherous grin and winked and cast his blue-eyed gaze back behind his recruits to the empty powder wagon sitting there, and winked again at the three snickering young men in the wagon, Gance Chesney, Pieter Groot, and Claven Sadowski, their clothes still soaked with sweat from the labor completed no less than thirty minutes before.

"Me in a huff and a hurry in that very town to your stern, down the street me, and all lilac and sweet roses a doxie accosts me and says she will do me a Gullyupson then and there in the street, and I say I have no time for any of her Gullyupson, in such a hurry be I.

"So she says she will do me a Gullyupson standing up, and I tell her it is against my religious faith to do such things while standing, and she offers to give me a Gullyupson as I walk along, and damn me, lads, I was so curious to see if she could do such a thing, I might near agreed. But duty was stronger, lads."

Gunner's Mate Parker laughed like a seal whistling and slapped his leg with the knotted rattan punishment rope in his right hand, calling attention to his breeches and rather ragged white silk stockings, all of Revolutionary War vintage, and a pair of huge paste buckle shoes.

His young charges did not change expression at the conclusion of his story. They were a mixed lot, four white farm boys, four Africans, probably freedmen, and the ninth an older man obviously an Indian, probably a Seneca.

For this was on the western tip of the old Five Nation Iroquois country, being now a place called Presque Isle but soon to be Erie, Pennsylvania, when the citizens got around to changing the name.

Well, the three in Nalambigi Chesney's wagon appreciated the salty humor and laughed, and glances passed between them and the gunner's mate, glances in which an agreement was made to meet again that evening in the place they'd been meeting for the past two nights. The Grand Erie Tavern and Grog Shoppe.

The ale and apple brandy and whitefish in the Grog Shoppe were excellent. They'd had plenty of it but not yet their fill, so they had more as they sat with the gunner in the dim taproom, dry now and bathed, having taken their accommodations upstairs in this same establishment and since concluding their work of the day paused to refresh themselves and put on clean trousers and sailorman shirts of blue-and-white horizonal stripes provided by Theolonious Parker himself.

Their trip from Cincinnati had been long and boring, no Englishmen jumping out from behind trees to hold their arms while screeching Indians disemboweled them, as Claven Sadowski figured was sure to happen at any moment.

They had trundled across all of Ohio along the south shore of

Lake Erie, finally arriving at Presque Isle only a short while after twenty-eight-year-old Commodore Oliver Hazard Perry and some of his people had arrived to build a fleet and win this lake so Commanding General William Henry Harrison could safely get at the British north of Lake Erie in Ontario without having enemy naval units in his rear.

Nalambigi Chesney's gunpowder was more than welcome, and the three of them remained to help get it aboard the two largest of Perry's ships, the *Lawrence* and the *Niagara*. This involved making cartridges and lightering them to the anchored vessels.

Making cartridges was a dangerous business and left fingers feeling sticky and raw at the same time. It involved using wooden spoons to fill felt bags of the appropriate caliber with gunpowder, then sewing these bags shut with a bone needle. No metal, please. Sparks at such a time being the dangerous part of the job.

"You can't have loose powder being shoveled into cannons on a gun deck during battle," explained the gunner. "So you make cartridges of felt bags, and the loader shoves them bags into the muzzle, slices a hole top of the bag with a mussel shell so the fuse will be sure to ignite the charge, and as he makes his little slice the rammer takes his rammer, see, and rams the bag home.

"Then in with solid shot, chain shot, grape, or a bucketful of musket balls, dependin on what the gunnery cap'n wants to chew up. The other ship's hull or its rigging or its people."

So they'd sat on the beach spooning gunpowder into the cartridge bags, loaded them in a flat barge, been rowed out to one of the ships, hoisted the cartridges aboard, and carried them below to either the forward or aft powder magazine, small, completely unlighted rooms below deck draped on all sides with felt cloth.

"Sailormen call it the Felt Room," said the gunner. "That felt would catch and hold any spark flyin about below decks during battle, hold it until the spark died. At least, you hope it will."

And that job was finished now, so they relaxed for what they believed would be the last time for one more round of whitefish and ale and talked with the gunner and admired his chewed-off ear.

"Now lads, you need to do like I've advised," said the gunner, leaning across the table and from time to time picking up a piece of whitefish from one plate or the other. "You need to take ship with me and the commodore so's you can help whip hell out of the God-damned bloody British. We've got a fine little navy here, lads. A fine little navy."

Well, it was a fine little navy. There were six gunboats, like barges with one mast and one heavy gun; a schooner fore and aft rigged with two masts and six guns, all twelve pounders.

But the power was in *Lawrence* and *Niagara* which the gunner said would be classed as brigs in any naval code book. They were sis-ter ships, identical, and built right here on the shores of Lake Erie, and in a short time, everybody proud of the fact that in the morning there would be a growing tree with leaves in the forest and by night-fall that tree would be planking and decking and sheathing and bulk-heads and scantlings and rails and stanchions. Spars and masts and yard arms took longer.

"They look fatter than brigs I've seen," said Pieter Groot. "And lower in the water."

"At the widest, the beam is about thirty feet on a hull about one hundred feet long," said the gunner. "They sit low and the keel will run only deep enough to get a good bite in the water, but you don't need a lot of below-deck space on a lake ship."

"Why?" asked Gance. "What difference does it make, lake or sea?"

"Hell, lad, a lake ship's always close to shore so you don't have to victual for long voyages," said the gunner. "You been below on *Lawrence* and seen. Ain't a thang on the orlop deck but a small cabin for the capt'n, the surgeon's cockpit, and them two powder maga-zines. No water casks, no victual bins. There's a fo'c'sle gallery to fry fish. You want fancy grub, you go ashore. You want fresh water, you drop a line overboard with a bucket on the end of it."

"Where do the sailormen sleep?" asked Claven Sadowski.

"Wherever they can," the gunner said and laughed. "She ain't built for comfort. Remember again, you ain't gonna be at sea a long spell. And they's clews in below-deck stanchions where you can swing a hammock. But mostly, you sleep on deck."

"Where do the sailormen go to the toilet?" asked the boy.

"The heads are at the bowsprit," the gunner said. "A hole in aslant bulwarks. Now, the whole crew on deck can watch you at your business, in daylight, but sailors don't mind such a thing. And at the bowsprit, if a man's business leaves a dribble of shit down the sides, it's quick to wash off as the ship makes way through the water."

"They're handsome little ships," said Pieter Groot. "And they look pugnacious."

"They damned well be that, lad!"

The *Lawrence* was Commodore Perry's flagship. Named in honor of Captain James Lawrence, killed in action, who had said in battle, "Don't give up the ship." Perry now had that motto embroidered on a blue banner, and it hung at the stern staff.

Lawrence and *Niagara* had two masts, fore and main, each with three yards of mainsail, topsail, and topgallant. There were booms for a spanker sail off the mainmast, but it was short and left the stern standing clear of any rigging directly overhead, and that gave the ship an upswept look at the fantail which wasn't really the case.

The deck was flat horizontal, stern to bow, main deck and gun deck in one, like some frigates, Pieter Groot told Gance. The upswept look was repeated at the bow with a high-pitched long bowsprit rigged with lines for a foremast staysail, a jib sail, and a very large flying jib.

"If you squint a little," said Claven Sadowski, "they look kinda like canoes, only fat ones."

"For God's sake, Claven," Gance said. "Don't tell the gunner two of his ships look like canoes."

"There is one thing about those two ships," said Pieter Groot. "The guns. Those are bigger guns than many you'll find on a frigate."

It was true. Each brig had broadsides of two twenty-four pounders forward, three of the same aft, and amidship there were five thirty-two pounders. Ten guns starboard, ten guns port, a complement of twenty guns.

"Now the God-damned bloody British," said Theolonious Parker through the haze of ale and applejack fumes, "they got these lake ships of theirs armed with nine and twelve pounders, mostly. Which can stand off and shoot at you a mile away and maybe hit you now and then and make a hole the size of a good apple like made this calvados, or whatever this horse piss is we're drinkin.

"The commodore, now, he's got them belly busters where you get close and fair blow the bloody bastards to splinters."

"How close?" asked Gance, well aware of shooting ranges with a rifle.

"So close," said the gunner, "that your yard arm blocks and braces are kissin his."

They'd been with the gunner and on the ships enough to understand the terms and knew that he was speaking of very close, indeed.

That last evening in the Grog Shoppe remained in Gance's memory as a kind of applejack-colored haze, pale yellow but transparent so everything that happened was viewed through a wavy mirror.

He recalled most vividly the moment when Gunner's Mate Theolonious Parker pulled up his sailorman's striped shirt to reveal his belly, and there in garish colors was the tattoo of a young woman with almond eyes and black hair piled high on a dainty little head.

Nobody was looking at the eyes or hair. For this was a woman naked from the waist, and Claven Sadowski almost choked on a mouthful of beer.

"I reckon you've seen the tattoos of various savages hereabouts," said the gunner. "These poor innocent infidels! Now in China, they know how to make *real* tattoos, and I show you a sample."

"You been to China?" asked Claven Sadowski, trying desperately to focus a rather drunken gaze on the woman of the gunner's belly.

"Yes, in the fur trade, and to Africa, too, not just the coast of Moroccan bandits but under the horn, in a slaver, and the black kings bringing down captives from their latest war and selling them to the Portuguese or the Arabs and then them to us, under a Dutch flag I was then, and us loaded with that stinking cargo, off to the Indies to trade our slaves for molasses and on to Boston to trade the molasses for rum and off to Amsterdam to trade the rum for guns and back then to the Ivory Coast to trade the guns for more Africans."

"Perhaps these freshwater lakes are confining after all that worldwide sailing," said Pieter Groot.

"It don't matter, lad," said the gunner, pulling down his shirt and taking a long drink of whatever it was he was drinking at the moment. "I served a time in the British navy before the Revolution, then in smugglers for years, and then found my bonny Oliver Hazard aboard an American sloop in the Mediterranean and says, 'This is the man for me,' and have been with him since."

The gunner leaned forward and nodded and said in the low tones of a conspirator, "Don't you think he's a fair young man? That little curl of brown hair on his high, shining forehead, such a little man but full of fire and ice and ready to bound into the jaws of hell, by God! Don't you think so, lads?"

"Without question," said Pieter Groot. "Perhaps his middle name prophetic."

"The God-damned bloody British on this lake will know him soon when he gives them a kiss," roared the gunner.

"Where are these British you speak of, Cap'n?" asked a listening militia soldier.

"No captain me, you bloody fool, but a petty officer, see?" Parker snarled but once said all heat gone and smiling again and tossing yellow curls. "They be on that lake yonder, two big ships, big as our big ones, I reckon. The *Detroit* and the *Charlotte*. More guns than we, only not so big, maybe.

"They got another ship nearly as big. They call her a brig, like we call orn. I can't name her ordnance nor size, but except she'll displace the same tonnage our large ones do maybe. Maybe.

"But no fear, lads, the brothers Brown, Adam and Noah, they built our ships, and no man walks this earth or swims its seas can build better than them two.

"We know the British commodore, too, me and Hazard Perry the lovely lad. He be a Captain Robert Barclay. A fine naval officer. A one-armed man. Lost his other one fighting with Lord Nelson at Trafalgar."

"With Nelson? At Trafalgar?" Pieter Groot asked. "Those are good references."

"Good indeed, lad," shouted the gunner. "He'll need them and more, too, when our lovely Oliver Hazard puts the gaff into him."

It was wonderful, salty conversation. Listening to Gunner's Mate Theolonious Parker, they could almost hear the swell breaking against the bow of some dark ship probing the shallows off Tripoli.

But for Gance Chesney there was a woman, a very young woman, one of the gunner's doxies, and he could never recall anything about her except the soft lips and a golden curl falling in front of each ear. And there was a dock over water, he almost falling in the lake, then shirt off and it was cold, he remembered that, and then back into the stifling heat of the Grog Shoppe where the gunner was regaling a group of soldiers from William Henry Harrison's army with stories of smuggling tea into hidden ports near Boston for John Hancock.

And then a sodden, hot bed and swirling clouds and walls that pressed in and then expanded and a blazing light in his eyes, and when he finally opened them he was lying on a bundle of hammock netting at the taffrail of some ship, the sunlight in his eyes, and Gunner's Mate Theolonious Parker bending over him and grinning and shouting into the breeze.

"Back amongst the living, I see, lad. Good!

"We're running before a fair wind to the Bass Islands. And the commodore thinks with me that you and your mates will be fine marksmen in the tops when we meet the God-damned bloody British. And we're sailing to meet them now. Look to your long rifle, lad.

"And welcome aboard the *Lawrence*!"

Chapter 19

You could pretty much assume that everybody knew where everybody else was on Lake Erie. At least, in general.

There were fishing vessels out from the American and Canadian shore almost every day. If one of these was hailed by a warship, say a schooner, either United States flag or British, the fishermen were usually willing to pass the time of day, as it were, and tell what they had seen in the way of other ships and boats. For the safety of navigation, they would tell you.

So in the first week of September, 1813, the Americans knew that Captain Barclay and his flotilla were at the western end of the lake, probably carrying supplies from the Niagara area in to the British garrison at Fort Malden just south of Detroit. And the British knew that Commodore Perry's ships had begun running short patrols from an anchorage he had selected to the lee of Bass Islands.

"Do the English know we're here?" asked Gance.

"If they don't," the gunner said, "they're sure in for a damned noisy surprise!"

"We play a game of cat and mouse," said Pieter Groot. "When the British mouse comes out of his hole, the American cat will be waiting."

Oliver Hazard Perry happened to overhear that comment and liked it so well he used it in his short inspirational orations to the men on board the *Lawrence*. He liked it so well that he instructed Gunner's Mate Theolonious Parker to have the author of it assigned to the stern rail as custodian of the blue banner on the stern staff. The banner with the motto Don't give up the ship.

"He likes inspirational things," explained the gunner.

"God, he looks so young!" said Gance.

The commodore also ordered that Groot learn crew duty on one of the aft twenty-four pounders. And at the same time noted the fine Pennsylvania rifles and instructed the gunner to have Gance Chesney perform duty as a marine sniper in the rigging.

"Ain't he the one to see talent at a glance now," observed the gunner, winking.

"Well, he's certainly more attractive in all ways," said Pieter Groot, "than that captain on the *Niagara*, what's his name?"

"Lieutenant Jesse Elliot," the gunner growled, and his face took on its rare cloudy expression. "He's a bastard, and jealous as a green lizard of our Master Perry."

There was an ominous ring in Parker's voice that Gance Chesney found disturbing, and from his expression knew that Pieter Groot had caught the same vibration. And for some reason he could not fathom, he was silently glad that back in Presque Isle, the gunner had not taken Claven Sadowski on board the *Lawrence* but left him to look after the team and wagon of Nalambigi Chesney until Gance's return.

Gance felt some weight of responsibility for that boy and was happy now that the most serious threat to young Sadowski would be the gunner's lakeside doxies.

While this game of cat and mouse continued, the crew of *Lawrence* and the other vessels trained. They needed it. Only a few of these people had ever been on a ship of any kind, much less a ship of war.

Oliver Perry was a dynamo of bustling activity. He was everywhere up and down the deck, adding his own personal explosive energy as example for the crews sweating under petty officer's instructions, or with megaphone shouting orders to other ships in the flotilla, or laying hands to ropes and rigging, or even going up ratlines to shout encouragement from above.

Frontiersmen and farmers and Africans and taproom hangers-on and a few seasoned sailors were burning their hands on the lines, reefing sails, hauling on halyards to trim yards, taunting or loosening stay braces, running down the big spanker sail set abaft the mainmast, then running it up again. Everything for speed, speed, speed.

Gunner's Mate Parker drilled his powder boys, running them up and down the ladders from the Felt Rooms to the bulwark readyracks for shot and cartridges. There were six of them, all about ten years old, urchins bright eyed with excitement.

"Little buggers," the gunner said to Pieter Groot. "They be eager now for action and not one of them blooded. Not one ever seen a man tore in half with solid shot. Little buggers. They be in for a terrible shock soon."

Gance Chesney had a hell of a time with the mainmast ratlines. A wooden ladder he could negotiate as well as anybody. But one of rope, growing narrower and narrower as it ascended sixty feet up from aft railings to the mainsail yard and then to the top, was something else. The top was a platform on the mast used by lookouts and as a shooting station for marksmen during battle.

First, he had to rig a sling for the rifle because he couldn't climb that damned swaying, spongy rope ladder without the use of both hands. Then he took a terrible tongue lashing from the various petty officers who supervised all these exercises.

"You damned dumb ox landman featherhead, hand holds on the lift lines, not the foot lines. If there's a man going aloft before you, he'll step all over your fingers when you grab with your God-bleeding stupid hands the same thread he's grabbin with his toes!"

And once aloft, even with the ship sitting quietly at anchor, he found himself being swung round and round in a wide arc like a June bug on the end of a switch and wondered how in hell he was supposed to take aim at anything smaller than a Canadian windmill under such conditions.

"Ahoy, you in the maintop, get that musket off your back and simulate firing it; you ain't up there to fornicate with the God-damned yard!"

And it meant making a lot of paper cartridges because it would be impossible up there in the tops, with the wind blowing and the mast jerking round, to pour powder from a horn into a muzzle. Hard enough to prime the pan under such conditions. Anyway, the gunner had paper for the purpose, and Gance realized that on shipboard, cartridges were as important for small arms as for cannon.

For Pieter Groot, practice was better understood but a lot hotter. Gun drill.

Ready shot box and powder box on either side of the gun at the bulwark. Pull the truck back, wooden wheels squealing, water bucket, sponge the bore to swallow hot embers from the last shot, ram in a slit felt cartridge, ram in a solid shot, run the truck out, heaving on the ropes, the blocks and tackles groaning, aligning with crowbar and handspike, adjusting the elevation screw, gunner sighting along the tube.

You got elevation on the trunnion with the screw, but for ranging you had to manhandle three tons of gun and truck with crowbar and handspike. That's where the real sweating began.

Then the powder horn, pour primer into the hole, the hammer a spring-loaded flintlock instead of old slow-match, and when the whole thing was laid and on target, the gunner yanked the lanyard, and all of it had to be done over again. And the faster the better.

The commodore had each crew fire four live shots. When the first of these exploded furious sound across the deck, followed by the dense cloud of dirty white smoke, all the gulls wheeling above squawked and flew away.

And the gun and truck leaped back hard against the lashings and wedges. When the crew moved in to reload and realign after the third shot, already the barrel was hot enough to blister so you learned in a hurry to touch the metal parts of this monster only with a handspike or with thick gloves like the gunner wore.

The smell of burned gunpowder was a thing to get used to, else it was pretty distasteful. Like rotten eggs. Yet, with that first firing, that first evidence of the savage bite of this little vessel, the crew cheered.

Indeed, said Pieter Groot, it was exhilarating!

Early in the day, September 10, the long, sleek sloop came sliding past the *Lawrence* with certain colored flags on the signal halyards, the little spots of color dancing high up, at a level with the fore gaff topsail, and of course, Gance Chesney had no idea what message they conveyed.

He didn't need to read the flags. The master of the sloop, with megaphone, shouted across to the officers and men on the quarter-deck of *Lawrence*.

"Enemy under weigh with a bearing to cross to the lee of Pelee Point."

There was more, but Gance didn't hear it. *Lawrence*'s first mate was bellowing orders, no megaphone required.

"Deck, up anchor. All hands aloft, make all sail. Gun crews clear for action. Powder boys fill your ready-racks. Run up the national ensign!"

There was a lot more; no way a landsman could keep up with it. The ship had exploded with motion, the ratlines suddenly filled with men scrambling toward the yards like frantic flies going up window-panes. Forward, the anchor chain scraped the hawsehole as the capstan was turned by half a dozen straining sailors.

"Fast lads, fast," Commodore Perry was shouting from his place near the quartermaster at the helm just aft of the mainmast. "Speed wins, lads, speed wins!"

At the gun stations, powder cartridges for each piece, and chain shot rammed home except for two twenty-four pounders at the bow starboard and port broadsides, and each of those loaded with a bucket of musket balls.

The forward guns would come into alignment first, and musket balls would sweep enemy decks clear of sailors and gunners before enemy guns came to bear on *Lawrence*. And the chain shot to cut masts, yards, and rigging, all the guns elevated to aim accordingly.

"The commodore wants to put the British dead in the water," said the gunner. "So they can't maneuver to longer range where their guns work best and ours work worst. Then when they're like ducks sittin, smash em with round shot."

At least, they hoped that's how it would work.

The ship was swinging out from the islands under nothing but jibs and shaker so when the mains and tops and top gallants came down, they caught the wind suddenly and fully and popped like gunfire, filling the sails and driving the brig's fat bow through the lake's placid water with a gurgling hiss.

They were well under weigh when the last of the gun trucks rumbled up to the ports, and the lashings were made fast, and the gunners adjusted their elevation screws and then stood ready to cock the flintlock hammer.

"Lads, no one fires until my order," Commodore Perry said, with hardly more than conversational volume but everybody on deck heard him clearly.

They were moving fast, and Gance heard Perry order his signalman to make to Elliot following in *Niagara* to stay close. "We go in together," Perry said.

The entire flotilla was strung out over the blue water of Lake Erie, like ducks following one by one. The same signal went to all, stay close, we go in together, and further, that Elliot would control the smaller vessels, feeding them in close behind the flagship when contact was made.

Gunner's Mate Theolonious Parker was at his station near the port broadside astern, close to where Gance Chesney waited at the portside mainmast ratline, and the gunner relayed the messages as the signalman made them so Gance might know a little better what was happening.

A seaman in the tops sang out a sighting, and the first mate called for minor adjustments on the braces, and Commodore Perry at the helm gave the quartermaster a course.

Then the chief gunnery petty officer called out, "All marksmen into the tops."

And with his rifle slung over his shoulder, Gance Chesney started up the ratline, his shirt tearing at the shoulders as *Lawrence* leveled out running hard before the wind, whistle in the rigging, humming in the sails, and the pop of spray around the bow.

Gance was past the main yard, then onto the maintop, arriving there along with two Kentuckians up along the starboard shrouds. These men were part of the contingent sent by General Harrison. The three men took kneeling positions on the top and unlimbered their weapons.

It was amazing. With the ship charging forward before a good wind and the keel biting hard into the lake's water, this perch high above the deck was more stable now than it ever had been when they lay at anchor.

Above them, at the topgallant yard, was one of Perry's petty officers. Now, he called out.

"Sail ho! Leeward on the port quarter. Four . . . five. Six ships, all sail set beating back against the wind."

Gance saw them. White patches across the blue horizon of the lake. The petty officer climbed down past them, going to his deck station.

"Sing out, lads, if they veer off. But we're bearing down on them so fast, I judge the commodore will be able to see them from the deck in half a minute. Good luck. Aim for officers. They'll be the ones with the big hats."

And he was on down the ratline, hardly seeming to touch them as he went.

Gance Chesney watched the white sails, seeming to grow larger by the moment, coming directly at him, or rather him directly at them, and his heart pounded so hard he was sure it vibrated through the top and down the mast to the deck below.

"By George," said one of the Kentuckians, "this here is gone be the first time I ever had a chanct to shoot a sailorman."

"I declare some sho deserve it," said the other. "I ain't ever heared men with such vile cuss words in their mouth."

Gance Chesney looked down at the deck below him. It looked so small. Except for the black, monstrous guns, and around each of them, the gun crews. And he saw the officers standing near the helm and Perry at one railing peering with a long glass toward the west. And Parker's powder boys were running back and forth with buckets, making the motions of farmers sowing wheat. And he understood.

They were spreading sand so the deck would not become slippery with blood.

The British squadron was coming in line against a wind that had gone slack. Barclay had to know the Americans with the weather gauge could strike him wherever they pleased. So he began to deploy his ships, bringing *Charlotte* up alongside his own *Detroit*, and the sloop and gunboats and the brig ranged on either side of that so wherever the *Lawrence* came, he could wear around into line so that the broadsides of more than one British vessel would bear.

The brig was moving well into position, having more of the wind, but *Charlotte* seemed to be having trouble and although she had moved out from the wake of the *Detroit*, she was almost a cable length behind. And in slackening wind, the British were going to have trouble wearing into a classic in-line-ahead to broadside Perry's charge.

Lawrence was coming down fast, and Perry sent men aloft to reef mainsails, taking off enough surface to slow his charge else he would dash through the British formation with only enough time for one broadside. Still, the American brig was moving fast enough to pitch spray up across the forecastle when the ship dipped into an occasional swell.

Perry was hoping to arrive at the British flotilla before they were ready, catching them as they were still trying to turn to meet him.

Gance Chesney, from his perch in the tops, could already see details on decks of the British ships. The iron hoops of the masts were painted yellow, a tradition from Trafalgar.

Astern, Gance wasn't too happy with what he saw. The *Niagara* and the rest of Elliot's section were lagging far behind, and he could see that the American brig there wasn't running under full sail.

"Howdee, boys, they shootin at us now," one of the Kentuckians shouted, and Gance saw the little puff of white smoke from the bow of the British brig. But they saw no splash of shot. And the sound of the gun was a soft thump.

Gance figured this was a wonderful way to watch a battle, up high, where he could look down on everything. He could remember Pap talking about battles on land during the Revolution when it was hard to figure out what was happening because there were always trees or hills or houses cutting off line of sight.

Not here, he thought. No trees or hills or houses, and high on the mast, safe, looking down on everything.

Then there was a second shot from the British squadron, and in a few seconds, before they heard the soft thump of the firing, there was a hiss and pop and suddenly a hole the size of a man's head appeared in the foremast topsail only a few feet in front of Gance's face.

Well, maybe it wasn't so safe as he'd expected.

Seeing the direction of *Lawrence*'s charge, Barclay still tried to claw *Detroit* round to get a broadside in position receiving Perry's first shot. But with his disadvantage of wind, he didn't make it, and the American brig dashed less than three rods abeam of *Detroit*'s starboard rail, and when the gunnery officer gave the command, a sheet of yellow-orange flame leaped from the ports of *Lawrence*, the entire broadside at once.

The crash of sound slammed against Gance Chesney's ears, the mast heaved, billows of dense smoke belched up in sulphuric fury to obscure the British ship, but not before he saw wood splintering and ropes going slack and blocks flying like cannonballs across the deck of the *Detroit* and two broad swaths cut through the ranks of men in light blue jackets unlucky enough to be in the path of the musket balls from the forward twenty-four pounders.

And Perry's insistence on speed paid profit now because before *Detroit* fell away, half the broadside got in another blow, this time with round shot, and Gance watched through the growing gauze veil of smoke the explosion of splinters from the British hull and bulwarks.

One of the nine pounders on the *Detroit,* struck fair on the muzzle by a thirty-two-pound solid shot, reared and flipped over on its gun crew. A great bite was taken from the mainmast just above one of those yellow bands. A boat, lashed keel up on the main deck amidship, disappeared in an explosion of splinters. At the bowsprit, the bobstay was shot away and the foremast staysail was cut loose and fell across the forward gun crews in the port-side gun battery.

And he heard screams, some from directly below because the *Detroit* had gotten in her own blows with twelve pounders, ball and grape shot. Men were wallowing on *Lawrence*'s deck beside the guns, turning the sand beneath them red.

But now his attention turned to the *Charlotte,* still coming around on the port side. And trying to wear in the still-lessening wind, had almost lost steering way for a moment, at least.

Perry used the helm to lurch away from *Detroit* and toward the other British ship, *Lawrence* responding with a sudden reach to port and then straightening again to bring her port guns quickly to bear and they crossed *Charlotte*'s bow, Perry's broadside muzzle flashes running like a ripple of orange lightning along the side of his ship.

Gance saw the *Charlotte*'s bowsprit shattered and jib sails and lines falling in a tangle, and part of the foremast went, too, and there were sails hanging across some of her ports when she returned the fire and the muzzle blasts of her guns set fire to the dragging sails, and *Lawrence* sent in a second round of shot as both ships were shrouded in smoke.

There was a sharp, cracking sound, like thunder from close by, and the topgallant sail and yard came smashing down on the starboard extension of the maintop where the Kentuckians were, and one went down toward the deck in a tangle of lines and blocks and canvas. The other seemed to stiffen for an instant at the top rail, then pitched forward, a splinter long as a hoe handle through his head.

The mast was swaying wildly and popping like a fusillade of musketry, and Gance Chesney lost any purchase he'd had on the buckling top platform and he grabbed for the yard arm, big around as a man's waist here, and clung to it with all the strength of his arms. The Pennsylvania rifle had fallen, without ever having been fired.

Now, through the dense smoke pall below, he saw the shape of the British brig just off the port bow. He could even see the frantic sailors there, trying to get her turned to meet the *Lawrence* because the American ship had burst from the smoke where the master of the British brig apparently hadn't expected her.

The American guns ravaged all standing timber on deck the British brig and after three broadsides at a range of less than twenty yards, *Lawrence* passing along the brig's bow and then her port side, shooting all the way, hardly a thing that could be called a mast left standing.

But *Lawrence* had begun to take a pounding. Badly wounded as they were, both *Detroit* and *Charlotte* were still very seaworthy indeed, and they were coming at Perry's flagship more effectively as they gained some of the wind after he passed to the lee of their formation.

Gance Chesney, clinging to his swaying, popping mast, looked to the east and swore. The *Niagara*, the American sloop, and all the gunboats were still being held back by Elliot, or else the wind there had gone calm. That part of this squadron was going to be of no help as the British closed on the single American ship fighting them.

But he had no time now to damn Lieutenant Elliot. There was a violent shock along the mainmast and yard, and all the wood under his hands seemed to split apart and he was spinning backward and a mass of twisting lines were whipping around his feet, and he saw the big wooden block from the end of the topsail yard coming but he couldn't duck and it struck his head a glancing blow above the left ear, and as he fell he was vaguely aware that the mast had begun to fall off to the port side.

All else that he could ever remember aboard *Lawrence* was a fall through the dense, almost liquid cloud of gray powder smoke that throbbed with the explosions of the guns and glowed with their muzzle flashes. Then into water that was amazingly cold. Then a gasp of air and an arm thrown over a floating spar in all the debris on the surface of this placid lake.

Then watched as the British closed in to batter the *Lawrence* into a dead-in-the-water hulk. But not helpless yet. For through it all, her guns were still roaring, and as the three large British ships struggled to come near, they were themselves being turned into matchwood by *Lawrence*'s heavy batteries.

To Gance Chesney, it was like being in a sulphur rainstorm, the flaming guns making red and orange and blue lights flash in the thick gray clouds of smoke and the wooden splinters from the ship's hulls and decks and bulwarks struck by shot showering down into the water around him with the exact same sound that raindrops would make falling in a barrel of water under a downspout drain at the corner of his mother's house.

Then they were lowering a boat from *Lawrence*. Or rather throwing it into the water, what with the ship's small freeboard, and a number of men were scrambling down and into the boat and taking up oars. His eyes were filmed with water fouled by powder smoke, but he was sure he saw Pieter Groot.

And it was Groot, who had taken the blue flag from the stern and with the commodore and about twenty men went into the boat rowing away, *Lawrence*'s guns behind them still roaring.

Gance Chesney shouted at them to come to him, but there was

still a bedlam of cannon fire, and the boat passed under the dismantled bowsprit of the ship and moved beneath the clouds of murky smoke and toward the east where the rest of the American squadron still lay.

Gance Chesney was crying with rage. Not because he'd been left with all the other flotsam of the battle, but because the others had not come to support Perry and now poor *Lawrence*, though she was still firing, abandoned to the mercy of the British. Along with the few men left alive on her.

"Dammit, dammit, dammit," he shouted against the still-thundering cannon fire. "It's all over! It's all God-damned over! Stop shooting, stop it, it's all over!"

But he was wrong.

When they returned to Cincinnati, Pieter Groot would tell it to his wife, and then to Nalambigi Chesney, because her son Gance would think about it for almost two years before he'd mention it.

"Gance saw the battle best," Pieter Groot said. "The first part a bird's eyeview from the maintop. The last part a fish's eyeview from the lake. It was only later we knew he was alive to see any of it.

"The first part, I saw almost none at all. Busy on that starboard twenty-four pounder. It's just shoot, shoot, shoot, and sometimes rigging or spars or a dead man would fall on the deck, and sometimes an English shot would tear open the bulwark or hit a gun truck and turn it over or take a man's head from him even as he spoke.

"A practice old in navies, I suppose, was distasteful at first bite. When the body of one of our sailors lay on the deck where we were working the guns, it was simply picked up and thrown overboard, the quicker the better, our gunner's mate yelled at us, to get it out of the way. I only hope we didn't throw too many men into Lake Erie who were still alive.

"When we left the ship, she was dead still in the water, her upper works shot away. The gunner and I figured that Gance was buried somewhere under all the fallen timbers and lines on deck. Else over the side and drowned in a tangle of rope.

"I never saw a man angry as Oliver Perry. He was at us to work the oars in that boat, and we all knew it wasn't to get clear of his flagship. It was to reach the other brig. And the gunner said Perry might just shoot Lieutenant Elliot on the spot for holding back all the squadron while the English were beating us to death in *Lawrence*.

"I know this. Every sailor in that boat was ready to support the commodore if he did. The quickest court martial in naval history, the gunner said, judge, jury, and high executioner.

"Perry always carried a pistol in his belt. If he'd shot Elliot, it wouldn't have surprised me. Or run him through with the cutlass he had that day.

"The miracle was that we got clear without English sailors spraying us with grapeshot. The gunner reckoned they were so busy closing in for the kill on our flagship, they didn't notice our boat, or if they did, figured it was a few deserting seamen escaping the carnage aboard *Lawrence*.

"At the *Niagara*, Perry sent Elliot in the boat to take command of the sloop and bring the rest of the squadron into the fight, and Elliot was falling over his tongue making excuses about loss of wind. His sails were mostly reefed, and the gunner said Elliot was likely hoping Perry would be killed on *Lawrence*, and that would make Elliot ranking naval officer on Lake Erie.

"Maybe so. There are men so low.

"It was soon apparent to everybody what Perry was up to. He broke out all sail on *Niagara*, and the English were suddenly being descended upon with a second raging American brig, and she was untouched by battle while the English ships were shot all to hell. I suspect they were a little startled. I suspect they thought the fight was over.

"It was a short story. Their two biggest ships got tangled and hung together in the fallen lines and they lay there unable to move very much—aboard one another, sailors say—and Perry simply sailed past them and wore around and past them again and wore around again, blowing them to pieces each time with first one broadside then the other. Then again.

"It was a thing I will never forget. On their flagship *Detroit*, we could see blood running down the sides of the ship from the scuppers. In those ships that get into a fight like that, the sailors are caught in their wooden pen and there is no place to hide, no place to run. They are slaughtered like Campbell Chesney's hogs, squealing and kicking and spurting blood.

"It was a thing I will never forget!"

As Captain Barclay struck his colors, if it could be called that when he had a sailor pull the ensign down from the splintered stump of the mainmast and wave a bloody white shirt, Commodore Perry's first concern was for his men on *Lawrence*.

Gunner's Mate Theolonious Parker and Pieter Groot were in the first boat rowed over to the battered American brig. It was then they found Gance Chesney and pulled him from the water, shivering but unwounded, and laughing and gripping their shoulders and hugging them and praising the commodore to heaven for coming back.

But as they went on deck of the *Lawrence*, Gance Chesney stopped laughing.

For during this fight he had either been high above it or at water level and in no position to observe the carnage in all its ghastly detail. Now, stepping on that deck, it was all around him. And the first thing that struck him was the smell.

And it was not the overpowering scent of burned black powder but rather an odor he'd not thought about for years, the odor he'd first experienced in the Kentucky woods when his pap dressed a deer just shot and hung from a tree limb, the entrails and feces and blood splattering on the leaf mold.

He'd been a very young boy then. And he'd vomited. Now, he had to set his jaw hard and grind his teeth together to keep from vomiting again.

From stem to stern, the deck was a rubble of cordage and lines, splintered and split masts and spars and yards, shredded sails, gun barrels lying loose and gun carriages shattered, dead bodies and parts of dead bodies in all of that, shattered and red and grotesque and horrible.

Many of her sailors had been struck down by grapeshot or musket balls, but most had been killed or maimed by flying wooden splinters, torn, slashed, impaled with chunks of rail or bulwark or mast, and some, too, crushed under overturned gun trucks or else caught beneath falling yards and masts.

There was no evidence that any wheel had ever stood at the helm, both masts had been sheared off at deck level, great gaps had been torn in her bulwark, bowsprit and most of the bow were in the water, held close against the hull by the tangle of jib sail lines, and along each side the hull itself was holed by solid shot like a Swiss cheese.

The survivors sat with vacant, staring eyes in faces coal black from powder smoke. In fact, on board that ship then, Gance Chesney was the only man with a white face. For black powder smoke is a sticky, clinging, almost liquid thing, and Gance Chesney's only close contact with it had been his falling through it when he went into the water from *Lawrence*'s shattered mainmast.

When the count was taken, it was reported to Commodore Perry that for every ten men who went in *Lawrence* at the time she cleared the Bass Islands, eight had fallen.

Lawrence's surgeon was still in the orlop, working, and they could hear the cries of men there, and when they went below, beside the commodore's mess table, which had been dragged out to lay men on as the surgeon worked, there was a pile of hands and arms and legs.

The *Detroit* and *Charlotte* and the British brig were as badly used. Their personnel had been even more severely battered. Barclay, the man who had served with Nelson, started this action with only one arm. He finished it with no arms at all. Throughout the British squadron, every ship's captain and second in command had fallen.

On the British brig, the Americans boarding found an English sailor dazed and mostly incoherent, who said he had served with Barclay and Lord Nelson off Spain, and compared to this Lake Erie action, what he had seen at Trafalgar had been a Sunday stroll.

On the same ship, in the orlop deck, they found Shawnees who had been brought aboard as marine sharpshooters but who had taken refuge below when the cannons started to shoot. From this day forward, they said, they would owe their undying allegiance to the Great Father in Washington City.

They found somebody's pet brown bear licking at the gummy red sludge on the deck. One of the Kentucky soldiers shot him, and the carcass was thrown overboard to float for a time with all the debris there, the wood and hemp that would float. And the bodies of men, back-up in the water.

"They float like that, dead men in the water," said the gunner. "Facedown with arms and legs dangling like the tentacles of a Portuguese man-o-war. The gas holds them afloat, lads, but when that busts out, what's left sinks out of sight."

There were so many dead, and something needed doing about them quickly. So Elliot was given the job of supervising men from all the ships of the American squadron and the small boats of the British one, too, in the detail of bundling bodies and body parts in sails, weighing them with round shot, sewing them into bundles. And dumping them in the lake.

Various other officers were used to read the funeral services at sea from a book of British naval regulations found in Captain Barclay's shattered cabin. American and British officers alike, reading over American and British dead alike committed to the deep.

But before all this, Perry.

Quickly, because he was still concerned with speed, the commodore penciled a message that he dispatched to General William Henry Harrison, waiting anxiously with his army south of Fort Malden.

This is what Oliver Hazard Perry wrote: "We have met the enemy and they are ours!"

And a long time afterward, Pieter Groot could say, "I never would have thought it possible. I leave the seacoast to make my way as a pioneer in the jungles of Ohio, and in process thereof, I am awarded prize money for a naval victory.

"The Congress, like us all, was so overjoyed with Commodore Perry and his Lake Erie victory, they appropriated prize money to everyone on those ships. Just like Sir Francis Drake being knighted by Queen Elizabeth for capturing all those Spanish bullion ships. And even though the British ships we captured were mostly shot so badly to hell they were no good to anybody. No matter. The prize money was just a measure of joy at having a victory.

"Even that bastard Elliot, who stayed back from the fight, got more than a thousand dollars. For us? Well, Gance Chesney got two hundred fifteen dollars. Me? Three hundred.

"Why the difference? I expect because it was me who carried the commodore's flag from the *Lawrence* to the *Niagara*. The flag that said, 'Don't give up the ship.'

"Well, you might argue Perry gave up the *Lawrence*. But remember. He didn't leave her there. He went back and got her. She was no longer any use to anyone, except maybe as firewood, and he knew that, but he went back for her just the same. He felt as we all did who served in her. She was damned precious firewood!"

Chapter 20

One of the Kentucky volunteers who had come to join William Henry Harrison's army remarked on the general's appearance.

"He be mite near as handsome as any man, with his bushy eyebrows and his little curlicue hair on his forehead and his nose, which be about as long as a hatchet handle."

For those who attended such things as the *Farmer's Almanac,* it was noted that, with the autumnal equinox, Harrison's army had become a rather impressive force and that great things might be expected, as is always the case with the turn of the seasons.

Most of Harrison's soldiers were spoiling for a fight. And maybe not so much to get in a whack at the British. Maybe they were eager for a chance to settle all of what they figured were past-due accounts with the redskin rascal who had been giving them pause for a long time, the Shawnee Tecumseh.

The British had made Tecumseh a brigadier general. And he had with him a following of about a thousand men from various tribes, but mostly his own Shawnees. The whole thing was a bad taste in the mouths of Harrison's men.

It didn't matter that now, with the advent of fall 1813, Tecumseh hated the British commander at Detroit almost as much as Americans did because in recent fights, this man, a certain Colonel Henry Proctor, had not tried to prevent but indeed had seemed to encourage his auxillaries killing wounded and captured Americans, a practice Tecumseh had been preaching against for years.

So when Commodore Oliver Hazard Perry won Lake Erie, thus making Proctor's position at Detroit and Fort Malden untenable with no way to provision his forces by water and an American navy in his rear, and Colonel Proctor decided to retreat deeper into Canada, everybody was saying, "Let's get after the rascals and scald their arse, redcoat and redskin alike."

It sounded right to General William Henry Harrison, so with an army of perhaps four thousand men, counting all bits and pieces, he invaded Canada and moved upstream along the Thames River which rises in Ontario and empties into Lake St. Clair just north of Detroit.

This was in pursuit of Colonel Proctor and his force of about eight hundred British regulars, who were rather leisurely making their retreat along that same route with Tecumseh and his thousand warriors covering their rear.

Apparently, it was Proctor's idea to move his regulars without breaking much of a sweat while his Indians kept their eye on any Americans who might decide to follow. All of which might have been just fine except that Proctor forgot to take into account an American characteristic already well known. Impatience.

"Even to be in the company of great men," said Gunner's Mate Theolonious Parker, "it is not worth having to ride a God-damned mule!"

But the gunner didn't say it loud enough for the remark to be heard by the command group of officers riding just ahead of them, on horses, through this woodland of sycamore and sugar maple and burr oak, the canopy colored with the scarlets and yellows of fall.

It was an impressive horseback entourage. There was General Harrison, seeming to sniff the air for danger with his remarkable nose, his stature emphasized by a hat large as a one-hole privy, as the gunner described it, and his officers. And there was Commodore Perry and one of his lieutenants.

For Harrison had invited the naval victor of the battle of Lake Erie to join him in this campaign, at least for a while, and with no more British ships to conquer on the lake and no duty except repair of wounds to the fleet, Perry had accepted the invitation, leaving his subordinate officers to patch up the ships and from time to time send supplies directly across the lake to Harrison's army.

Gunner's Mate Theolonious Parker had apparently been detailed to persuade Pieter Groot that he should remain in Perry's service, for the commodore had taken a liking to the African, and recognizing that without Gance Chesney beside him, Pieter Groot would not even consider accepting the commodore's invitation to accompany him on the army campaign, much less agree to being recruited into official naval service, Gance had been asked to go on this little outing into Canada as well.

Whatever the tangled motives, there they were. On mules. Immediately behind the command group of Harrison's army as they felt their way up the Thames. From time to time, they heard the rattle of musketry somewhere ahead in the woods or bordering fields. From time to time, they passed a wounded soldier, usually leaning against a tree and chewing tobacco as a comrade saw to his wounds. Now and then there was a dead man.

"Their Indians are the rear guard," someone said. "And when our boys wound or kill one, they drag him off. So we see only our own who are struck."

Sometimes they heard men shouting in unison, like holloing a fox on the hunt. Sometimes they saw a few of the Kentucky cavalrymen ride nearby.

It was true. Harrison had cavalry in his army.

Well, in the age of great regiments of horse in France and Britain, you would hardly qualify these formations as cavalry. Of course, that's what they called themselves because of the romance in the name. But there were no sabers. There were no lances. There were few pistols. Their weapons were smoothbore muskets.

You could call them dragoons. Because it was expected that when they got to the place where a fight was happening or about to happen, they would dismount and fight as infantry.

But General Harrison called these Kentucky frontiersmen "My Cavalry." With the same pride, you would suppose, that during this era Napoleon said of the magnificent Grenadiers à Cheval of the Imperial Guard, "My Cavalry."

Regardless of what Harrison called anything, this ride was becoming very boring indeed. They saw almost nothing, except what happened immediately around the command group. Their butts were beginning to burn and ache, they were very hungry, they were thirsty, having to share a single canteen.

Besides all of which Gance Chesney felt near to naked being in the woods without a rifle. He had already begun to overcome the images of mutilated corpses and crimson decks and think instead of the calamity of losing two of Nalambigi Chesney's rifles in the deep water of Lake Erie.

There was one short and rather unpleasant surprise. When one of the Ohio battalions passed nearby, Gance Chesney was hailed by one of the soldiers. It was Bedford Croft, and marching behind him, musket on shoulder, grinning through a ragged stubble of beard, Corliss Hooten.

"My, my," said Pieter Groot. "We've come across old friends from Cincinnati."

"Hey there, Chesney," Bedford Croft shouted, waving his hat. "Does your big brother know you're here gnawing at the tail of his English friends?"

"Hey there, Chesney," bellowed Corliss Hooten. "Your redskin mother ain't here now to sharpen your hatchet."

Gance Chesney said nothing, but Pieter Groot could hear him

grinding his teeth. Happily, the marching troops were soon gone into the trees, leaving Gance Chesney riding silently along with a grim, hard-set mouth.

"Do I get the feelin," said Gunner's Mate Theolonious Parker, "that you young gentlemen has had some social intercourse with them ugly soldiers?"

Pieter Groot laughed. "We have addressed their heads with ax handles, and Gance's older brother very nearly sliced the jaw off one of them once, with a D-ring shovel."

"Well now," said the gunner. "I would enjoy meeting this brother. Sounds like your typical bos'n's mate."

In night encampment, everyone spooky about some of Tecumseh's Indians slipping into their lines and sticking knives under their ribs, their rears throbbing now with mule-ride pain, bellies choked with raw bacon and hard navy biscuits, Gance Chesney wondered what in the name of God he was doing here.

"Pete," he whispered, shivering under the one blanket they had to share, "why the hell did you agree to come along on this damn fool jaunt?"

"It's the great adventure."

"Oh?" snorted the gunner from his own blanket. "I'll take my bloody adventure on the water, in a good ship."

"Well, I don't see why the general won't let us light fires," Gance said. "My sore behind is froze off."

"Why, with fires to guide them, the English and their Shawnees would know just where to slip in and disembowel us, now wouldn't they?"

"Shit! They know where we are. If the English have got even just one Indian with them, they know where we are."

"True. And I fear they've got more than one."

"Well, it's you Perry wants in his navy," whispered Gance. "So if one of Tecumseh's bucks slides in here tonight with a butcher knife, please tell him I'm not supposed to be here."

"I'd be glad to."

"For God's sweet love," the gunner hissed. "Will you two stop hawkin and get to sleep!"

The road that followed the course of the Thames River was a good road and the British had disdained destroying any of the bridges along it, so Harrison's army moved quickly and was soon seriously engaged with the Indian rear guard. There was increasing evidence that Proctor had finally come to realize the obvious, that if he continued his leisurely pace, the Americans were going to catch him.

They began to find wagons and carts left behind, and soon their path was littered with the debris of an army in headlong retreat. A sure sign was the abundance of powder and ball abandoned, which meant the British soldiers were not as much interested in fighting as getting away.

Near a place called Moravian Town, Proctor decided to make a stand, halting his retreat to form his battalions in a line of battle across the route of Harrison's advance.

Harrison's column simply flattened itself out against the British line, overlapping at both ends like a flood of water against a solitary rock. On his right flank, Harrison sent in the Kentucky mounted men and they drove forward, apparently frightening or surprising the British, most of whom threw down their weapons and ran.

The Kentucky men dismounted with their long rifles and proceeded to shoot down the redcoat soldiers trying to get away. Those who escaped the sharpshooters surrendered.

Some of the British prisoners were moved past the command group, and Gance Chesney for the first time saw the hated enemy. They looked just like everyone else.

You might suppose that by this time Colonel Proctor lost his nerve and led the route toward Lake Ontario and upper Canada, leaving his Indians to hold back the Americans.

That's what his own people supposed, and later everyone heard that Proctor was court martialed for cowardice and by order of the prince regent his name was read out in dishonor before every regiment in the British army. Worldwide.

But on the spot, as Proctor and what few of his soldiers got free and fled to the east, Harrison's force ran into the toughest fighting they'd seen thus far. The Indians, led by Tecumseh, fought for each tree and stump trying to keep the Americans off the straggling rear of the retreating British army.

And they succeeded.

During that hour, Gance Chesney was close enough to the fight to hear an occasional ball hissing through the foliage. Close enough to smell the powder smoke. Close enough to come across men just wounded and crying on the ground, crawling through the brush, hunkered against tree trunks.

But after the deck of the *Lawrence*, this combat seemed almost casual. Then he was ashamed to think of it like that as he watched men die. It was not casual to them.

William Henry Harrison probably did all he could to get his army moving after Proctor again, to completely destroy the British force. Gance and Pieter Groot and the gunner watched as the general charged about, shouting orders which were mostly ignored. And Oliver Hazard Perry watched as well, an expression of amazement on his face.

You might expect that Perry had images of a lot of people hanging from yard arms for disobedience of orders.

But the men of that army were not too much interested in Proctor and his men. Their attention was centered on the Shawnees and Tecumseh. This is where they wanted to do the work of annihilation.

In all the years that went down after this Battle of the Thames, surely every soldier who fought there claimed he saw Tecumseh himself, dashing about among his Indians giving orders, firing a weapon, chopping with a great tomahawk.

Well, there's no doubt that Tecumseh was there, Pieter Groot would tell Willimena. A great battle leader. Because it was one of the few actions in all memory when Indians stood and fought like Europeans, defending positions to the death. The only kind of tactic that would succeed in keeping a superior force from falling on the rear of a staggering, stumbling retreating army in rout.

"Only a strong man could hold them to that kind of fight," Pieter Groot would say. "It flies in the face of everything all those warriors ever learned about how to make war successfully."

Tecumseh was killed, of course. Some said pierced by many bullets before he fell. Some of those American veterans as they grew old undoubtedly came to believe they had been the marksman who delivered the lethal ball.

Gance and Pieter Groot and the gunner dismounted, glad for the chance, and walked about the battlefield, through the stands of oak and beech, and watched the soldiers taking souvenirs and scalps from the Indian bodies. And there were plenty of bodies to be found now, none of them carried off by comrades. There had been no comrades left to do it.

It was in a thick grove of young sycamores close to where the forward edge of battle had been when they saw Corliss Hooten and Bedford Croft on their knees behind a fallen log, working feverishly at something. As Gance and his two companions drew nearer, they could see the bloody arms of both men, scarlet to the elbows.

"What have we here," Pieter Groot muttered, and they stepped closer to see over the log.

Croft and Hooten had knives in their hands. They were bent over the body of a man, although much of it was not recognizable, lying on old leaf mold become sodden and red. They were skinning it.

Looking up as Gance Chesney came near, Corliss Hooten laughed and held up a grisly trophy.

"You want a piece, Chesney, take home to your redskin mama?" he said. "This here is what's left of old Tecumseh, sos me and Bedford is gonna have a few patches of his hide to take back for our sweethearts!"

All of it, the whole scene, turned into a red haze for Gance Chesney as he started for them, but Pieter Groot had his arms and was

421

pulling him back, and he heard the laughter of Corliss Hooten and the swearing of Gunner's Mate Parker.

"They're not worth trouble, they're not worth trouble," Pieter Groot kept saying.

"God, I wish I had my rifle," Gance panted.

"I'm glad you don't," Pieter Groot said. "And settle your temper. It was likely not Tecumseh. How would either of those ugly mutts know Tecumseh?"

"It doesn't matter if it was Tecumseh or not," Gance snapped. "Don't you understand, for God's sake? It was *somebody*!"

They sailed back across Lake Erie to Presque Isle, where Perry's fleet was being refurbished, and there said their good-byes.

The commodore thanked them for lending their hands to his work in clearing the British out of the old Northwest Territory and said to Pieter Groot that if he ever changed his mind and decided to become a professional sailor, to come looking for Oliver Hazard Perry.

"The lovely man will be trying his damnedest now," said Gunner's Mate Theolonious Parker, "to get a posting back in the saltwater navy."

Later, Pieter Groot would say he saw a glistening of moisture in the gunner's eyes as he bid the young men of Ohio good-bye.

"By God, lads, an old salt always remembers the shipmates of a grand battle. So me with you. Now, I hope you both fare well," said Parker, and he turned and stomped away along one of the docks where new spars and coils of hemp rope and blocks and tackles and folded sail lay in great confusion.

Perry shook Gance Chesney's hand warmly and told him to express profound appreciation to his mother for having sent the fine Cincinnati gunpowder. And even though, according to her instructions, it had been offered free of charge, Perry paid Gance seventy-five pounds sterling, part of the booty taken from the cabin of Captain Barclay on the *Detroit*.

It was a good thing, being all the money they had, for on investigation they discovered that young Claven Sadowski had sold Nalambigi Chesney's powder wagon and her team of horses and taken the money and stated his intention of going to Pittsburgh and thence to the East in search of fame and fortune.

"That little son of a bitch," said Gance Chesney. "I leave him here to keep him free of danger, and he shows his appreciation by stealing our rig and horses. What the hell am I going to tell his pap?"

"Only the truth," said Pieter Groot.

"More important, what am I going to tell my mother?"

"Only the truth. But please do so when I am safely outside or better still, when I have had time to get to the Kentucky side of the river."

"Sometimes I'm not sure I like your sense of what is funny, Pete."

"Look on the shining side. We aren't without means."

"Yeah, thanks to the commodore, we can at least afford to buy a couple of rifles before we start home. There might be a stray Shawnee hiding in the woods twix here and there."

"And horses. There's enough to buy horses as well."

"No. I'm not going into my mother's house after giving away her gunpowder then losing two of her fine rifles and then having her wagon and a good team of horses stolen without at least a few coins to show for it. Maybe the fact that it will be coins taken away from the English will dissuade her from hanging me by my thumbs in a corner of her lodge. So I'm not spending that money on horses."

"But you could replace the horses stolen."

"No. Those were Kentucky horses and she bought them herself. I can't replace them here. Even if I could, I wouldn't. I don't want her thinking I imagine myself as good at buying horses as she is."

"Then how do we get home?"

"We walk."

As far as most people in Ohio were concerned, the war was won. Perry and Harrison had won it. Now the British weren't threatening them, and the Indians had been beaten down so badly that the remnants of all the old hostile tribes were scrambling to vow their love of the Great Father President Madison in Washington City.

Maybe, folks figured, we can get on with settling the land from Niagara to the Big River without the threat of some wild bunch of savages full of English rum swooping down on hill and dale with murder in their red hearts.

And they were right. There would be a few minor kickups over the next decade, but nothing serious anywhere along Lake Erie west of New York State. For the first time since European white men had come into that vast area, there would be no foreign power encouraging the local tribesmen to use their ancient methods of warfare on whoever happened to be settling north of the Ohio River.

After Thames, the old settlers along the lower Ohio watched the rest of the British war as they might a conflict happening on another continent. Of course, as the news of a continuing war came to them, they reacted alternately with joy or despondency. Pride or shame.

If it's bad news, they said, Nalambigi Chesney cooks a goose, and everybody on the riverfront gets drunk. If it's good news, Nalambigi Chesney runs out on her cliff-top porch and shoots off a pistol in the air, and everybody on the riverfront gets drunk.

Nobody outside the family ever understood the goose the widow cooked, or rather that her colored woman cooked, represented something or somebody Nalambigi Chesney was in a particular state of mind to despise, hence taking great satisfaction in devouring.

But as this war wore on, it was a good thing, said Gance Chesney, that his mother started with a very large gaggle of geese because it seemed hardly a month went by that Nalambigi Chesney didn't find soul, spirit, or symbol of somebody or something or someplace to sacrifice due to its repugnance to her and to the memory of her husband who was a hero of the Revolution, a fact she was most happy to point out to anyone who wasn't aware of it. Or in fact to anybody who stood still long enough to listen.

Relative calm may have descended on Lake Erie's western shores, but there was still a lot of action at the eastern end. There were any number of fights along the Niagara River, the most bloody being Lundy's Lane, which both sides claimed as a victory.

Nalambigi Chesney's geese were safe when the town heard about the battle on Lake Champlain. It, like Erie, had been a sound victory for the United States. But the gaggle took a severe beating when the British sailed up Chesapeake Bay and burned Washington City, and the fact that they failed to burn as much of Baltimore as they had the nation's capital didn't salve the pain.

In Judith Dwyer's hotel dining room, Carter Purcell from the land office said he was ashamed to be an American what with our soldiers running like stampeding cattle at Bladensburg and then having our capital city torched, and the president hiding in a goat shed someplace.

Doc Claudes Insel's wife Pauline overheard the remark from a nearby table and almost beat one of Carter Purcell's ears off with a rare beefsteak.

"Ma'am," Sheriff McCracken said, "you almost beat this gentleman's ear off."

"I would have, too," she said, "except I'd already carved the bone out when I picked it up. Of all things! That kind of talk!"

Emerging as a hero to rank with Perry and Harrison was Andrew Jackson, who was going about the Southeast thrashing people he called Red Sticks. Mostly Creeks.

"If your pap was still alive," Nalambigi Chesney told Gance, "he'd be off down there with this General Jackson."

"Well, I don't propose to go join him. I don't propose to go join anybody in this war. I already feel like an old man."

"Oh no, I don't mention your pap to encourage you to go off to fight. If you did that, I'd be bound to give you a horse to ride, and I can't afford to lose any more horses," she said with a laugh.

Everybody in the family had been astonished at the widow's reaction to losing that team of Kentucky horses. She'd passed it off almost as a joke and even patted Gance's back once as Pieter Groot explained what all had happened, his having been dragooned into telling it on threat by Gance of revealing to Willimena certain aspects of that last drunken evening in Erie, whether true or not, before they shipped on the *Lawrence*.

"I did nothing for which I am ashamed," Pieter Groot said.

"Don't be too sure."

"Certainly you wouldn't lie about it."

"I might. To avoid my mother's wrath, one does all kinds of strange things."

So in a mood of adventure, Pieter Groot told about all of it, except the night in Erie, and Nalambigi Chesney laughed.

"It was that English coin you brought her," Campbell said. "The last time she had English gold in her pouch, real English gold from an enemy Englishman, was when Pap looted that carriage at Saratoga during the Revolution."

"Blood money, huh? Mother enjoys having blood money."

"Sure. As long as it's English blood."

Anyway, southern hero Jackson really had them whooping and hollering in the Crock and Bottle and other grog shops on the day news came of the fight at New Orleans.

"Yah, dem English," said gunsmith Steinhartz, "I seen em line up like dat, all in a row of dem damned redcoats, and come right forward at you when we fight at Brandywine. Now, dey come, ole Jackson shoot em down like dogs, English band tootles, English drums thump thump, they come right on, an ole Jackson shoot em down like dogs!"

They fought that battle on the last day of the first week of 1815. What they didn't know was that the war had been over since Christmas Eve, 1814. Nobody on the American side of the Atlantic had received word of the treaty made at Ghent, Belgium. Including the commanding general of the British expeditionary force trying to take the mouth of the Mississippi. He was killed. Along with over two hundred of his soldiers. Who didn't know about the treaty, either.

"It don't matter that the war was over," said Sheriff McCracken.

"They come at us with their regular army, and we whomped their arse for em!"

That was pretty much what everybody else thought. So the war, which had started with such miserable bungling and hadn't gotten much better as it went along, finally ended on a high note. But neither side really won. They were tired of fighting. And the United States was broke. So they just quit.

Campbell Chesney could have done a little crowing about it, pointing out that he'd said all along there was nothing to be gained. Maybe he considered it. But he kept his mouth shut, more to avoid throwing cold water on his mother's elation than from fear of renewing anger against his views among the townspeople.

So it was finished.

And it turned out that New England hadn't really considered secession, and those who wanted to annex Canada said they really didn't want all those Frenchmen sending representatives to the United States Congress, and although it wasn't in the treaty, Great Britain ceased stopping American ships on the high seas, and the Indian menace in the old Northwest was taken care of, so now everybody could really pitch in to make Cincinnati better than St. Louis as the jump-off place for all those folks westering.

It was time for them to do what Americans did best. Make a lot of money. And have a hell of a lot of fun doing it, too!

Part V

SHADOWS
OF THE MOON

Chapter 21

"We can't let St. Louis get ahead of us," said Campbell Chesney. "We've got to put some of our profit back into the businesses. With the war over, a lot of people will be going along the river, and we don't want them to pass right on by and fill out their outfits in Missouri. In fact, we want St. Louis to be a customer, too."

"A lot of people went along the river when the war was going on, too," said his mother.

"All right. But now, there will be more."

"You're beginning to talk like General Putnam, all that business this and business that. And how can a town be a customer? Does it walk in and hand you some coins? I'd like to see that, a town acting like a man."

"All right. What I mean is, if somebody in St. Louis wants to start a business selling matches, he gets them from Cincinnati. If somebody in St. Louis wants to start a shoe store, he buys his shoes in Cincinnati," Campbell Chesney said, showing only that amount of impatience he knew his mother expected.

"If they want to start a shoe store, why don't they make their own shoes?"

"Because it's easier to buy them from somebody else, in large quantities and therefore at a low price. That's called wholesale."

"Wholesale. Because they buy a whole lot of shoes."

"Yes. Then sell them to people at a higher price, for their profit. They call that retail."

"Why don't they call it resale?"

"I don't know, Mother. I'm going home to supper now," which is what he always said, whether it was suppertime or not, when his mother had so exasperated him that he could see the end of patience coming. And of course, he had the sense that his mother knew exactly how the game was played, and her part in it was to drive him close to hot temper and hence end the conversation.

He knew this because at such times, he could see the shine of a smile in her eyes if not on her lips. His mother smiled more with Campbell now than she ever had before. Once, she had smiled easily with Clariese, and then when he was old enough to be a portrait of his father, she smiled a great deal with Gance. But now, she was coming round to smiling with her eldest.

Or maybe, Campbell figured, smiling *at* him.

Gance Chesney always listened to these exchanges, but he never entered into them. Sometimes, later, he would come to Campbell and ask questions about what Campbell had been trying to explain. Sometimes not.

Then Nalambigi Chesney would agree with Campbell, or not, and it didn't take the older brother long to realize that after he'd proposed something, his mother conferred with the younger brother before she decided.

Strangely, he didn't mind that arrangement. Once, he would have resented it hotly, but now, it worked well. He began to realize that he was becoming head of this family and that Gance not only accepted it but welcomed it because he, Gance, sure as hell didn't want to be any patriarch himself. To be adviser was good enough for him.

432

Besides all of which, Campbell was not likely to forget that it had been his little brother who was largely responsible for the success of their abduction of Sarah McCallum from the man who had tried to kill Pap. And that when the die' was cast in the affair on the island upriver, it had been Gance ready with pistols in his hand.

And Nalambigi accepted it, too. That Campbell should make important decisions now, with her concurrence, of course. Or maybe even without her concurrence, but still expecting to be asked because after all she owned most of the capital. And when he thought like this, Campbell began to suspect that his mother understood the game better than he did.

Judith Dwyer observed that a lot of things had changed on the Bluff, as most of the town people had begun to call the Chesney home above the river. The widow wasn't out in a hack drawn by a matched team of Kentucky bay horses, seeing to her various enterprises almost every day, as she once had been. When she appeared in town, it was usually social, to visit with whomever she might find in Judith Dwyer's taproom.

Everybody had gotten over their initial shock that the woman could walk into a taproom and sit down and make herself at home, calm as any man you'd ever see, said Stan Lewicki.

And why not, asked Doc Insel, who often sat with the widow while they sipped dark beer and smoked clay pipes in a cool corner of Judith Dwyer's saloon, or in winter sat near the fireplace and had hot coffee.

"She can do as she pleases," said Doc. "You know she employs more people than any other entrepreneur in this town, if you include Campbell's hog factory."

"Yah, by God," seconded Able Steinhartz, "and she's a hero of Revolution, by George, her an Sergeant Bobby, so she sit where she damn well want to sit, you know. She ain't like no other of dese hausfrau besen kehren!"

"Able, what the hell is a hausfrau besen kehren?"

And Able's youngest son Helmuth, who was usually standing by for just such assistance, said, "It's a married woman using a broom to sweep her house."

"And I tell you," said Sheriff McCracken, "when she gets started on the Revolution, she can spin off more tales about Old Sergeant Bobby and what he done than you can imagine, and the one she likes best is when Sergeant Bobby found that gold coin in them English women's coach at the Battle of Saratoga. She gets started on that, and it draws a crowd, boys, it draws a crowd!"

Looking in on all the Chesney operations had become Campbell's duty, and he did it with intensity. Such as on the shoe factory, where Clariese's husband, Otto Black, was now majordomo. Campbell and Otto sometimes paused to reminisce about the trip to Kentucky to deliver the Aaron Burr letter.

But Campbell didn't pause long. Then off to see about the gunpowder works, the match factory, the land office, the distillery, and then back to the sausage mills.

Every one of those Chesney enterprises had become well-known on the river. And already, before Campbell made his wholesale speech to his mother, St. Louis and other places had merchants shopping in Cincinnati for their trade goods.

And Chesney's wife Sarah was just as busy as her husband. Being a devout Presbyterian and booster of the University of Cincinnati, which a group of good citizens had only recently established.

Campbell had joined the church, too, but his wife sometimes embarrassed him with her outspoken disdain for the Baptists and Methodists, all of whom she characterized as barbarians. She was a charter member of the Cincinnati chapter of the new American Bible Society.

"That wife of Campbell's is a feisty one all right and a mighty good looker, too," said Carter Purcell in the federal land office. "When she first came here, she was a timid little thing, until her papa went off downriver. No bigger than a wart. But she produces. How many young uns do they have now?"

"Six," said Judith Dwyer. "No wonder she's interested in a university. Her own children are gettin old enough for it, and they's enough of em to fill out a whole class."

Steamboats were coming down the river in coveys, said Gus Staufer, who spent all his spare time away from the Chesney livestock pens hunting quail in the cleared upland fields along the Miami River. And Carter Purcell could tell you, there were more and more cleared fields and settlements along all the roads that led to Lake Erie.

National roads everywhere now. When one had been completed from their town to Chillicothe, one that you could travel without losing a wagon in mudholes, it was the talk of all the saloons. But before long, it became so common nobody paid any attention to it except the people who depended on river traffic to make a living.

It was the steamboats that took Pieter Groot and Willimena away. After the Battle of Lake Erie, he couldn't resist things that moved about on the water. He wanted to build them or sail them. So he decided to go upriver to Pittsburgh and find a job in one of the boatyards there.

That had been a very tearful occasion. On the day the African and Willimena departed, she had cried and Sarah had cried and half of Sarah's children had cried, and the women were all hugging, and Pieter was shaking hands with Gance and Campbell and Otto and then back to Gance again. Then at the very last Gance and Pieter embraced. And Gance had to take a swipe at his eyes with his sleeve.

Gance had been at the bottle pretty seriously since early morning, but Campbell figured Gance would have acted the same even wedge-cold sober.

So now Nalambigi Chesney had to train herself another housemaid, and Able Steinhartz sent her his youngest daughter, a stout, tough, healthy flaxen-haired girl with the strength of a two-year-old mule and energy enough as well to do Nalambigi Chesney's housework and cooking and still have plenty of time to try luring Nalambigi Chesney's youngest son into the hayloft.

435

Except for her and Gance, nobody ever knew if she succeeded. Her name was Herta.

And Gance?

Some of the early settlers, those who could remember Robert Chesney in his youth, said Gance looked so much like his pap that it would take your breath away when he walked into a room. Of course, he wasn't missing those two front teeth, but so long as he kept his mouth shut, you'd almost bet it was Sergeant Bobby come back from his grave.

Nalambigi Chesney thought so, too.

Gance had moved into the quarters vacated by the Groots, the rooms just off the kitchen, and so he was in the main house most of the time. When he came in from a trip to the headwater of the Miami, where there were still turkey and deer, his mother would look at him in wilderness gear and her heart would almost stop.

He spent a lot of time on the Bluff now. Sometimes he would go down to the town for his afternoon drinking. Sometimes not. He would repair harness or sharpen the knives and the hatchets and axes or clean all the firearms or put up a shelf or build a woodbox in his mother's kitchen, warding off Herta's advances like an army protecting its flanks.

Sometimes one of his nephews or nieces would come to be with him, and he'd make toys for the little ones and teach the older ones how to use a flintlock weapon. He taught Campbell Junior to shoot in the lot behind the horse barn.

And sometimes he would whittle a toy boat and put masts on it and sails that he made from cotton sheeting his mother gave him, and he and the nieces and nephews would sail it in the horse trough. Usually the boats capsized until he learned to make them with deep keels and ballast embedded in the hull to counteract the top-heavy weight of the masts and sails. For ballast he used .50-caliber lead musket balls.

436

And sometimes he would drink in his room all afternoon and be unable to come out for supper, and Nalambigi would go in and put a cool wet towel on his forehead. But usually, when he was drunk, he would come in from the town taprooms and want to talk, and in summer they would go to the porch overlooking the river and in winter would stay near the fireplace in the kitchen.

On one such night, she told him about her dreams.

"I think I've become too much of a white man," she said. "My dreams don't mean anything any more."

But then another time:

"I dreamed of Willimena," she said.

"And Pieter?" he asked. He was lying on his back on the inlaid stones of her promontory porch, staring at the moon.

"No. Only Willimena," she said. "She was watching this great war. As great as the Revolution. Maybe even a greater war than that."

"The English again, Mother?"

"No. There were no English. And no red savages."

"What was the war about?"

"I don't know. It had something to do with Willimena's people. It was a terrible war."

There may have been others with dreams similar to the one of Nalambigi Chesney.

States had been joining the Union like soldiers marching through the gate. Indiana and Mississippi. Then Illinois and Alabama. Anybody paying attention to politics knew why they came in two-by-two more or less, one from North, one from South.

Now, even for those who hadn't been paying attention, it was brought home with a vengeance. Missouri was ready to come in, with a constitution that allowed slavery. All hell broke loose in the Congress, and the whooping and hollering spread across the country, coming down the Ohio River like a riptide.

"Mother's confused about all this," Campbell said to his younger brother. "Why don't you take her on a boat trip to Marietta to see General Putnam? She always listens to him about such things."

"Why don't you explain it to her?" asked Gance.

"When I try to explain something," Campbell said, "it always ends in a wrangle. You know that. I'd take her myself, but it's a busy time of year and I need to stay here and keep my eye on business."

Nalambigi Chesney surprised them all by agreeing at once to go. She'd never been on a steamboat. Gance thought he sensed a bit of excitement in it, especially when he said it would be their first steamboat trip together.

When the day came, the whole tribe was at the riverfront, on the dock to say good-bye. Otto and Clariese and all their children, one with a big bunch of wildflowers for his grandmother.

Sarah Chesney was there, too, and she slipped a small Bible into Nalambigi's hand.

"Take this with you," she said.

"It's not my book," said Nalambigi. "I won't read it."

"You don't have to read it, Mother," Sarah said. "Just take it, just have it with you. I'd like that."

"Good," Nalambigi said and put the Bible in a large shoulder-strap pouch where she carried some money and a Harpers Ferry flintlock pistol.

Campbell helped her up the bow gangway and onto the lower deck of the boat.

"My legs are old," she said. "And stiff now from all that cold water we waded when we went up the Kennebec."

"Mother, that was almost fifty years ago."

"To me and my legs, it was only yesterday."

They were on the boat overnight, but she did not go to the cabin they had arranged for her. She slept in a chair on the pilot house deck, and maybe she didn't sleep at all but watched the dark shoreline glide past under the soft black canopy sprinkled with a million stars.

It was obvious that General Rufus Putnam had only a short bit left of life. But his mind was still keen, and when he saw Nalambigi Chesney walk into his parlor, his old eyes sparkled as they had when he first looked at her.

And he explained the Missouri Compromise.

So long as the states were more or less equally divided between those barring slavery and those allowing it, there was an uneasy peace in the Senate of the United States of America. It was urban, Federalist, industrial, high tariff, nonslave North opposed to rural, Jeffersonian States-Rights, farming, low-tariff, slave South. To over-simplify fantastically, completely overlooking the fact that a lot of border states were hard to tell apart, free or slave, and many of the slave states at this stage were trying to think of a way to end slavery as much as were northerners, General Putnam said.

Except for South Carolina, as General Putnam had always pointed out. South Carolina was a completely separate country, he said.

"Let them be what they want," said Nalambigi Chesney.

"A noble sentiment, my dear, but it will cause all kinds of trouble one of these days."

Anyway, if Missouri came in slave, as it wanted to do, the South would gain an advantage in the Senate that northern states would not abide.

So they came up with the Missouri Compromise, which in simple effect declared that Missouri would come in slave and the northern province part of Massachusetts would become another state, non-slave, called Maine. And that no new state north of thirty-six degrees thirty minutes north latitude could enter the Union as a slave state.

Wonderful! Two more slave state senators, but also two nonslave state senators.

"Most of them don't care a spank about slavery, one way or the other. It's all about power in the Senate."

And, General Putnam told Nalambigi Chesney, "They all think this closes the book on the question. For now, maybe so. But it has given hint of dark and bloody secrets we will be forced to read some-day. Because this is from a book that refuses to stay closed!"

"I would like to have some of my family far from here if such a time comes," she said. "I have had dreams of how terrible this time could be."

"My dear, it may be impossible to hide from such a time."

And two nights later, during a thunderstorm, she dreamed of Willimena once more.

Sheriff McCracken said, "Are things moving faster now, or is it just that I'm getting old?"

"Things might not be moving faster, but we hear of them quicker," said Stanislas Lewicki. "But you're getting old, too. We all are. I look around, and by God, there is here hardly a soul left who was alive during the Revolution. And I can remember every wart on Count Pulaski's face!"

"He was a count?"

"Of course. He was one of our great Polish noblemen."

"Well, I knew von Steuben was a baron, but I never heard Pulaski was a count. Speaking of noblemen, did you read in the newspaper that Lafayette come over recently to visit General Washington's grave?"

"He was a marquis. That's just above a count in the old country. And I tell you, this Frenchman was lucky they didn't cut off his head during that French Revolution they had, and maybe he was lucky Napoleon didn't have him shot."

"No worry about Napoleon now. They got him on some island away from everything."

"We need an island where we could send Corliss Hooten and Bedford Croft and other men of that stripe. Since they come home from the war, they are a big noisy pain in the arse, fighting and disrupting business and breaking windows because they think they are heroes."

Well, the community was at least spared the humiliation of having Hooten and Croft showing off chunks of what they claimed was Tecumseh's skin. After discharge from Harrison's army in Illinois, they had made a tour of taverns along the way home, and soon their mustering-out pay was gone and they ended trading their trophies of the Battle of the Thames for a half gallon of clear whiskey.

Sometimes, Gance Chesney would get drunk at one of the river-front taprooms and go looking for these two, taking no pain to hide his intention of administering a good beating with the heavy walking stick he always carried now. In lieu of carrying a rifle, everybody said, because Cincinnati was getting so civilized few inhabitants of the town went about on the streets in daylight carrying a firearm.

Gance never told anyone about what he and Pieter Groot had seen on that Canadian battlefield, and so everyone just figured he was out to put lumps on Hooten's and Croft's heads because of all that ill feeling before the war when they'd probably been an impor-tant part of the mob that set fire to Campbell Chesney's house.

But Hooten and Croft knew what Gance had seen and that he was the kind of unreasonable man who would remember such a thing and make trouble for them just to show how much they disgusted them.

In any case, Hooten and Croft were very attentive to Gance Ches-ney's visits to riverfront taprooms, and if he showed signs of aggres-sion, as when he began to hold his cane like a club instead of like a walking stick, they always remembered urgent business in Kentucky and took the ferry to Covington.

"Mother has relaxed, finally," said Sarah Chesney. "She sits in that rocking chair you bought her, out on her porch, looking down at the river and the town, and she isn't always yelling about something."

"She's not relaxed," Campbell said. "She's getting old, and she's only resting, watching and waiting, but storing up energy for times when she sees something she needs to erupt about."

"You said nobody would ever get her to put money or legal papers or anything else in a bank," Sarah said. "But she does."

"The smartest move the First State Bank of Southwest Ohio ever made was to name her a director," he said. "She has never been to a board meeting, but she thinks the white man has made her a chief in one of his important councils and any time she wanted to, she could go in and smoke with them."

"Well, she might just do that, if she takes a notion."

"Christ, I hope not," Campbell said. "I hope the time has come when she's satisfied to just sit and watch it all go by until something she doesn't like comes near enough for her to swat it without leaving her rocking chair."

"My dear, please don't use the Lord's name."

Well, Nalambigi Chesney wasn't completely calmed. When old King George III died, she treated it like a victory in warfare against the English, startling everybody in the lower end of town when she ran out onto her promontory and fired a pistol in the air.

Then killed a goose, which she named King George IV, and directed Herta's cooking of it, and called all the family in for a feast, and of course, she ate the heart.

"With President Monroe's new doctrine," she said as they all sat at table that night, "we don't need to worry anymore about the damned English starting new colonies someplace."

"Mother, where would they find a place to start new colonies?" Campbell asked.

"Don't start with me, boy! See to my grandchildren. Give them more stuffing. Give them more corn. Are you trying to starve them? And Clariese's children, look at them, give them more of that goose."

It was very strange, but Nalambigi Chesney at no time other than at her supper table paid the slightest attention to any of her grandchildren. She always regarded them with an impersonal gaze, not at all hostile, but as though she were trying to figure out where they might have come from.

She went less and less into the town to sip beer in Judith Dwyer's tavern. Sometimes in good weather, she was the whole afternoon on her porch looking at Kentucky, and if Gance came near complained that she had really become a white man now, what with taking so much interest in such a thing as a rocking chair.

They often had lemons now, in the greengrocers, these and other exotic things coming upriver on the steamboats all the way from New Orleans. In summer, as she rocked and watched the sun in its march across the dim blue highlands to the south, she enjoyed having Gance make lemonade.

"Spill a little of your clear whiskey in it," she would say.

Gance gave her the news almost daily. Mexico was now a free country, having separated itself from Spain. Nalambigi Chesney swore a mighty oath with the mention of Spain, remembering Mendez, the man who had tried to kill her Sergeant Bobby.

And Campbell had joined the Masonic lodge.

"Masonic lodge?" she asked. "What's that? Like a Mohawk long-house?"

"No, Mother, the word means something else here," Gance said. "It's like a club, for men. Or a kind of church."

"How many churches does he need?" she asked. "He's already a Presbyterian, as his wife keeps reminding me. What do they do in this Masonic lodge?"

"I don't have any idea, Mother."

And there was always news about the Erie Canal, now building from Albany and up the Mohawk Valley to Buffalo, a water connection from the Hudson to Lake Erie. Nalambigi was always interested in things happening in the old Iroquois country, but the idea of men digging a ditch more than two hundred miles long she found hilariously funny.

In 1824, a son was born to Campbell and Sarah Chesney. Although she had gone to term, he weighed only five pounds four ounces. They named him for his grandfather, Robert Chesney. He cried a great deal and was unable to digest his mother's milk. Doc Insel devised a formula of goat's milk and honey that would stay down.

Sarah wanted to call him Robert II, but Campbell said his mother would raise a storm over such a name because it would remind her of the succession of English kings.

Nalambigi Chesney walked down the hill to her son's home and looked at the child while Sarah was still confined. This had never happened before.

However, standing above the cradle looking down at the baby, she showed no enthusiasm for picking little Robert up and didn't. At least, said Campbell, she'd come to look. Without having spoken a word, she left and walked back up the bluff to her rocking chair and a glass of Gance's lemonade.

"She only came because she wanted to see the freak," Sarah cried.

Little Robert had a badly deformed left foot. And Doc Insel had let slip this information in Judith Dwyer's taproom so soon it was common knowledge in the town.

Some of Nalambigi Chesney's old enemies said, "Well now the high-and-mighty red Indian princess has a grandson with a clubfoot. That's a good comeuppance!"

Chapter 22

Gance Chesney had been dreading the day.

It was a dark and gray afternoon when the news came downriver. Gance was in Judith Dwyer's taproom, and he left at once to climb the bluff in the rain and tell his mother that General Rufus Putnam had passed.

Nalambigi Chesney watched her son come up the hill, and she knew from his stooped, purposeful stride that something bad had happened. When he came into her kitchen, her face was set in hard lines, and as he told her, her expression did not change.

For a long moment, they wordlessly looked at one another, and then she rose and went to her porch. He hurried after, catching up an umbrella. He held it over her as she stood staring across the gray river into the mists of Kentucky.

The town militia had dragged one of their old cannons out of its shed and wedged it with timbers on a river dock and began to fire a salute. Nobody in charge knew how many shots might be appropriate so they fired until all their powder was exhausted.

The booming voice of the gun came through the rain like a mournful thump and each time was echoed back from the far shore of the Ohio and then died softly as though muffled in wet cotton, faint and distant as the guns of Yorktown.

"He fought with your pap and me in the Revolution," she said. "He always loved the Republic."

And then she turned and went inside.

It was almost a month later when the brown package came, delivered to the local postmaster off the steam packet from Pittsburgh that came twice each week.

Jude McCracken, the sheriff's brother and an old-fashioned kind of Federalist and hence appointed postmaster by the new president John Quincy Adams, who appreciated Federalists old-fashioned or any other kind, saw the addressee and the red wax seal with the imprint of a signet ring and immediately called an urchin off the street and paid him a penny to hand-carry the package up the bluff to Nalambigi Chesney.

"You know the Widow Chesney, don't you, son?"

"Yeah, she's that old Indian squaw, ain't she?"

"You say that too many times, Son, you'll get squawed yourself good and proper. Hand this to her. No other."

Nalambigi Chesney recognized the seal. Rufus Putnam had sent her letters before. What she found inside made her pause after reading the first few sentences. She thought it best to share it from the outset with someone she trusted, someone who could help her digest its full meaning. So she put it in her kitchen bread safe for Gance to translate when he got home.

But she changed her mind. Gance and Otto Black were in Illinois hunting turkey, and they might be gone another week. She'd have Campbell do it.

Then changed her mind again because she decided that if General Putnam had sent her all these official-looking papers, she'd better know what they were before sharing them with the rest of the family. So she dispatched Herta down the hill to find Doc Claudes Insel, asking him to come at once.

The doctor came flogging his old horse up the bluff road because he thought he was needed for his professional services. Over the past couple of years, Nalambigi Chesney had complained of difficulty in breathing and she coughed a great deal and she was no longer a young woman, so Doc Insel feared the worst.

Instead, he found her alert and as intense as ever, and at her kitchen table she swore him to secrecy and then shoved the brown package to him and asked him to read it and tell her what it meant.

Immediately cautious, Doc Insel said he'd be glad to read it if she could assure him that by doing so he wouldn't be getting involved in something against the law.

"How do I know if it's against the law?" she asked, producing a squat, black bottle bought from Judith Dwyer only a few days hence. "That's what I got you up here for, to tell me."

Doc Insel looked at the brown package with the red seal, and he looked at the black bottle with a white label identifying a full quart of Braugh's Genuine Irish Whiskey. He blinked rapidly and licked his lips.

"I would be more than happy to oblige," he said. "And be assured that any word of this meeting and what it may produce will be safeguarded from any other person even with threat of horrible torture. Do you happen to have some nice hot coffee I might take with a dose of this stimulant?"

"No. Read the papers in that package."

TO: Nalambigi Chesney, Cincinnati, Ohio

In furtherance of my duties as Executor of the Last Will and Testament for Rufus Putnam, Esq., Justice of the Supreme Court of Ohio; Surveyor General of the United

447

States of America; and Major General of Engineers, Army of the United States, extract therefrom to her:

To All Who Shall See These Presents, Greeting:

It is the bequest of Rufus Putnam that said Nalambigi Chesney aforementioned have from his estate one Quarter Section, or one hundred sixty acres, of Real Estate as hereinafter identified, and necessary documentation for establishing it officially as hers to have and to hold from this date forward:

1. Receive in hand a quit claim deed that describes this grant of land in fee simple as inheritance unqualified ownership and power of disposition thereof;
2. Report of the Solicitor General of the United States to the Congress, as it applies to the time and place of this bequest;
3. To have, after his decease, his personal message written in his hand.

My Signature: Thadeous Proctor, Attorney at Law, Marietta, Ohio. Executed on this 12th day of March, Anno Domini 1825.

"All right," she said. "I can understand enough of that for now. Why would he give me a quarter section of land? Well, read on."

"Madam, are you sure there isn't just a tad of cold coffee in that pot on the stove?"

"Just take a little by itself," she said and poured a dribble of the Irish whiskey into a cup. "Now get on with it. Read the next one."

"It's a deed," he said. "But there's a paper attached to it which I think we need to read. All deeds look alike to me. Perhaps we have an explanation, yes, yes, I think we do."

"Well, *read* it!"

United States Land Office
Marietta, Ohio

Disposition of Public Domain: NW Quadrant Arkansas Territory. Formerly Upper Louisiana; Territory of Missouri; the Indian Territory.

Sale: Recorded under Ark 231-44824 this office, filed in the Office of the Solicitor General of the United States, in consideration of three hundred and twenty dollars.

One hundred sixty acres, a Quarter Section, to wit:

On Earth Grid determined by Prime Meridian, Greenwich, at 94 degrees 14 minutes West Longitude, 36 degrees 15 minutes North Latitude, from benchmark one half mile north and one half mile east, as in chart below:

SECTION 31 TOWNSHIP & RANGE SYSTEM Land Ord 1785

"My God, where do they find people who can do all this higgly-piggly?" Doc Insel asked.

"Let me heat up some of that cold coffee," she said, and as she stoked the embers in her cookstove, she kept muttering. "Arkansas? Arkansas? Where is Arkansas?"

"It's just south of Missouri. Here's a sketch map," Doc Insel said, and she hurried back to the table, bending over him, grunting a little with the pain such quick movements always brought now.

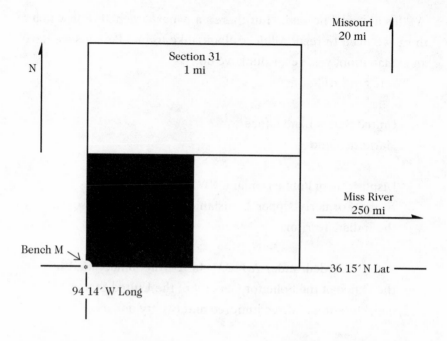

It was a pencil copy of one of the current maps of the Mississippi Valley. There was considerable detail at the mouth of the Mississippi and north to Red River, showing a scatter of towns and smaller streams and lakes. There was some detail along the river, particularly near Natchez, the mouth of the Ohio, and at St. Louis. The Arkansas River was shown with only three towns along its entire length. Arkansas Post, Little Rock, and the military Fort Smith. Everything else west of the Mississippi was blank. A small X had been marked in the blank space north of Fort Smith.

"My God, your little X is a wilderness," the doc said.

Now, Nalambigi Chesney's eyes had begun to shine, and she was smiling.

"A wilderness," she said softly. "Now I know why he willed it to me. A wilderness, where nobody is. Away from trouble!"

"Away from trouble?" Doc Insel said. "Woman, this end of Ohio is just beginning to get filled up with enough people to make civilized living natural and to be expected. We've finally got houses with windows in them. We've got churches instead of those circuit-riding

Methodists trying to save our souls; we've got a fire department and a university. We elect public officials. We've got representatives in Congress. Our bottle has filled up.

"And you're talking about starting all over again in a primitive place that belongs to the savages and beasts? You want to start with an empty bottle again? So you can fill it up once more? By the way, I suspect that coffee's hot enough by now, don't you?"

"I'm not going anywhere," she said and laughed. "But somebody else can."

"Who, one of the boys?"

"We'll see," she said and handed him the bottle. "You take this and let me read the general's letter myself."

"I'd be glad to do it," he said, but she was pulling on his chair and there wasn't much doubt but that she wanted him gone. "Well, I'll go then, madam, and thank you for the Irish."

And then, alone under her lamp at the table, because now she needed the light of the lamp even in daytime, she sat and read the letter from her friend.

My Dear Lady Nalambigi:

This land I leave to you is not yet surveyed but soon will be. A Principle Meridian and Base Line have been established in the territory of Arkansas not far from Chickasaw Bluff on the Mississippi, and lands through much of President Jefferson's Louisiana Purchase will be marked from there.

Your quarter section is in a wild, mountainous, timbered area. The nearest settlement that can be called such is at Fort Smith about seventy miles south. It is as far away from everything as it was possible for me to obtain now. At present, it is ceded to the Cherokees but that cession will soon be reversed. I hope it is useful to you.

When you read this, I will have gone beyond, hoping that the God of my fathers accepts me in his paradise. But it will be small comfort if I go to that place and am not allowed to visit with you someday in the land beyond the sun of your father's Gods.

We have seen many things together. They have been enriched for me because I have been able to share so many with you. I look back proudly on that land which I must leave and where you will still live for many years, I hope, and know that we had some small part in making it what it is now.

It has been my honor and pleasure to have known you.

I am, as always, your obedient servant, Rufus Putnam.

Postscript: You should see your banker about arranging a trust fund to fulfill tax obligations on the land now and after you have joined me. And until then, I hope you fare well, my dear.

It was a noteworthy winter.

Of great interest to the tavern and taproom owners of the lower class of saloons along the riverfront was the Corliss Hooten affair.

Corliss, on the coldest night of the year, got drunk and fell in the river and was able to pull himself from the water but with no energy left to get him home to his wife Ernestine, a frail little Kentucky woman he had married during the past autumn, lay in an alley behind the Crock and Bottle and froze to death.

On the occasion of his funeral, it was remarked by the more observant mourners that the only emotion Ernestine displayed was one of relief.

The other event was in a different part of town. It was the next day before Campbell Chesney heard about it, and it horrified him. His mother had gone to a meeting of the Bank of Southwest Ohio Board of Directors. She smoked her pipe there, too.

452

Gance had driven her into town. She had become more and more housebound, walking being a terrible chore and breathing noisy and labored. She spent most of each waking hour in her rocking chairs.

Gance had contracted to have a second one made for her because he was tired of carrying back and forth from porch to kitchen the one Campbell had given her. After a full afternoon sitting in one or the other of them, either Gance or Herta had to help her move to the table for supper because her joints would swell and go stiff.

Anyway, the Board of Directors.

"What the hell is she up to anyway?" Campbell asked.

"I have no notion," said Gance. "I thought maybe you did, all this bank business. That's your side of things around here."

"I think she made them swear a blood oath to keep their mouths shut on pain of being scalped maybe," Campbell said. "All I know is the bank has set up a trust fund for her and they are the trustees, and half, you understand that, *half* of the profits from the distillery go into the damned thing."

"Well, she asked me a long rigmarole of questions about how I'd like to go west to some new country."

"Oh Christ, she's not able to go anywhere. She may be a tough one, but she's got trouble moving from her table to her bed," Campbell said.

"I don't think she's considering going anywhere," said Gance. "Somebody else. That's what all her questions were about. If I'd like to go."

"What did you tell her?"

"Hell no, I got no interest in leaving here. I think it disappointed her because I'm not like Pap, always thinkin of heading off for new stomp grounds."

"She hasn't said a word to me about any such thing."

"She knows you'd never leave all these Cincinnati ledger books," Gance said and laughed.

"I wouldn't, either, but she might at least ask," said Campbell, and he was smiling, too. "That has to be it, though. Going west. Some-

453

body. And I suspect the trust fund has something to do with it. Why else would she be squirreling money away."

There was another thing. His mother was constantly asking Gance if he ever saw anybody going up the river, or down either for that matter, who knew anything about Arkansas Territory. And she had a map she took out to study, almost every day.

When he told his brother about it, Campbell snapped his fingers.

"That's it, then, isn't it?" he asked. "She's set on getting back in touch with the wilderness somehow or other. But God, can you imagine? An old-line red savage heathen getting all tied up with bankers and trust funds."

"Well, those men on that Board of Directors best watch their step now, or one morning they'll wake up and Mother will own their damned bank."

They both laughed. Gance because he thought it was a funny little thing going on, whatever it was, and Campbell laughed because it was driving him crazy trying to figure it all out, and making light of it was his only defense.

So the winter went down, and a deputation of athletic citizens visited from Rochester and said they'd started a baseball club and maybe Cincinnati would like to do the same so the two towns could have a few friendly contests during the coming summer.

Everybody who tended toward eastern sophistication read James Fenimore Cooper's *The Pioneers* or Washington Irving's *Bracebridge Hall*. Sarah Chesney read them both. And of course, she and her children joined the new Sunday School Union of the United States.

The Erie Canal was finally finished. Stonemasons decried the new construction material called cement.

And Thomas Jefferson died.

It wasn't Gance who found the Arkansas man. It was Herta. On a blustery April morning she had been in the town visiting her father,

Able Steinhartz, at the gun shop and saw there a tall, raw-boned, thatch-haired man who called himself Beverly Yoes.

The man was looking for a job, just mustered out of the army, so he claimed. He was dressed in what appeared to be army trousers and jacket and the clumsy brogans sometimes issued, shoes that would fit either foot, and a little billed cap with a chin strap.

Herta escorted Mr. Yoes up the bluff, chattering like a blackbird the whole way, some of it in English, some in German. When Yoes spoke at all, it was in the short, clipped phrases of what you might expect from a Tennessee mountain man, which was what he had been before joining the army.

They found Nalambigi Chesney and her son in the kitchen sipping spiced sassafras tea and eating a pound cake Judith Dwyer had sent up that morning to celebrate something or other, nobody other than Judith Dwyer was sure what.

It quickly being established that Mr. Beverly Yoes had indeed been in the territory of Arkansas, he was asked to sit and have tea and cake, and as Gance and Herta moved back to sit as spectators against one wall, Nalambigi Chesney, after first getting the map General Putnam had sent and laying it on the table, began her interrogation.

"Yes ma'am," said Mr. Yoes. "I was enlisted in the Army Rifle Regiment, and we took keelboats from St. Louis down the Mississippi to the Arkansas and up that river to a place called Belle Point, a bluff where the Poteau River runs into the Arkansas. That was 1817."

"It was a wilderness?" she asked.

"Pretty much so," Mr. Yoes said. "That wasn't even Arkansas Territory yet. The country all around had been ceded to the tribes. They were always fighting one another, and we were sent out there mostly to keep the Cherokees and the Osages from murdering one another."

Nalambigi turned and looked back at Gance, and she was smiling.

"The kind of country where your pap and me first seen one an-

455

other," she said. Then she was back with Yoes, bent toward him, urging him on.

"Whites were moving in," he said. "They started a town at the fort. They was some of them up in the mountains north of us, about where your little *X* is on the chart here. Twice, we marched up there to run them off because it was Indian land and we'd burn their crops, but as soon as we left they'd come right back.

"Of course, before long, the cessions to the Indians was took off and it was all Arkansas Territory and whites could come in, at their own risk sometimes."

This last, and at other times, Mr. Yoes spoke with a faint expression of concern, obviously seeing the person to whom he was telling all this was an Indian. At least in large part.

But her encouragement and delight at his recitation were real, and he plunged ahead. From his place at one corner of the room, Gance had to admire the old soldier for having the guts to speak on subjects of which an Indian might be irritated or downright belligerent at hearing.

"We started building forts upriver, then. But we still operated out of Fort Smith. I guess they still do."

"This country," Nalambigi Chesney, stabbing a finger at the *X* on the chart map. "What kind of country is it?"

"Mostly empty right now," he said. "Osage and Cherokee hunting parties in there. But it's mountain country. Deep valleys. All kinds of game. Good water. One big river heads up there. The White. Its mouth is on the Mississippi just about where the Arkansas empties."

"Timber?"

"Oh my stars, it's a jungle. Hardwoods. South of the Arkansas, there's pine. But up in what they call the Ozarks, it's hardwoods. A few scattered cedar. The Osage say Ozark was a name the French gave those mountains, and the French took it from what the Osage called it. Place of the Bows. Because they get the wood to make their bows from a particular tree there."

456

"You said a lot of running water and this White River. Do the Osage and these others go in bark canoes?"

Mr. Yoes looked blank for a minute, then shook his head.

"No, they go in dugouts if they travel on water at all. There's not any paper birch there for making bark boats. Not much bark there that will work. Streams are pretty swift, too. No, people there move on foot. Or horseback."

"You said game. What kind?"

"Deer, turkey, black bear, all the small game like rabbit, squirrel, and all your upland birds like quail, ducks, and geese along the Arkansas and White in migrating season. Fish, too. And along the wider valleys, even deep in the mountains, you can find a few buffalo. Of course, if you want to travel west of the Arkansas line into Indian Territory, there are plenty of buffalo."

"I'd like to see one of those. One of those buffalo."

She put her finger on the X again.

"You said a few white men were here now," she said.

"Yes," he nodded. "A few. They've got a settlement up there, and it's about the center of one of their counties. Washington County. They've got a judge who rides on circuit, and he goes up there once a year. When I left it was once a year. And they hold court in a log cabin saloon. They call the settlement Washington Court House.

"So there's a few people in that country. It's fine country if you want to be left alone. Not really any Indian problems . . ."

Beverly Yoes stopped and blushed, looking at her, and she shook her head.

"It's all right, Son, it's all right. I've fought more red savage heathens than you have. Go on."

"Well, I was sayin, not really any Indian problem up in the mountains. Down along the river and west of there, where prairie land starts. There's trouble there sometimes, but in the mountains, it's quiet."

So she found out about her inheritance from General Putnam. And she was satisfied.

When Beverly Yoes left, Nalambigi Chesney sent Herta back down into the town with him, instructing the girl to tell her father that if he was a friend to the Chesneys, he would hire this old soldier.

"Thank you, Mrs. Chesney," he said, a little startled that she shook his hand. "I am much obliged to you."

"All right," she said. "I understand this Rifle Regiment is good."

"It's the best outfit in the army," Yoes said. "They take only the best men, and you have to be a marksman."

"Good," she said. "I was in the army once. When my husband and me fought the Revolution. We was riflemen with Danny Morgan and General Benedict Arnold."

Gance almost laughed aloud with Beverly Yoes's expression on that one. And when his mother turned to him and winked, he knew that as much as she ever did, she enjoyed making a white man raise his eyebrows.

The visit of the old soldier who had seen Arkansas Territory was only a temporary return to her old familiar enthusiasm for what went on around her. But then, after a few days, she sank again into an almost apathetic inactivity when all that mattered was to sit in her rocking chair and look down on the town, even though perceiving it dimly now and maybe seeing more in her mind than in her eye.

It was still cold outside, but she would have Gance or Herta bundle her in blankets and she would sit in the sun with not much more exposed than her nose.

"I like the cold," she said. "It reminds me of my mother's country, where sometimes there would still be snow as late as June in the deep woods of the high mountains."

Sarah Chesney was well aware of her mother-in-law's condition, not from seeing much of the old lady but from what she heard from

Campbell and Gance. She began to feel guilty about avoiding her mother-in-law, she knew it was un-Christian. So the day came when she walked up the hill for a visit alone. Without children, without husband. Just herself to visit Nalambigi.

If Nalambigi was surprised, she didn't show it. Only Herta was there, for Sarah had chosen her time to coincide with a trip she knew Gance was taking across the river into Kentucky, accompanying Otto Black to buy cowhides. So it was Herta who stewed and brought the spiced tea for them on the promontory porch. There was also a batch of Herta's oatmeal-and-black-walnut cookies.

It was rather cool, but Sarah didn't complain or suggest they go inside. She left her coat on. She sat near the older woman's rocker and worked with string and needle, crocheting little doilies which she used to decorate all the new horsehair-stuffed furniture Campbell was now having shipped in for her from Pittsburgh.

They spoke the usual female small talk, only Sarah did most of the speaking. Weather and children's bad colds and how quickly men wore holes in the elbows of their shirts and some of the new recipes for various stews that were escaping from the small settlement of Irish immigrants just now coming from the old country.

But finally she could put it off no longer, so Sarah came to the real point of her visit.

"Mother," she said. "We thought you might like it if Pastor Mac-Daniel came to visit and talk with you. He could be of great comfort."

For the first time, a small light flickered in Nalambigi's eyes as she looked at her daughter-in-law. Maybe there was a tiny smile at the corners of her mouth.

"Yes," she said. "Pastor MacDaniel, your priest."

"No, we don't call him a priest. He doesn't have the heretical powers the papists say priests have."

The expression of half-sleep returned to Nalambigi's face. After a few moments, she drew a clay pipe and a pouch of tobacco from beneath her blankets, and after loading the pipe, she lit it with an old-fashioned flint fire starter.

Sarah Chesney could not help but be impressed with this operation, firing a pipe with a flint starter in the breeze that was coming up from the river.

Nalambigi took a few puffs and seemed to enjoy greatly the flavor of the tobacco.

"My mother once told me about the time when she was a young girl," Nalambigi said. "Some of her people were friends of the French. Some of her people were friends of the English. They were friends to whichever white man could give them the trade goods they needed, like iron pots and woolen coats and guns. And also the white man who happened to be where the various people of my mother lived. And to have these things, my mother's people had furs to trade. And also they could help either the French or the English in the wars, depending on which was their friends."

Nalambigi rocked slowly and puffed her pipe and looked across the great valley toward Kentucky, only now she could no longer see much of that far shore. Sarah Chesney's fingers were moving like writhing white worms at her crocheting. At least Nalambigi thought they looked like writhing white worms.

"And when my mother's people were with the English, the English holy men who wore large hats and always carried one of your books would tell my mother's people that the only way they could defeat death when it comes was to become their kind of Calvinist Christian."

Sarah gave a little start of surprise that this Indian woman should know anything about Calvinists. Which, of course, Sarah herself was one.

"And when my mother's people were friends of the French, or captured by them, their holy men called Black Robes said to my mother's people that the only way they could defeat death was to become a Black Robe's kind of Christian."

There was a small sound in Nalambigi's throat, and Sarah wasn't sure whether it was a cough or a laugh.

"So almost all of my mother's people, whether they were friends

460

of the French or friends of the English, said fine, they would become white man Christians, either the French kind or the English kind, depending on where my mother's people happened to be."

Now, when the same sound came, Sarah Chesney knew it was a laugh.

"Of course, my mother's people were not stupid," said Nalambigi. "They wanted to keep their friends friendly because they wanted to continue to get the trade goods, like the iron pots and the woolen blankets and the guns.

"But only a few of them really took either the French or the English kind of Christian religion. They said they did, but they had the spirit of their grandmothers, and that's what they kept. Because to them, this spirit was truth. To them, there was no truth in the French Black Robe religion or the English Puritan religion."

Now Nalambigi Chesney looked into her daughter-in-law's eyes and there was no dimness in her own, but rather a smolder of red heat.

"I know you believe the truth is with your Pastor MacDaniel," she said. "This is good. I would never try to change you.

"But for me, I am still one of my mother's people. And I am not one of her people who would say I am something that I am not just to be sure I will still have somebody who will provide me iron pots and woolen coats and guns."

Sarah Chesney's finger flew at the needle and yarn. Her eyes were downcast, and she raised them only when she heard Nalambigi heave a great sigh.

"Everybody has to come to their power in their own way. And decide how to think about life and death."

Sarah waited only a little while. Then she folded her crochet, put it in a small bag, and rose.

"Mother, it's been pleasant talking with you," she said.

There was no answer, and Sarah saw that Nalambigi's eyes were closed, as though she had gone to sleep. She turned to the house, but the voice stopped her.

"Sarah," Nalambigi said. Her eyes were still closed. "It was kind of you to come and talk to this mean old woman."

As she hurried out, Sarah Chesney found an irritable mistiness in her vision.

She seemed to turn inward. When she sat on her porch, her dim eyes might appear to be observing all the activity along the river below, but Gance Chesney had the sense that she was seeing nothing. Not anything that he, or anybody else, could see. She spoke infrequently. When geese went north that year, she appeared not to hear the honking as it marked their passage across the night sky.

Once, she said, "I dreamed of Pap."

But nothing more, and he didn't ask how she had seen him because he figured if she wanted him to know, she would tell him. And she didn't.

Once she said, "I dreamed of the forest and lakes and mountains in a far place."

But nothing more, and he didn't pursue it. The time had come when it was almost as though great effort was required for her to make conversation with him, or with anybody, even as though it were painful for her to try.

Gance believed his mother had begun to die. He didn't tell Campbell because Campbell would have asked a lot of questions and argued about it and tried to make everything as neat and logical as a column of figures in a ledger book.

He stopped going into town for his afternoon drinking. He did it at home, now, and he did less of it. He watched his mother carefully, and at one time she would have noticed it and demanded what he was doing, but now it was too subtle for her to detect. Or maybe she saw but chose not to mention it.

She had to be physically moved everywhere. As he carried her, on each of the days of that advancing spring, he could feel her weight growing less and less, like a flower still with color but fading into a husk of its former self.

Herta stopped teasing and poking and pinching and trying to kiss him. Instead, now she helped him move Nalambigi about, from bed to table to rocking chair, either the one in the kitchen or the one on the porch. And now Herta made herself a pallet behind the kitchen stove and remained in the house at night.

Gance went into his mother's bedroom often, always somehow grateful when he heard her labored breathing in darkness, telling him she was still alive.

Sometimes when he went to her room, he would find her sitting up, and he could see the shine of her open eyes in the gloom. He always asked if she wanted something, but she seldom did.

Once, during a thunderstorm, she asked him to make some lemonade and bring her a cup with a little of his clear whiskey splashed in it.

Almost every morning, she would sit at the table with Gance and Herta and sip spiced tea and tell them she had dreamed. That was all. Just that she had dreamed. And Gance wondered if she had dreamed of places she had seen. Or maybe she had dreamed of places she expected soon to see.

It was June. The moon was coming full. There was a dogwood tree at the eastern end of Nalambigi's promontory porch, and the shadows of the leaves and branches were like the lace of a widow's veil moving inexorably across silvery flagstones.

Gance carried his mother there and lowered her into her rocking chair and stood bedside her and watched the light of a steamboat moving up the Ohio. They could hear the boat's bell ringing, a faint chime like the tap of a fingernail against the thin crystal of a stemmed wineglass. They were too far away to hear the labored coughing of the steam engine.

There were many lights below them in the town, for it was early in the evening. These were orange glows that stood in sharp contrast to the white, snowlike moonscape bathing all the houses and trees. Even the ridgelines of Kentucky across the river seemed to have halos of silver light.

When his mother spoke, it startled him a little.

"Go to your brother's house," she said. "Tell him I want the child here, the little Sergeant Bobby of the bad foot. No one else."

"Only those two, then?"

"Yes."

"Not Sarah?"

"No."

"How do I explain that to Sarah?"

"However you want to. Well, you might say I thought she should stay with the other children. This won't take long. Send Herta out here."

It wasn't so bad as Gance had thought it would be. Mostly because Campbell made no fuss about it. And as they came back up the hill to Nalambigi's house, him carrying the blanket bundle of little Robert Chesney, he made Gance ashamed for underestimating him.

"She's dying, isn't she?" Campbell asked.

"I think so," said Gance. He was unable to come right out and say it, as though to avoid the utterance could avoid the fact.

When they came onto the porch, Herta was there and immediately moved back into the house. Nalambigi held up her arms, and Campbell stood a moment uncertainly.

"Give me the little Sergeant Bobby of the bad foot," she said.

She took the baby and held him close against her, and he had begun to cry, a tiny, snuffling cry. She started to rock, the chair making a soft rhythmic squeak. She glared at her sons.

"Well, go," she whispered. "Leave me with my grandson."

There was a lamp burning in the kitchen, but Gance blew it out and the three of them sat in the dark and heard the singing start. It was a low, quavering sound, and it made chills of gooseflesh run up Gance's back.

464

She sat for a long time, rocking the child. She had never rocked a child before. Her sons could never remember her ever having held one of the grandchildren in her arms before. Now, soon, the child stopped crying, but her crooning chant went on.

Maybe it was an old Narragansett lullaby, or one from the Penobscots or the Abenakis. Maybe it was none of these. But from wherever it came, there was in it the mystic, ancient, neolithic murmur of deep woods and high green mountains, head-waters country of the Connecticut and the St. Francis and the Kennebec.

As she sang, she rocked and held the baby close to her breasts and watched the shadow of the moon slowly march across the flag-stones.

When he walked into his home carrying the baby, Sarah was waiting for him, pacing and muttering to herself in the lamplight. She stopped when she saw him, and from the look on his face she knew it might be best to forget the angry outburst she'd planned. Instead she asked if his mother was dead.

"No," he said, handing her the child. "But nearly so."

Sarah frowned as she held the bundled baby, and then from his blankets she took a long, brown envelope.

"What on earth?"

Campbell took the package and saw the broken red seal and knew where it came from, and he sat at his kitchen table and finally discovered what all that bank business had been about.

By the time Sarah had little Robert in his cradle and was back with him, he had seen enough to understand that the trust fund was to pay taxes on land. A quarter section in Arkansas.

"Arkansas?" he said. "My God, what was she thinking? What was old Putnam thinking?"

Then beneath the last of the paper he found the letter, written with cramped penmanship in brown ink. It was folded, and he assumed his mother had addressed it to him because on the sheet was the single word *Campbell*.

He unfolded it and read aloud with Sarah bending over him.

> This is my will. Campbell, I expect you to do all these things. You have always been dependable and true. And I have always trusted you.
>
> My house and all in it I leave to Gance. Watch out for him, Campbell. Try to make him marry that Herta. She's good and will take care of him. He is going to need somebody to take care of him.
>
> All the leather works and shoe business, I want Clariese and her family to have it.
>
> Everything else is yours.
>
> Except for the land General Putnam my friend gave me when he died. It is for the little one of the bad foot who you named after my Sergeant Bobby. Try to get him grown up well and then try to let him go there and see what freedom from this white man's place is all about.
>
> Remember, this is my last will. So it has much power.

After he took his mother in to her bed, Gance Chesney sat at the kitchen table in the dark. He could hear Herta breathing from where she lay on the pallet she'd made for herself behind the stove.

He must have dozed, but came awake with a start, thinking he'd heard his name called. But the house was quiet. He saw the windows were going gray with the coming dawn, and he went into his mother's room.

She was lying on her back, her eyes open. He bent toward her face.

"Sit with me," she whispered.

Gance sat on the edge of his mother's bed and took her hand in his. It felt as light as an empty corn shuck. Her breathing seemed normal. She tried to speak, and he had to bend close to her lips.

"I can hear Sergeant Bobby speaking to me," she whispered. Then she slowly turned her head on the pillow so the gray light from the window shone in her eyes. "Dawn is the best time to begin a long journey."

In a moment, he felt her fingers tighten and then her hand went loose. Her eyes had closed, and he was glad for that. He held her hand for a while, but not too long. He didn't want to feel his mother's hand turning cold in his.

In the kitchen, where it was darker, he could make out the form of Herta standing before him. He reached out to her and she came to him and they embraced. They did not speak or kiss but only held one another for a moment.

And then he pulled free of her and got his hat and went down the hill to tell his brother and sister that their mother had gone.

Afterword

Maybe Nalambigi Chesney's will had all the power she claimed was invested in it. For its provisions were as well accomplished as can be expected from any such instrument.

Herta did indeed stay on the bluff in the widow's house and become its mistress and took care of Gance, who, as his mother prophesied, needed plenty of taking care of, but she gave him no children.

He became known among generations of the town's urchins as Uncle Gance, just as he was to his own nieces and nephews, and in summer they walked up the hill to hear him tell stories of Indian chiefs and Great Lake battles, and sometimes he whittled boats for them, modeling each one after his memory of the flagship of Oliver Hazard Perry, and he was still doing it right up to the time newspapers were telling of the battle between ironclads *Virginia* and *Monitor* in Hampton Roads.

And Otto Black became known for the quality of his shoes, as good as any manufactured in New England.

And Campbell. Well, he was always Campbell, and he knew how to cure hams and bacon and how to distill good whiskey and where to find markets for all of it.

And Little Sergeant Bobby did go to claim his grandmother's inheritance in the wilderness of Arkansas, which was by the time he got there no longer a wilderness such as Nalambigi Chesney had visualized but maybe a wilderness of a different kind.

And he was no longer Little Sergeant Bobby by then but Robert Chesney, the dour cripple who had many sorrows but some happiness, too, and took to himself the religion of his mother and brought to Arkansas a woman most observers said was the most beautiful creature they had ever seen in that land, even though she did not speak English and was an Orthodox Catholic and a Greek besides.

A long time before all that, Campbell Chesney buried his mother where he was sure she wanted to be buried, on the bluff near her house, so she could look down on the valley of the Ohio as she had always done and watch the steamboats go by and later the steam locomotives that drew cars along steel tracks.

"She watches nothing from that hole in the ground," said Gance. "My mother is not there. She is with Pap in the north woods, where sometimes among the pines on the high ridges there is still snow on the ground in June."

Campbell ordered a wrought-iron fence from Pittsburgh and placed it around the grave, and for a long time it was only this enclosure that indicated any grave was there.

Then they went to Pittsburgh together, Campbell and Gance, although they could as easily have done it in Cincinnati, and contracted with a stonecutter for an obelisk. About four feet high, the tip reaching toward the stars, so Sarah Chesney said.

There was a long discussion about the inscription. But finally they had the engraver perform his artwork:

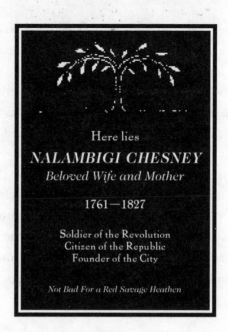

Here lies
NALAMBIGI CHESNEY
Beloved Wife and Mother

1761—1827

Soldier of the Revolution
Citizen of the Republic
Founder of the City

Not Bad For a Red Savage Heathen

And maybe the best part: the stone was genuine Vermont marble, quarried from the earth less than a day's march from the headwaters of the Kennebec!

Jones, Douglas C. 1924-
Shadow of the moon

4/30/21	DATE DUE		

Member Of
Chautauqua-Cattaraugus Library System